MASTER OF HER HEART

"What I desire is you. Just you. Willing and eager in my arms. *Begging* me to make love to you."

"Tell me what I must say. I will say it, for I am bound to obey you. But what I *feel,* you will *never* control."

He rose to his feet. The table stood between them, but the barrier suddenly seemed insufficient. "Shall we put that to the test? Kiss me, Maria. Then tell me you feel nothing."

He came swiftly 'round the table and drew her to him.

"No! No, don't . . ." she pleaded.

As he molded himself against her, she could feel her resistance slipping away. His lips brushed her cheek—gentle as a butterfly's wing. Releasing a little sob, she gave up and clung to him. He was strong and solid. Gentle and kind. Beautiful in a rough, masculine way. She could not fight his strength or her own inner needs. She *needed* to be held. What could be the harm in a single kiss?

SUPER ROMANCE

MASTER OF HORSES

Katharine Kincaid

Zebra Books
Kensington Publishing Corp.

http://www.zebrabooks.com

ZEBRA BOOKS are published by

Kensington Publishing Corp.
850 Third Avenue
New York, NY 10022

First Zebra Printing: June, 1999
10 9 8 7 6 5 4 3 2 1

Printed in the United States of America

For Christina,
My youngest daughter
With love and thanks
For all we have shared over the years.

Special thanks to Peggy Brown
For the use of her library
And for sharing her love and knowledge of horses
With me and my family.

Chapter One

Dehesa de Oro, New Spain
1580

"I *must* have a son—a legitimate, highborn son, and *this* may be my last opportunity!"

The exclamation brought Maria to a standstill outside the door of the large salon wherein her father and stepmother awaited her appearance. She had no idea why she had been summoned from the laundry shed, and expected that once again her stepmother had found her lacking in some necessary virtue.

In the best of circumstances, Maria avoided meeting with Don Gonzalo and Doña Inez. If the subject of discussion had anything to do with sons—or the lack thereof—she was doubly reluctant to appear. What could have raised the explosive issue this time?

"Calm yourself, my husband," came the measured, even tones of Doña Inez. " 'Tis never wise to stir up bad humors in the body. I know how much you long for a son and heir. Believe me, I share your pain over the loss of our dear little Antonio. As his mother, how could I not? If not for that Worthless One, that half-breed abomination . . . *Madre de Dios!* Do you not see the justice of it? This is how she can *pay* for her crime! She should be delighted to have an opportunity to redeem herself in our eyes at long last. Consider not *her* reaction— but *his,* the only one that counts.''

''What you say is true, but I don't know,'' her father muttered. ''I just don't know. Granted, she is my daughter and a beauty, but she has no knowledge of men, certainly not the sort to stir the appetites of a sophisticated nobleman and ensure enthrallment, as you suggest.''

''Nonsense. It is her very innocence which will attract him. Would you dare offer Don Diego an experienced courtesan— a female who is nothing more than the leavings of other men? It is *because* she is your daughter—and untouched—that he will most appreciate her. And while she distracts him from his own losses, we can use the time to find him a suitable wife— a woman of refinement and good breeding to produce the grand-children you so much desire—young ones who will ensure that your beloved *Dehesa de Oro* continues to thrive and prosper.''

''Ah ... *Dehesa de Oro,* my legacy, my life's blood ... the future of the New World!'' Don Gonzalo's voice rose in agitation. ''Your plan must not fail! Diego is the answer to our prayers. Doubtless he considers his banishment to the New World the worst tragedy of his life. Little does he know what a grand destiny awaits him here! For I intend to entrust not only my beloved *Dehesa de Oro* to him, but also my silver mine at San Martin. After I am gone, my dreams will live on. And if this blasted ague from which I suffer renders me any more infirm, he may take possession—and responsibility— even sooner. He can live here, while we retire to our villa at Santa Barbola, as you have always wanted. We'll take our ease among those of our own kind, away from these wretched *Indios* who are always plotting and scheming against us.''

''Don Diego *is* the answer to our prayers,'' Doña Inez fervently agreed. ''He is a grand *hidalgo,* an aristocrat to the bone, from one of the oldest, most respected families in all Spain. 'Tis a pity he can never return there, never inherit his father's lands and titles—not when he's been branded a murderer. He may be innocent as a newborn lamb, but he *was* found bending over the body of King Philip's most trusted advisor—and in the middle of the night. No wonder his own father doubts his story.''

"I care little if he *is* a murderer. What matters more to me is *why* he did it. Honor demands many things of a man— sometimes even murder. If honor demanded it—''

"Oh, honor, yes. A man must always uphold his honor. But in this case, the scandal will *never* blow over. He and his family must accept the inevitable—he can never go home again—but their tragedy is our good fortune. We are lucky that Don Francisco thought of us. For once—just this once, mind you—I am glad we live on the Edge of the World, a full thirty-nine days journey from the center of civilization in the New World, and six days just to Santa Barbola. We have been given a second chance, Gonzalo. Now, it is up to us to make certain Diego *wants* to remain in the New World, to replace the son we so tragically lost ... and if the Worthless One can help persuade him, I see no conflict of conscience, dear husband. No conflict whatsoever.''

How? Maria thought despairingly. Anger pricked her. *She* was the Worthless One, the half-breed abomination to whom her stepmother referred. How was she to persuade a Spanish nobleman banished from his own country for the crime of murder—a man who didn't want to come to *Dehesa de Oro* in the first place—to be happy enough to remain here? She lacked experience in charming gentlemen, highborn or lowborn. Until now, she had not been permitted to speak to one unless he was old enough to be her grandfather or young enough to be her son. Whatever would she find to discuss with a Spanish aristocrat from the other side of the world? Perhaps he would enjoy explaining how he had come to be branded a murderer.

She greatly doubted he would be dazzled by her beauty; before this, no one had ever remarked upon it. Her stepmother had often told her that her Indian features rendered her ugly. As for happiness, she could scarcely provide something she herself did not possess. For the last twelve years of her life, misery had been a familiar companion. When she was a child, while her mother still lived and Don Gonzalo had actually seemed to care for her and her two older brothers, Santelmo and Lorenzo, she had felt joy and contentment. But her mother and Lorenzo had died long ago, Santelmo lived somewhere far away on the Sea of Grass, and she herself was little more than a slave in her father's house—a person nearly everyone despised and ridiculed.

It was all because of Antonio's death, which had been a tragic accident, not a crime. She more than anyone grieved over the loss of the sweet little boy entrusted to her care. She had not meant to startle the stallion in whose box the child had playfully hidden; all she had done was shout Antonio's name, and the stallion had reared up in fright, pawed the air above the boy's tousled black curls, and . . .

"Maria Encanta! Where is that willful girl? I sent for her three quarters of an hour ago, and she has yet to show her face! Her insolence is not to be borne."

Maria leapt into the room. The last time she had kept Doña Inez waiting too long, she'd had to scrub all the stones in the courtyard on her hands and knees—using lye water that made her skin burn for a week. Doña Inez had claimed ignorance of the lye's effects, maintaining that since Maria was half-Indian—the daughter of an *Indio* with whom Gonzalo had eased his loneliness until a worthy mate of his own race could be found—the lye water couldn't possibly hurt her. Indians, being little more than animals, supposedly had skin with the properties of leather.

"Well, there you are . . . finally," Doña Inez hissed, narrowing her eyes at Maria.

Squaring her shoulders beneath the scrutiny, Maria coolly returned her stepmother's gaze. From the moment of their first acquaintance, the woman had had the power to cause a frantic fluttering sensation in her lower abdomen. Determined to hide the reaction, Maria focused on Doña Inez's physical appearance rather than her power or position. Doña Inez was tall and slender, straight as a stick, and gowned in stark black. Even before the death of her four-year-old son, the woman had worn black, as if she had divined ahead of time that her life would be one of bitterness and bereavement. She had black hair, black eyes, and skin even darker than Maria's. In an effort to lighten it, she was constantly bathing her face and arms in a mixture of milk, aloe, and honey—so far without success.

Doña Inez was as plain and thorny as a mesquite bush in the dead of summer. She almost never laughed or smiled. She hated *Dehesa de Oro's* isolation and primitive comforts, and couldn't understand her husband's love for the land. She had probably never envisioned spending her entire life here. Maria might have felt pity for her—even compassion—had the woman not inspired rebellion instead. The sad truth was: Doña Inez hadn't liked her much even *before* Antonio's death.

"Maria, child," her father muttered, "stop bristling so. Don't look at me like that. . . . There, that's better. A man doesn't wish to woo some defiant hellion whose disdain threatens to singe his soul. . . . It won't work, Inez, you see? She lacks the most rudimentary skills of flirtation. And she must dress better, too. Diego will think she's some rank-smelling kitchen maid, rather than my own daughter."

"Do not despair, Gonzalo. I will have a new wardrobe sewn for her. There will be time, I think. And I will teach her how to lower her eyes and wield a fan to good advantage, too."

"Yes, a fan! Flashing black eyes peeping over a fan never fail to capture a man's interest. You captured mine when you first peeped at me. I was enchanted. You were so demure and shy. So sweet and elusive. That's the combination a man desires in a woman."

Maria could not imagine her stepmother being shy and elusive. Doña Inez had taken command of the household from the moment of her arrival. It had been a mere three months after Maria's mother had bled to death trying to bear a fourth child, which had been stillborn. Her father had neglected to tell his new bride about Maria and her brothers, and Doña Inez hadn't been pleased to discover she'd had an Indian predecessor. Maria had been very young then, not yet in her teens. Being much older, her brothers had greatly resented this interloper. The troubles between them had started immediately.

"Well, what do you think, girl?" Doña Inez snapped. "I asked you a question. I want an answer."

Lost in her own thoughts, where she often retreated to escape unpleasantness, Maria had missed the question.

"Pardon. I was not paying attention."

"You *never* pay attention. That is the problem! Your mind is always wandering—plotting mischief and mayhem." Doña Inez turned to Maria's father. "It's the *Indio* in her! I blame it all on that. Despite the tragedy she's caused, she has still learned nothing. She stares at me with those fox fire eyes of hers, but her thoughts are a hundred leagues away. With every breath she takes, she defies me. I may have to beat her to gain her cooperation in this endeavor—or deprive her of food and water. Do I have your permission to do whatever is necessary, husband?"

Her father sighed. For the first time since she had entered the salon, Maria gave him her full attention. She wished that just once he would defend her against her stepmother's unfair tirades. One had only to look at him to be aware of his power. Don Gonzalo was short and built like his best bull, Old Lope, who serviced the cows at *Dehesa de Oro*. His green velvet doublet did little to conceal his huge stomach, the result of prosperous living, and his fawn-colored trunk hose only served to emphasize the enormity of his thighs. He had gray hair, spiked mustachios, and a patrician air.

Before his marriage to Doña Inez, he had often been jovial. The father of Maria's childhood had been a loud, boisterous, enthusiastic horseman. The father of her womanhood constantly complained, and was often in pain. Only when he gazed at his precious horses did Maria see a hint of the man she had once known, respected, and yes, even loved. Then, his eyes softened, and sometimes, he smiled. She knew he would be far more content if he could still spend his days on horseback, exploring the Ocean of Grass as he had done in the old days. But advancing age and girth, his many aches and pains, and his fear of the *Indios* kept him housebound now—and too much in the company of his tyrannical wife.

"Maria," he finally said. "We are not asking all that much of you."

"Humph! We're not *asking* anything," Doña Inez corrected. "We are demanding."

"Demanding, yes," her father agreed.

"Demanding what, exactly?" Maria still did not fully understand. They wanted her to entertain a guest—be pleasant to him, enough so he would want to remain at *Dehesa de Oro*, marry, and become her father's heir. At the moment, she wasn't trying to be disobedient; she simply had no idea how she might accomplish such an impossible feat. From morning 'til night, she labored alongside the slaves and servants in her father's household. A mountain of laundry awaited her attention this very moment. She had no time to sit and charm a stranger.

"You will share his bed!" Doña Inez bluntly announced. "And you will give him reason to want to sleep in that bed every single night until a proper wife can be found to take your place."

Maria could not conceal the small gasp that escaped her. At the sound of it, her father looked sheepish, Doña Inez triumphant. Was that what a courtesan did—share a man's bed, and . . . and . . . remain still and compliant like the cows when Old Lope wished to mount them?

Maria knew little of what occurred between males and females of the human species, but she'd had ample opportunity to observe the mysteries of mating among cattle, horses, and dogs. She had just never considered that *she* might be permitted—*forced*—to mate. For her, marriage was out of the question. Her bloodlines were impure, so no Spaniard would ever want her. Nor would her father be likely to give her to an *Indio*. Don Gonzalo had no use for Indians, except to work them to death in his silver mine. In his house, he preferred Spanish-speaking peasants as servants. If they had a little mixed blood, he could overlook it, as long as their loyalties remained Spanish. Her mother had been the one exception—an *Indio*, but too kind and beautiful for him to resist.

"You are of an age to be bred," her father said gently, referring to her as if she were one of his prized fillies. "The nature of a female is to serve a man and bear young. Until today, I had despaired of what I might do with you—how best to arrange your future. If you please young Diego, he will ensure you are well taken care of when we are gone. You will never lack for food and shelter, nor will any offspring that might result from your . . . ah . . . liaison. To have the protection of a man of his stripe is the best I can hope for you, Maria. This is your chance to secure your future. Please Don Diego, and he will become your protector. Offend him, and he will put you out to starve. 'Tis that simple, daughter. Now then, do we have your cooperation?''

Maria grappled with shock, despair, and outrage. She could hardly grasp the situation—or believe it. Did they think Don Diego would actually keep her when he took a wife? If she pleased him too much, the wife would become her enemy, and if she pleased him not enough, he would cast her out. The mere idea that they expected her to bed a man she had never even met stunned and sickened her. He could be ugly as an old goat, and cruel besides. He could make her life more of a misery than it already was. Yet what choice did she have? To refuse would only incur the wrath of Doña Inez, whose punishments were most inventive.

She could run away—now, a bit sooner than she had antici-pated. She did plan to run away as soon as she was ready. Dreams of escape were what fed her spirit; one day, she would be free of the Spanish, able to seek her own destiny and happi-ness far away from all those who judged a person solely by the accident of birth. To that end, she had been sneaking out in the middle of the night and teaching herself to ride her father's swiftest horse, a fiery, young mare called La Reina.

Mounted on such a horse, she could elude her father and his *vaqueros.* They would never catch her. She wouldn't make the same mistake as her brothers: They had not been able to ride well enough to elude their pursuers—and they had known nothing about managing or training their stolen animals.

When *she* finally left *Dehesa de Oro,* Maria intended to know all the secrets of horse handling, and to take her father's best horses with her. She would search for her brother, San-telmo, and live forever among the Indians, teaching them all she knew. Never again would they be the helpless victims of the Spanish. Horses would make the Indians equal to their conquerors . . . *only she was not yet ready!*

"I . . . I will do all I can to . . . to win his favor," she finally said, half-choking on the hateful words.

Tears threatened, but she reminded herself that to flee before she was fully prepared was to ensure her own defeat. The cause she had undertaken—to bring the horse to the Indian—was far greater than any paltry concern for her virtue. Her virginity seemed a small price to pay for the deliverance of an entire people.

"Excellent!" her father crowed. "Serving this man will be an honor, Maria. You will see. Don Diego de Iberra is a grand *caballero,* a horseman without equal, like his father before him. He was trained by the best, a master of horses with the hands of a true reinsman. None could compare with his father—not even myself. That is why I am so excited! When young Diego sees this land—the immensity of the Sea of Grass—he will know at once that it was created to support livestock without number. The horses his father gave me when I first journeyed to the New World have all flourished here, at least those who survived that horrible ocean crossing. The pasture in Andalusia where the mare bands of Diego's family graze is called *Dehesa de Oro.* I thought never to see its equal, but when I arrived here in the New World I knew at once I had found even better, so I gave my lands the same name: *Dehesa de Oro,* Pasture of Gold."

Don Gonzalo gazed rapturously at the scenery outside the unshuttered window. "I never dreamed the son of my old friend would come here, yet fate has decreed it. Diego will yet inherit *Dehesa de Oro,* only it will be here in the *Nueva Vizcaya,* the land of the future, not of the past. I will immediately offer him the position of *arrendador*—no, he will be Master of Horses! He will teach my great and beautiful ones the subtleties of fine reinsmanship and even the advanced movements, the *curvet* and the *levade.* This, he probably did at home, anyway."

Her father turned back to her, his gaze piercing. " 'Tis *you* who must make him want to stay, Maria. I doubt his father permitted him the luxury of his own mistress. By now, they must have been planning his marriage. It will doubtless be a sore subject with him, so we will not mention it. In time, when he realizes he can never go home again, he will be content to think of taking a wife here—but until then, his happiness is in your hands, daughter.''

Madre de Dios! She was now responsible for the happiness of an accused murderer.

''You had better not fail us!'' Doña Inez snapped. ''I will strangle you with my own hands if you do not meet our expectations.''

''Now, now . . .'' her father placated. ''Of course, she will. Maria understands what is at stake here—not simply our futures but her own.''

''We must begin at once to prepare her. Listen well, Worthless One! Beginning today, you will see to your skin. I will give you creams and unguents to soften and lighten it. No more laundry. No more scrubbing. No more tasks to roughen your hands. You must brush that wild tangle of hair one hundred strokes, morning and night, until it shines like a raven's wing, and . . .''

Maria's thoughts wandered. *At least, he was a fine reinsman—a Master of Horses.* If she succeeded in enchanting him, as they wished, what might he be willing to teach her? From him, she could learn all the techniques her father and his *vaqueros* kept hidden from her—and indeed, from *all* Indians, so fearful were they of what might happen if the savages ever obtained horses.

''Oh, my husband!'' Doña Inez's cry interrupted Maria's vision of herself and Santelmo galloping across the prairie, chasing the wooly cows she had only seen at a distance. ''How long before Diego arrives, do you think? What was the date on that letter his father sent?''

''Wait a moment. Let me fetch it.''

Maria watched, plotting the future, while her father rummaged through the drawers of a cabinet. Seizing a scroll, he unrolled it, and held it up to the window's light.

''The date . . . I don't see a date. Ah, but Don Francisco says it will take at least a week to rig a ship to carry Diego's stallion. He refuses to leave his favorite mount—and a small number of mares—behind. He and the horses are sheltering in a warehouse on the wharf at Cadiz until the ship is ready. Francisco sent this missive by the first available transport. You will remember the voyage from Cadiz requires sixty-eight days at sea. Add to that the number of days to travel from Mexico City to Santa Barbola, and—''

''Oh, never mind!'' Doña Inez burst out impatiently. ''I would guess we have no more than a fortnight to effect some sort of transformation in this wretched girl. Diego must not think we are scheming to foist a common *Indio* upon him, but a creature of rare grace and comeliness, regardless of her origins. Stay out of the sun, Maria, do you hear me? We will prepare excellent quarters for Don Diego—the entire west wing of the house. You will occupy the very same rooms, and see to his every comfort. Go now and assemble your things—no, forget your things. None will suffice, anyway. You must have new things. By all the saints! There's so much to do.''

As her stepmother shrieked for Juana and the other servants, Maria seized the opportunity to escape. She hurried to the laundry shed, where she was now forbidden to finish the day's chores. Once there, she paused, trembling, near the washtub to reassess her situation. It was all well and good to dream of turning this tragedy to her advantage, but when she tried to imagine herself in bed with a stranger, a sick feeling again consumed her. If she had to spend every night in the bed of the new Master of Horses, how would she find the time or the opportunity to perfect her riding skills?

As yet, she still tumbled off La Reina with amazing frequency, especially at the faster paces. The mare preferred galloping to walking. Even though Maria grabbed her mane and hung on tightly, she could barely maintain her balance, and still could not control the animal's direction. What if she were *never* able to escape?

The thought made her shudder. If she failed, her life could only end in disaster and tragedy. Look what had happened to her mother! Don Gonzalo had called her his precious dove, his one perfect rose, but he had never acknowledged their union before his own countrymen, nor accepted their children as his heirs. Maria's mother had been devastated, for she had truly cared for Don Gonzalo and lived only to please him.

After her death, when Maria's brothers stole a few precious horses and sought refuge among the Indians, her father had flown into a rage, pursued them onto the Ocean of Grass, and slain Lorenzo. He would have killed Santelmo, too, but the People Who Follow the Woolly Cows had hidden him too well. Even under torture, the two Indians her father had captured had refused to reveal her brother's whereabouts.

For days after the incident, Maria had wept bitterly and dreamed of her dead mother weeping for her lost sons. By then, of course, Doña Inez was in charge, and *she* had loudly lamented that Santelmo hadn't died alongside Lorenzo! No, the last thing Maria wanted was to follow in her mother's footsteps and become the personal slave of a man who would never openly claim her or her children. She could not bear to see the father of her children marry another woman—a highborn Spaniard— and watch him fawn over his legitimate offspring while her own suffered scorn and neglect. She would rather die than suffer such a fate! Somehow, some way, she *must* learn all she needed to know and escape with a small band of horses.

Santelmo had explained it to her long ago: On horseback a man could win battles, elude his enemies, and follow his prey. Horses gave men power over other men and animals. On a horse, a man became a god.

It was up to her to bring horses to her mother's people. No one else could do it. She must be brave and courageous, and never count any sacrifice as too great or difficult. The new Master of Horses must become *her* slave, eager to reveal every secret of equestrian accomplishment. Once she knew all the tricks to compel a horse to obey its rider . . .

Through the open shed door, Maria suddenly spotted La Reina, prancing back and forth in her wooden-barred enclosure. The mare's coat shone like sun-burnished gold, but her mane, tail, and stockings were purest ebony. Head lifted, ears pricked, she scented the wind, and every muscle quivered, as if she, too, longed for freedom.

I will give it to you, Maria silently vowed. *We are sisters, you and I, and together we will fly beneath the stars and moon, and discover our own happiness.*

"There! There it is, Don Diego—*Dehesa de Oro!*"

The voice belonged to Basilio, the *vaquero* Diego had hired in Mexico City to guide him north to the vast holdings of Don Gonzalo de Andalusia, his father's friend.

Turning on his skinny pony, Basilio pointed to the collection of adobe buildings lying below them on the grassy plain. Don Gonzalo's *hacienda* was indeed at the Edge of the World—a perfect refuge from the long arm of Spanish justice and the vengeance sworn by the family of Don Toribio, the man he was accused of killing.

At least, his new prison wasn't lacking in beauty. As the rays of the setting sun brushed the landscape with liquid fire, Diego could understand why it bore the same name as the lands now lost to him, possibly for all time—the Pasture of Gold in faraway Spain. A haze of iridescent dust hung above the yellow-green grass in the mellow light of day's end—exactly as it had done at home at this hour.

Diego's heart clenched with longing. Better not to think of what he had left behind; he must focus on the reality of what lay before him. In the immensity of these endless grasslands, framed by shadowy mountains in the far distance, man's encroachment looked poor and humble.

Plain square walls enclosed a sprawling, single-story house surrounded by outbuildings and lean-to sheds, a round granary, and numerous grass-thatched huts. Only the main house had a tiled roof of faded red *azulejos,* but a waterpond glinted among the emerald green of poplars and willows. At one end, a dam captured the precious liquid and divided it among neatly planted fields. Diego could also see animal pens and corrals fashioned from dry-laid rocks, with a few built of wood, and these very small. Horses and cattle moved within the enclosures. However, the animals were still too far away for careful scrutiny.

The staghound he had plucked from the streets in Santa Barbola stood sniffing the wind. Abruptly, the dog started down the hill ahead of them until Diego called him back with a curt, "Caobo!"

It was the name of his dog at home—an animal he loved too well to expose to the hazards of this journey. Just saying the dog's name was like a jab in the stomach: Would he ever see him again? Surely one day, all would be restored to him, including his ailing father's esteem. The withdrawal of the latter still stung, feeding his bitterness. He could never forget that Don Francisco had flatly refused to listen to his explanations. It was enough he had been found in Don Toribio's bedchamber; why he had gone there and what he had done—or *not* done—mattered not at all to the old patriarch.

His father had not even come to say farewell before Diego's ship sailed for the New World. He had been too busy rearranging all his affairs so that Diego's cousin, Evaristo, could take over the family's interests and inherit everything upon his death. Only Diego's mother had appeared at the wharf. She had clung to him wordlessly, never daring to express the hope that she might lay eyes on him again. Even now, half a world away from that dismal scene, Diego could recall the painful parting with perfect clarity.

"God go with you, my son," was all his mother had said, and he had been forced to sail into the unknown, bidding farewell to all but his stallion and the half dozen mares he had insisted upon taking—or he wouldn't go at all—no matter the consequences.

As the ship sailed away from Spain he had wanted to shout, "I am not a murderer! Evaristo is behind all this! Tell my father."

He had said nothing. Pride prevented such a boyish outburst. Besides, he had no proof, only an instinct borne of years of silently combatting his cousin's rivalry and jealousy. His only recourse now was to discover gold in this misbegotten country and return in triumph to win King Philip's pardon and expose his cousin's wickedness. The king would forgive anything for gold; gold could also break the silence of anyone protecting Evaristo.

In the meantime, the once mighty Don Diego de Iberra must

make his peace with life in this . . . this unspoiled Eden. In truth, the land pleased him far more than the plain fortress overlooking it. Twin stone blockhouses with tiny apertures stood sentinel over the house and corrals. Apparently, the threat of Indian attack had driven Don Gonzalo to secure his kingdom in whatever modest way he could. The blockhouses faced the north, in whose limitless reaches the unconquered savages yet resided. Diego had been reading about them, and was most curious to make their acquaintance.

On the long voyage over, when he wasn't busy consoling his horses in their confinement, he had amused himself by studying conflicting accounts of the Spanish settlement of the New World. The sight of the blockhouses brought back the words of Fray Bartolome de las Casas in *La Destruccion de los Indios:* ''The Spanish entered the *Nueva Vizcaya* like the cruelest of wolves, tigers, and lions. But the Indians were simple people, devoid of evil or duplicity . . . humble, patient, peaceful and quiet.''

It was obvious Don Gonzalo didn't hold with this simplistic notion; more likely, he agreed with Gines de Sepulveda, who as late as 1555 had claimed that Indians often slaughtered and ate Spaniards, therefore necessitating their complete and total subjugation.

Diego suspected that his host at *Dehesa de Oro* would fervently agree that Indians were dangerous and should be converted and then held beneath the Spanish thumb and made to earn their daily bread dredging precious metals from the earth to send back to the king for use in his religious wars.

Studying the wilderness beyond this last outpost of civilization, Diego couldn't help wondering what manner of men and beasts lived out there on the Sea of Grass. To date, no one really knew, or if anyone did, he had not returned to tell of it. There were no maps, nor reliable eyewitness accounts . . . only rumors, tales of unbelievable wealth, such as entire cities built of gold. He had read of this, too, but rather doubted it. Until now, he had never quite believed that such wilderness as the books described actually existed. He had not been able to imagine a land so vast and empty that a man could ride away and be swallowed up in it, never to be seen again. . . . He felt a bit like a child at his first sighting of the ocean. Until a man saw it with his own eyes, he could read all he wished without comprehending its awesome immensity.

"Don Diego, shall we go down now?" Having ridden back to join him, Basilio waited at his elbow. The three other *vaqueros* in his little caravan were also awaiting his direction. He had hired them to help guard his priceless horses, but the difficult ocean crossing had already proven fatal to two of his charges—prime, young mares whose loss he deeply mourned, for they were irreplaceable.

"It will soon be dark," Basilio warned. "This near the Ocean of Grass, the men are growing anxious."

Diego saw that it was true. The men looked uneasy. Uneducated men often feared the unfamiliar, he knew, but these seemed more worried than circumstances warranted. He suspected they wouldn't relax until they were safe inside the walls below. He nodded his permission, and the little party surged forward—spilling down the golden slope toward *Dehesa de Oro.*

With much less enthusiasm, Diego followed. He would have preferred galloping El Cid down the slope and straight into the wilderness, bypassing the settlement altogether. It would have been far more exciting than an encounter with Don Gonzalo, his father's old friend. Unfortunately, both men and horses needed food and rest. He wondered if Don Gonzalo had even received his father's missive, explaining the situation. If not, he himself would have to account for his sudden appearance out of nowhere.

Since his own father considered him capable of murder, what might a stranger think? Don Gonzalo might not welcome him. The moment had but one saving grace: He at least rode a horse worthy of any man's envy. Here, as in Spain, a man's horse defined him. If he rode well, exhibiting the proud carriage and equestrian finesse achieved only by the nobility—and then only by those who spent their lives on horseback—he was accorded respect. And if he rode a horse such as El Cid, whose every movement proclaimed magnificent bloodlines, he would never lack for followers, men who would gladly ride in his shadow in the hopes that some of his greatness might rub off on them.

If nothing else, he had El Cid. And four good mares had survived the grueling journey. Diego had begun to doubt his ability to attract good fortune, but he hoped that his host had other mares he would not regret breeding to El Cid. In this wilderness, he hardly dared expect real quality, but if his search for gold proved fruitless he must have some other means of earning his keep. Breeding, raising, and training young stock to meet the insatiable demand for horses were worthy tasks for any man who called himself a horseman.

Urging his stallion down the slope toward his new—and he hoped temporary—home, Diego could feel the blood rushing to his head. His heart pounded. He suddenly had a feeling of enormous anticipation. Whether this foreboding were for good or ill, he knew not, but his banishment had truly begun.

Chapter Two

He was here! The new Master of Horses had arrived at sunset, riding a magnificent white stallion that immediately drew the envy and admiration of every man at *Dehesa de Oro*. So splendid was the appearance of both man and horse that no one even thought to comment upon his tardiness; all Maria heard were exclamations regarding their elegance.

Before Maria had a chance to view the man for herself, Doña Inez sent for her and ordered her to see to the last minute details ensuring that his accommodations were as comfortable and inviting as possible. While the rest of the household rushed to prepare a fine meal for the long-awaited guest, Maria cut some of Doña Inez's preciously guarded flowers in the inner courtyard and arranged them in heavy clay pots to grace his rooms, which included a small private library in the west wing of the house.

She dusted everything not once but twice, for a fine layer of grit had sifted through the roof tiles and lay like a mantle on the heavy dark furnishings. After that, she made up the large bed with fresh linens, swept the tile floor, opened all the shutters to admit the cooling air of evening, and lit the tallow dips arranged throughout the suite of rooms so that a warm, golden glow bathed everything.

Having completed her preparations, she wondered what she might possibly do next. The evening meal was taken late, so it would be hours before Don Diego sought his bed. When guests were in residence, everyone lingered long in the dining hall. They would all be up early, however, before the heat of the day began, and would then return to their quarters to rest when the sun beat down like a hammer on an anvil.

Maria was sure she had several hours before she must obey the last of Doña Inez's orders, the one she most dreaded. The problem was how to stay busy until then, to keep fear at bay and resist the impulse to run to La Reina, climb on her back, and gallop off across the plain. The only thing that kept her from fleeing was the knowledge that she had fallen off twice the last time she had tried to ride the mare in the dead of night. Once, La Reina had jumped at a strange sound, and the second time she had stopped dead in her tracks, while Maria flew over her head.

How could she best occupy her hands and mind for the next several hours? Opening one of the clothes cupboards, Maria surveyed the meager contents and debated whether or not to strip off her worn and tattered garments and don one of the three brightly colored skirts and lacy white blouses that hung in the wardrobe. Their purpose was to enable her to better impress the new Master of Horses.

Such clothing and leather sandals seemed poor ammunition to win a battle for a man's heart . . . not that she had expected silk or velvet gowns such as the wives and daughters of the *hidalgos* wore. Still, she doubted that Don Diego would be enchanted by typical peasant clothing, even though it was of better quality than most peasants wore and certainly better than lowly Indians ever saw in their lifetimes.

She herself had been surprised that these were new and not cast off. Their colors were wonderfully vibrant. The blouses dripped lace at neckline and sleeve, the skirts sported deep ruffles at the hems, and the fabrics were soft and inviting to the touch.

However, she imagined that a man of Don Diego's lofty position would be more accustomed to the somber hues and expensive fabrics favored by the *hidalgos*—such as the black lace shawl Doña Inez had provided for her to wear on cool evenings. The shawl was an old one that reeked of the heavy musky scent her stepmother favored, and Maria grimly reminded herself to hang the thing in the sunlight to banish its offensive odor before she had to wear it right near her nose.

She had been given one other adornment: a plain wooden cross on a thong to be slipped over her head and nestled on her bosom as a sign of piety, modesty, and purity.

Taking the cross from where it hung on a small wooden peg in the cupboard, Maria wondered if a seductress was expected to be pious as well as beautiful. All of the Spanish were pious—none more than Doña Inez. Whenever Maria was punished for some infraction of the rules, Doña Inez always made her spend the remainder of the day on her knees before the statue of The Sorrowful Mother in the tiny chapel off the courtyard. Since The Sorrowful Mother had a kind, sweet face—reminiscent of Maria's own mother—Maria never much minded the penance. In any case, she would rather kneel there forever than beg for mercy.

She had always admired the jewel-studded crucifixes the Spanish often wore, but it seemed inappropriate to display a religious symbol in order to present a picture of false virtue. Fray Leonido, a fairly frequent visitor to *Dehesa de Oro,* often preached about "the sins of the flesh," and the eternal fires of hell awaiting those who indulged in them.

If she obeyed her father and stepmother, she would surely be damned—but she'd also be damned if she *disobeyed.* Fray Leonido also never lost an opportunity to lecture her regarding her defiant, rebellious nature. Damnation thus appeared inevitable.

Slipping the thong over her head, Maria noted that the cross rested exactly in the cleft of her bosom. *Cristo* was a Spanish God, but He had suffered and died at the hands of cruel enemies, so she felt a deep empathy for Him. Perhaps He would understand and forgive the actions of a lowly, half-*Indio,* since she truly meant no harm or malice to anyone, except perhaps Doña Inez. She did feel guilty over that, but only because her own mother had always advised her to reject hatred as a poison that destroyed one's own self, rather than the recipient.

Closing the double doors of the clothes cupboard with a snap, Maria turned toward the bed. She wouldn't don her new clothing tonight; there wasn't any sense to it—not when Doña Inez had taken her aside and instructed her to *remove* all her clothing and await her new master naked in his bed. She would wear only the cross in the hope that perhaps when Don Diego saw it, he would be inspired to send her away.

If he revered the cross as much as some did, he might recall the preachings of some clergyman such as Fray Leonido and refuse to lay a hand on her. Of course, he might also become violent. The Spaniards committed all sorts of atrocities in the name of the cross, a fact which had always puzzled Maria. How could these powerful conquerors be so horrid to their charges when they professed to worship a God of gentleness, peace, and love?

Worn out from her musings, she perched on the edge of the bed and yawned. Compared to the thin straw mattress on which she usually slept, the bed was a marvel of comfort. Its softness beckoned. She had risen before dawn and been working hard since. Doña Inez had insisted on bypassing the midday rest in favor of drilling her further in the feminine arts. On a small chest near the bed lay the red and black lace fan she had been exhorted to flutter in front of her face, snap open and closed, and peer over, allowing only her eyes to show—never her mouth or nose.

"Indio features, anyway," her stepmother had scoffed. "Best to keep them hidden while you beguile him with your fox fire eyes. They only serve to anger *me,* but I doubt not they'll intrigue a gentleman."

Doña Inez would probably tell her she should practice more with the fan, for she still did not have the knack of it and felt ridiculous waving it in front of her face. However, since she did not intend to use it, anyway, practice seemed a waste of time. The night ahead would likely be arduous, embarrassing, and possibly painful, so she might as well seize what rest she could. She decided she had better undress first, so that she could not be accused of disobedience or laziness if Doña Inez came to check on her.

Peeling out of her work-stained garments, Maria suddenly remembered the wash water she had hauled into the room earlier. She had filled a large clay pitcher and left clean linens and sweet-scented soap on the wooden shelf above the table. A basin also awaited the new Master of Horses. No one would notice if she sampled these small luxuries.

She squeezed water from a washrag over her naked breasts and hurriedly cleansed herself, then turned back the bed linens and stretched out on one side of the big, soft bed.

Unknown to anyone, she often slept naked because of the heat. Her mother had taught her that the human body was neither shameful nor ugly, so she felt quite comfortable. She just wished she could lie there undisturbed until morning. The moment she heard a footfall in the hallway outside the bedchamber, she planned to pull up the bed clothing and shield herself from the gaze of her new master.

Weariness won out over good intentions. No sooner had Maria closed her eyes for a moment than she was lost, and remembered nothing more until . . .

Diego was sure he must have drunk an entire kilderkin of fine old Jerez brandy, the equal of any he had enjoyed in Spain. Still, his grinning host kept filling his cup to the brim, as if to let it go dry would be the greatest of insults. The old man's image was now blurring before his eyes. Don Gonzalo seemed to be wearing *two* ornate silver crucifixes that thumped on his velvet-clad belly whenever he leaned back in his chair to regard Diego with fawning delight.

Diego's welcome had far exceeded his expectations. Don Gonzalo and his thin, haughty wife had effusively assured him that they considered themselves honored to give him shelter. He had been served a meal fit for King Philip—not perhaps in the number of dishes served, but certainly in the quality. He hadn't eaten so well since he'd left Spain. The beef, in particular, had been excellent, a fact his host attributed to the abundance of good forage for his cattle.

Tomorrow, Diego would have a chance to view Gonzalo's horses and determine for himself whether or not his host's mares were good matches for El Cid. Tonight, the talk had all been of horses. The fact that no explanations for his presence had been necessary greatly heartened him. He still could not get over it. Don Gonzalo had hugged him as if he were a long-lost son! And Doña Inez had clutched his hand with the glint of tears in her piercing black eyes.

"Do not worry about the past, Diego," she had earnestly entreated. "The past is finished. Now that you have safely arrived, your future awaits you—and you may be certain it will be a good one."

Gazing now into Don Gonzalo's avid face, Diego wondered if the man had any misgivings at all about him. Had his father not told Gonzalo he was accused of murder? If so, he seemed unaffected, so great was his joy in welcoming a man of his own class into his rustic home in the New World.

Perhaps it was only the brandy, but he was beginning to think his banishment might have its advantages—gold or no gold. If Gonzalo's horses were as good as he claimed—truly descendants of El Toreador, his father's best stallion, dead five years past—he might even find reason to rejoice that he'd been sent here! If he could cross El Cid's line with El Toreador's . . .

"Drink up, Diego!" Gonzalo urged, expectantly watching him. "Surely, you would not refuse to drink to the well-angled pasterns of our beloved Iberran horses!"

Diego struggled to remember: Hadn't they already drunk to the pasterns? They had started out by toasting their heads, known for being broad of cheek and narrow of muzzle. Next, they had drunk to their necks, which outshone other horses' necks by being thick and well-set on fitly sloped shoulders. They had drunk to their short backs and long hips, springy, smooth gaits and perfect heights. Iberrans usually stood about fifteen hands high, and were thus ideal for the sake of agility and stamina. . . . By the blood of *Cristo!* They had even drunk to the goose-rumped, Spanish-Barbary strain from which the Iberran horse had evolved.

Surely, they had drunk to the pasterns.

"I have had enough. Forgive me, Gonzalo." Diego tried to speak distinctly, but he could hear his words slurring together. "If we find another noble trait to salute, I may die of excessive admiration."

"Ah, but this is the last one, I promise. One last toast, and we will have mentioned all the most notable qualities of our most wondrous and glorious breed."

Diego squinted into the darkened corners of the room. "Where is your wife? What hour is it?"

"Have you forgotten? She retired two hours ago. I sent all the servants to bed as well. How can a man talk horses properly with a kinsman of his soul, if not his blood, when surrounded by ignorant nonbelievers?"

So they had progressed to being kinsmen.

Diego decided they must have drunk a great deal for Gonzalo to be claiming an accused murderer as a member of the family. This was only his first night beneath the man's roof. Raising his cup, he toasted the pasterns of the Iberran horse, then quickly downed the fiery contents. Before Gonzalo could think of yet another toast, he rose to his feet and stood swaying a moment, desperately wishing for the room to stop spinning.

"Where is my bed, Gonzalo? Show me the way. I must go there now, or I will fall asleep in my chair."

"What is wrong, my friend? Is the brandy not to your liking? We will switch to *Madera* instead. The night is long yet. We have hours before sunrise."

"No . . . no. I mean, yes, the brandy is excellent. But I can hold no more. I am unaccustomed to heavy drinking. A horseman needs all his faculties, and brandy has a way of dulling them. Besides, the journey has wearied me."

Don Gonzalo sighed. "Come then, I will show you to your quarters. My wife has prepared the entire west wing of the house for your use. You will want for nothing. You have only to mention the least little thing, and it will be provided."

Panting from exertion, Gonzalo heaved himself upright. He

had to grab hold of the table to steady himself. Diego was glad to see he wasn't the only one affected by the potent brandy.

"You are too kind, Gonzalo. I never dreamed to find such hospitality on the other side of the world from my home."

And what will be the price? asked a little voice inside Diego's spinning head.

"Why should I *not* be hospitable to the son of my oldest and dearest friend? In this part of the world, my wife and I have little opportunity to converse with our own kind. Great distances separate the *hidalgos*. When we do come together, we sometimes squabble over petty differences. You are a refreshing breeze into our stuffy lives, my son. So of course, we relish your coming."

"Gonzalo . . . let me be blunt. I am a fugitive. Have you no fear of harboring an accused murderer beneath your roof?"

"*Are* you a murderer, Diego?" Gonzalo rocked back on his heels and studied him in the wavering light from the wall sconces. "I cannot believe you committed some heinous crime, unless, of course, honor demanded it. I myself have killed in the name of honor, so I can hardly condemn another man for doing the same."

"You have?" Shock lanced Diego. He would never have suspected it. His host seemed too congenial to ever lose his temper to the extent of taking a life.

"I once killed a horse thief, and make no apology for it. Horse thieves must be taught harsh lessons as a warning to others." Gonzalo's jowls quivered with remembered outrage. "I only did what needed to be done."

"The man I am accused of murdering was a horse thief." Diego found it a relief to have a willing audience. "I discovered his name on a bill of lading for a mare bound for the New World. She was one of several stolen from my family. I went to Don Toribio's home in the middle of the night to confront him with the evidence and discovered him stone dead, with a dagger in his heart. His wife walked in, started screaming, and accused *me* of killing him. 'Twas impossible to reason with her, so I fled the scene—a grave mistake, I later learned. I was condemned before I ever had the chance to defend myself."

"A sad tale, indeed. But if you *had* killed him, you would have done no wrong. We dare not tolerate the theft of anything so valuable as a horse, especially an Iberran horse. We will speak no more of the tragedy that brought you here, nor will the name of the thief be mentioned in my household. I spit on his name. Don Toribio's family always thought themselves better than anyone else, anyway. 'Tis one of the reasons why I came to the New World—to escape the disdain of those who consider themselves superior to me and mine—and of course, to make my own fortune, which God knows I have done."

"But Toribio is—was—from a powerful family. He was an advisor to King Philip."

"What does that matter to me?" Gonzalo waved a hand dismissively. "Our beloved monarch lives far away, across the sea. He receives his share of silver from my silver mine at San Martin, but here, at the Edge of the World, on the lip of the great Ocean of Grass, *I* am king. My word is law. I do whatever I wish. No one tells me yea or nay. 'Tis I who do the telling. I decide who may live and who may die . . . and I say *you* are my friend, Diego de Iberra, and nothing shall be denied you as long as you dwell in my house. I perceive you as a son to me—the son I lost some years ago."

'Tis the brandy talking, Diego thought. *He cannot mean what he is saying. Besides, I do not intend to stay here any longer than necessary. I must avoid becoming indebted to this man any more than I am already.*

"It was unnecessary to give me an entire wing of the house," he protested. "I assure you, my needs are simple."

"Nonsense. Your father is a great man, and you are his only flesh and blood. You deserve all I have to give, and more. When you see my horses tomorrow, you will understand. If your father had not provided me with the very best Spain had to offer, I would not now possess the finest horses to be found anywhere. Don Francisco first put his trust in me by allowing me to purchase some of his best breeding stock. Now, he entrusts his own son to me in his time of trouble. Think not you have come to a poor place, Diego. Here, a man can achieve all his heart desires."

Diego felt suddenly sober. *I want what I left behind in Spain. I want what I should have inherited from my father. Nothing can ever compensate for the loss of my good name and my heritage, all of which I will regain, or die trying.*

To Gonzalo, he said: "Tomorrow I will see your horses and more of your great Ocean of Grass. For what is left of tonight, I must sleep."

"Bah! Sleep is a waste of time. When you are old, you will realize that. A man's hours are numbered. Should he spend them snoring when he can use them eating, drinking, and conversing with good comrades?"

Diego smiled. From the look of him, Gonzalo had wasted little time sleeping, but his pursuit of wakefulness had curtailed his ability to enjoy more rigorous pursuits in his old age. What good did it do a man to own fine horses if he could no longer mount and ride them?

"Forgive me my weaknesses, Gonzalo. I can match you neither in energy nor appetite."

"Ah, but you outshine me in so much else, my friend. Permit me to savor a few small triumphs." Don Gonzalo gestured toward the doorway. "Come, I will show you the west wing. 'Tis about as far as I can walk. Already, I am winded."

"Simply point me in the proper direction. You need not accompany me. I'll fall into the first empty bed I find."

"A young man like you shouldn't have to sleep alone in an empty bed." Don Gonzalo winked at him. "Bed should be a place of exercise as well as rest."

"Not for me. I have no wife. When all of this happened, negotiations for my nuptials ceased."

"Then you had your heart set on someone?"

"More or less. She is a shy young beauty with a lineage that pleases my father. If not for her mother's pleas that she needed more time to mature, she would already have been mine. Our families approved of our alliance years ago, but she was too young for us to press the matter. I had to wait for her to grow up. Now, it seems, I will never have her."

"A pity." Don Gonzalo wagged his head as he led the way down the darkened hall and into a moonlit courtyard where a small fountain tinkled into a shallow basin. Flowers scented the air, and the night breeze was sweet as honey.

"You may not believe it, but 'tis for the best, Diego. A young man should be free to indulge himself. Once he marries, the chase is over—or at least more difficult to conduct."

"The chase? You mean the seduction of nubile young maids? My father frowned upon lewd behavior and warned me to leave the peasant girls alone. I had to go far from home to indulge myself, and could not spare the time from my horses. My experience with women is thus sorely limited."

"Too stiff-necked and devoted to duty, your father. 'Tis the only thing for which I fault him. I chafed against the restrictions of church and society, but your father embraced them. That's another reason why I live in the New World, while he still lives in the old. Here, our only restrictions are those we set upon ourselves. I try to set as few as possible, and expect you to do the same."

Don Gonzalo suddenly stopped and turned to Diego. Behind him stood an iron gate that opened onto another corridor illuminated by light from adjacent chambers.

"This is the entrance to the west wing. As I said, it has been prepared for you. Go and enjoy all you find."

Diego inclined his head. *"Gracias. Buenas noches,* Gonzalo. I will see you in the morning."

Entering the long corridor, Diego wondered if his host would sleep at all, or would simply continue drinking alone. If *he* had to join Doña Inez in bed, he, too, might prefer staying up all night. The mistress of the house had been kind to him, but he found it difficult to like—or trust—her. If she was indicative of the sort of women available for marriage in the New World, then he pitied the men forced to choose from such a limited selection. Not that the women of Spain were better. The young ones were often beauties, but as they aged—and if they didn't marry—they often became dull-minded, spiteful, and shrewish. He could hardly blame them. Unmarried women of the upper class had nothing to do all day but gossip, go to church, and dote on other people's children. There were high feast days, bullfights, and various other amusements, but in general, proper

Spanish women led boring lives and thus *became* boring. Except for the occasional lusty urge, Diego found horses of far greater interest than women.

After poking his head into several rooms, Diego finally located the bedchamber, where a large bed stood cloaked in dark shadows. Not sparing it a second glance, he strode into the room and began removing his clothing. He didn't see his belongings anywhere, but was too tired to search for them. He wanted only to strip off his stained traveling clothes and bathe the sweat from his face and upper body.

He had refreshed himself at the little fountain in the courtyard before the evening meal. Now, he needed a head-clearing, as the morning would probably bring a pounding headache. He wished he had called a halt to the drinking several toasts earlier.

His skull felt thick and heavy, already a burden for his neck and shoulders—and he was disoriented. Maintaining control at all times was important to him, and probably why he took great satisfaction in teaching young horses to respond to his slightest demands. In his present condition, he could not have trained a starving dog to steal a bone!

Luckily, there was water in the pitcher on the table, and he picked up the vessel and poured the water over his bare head and shoulders. It ran down his chest in rivulets. Closing his eyes, he gloried in the shock of the liquid on his heated skin. When he reopened them, he saw a stack of linens on the shelf above the table and helped himself to one of them.

Toweling himself dry, he grabbed the tallow dip in its iron holder, turned, and headed for the bed—only to stop short of it, riveted by the sight of a naked female sprawled across the bed linens. She was young, beautiful, golden-fleshed and glorious . . . and deeply asleep.

He thought he must be dreaming, or so inebriated that he had conjured her from the sultry air. In the dim light, she embodied all things feminine and mysterious, being the sort of creature a man might imagine but never be so fortunate to encounter except in some feverish dream.

She isn't real. She can't be. She's far too perfect—too incredibly exquisite.

Expecting her to vanish at any moment, he gingerly approached the bed. She didn't move, and he was able to walk right up to her. The closer he got, the more apparent her perfection became. She lay on her back, one arm draped across her mid-section, the other outstretched.

Diego feasted his eyes on flawless golden skin, delicate round breasts with roseate nipples, and gently flared hips. The latter cradled mysteries that eluded his gaze, shielded as they were by a wealth of glossy black curls at the junction of her thighs. She had long golden legs, artfully fashioned feet and toes, and abundant hair—straight as a waterfall and as black as his best velvet doublet. Hers was the face of a sleeping madonna, each feature innocent and fine. Her lips seemed to be sculptured from purest rose marble, and her nose and cheek bones utterly entranced him.

He hardly dared breathe for fear of awakening her. Even her hands enthralled him, for each finger was a marvel of grace and delicacy. She lacked but one thing, and his brandy-befuddled brain insisted that he remedy the slight defect.

Glancing about the shadowy room, he spotted flowers arranged in a clay pot. Among them was an *adormidera*—a poppy, scarlet as a sunset. Swiftly descending upon the blossom, he plucked it from the pot and tucked it into her hair next to the fan of her black lashes. *Now* she was perfect—the essence of femininity, Eve awaiting Adam to awaken her from the sleep of creation. How he longed to be her Adam!

Unable to resist, he knelt beside her on one knee, leaned over, and inhaled her scent. She smelled clean and sweet. Untouched. Virginal. Innocent. He suddenly noticed the small, wooden cross she wore. It lay between her perfect breasts, mocking his rising lust. As a gentleman and a guest in this house, he ought not to touch her.

Yet she slept naked in his bed.

Her presence could be no accident. She was here for his pleasure. A slave probably. An Indian? Perhaps a peasant girl with no choice in the matter. Don Gonzalo had boasted of the lack of constraints, and urged Diego to savor his freedom and enjoy all he found here.

Never had Diego wanted a woman more than he wanted this one. He didn't doubt she was untouched. His host didn't seem the type to offer anything less than the best to the son of his oldest friend. Still, it amazed Diego that Gonzalo hadn't enjoyed her himself. How could he resist the temptation?

The girl's nakedness gave proof of her complicity and willingness. There was nothing to stop him. Still, he hesitated. A frightened or abused young filly quickly learned resentment and would never be capable of the more advanced movements of equitation. So, too, with a young woman. Her first time with a man must be a good one or she would always be reluctant to give a lover all she was capable of giving.

From this young beauty, he wanted far more than a brief, frantic coupling. In a hidden room in Cordoba, he had once been fortunate to experience three days and nights of prolonged, exquisite lovemaking, a true feast for the senses. It was then he had discovered that making love to a woman could resemble a ride on El Cid—or one on a donkey. Both animals could eventually take a man where he wanted to go, but if he desired a truly wonderful journey, he would avoid the donkey at all costs.

If this lovely young woman was gently tutored in the amorous arts, she would be unforgettable, the sort of female he would dream about in old age when he lacked the stamina to make dreams a reality. Maybe that was why his host hadn't saved her for himself! He no longer had the stamina to satisfy a virgin. Simply walking to the west wing had tired him.

He himself was just the man to teach her.

Hurriedly shedding the remainder of his clothing, Diego eased himself onto the bed beside her. Then, leaning over her shoulder, he gently tongued her ear.

Chapter Three

Maria awoke with a startled cry. A warm rough hand immediately descended over her mouth to still her.

"Hush, now. I mean no harm, little one," someone crooned in her ear, the very ear that still tingled from some unexpectedly intimate contact.

Gruff and masculine, the voice had undertones of black velvet. It made her flesh prickle. Turning her head, Maria discovered the speaker as close as the end of her own nose.

"Don Diego?"

She stared into dark eyes that seemed lit from within. He was younger than she had expected, but no boy, either. His hair held the faintest whisper of gray, and his face had a sun-bronzed, weathered look that suggested constant exposure to the elements. He was more handsome than she had expected, too. His nose was straight and finely chiseled, his brow forceful, and his mouth . . . well, it was oddly gentle and appealing—and much too close to her own mouth.

Smiling, he spoke again. "You have named me correctly . . . but who might you be?"

"I . . . I am Maria."

"Simply Maria? Surely, there is more to your name."

"Maria Encanta." She would reveal nothing more. Did he know—had he been told—that she was the illegitimate daughter of Don Gonzalo?

"Maria Encanta ... the perfect name for you. You *are* enchanting, the loveliest woman I have ever seen."

He sounded sincere, but she doubted he was telling the truth. No Spaniard could find a half-breed *Indio* lovely. Belatedly, she remembered her nakedness and reached to pull the bedclothes over her, but he grabbed her hand. At the same moment, she glimpsed the rest of him.

Madre de Dios! He wore no more clothing than she did.

Alarmed, she rolled away from him, her whole body flushing with shame and embarrassment. It was bad enough *she* was naked; his nudity came as a great shock, a circumstance she had not expected and for which she was unprepared.

"What is it?" His hand covered her upper arm, halting her departure. She could hardly draw breath, let alone speak.

"What then? Are you so shy?" Low and husky, his tone soothed her better than his hand. Still, fearing his power over her, she shrank from his touch. "Little madonna, do not be afraid. I told you: I mean you no harm."

Rebellion bubbled up in her. Eluding his grasp, she snatched a linen bedsheet to shield herself from his gaze and scrambled off the bed. He managed to grab the end of it, halting her progress. She refused to look at him, but could contain her ire no longer. "How can you say you mean no harm to me? In the morning, will I still be who I am? ... Will I still own myself?"

"Own yourself?" He sounded puzzled. The rustle of the remaining bedclothes told her he was moving around on the bed. She resisted the impulse to raise her eyes to see what he was doing. "Look at me, Maria. 'Tis all right now. I am decent."

She dared a glance. If decent meant covering himself from waist to thigh, he was indeed decent—but the rest of him shouted his sex, as plainly as words hurled in anger. She noticed everything. The upper portion of his very masculine body was broad, bronze, and muscular, sporting dark, curly hair the same color as the short wavy hair on his head. He gave an impression of great strength, but closer inspection revealed that he was lean and lithe, with little meat to spare on his bones. Dark hair covered his legs, but rather than being coarse, his lower limbs, including his feet, looked finely made. His feet, in particular, in no way resembled the feet of Indians or peasants. They went barefoot most of the time or wore only crude sandals, but boots of the finest Spanish leather had probably protected *his* feet all his life.

"I am not afraid of you, *señor.*" She lifted her chin and glared at him. "I fear no man."

It was a lie, but she said it, anyway. That he was an accused murderer made him doubly frightening.

"If you do not fear me, you must despise me instead. Your eyes shine with an unholy light, the likes of which I've never before witnessed in a person's eyes."

"My stepmother calls them fox fire eyes. I know not why they shine so. I am powerless to control the effect."

"Your stepmother?"

"Doña—" She stopped, mindful of revealing too much, and only nodded. "Yes, my stepmother."

He watched her with a thoughtful expression on his elegant Spanish features, and she wished he were not so handsome. She wanted to hate him, or at least maintain a sense of detachment. Now, she realized that maintaining detachment might prove more difficult than she had anticipated.

"Why were you sleeping naked in my bed?" He acted as if the question barely interested him, but his eyes betrayed his curiosity. He watched her as intently as a hawk.

"I am . . . to be yours while you are here." She hated the slight tremor in her voice, but could no more control it than subdue the brilliancy of her eyes. "You may do with me whatever you wish, *señor.*"

"Whatever I wish? . . . But what of you? What do *you* wish?"

She bluntly stated the truth. "I am half *Indio,* so my wishes do not matter."

His brow rose in question. "Your parents. Your stepmother.

Where are they? Did they not protest this unusual arrangement?''

"My real mother is dead. She would not have liked it, but
she was full *Indio,* so she usually did as she was told.''

"And do you always do what you are told?''

Unable to guess his motive for all these questions, she hesitated. Perhaps it amused him to watch her squirm.

"I am here, am I not? And I am naked.''

A smile played about his mouth, and he glanced pointedly
at the sheet. "Not quite, little madonna.''

She closed her eyes a moment and drew a deep breath.
*Remember Santelmo and the Indians. If I do not assist them,
who will? This man has the power to help me help them. I must
not offend him. Indeed, I must enchant him, so he will teach
me all I need to know.*

Slowly, her hands shaking, she unwound the sheet, held it
away from her body, and let it slide to the floor.

"You are lovely . . . so very lovely.'' His tone hinted of
awe. "Open your eyes, Maria. Look at me. Don't be ashamed
of your body. I find you exquisite.''

She *wasn't* ashamed of her body—only of him seeing it.

Inhaling another deep breath, she opened her eyes. Fire
burned in her cheeks, and her heart thundered in her breast.
She summoned all her courage to meet his gaze. A warm glow
suffused his face and eyes. His lips were parted, and his bronze
skin gleamed with a light sheen of sweat. He had propped
himself in a half-sitting position against the pillows. Now, his
smoldering glance leisurely explored every part of her, from
head to toe.

"No man could look at you and not desire you.'' Roughness
edged his words. No longer smooth and caressing, his tone
suggested danger. "Since you have been sent here this night
expressly to serve me, I would be a fool not to enjoy you in
each and every way I can imagine, little Maria.''

She didn't know precisely what he meant—how many ways
could a man enjoy a woman? She had thought there was but
one way. Fear leapt in her belly—accompanied by a strange,

throbbing excitement that scared her all the more because the feeling wasn't totally unpleasant.

"Must I return to the bed now?" She barely managed to utter the question, and her knees felt wobbly.

His eyes searched her face. "Maria, have you ever been with a man? Do you know what to expect?"

"No, *señor*." She shook her head. "But I have seen how the bull mounts the cows, and the stallion mates with mares. I expect it will be like that."

He startled her by laughing, his reaction loud in the deep night silence. "You think I have no more finesse than a rutting bull, or a stallion pawing the air above a mare's hindquarters?"

"I . . . I pray it will be over quickly," she admitted. "But you must t-tell me—show me—how humans do it."

He sobered instantly. "And you will submit?"

Reluctantly, she nodded. "I have little choice in the matter."

He frowned as if the comment displeased him. "What if I tell you that submission is not what I want from you?"

She didn't know how to answer. As a man and a Spaniard, he dominated her entirely. She was at the very lowest level of authority. She could submit, fight, or flee. Those were her only choices. She was no match for him physically, and since she wasn't yet ready to flee she had to submit—grit her teeth and somehow get through this awful night. What more could he possibly want from her?

Leaning on one elbow, he appeared to be memorizing every aspect of her face and form. "What if I say I want your passion, Maria? When I plunge into your body, I want you to writhe in ecstasy and cry my name. To claw my back and urge me to thrust harder and faster, to give you all *my* passion, my pleasure, and my pain. What if I say I want *that,* little madonna? Submission alone will not suffice. Your body by itself can grant me no ease. Pleasure, yes, but I demand more than mere pleasure. I want you to desire me with the same fierce joy that you take in breathing . . . or being alive."

Her fears intensified. She struggled to subdue them, but a tremor passed through her. She never wanted to feel the way he was describing about anyone. He demanded too much—to own her soul as well as her body! Her body she was willing to sacrifice, but her soul? Her heart and all her feelings? *No!* Never. She longed for freedom, not bondage. No one deserved her innermost self. It was all she possessed that was truly and uniquely her own. All else belonged to the Spanish.

"I was ordered to offer you my body—to serve you in whatever way you wish. If that is not enough, then go to Don Gonzalo and tell him I displease you. What he will do then, I cannot say, but perhaps he will send you another maid—one more to your liking."

"You do not displease me!" Holding the sheet to his lower body, he rose from the bed in one swift, smooth motion. She couldn't stop herself from retreating a step. He towered over her—as magnificent and terrifying as a stallion in pursuit of a mare.

"I said I won't hurt you! You need not withdraw from me as if I were some ravenous beast about to tear you apart."

"You *will* hurt me, *señor*," she quietly disputed, holding her own though the effort cost her much. "You cannot avoid hurting me. For one thing, you are twice my size."

For another, he affected her in a way no man had ever done before, and that frightened her more than anything.

"I swear I will not touch you—at least not while you are frightened and cringing away from me. Were I to use your body while you were resisting me, I probably *would* hurt you. If 'tis pain you fear, you must allow yourself to relax and become more compliant. Then there will be no pain."

"Compliance is the same as submission, is it not?"

He stood very close to her now, one hand securing the sheet behind him. With his free hand, he reached around her waist and pulled her closer. The sensitive tips of her breasts grazed his naked chest. She trembled from the contact but could not retreat, for his hand held her steady. He kept her still while he gazed down at her, his mouth taut with anger.

"You are determined to make me a monster. I admit you have stirred my guilt. 'Tis almost stronger than my passion . . . *almost.*"

She suddenly noticed how the sheet jutted out in front of

him. A bull or a stallion could scarcely have tested the fragile barrier any more than he did. Her heart lurched painfully. He *would* tear her asunder if he jammed his great organ into her body . . . yet submit—comply—she must, if he demanded it.

"Take me quickly, and be done with it," she whispered. "This cruel anticipation must be far worse than the actual act. I have never known a woman to die of coupling, though I have known many who wept afterwards."

He jumped back from her as though scalded. "They *wept?*"

"They were captive *Indios,* not Spanish ladies. And they had no choice in the matter, either."

"You have never known a woman who *relished* a man's attentions?" he demanded incredulously.

She shrugged. She could not say she did, but then she had never spoken to another woman regarding the act of mating. She had noticed the maid, Juana, flirting and giggling around a certain *vaquero,* but she wasn't a close enough friend of the girl to discuss the issue. Except for a precious few, the servants tended to keep their distance. They feared her stepmother's reaction should they appear too friendly with her.

Since he seemed to be waiting for an answer, she gave him one. "My father's *vaqueros* once captured some Indian women alone on the plain. They brought them here before taking them to his silver mine to prepare food for the slaves who dig the metal from the bowels of the earth. The *vaqueros* received permission to use the women before they took them to the mines, and the women wept afterwards. They wailed far into the night, until they were beaten for it. That is all I know. I assumed then it was a painful, degrading experience. Certainly, no woman has ever told me differently."

"*Madre de Dios!* . . . your father . . . he is Don Gonzalo?"

Too late, Maria realized her slip of the tongue. "I did not say that, *señor.*"

"You referred to his *vaqueros* and his silver mine, so it can only be Don Gonzalo."

Shaken, she tried to pull away from him, but he held her too tightly. The strangeness of the entire situation had loosened her tongue; she had not guarded it as well as she had intended.

"If you are indeed his daughter, I am amazed he gave you to me. However, that also explains why he didn't keep you for himself."

Again, she couldn't resist the temptation to speak her mind. "Why amazed? I am his daughter by an *Indio,* and therefore hardly his daughter at all. He cares not what happens to me. I am less than the dust he shakes from his boots. If you beat me, he will say I deserve it, and my stepmother—Doña Inez—will applaud every welt you give me."

Don Diego sighed. Then—abruptly—he released her, stepped back, and wrapped the sheeting more tightly around his waist. "Clothe yourself, Maria. These disturbing revelations have dampened my ardor. I had guessed you were here for a reason. Until I know the truth of the matter, I want nothing more to do with you."

Maria snatched the sheet from the floor and hurriedly wound it around herself. When she finished, she raised her head to look at him and dared one last confession.

"You are right, Don Diego. I *am* here for a reason. My father wants you to remain here forever. He has no legitimate son to inherit his lands and his silver mine or to assist in their managing. You—a highborn Spaniard—could fulfill all his dreams. They are also the dreams of my stepmother, who hates this place and longs to live in the south. Many men would kill for such an opportunity as you have been handed. You, it seems, already have."

She bit her tongue. She had as much as accused him of murder. Now, he would surely beat her—and *then* use her.

To her amazement, he only stood watching her, his eyes dark and piercing. "Your father intends to force me to marry you. That's why he sent you—knowing I would have little choice in the matter once I had bedded you."

"Marry me?" It was her turn to laugh. "Have you not been listening? My father considers me unworthy of marriage to a highborn Spaniard. I am meant only to amuse you until a more suitable wife of your own race can be found."

"Your father has apparently thought of everything. His plan needs but one thing—my cooperation. Unfortunately, I don't wish to remain here forever. Generous though his offer is, I will not so willingly surrender my own plans. Look not so surprised, Maria. Does it shock you that a *murderer* could possibly have plans? No wonder you are so terrified—but also brave and courageous! You must have expected me to abuse you unmercifully.''

"I have little reason to expect anything other than abuse from a Spaniard."

"My poor little madonna. Life has dealt harshly with you, has it not? I can see from your face that it has. Others may have hurt you, but do not expect the same from me. I prefer more gentle methods to tame my conquests. Sensitive young fillies often resist their handlers, but if they are treated kindly they soon learn to trust a man and do all he asks of them. I will deal that way with you, in the hopes you will respond similarly.''

"I am no horse . . . and 'tis far too late for gentleness and kindness to win my trust. Just tell me what you would have me do, for I am still bound to obey you."

"Take your clothes—and the sheet—and go. The hour is late, and we both need sleep. When you dream, however, dream of me . . . holding you tenderly and touching you as gently as a mother caressing her newborn babe."

She stared at him in total disbelief. Men were rarely gentle, and Spaniards even less so. She could hardly dream of that which she had never experienced.

"I am not like the Spaniards you have known until now, little madonna. Give me a chance. I will show you how gentle and kind I can be."

Maria suddenly realized she had been given permission to depart. She rushed to gather her clothes and escape before he changed his mind. It took only a moment to locate her things, and as soon as she had found them she fled for the doorway.

"Maria!" The command was soft but compelling.

Her heart sank as she skidded to a stop and turned to face him.

"Señor?"

"Before you go, I do want one thing of you."

Her heart plunged to her toes. Now, it would come, something shameful, painful, and degrading.

"Whatever you wish. You have only to name it."

His grin flashed like lightning in the darkness of his shadowed face. "A smile, little madonna. I wish to see what you look like when you smile for me alone."

A smile should have been the easiest thing in the world to produce—but it wasn't. Maria had not had much practice smiling for Spaniards. She usually reserved her smiles for small children and animals—or for Indians, when she could find something to smile about.

She had to force herself.

"There," he said, "was that so hard? You really should smile more often, Maria. When you smile, your beauty dazzles like the sun shining through clouds on a stormy day. A smile transforms you from merely lovely to breathtaking. Together with your fox fire eyes, your smile could slay dragons or topple empires—or even warm the heart of an exiled and homesick Spaniard."

Her smile came more easily the second time. This Spaniard certainly knew how to make winning compliments. If she were not careful, she would believe he truly meant no harm. That would be like trusting a scorpion—allow one to get too close, and you were likely to be stung.

"*Buenas noches,* Don Diego," she whispered and fled.

After she had gone, Diego returned to the bed. The emptiness of the room now depressed him. Any sane man would have availed himself of the girl's luscious charms. Clearly, her father had intended that he do just that. He pictured himself plunging between her soft thighs and feeling her body spasm as it opened for him, and he released a heartfelt sigh. She had looked at him so bravely—fighting her fear. Her terror had been as plain as a brand stamped on her forehead.

Her courage and spirit roused his admiration. He hated to destroy either one. Rather, he yearned to see her smile at him

in genuine liking, with warmth and willingness in her eyes.
Only then could he enjoy taking her to the limits of ecstasy.

Her eyes are truly amazing, he thought as he snuffed the
candle flame with his fingers and stretched out in the dark on
the soft bed. Doña Inez was right; she had fox fire eyes. They
glowed with an almost eerie luminescence, suggesting mystery
and other-worldliness. If she ever fell into the clutches of an
Inquisitor, he would suspect her of a carnal association with
Satan himself.

He himself discounted such things as preposterous. No evil
abided in this little madonna; she radiated rebellion against her
circumstances, but no hatred or innate wickedness such as he
had always sensed in his cousin, Evaristo. Evaristo exuded
malevolence, while Maria's essential goodness and innocence
shone like a beacon, making him feel that if he took advantage
of her he really *would* be a monster.

Furthermore, he disliked being manipulated by Don Gonzalo.
No doubt there were men who would not mind being named
a son and granted an instant inheritance. But he preferred being
master of his own fate and deciding his own future. True, he
was nearly destitute, deprived of his birthright and banished to
a foreign country, but he still had his pride. Never again would
he allow another man—friend or foe—to chart his course in
life. He might fail at regaining his father's regard and his own
inheritance, but he intended to take his vengeance on Evaristo
and somehow carve out a good life for himself. No matter what
happened, he would choose his own destiny.

That included wooing Maria into his bed and winning her
wholehearted participation in the delightful games he intended
to teach her. Closing his eyes, he imagined how she would
look with her head tilted back, her black hair spilling down
her back and her mouth parted in anticipation of his full possession. He could almost hear her panting with passion.

When a cold, wet nose suddenly found his hand and a tongue
began to lick it, he realized Caobo had finally found him. A
dog, not a woman, eagerly sought his affection. He had left
the dog in the stable with El Cid and his other horses, but
Caobo had grown accustomed to sleeping near him, and must

have been silently searching the grounds and the house to discover his whereabouts.

Splaying his fingers, Diego patted the sleek head, and the dog wriggled and whined in delight, then leapt onto the bed and curled up next to him, pressed close to his side.

"So I must share my bed with a hound rather than a comely young woman, must I?" Diego groaned in mock disgust, but he was glad of the dog's company.

He didn't relish being alone tonight, thinking of what might have been. The dog's presence comforted him, and at last, he could relax and even ignore the throbbing sensation in his temples—a harbinger of tomorrow's sufferings. The encounter with Maria had cleared his head of the effects of over-imbibing, but now, he was again conscious of feeling dizzy and wooly-headed.

Caobo would keep watch over him, allowing him to sleep without constantly awakening to check his surroundings, a habit he had picked up before leaving Spain. In the warehouse at Cadiz, he had spent his nights tensely listening to every small sound. Here in the New World, he was presumably safe, but old habits died hard.

Tomorrow, he decided, he would seek out Maria and speak with her again. He would start the process of befriending her. He fell asleep wondering what small treasure or sweetmeat he might give her. He always trained his horses by offering them a tidbit they could not resist. Once a wary horse accepted a bit of cornmeal or cane sugar from his hand, the battle was half-won. Surely, it was the same with a woman. . . .

He awoke to the sound of voices—a man and a woman arguing. When he moved, his head nearly exploded, so he lay still, listening and attempting to get his bearings. He knew only that he lay in a strange bed, in a strange room, and when he opened his eyes he gazed up at an unfamiliar ceiling composed of heavy wooden beams and faded red tiles. Next to him, Caobo stretched and licked his arm.

Finally, he realized what he was hearing: Don Gonzalo and Doña Inez arguing.

"I tell you she did it deliberately. You must beat her as a

punishment! He would not have banished her from his quarters if she had not sorely aggravated him in some way.''

"You are right, Inez. I cannot believe he dismissed her, not if she greeted him naked in his bed, as you ordered. Are you certain she was naked?''

"Blessed saints! How can I be sure of that? But if she was not, that is all the more reason to beat her. Like your bastard sons, she has betrayed you and ruined all our plans. Beat her and send her to the silver mine! Since she scorns an *hidalgo,* let us see if she finds the prison guards more to her liking. I doubt not *they* will take the rebellion out of her. Once she has borne a string of bastards whose fathers cannot be named with certainty, she will wish she had done as she was told and spread her legs for a nobleman.''

"Lower your voice, Inez. Don Diego will hear us. If what you say is true—she provoked him into sending her away untouched—I *will* beat her and give her to the guards at the silver mine. I will not bear a daughter's betrayal any more than I'll bear a son's. Why do they all betray me? The accident with Antonio I could at least understand, but this I cannot. She has destroyed not only her own future, but mine and yours.''

"Wretched little savage! I could scarce believe my eyes when I found her sleeping as she always does on her pallet in the cook shed. I wanted to throttle her while she slept—looking innocent as a babe. But she heard my cry and awoke, then offered all those weak excuses. She lies as easily as she breathes, claiming he took one look at her and sent her away in disgust. I tell you he would *not* have done so, not a virile young man like Don Diego, unless she provoked him to it. We must beat her until she confesses!''

"Go and fetch my bullwhip. Summon the little rebel to the laundry shed. I'll strip her naked and judge for myself if her body could possibly disgust a man.''

"What do you expect to find—the pox? There is not a mark on her. But come, you will see for yourself.''

As their voices retreated, Diego rolled out of bed and struggled into the clothing he had worn the night before. The pounding in his head nearly blinded him, and he stumbled over poor

Caobo, causing the dog to yelp and seek refuge beneath the table. He ignored everything in his haste to stop Maria from being beaten and humiliated. What was wrong with Don Gonzalo and his wife? What sort of place *was* this?

Yet he knew even as he rushed to rescue the girl that fathers were sometimes the harshest judges of their own offspring. Witness how his own father had believed him capable of the vilest wickedness. Well, he would *not* let them punish Maria!

Chapter Four

"I have already told you. I do not know why he sent me away. He was not happy to find me naked in his bed."

Maria calmly faced her accusers, but inside, she was far from calm. Terror had dug its talons deep. Her father's face held the same degree of outrage and wounded pride she remembered seeing on the day he had ridden out to capture her brothers and killed one instead.

"Lying little savage!" her stepmother hissed. "You said— or did—something to offend him. 'Twas not your presence in his bed that did it. Before this day is done, we will have the truth of the matter."

"Your brothers betrayed me," growled her father. "Now you have done the same. You will pay dearly, daughter, even as they paid."

He uncoiled the bullwhip in his hand and gave it a snap. The thin, lethal leather bit into the beaten earth floor at her feet, raising a puff of dust. Maria eyed the closed door to the shed, her only means of escape, but Doña Inez stepped in front of it and leaned against the heavy wooden barrier. Triumph shone on her thin, sallow features. She had finally succeeded in discrediting Maria altogether. Maria wondered if she would leave the shed alive.

"Remove your clothing," her stepmother said. "Your father wishes to see for himself if anything is wrong with you."

Her father stepped forward, and before Maria could guess his intent he seized the front of her bodice and tore it open down the center. Warm air washed over her bare breasts. The violence of the action caused her to gasp, but she made no move to cover herself. She would not cower before her own father, nor this woman who was her mortal enemy.

"I did nothing wrong. I only followed orders." Maria searched her father's eyes for some connection or recognition of familial bond. She found none, and a feeling of desperation swept over her. "I awaited Don Diego naked in his bed. He did not want me, so he sent me away. I do not deserve a beating because he found me unattractive. I did not betray you, Father," she added softly.

Not this time, anyway. When I finally run away and steal horses to give to the Indians, then you will have just cause to hate me. Our blood bond will count for nothing.

"I did my best," she persisted, stopping short of begging. Still, she needed to say something in her own defense. Once her father started wielding the whip, he might not stop until she was dead.

Her father stared fixedly at her breasts, his face red and congested. "I see no ugliness to merit rejection, Daughter, so it stands to reason you must have done something. Remove the rest of your clothing. Turn your back and kneel down. When the lash licks your tender flesh, perhaps you will recall the truth of what happened last night."

Maria's hands trembled as she pushed off the remainder of her blouse and started on her skirt. But a commotion outside in the yard suddenly drew her father's attention.

"Where is the laundry shed? Is that it—that building over there?" thundered an angry male voice.

The door flew open, propelling Doña Inez across the shed, so that she stumbled and almost fell to her knees. Fully-dressed, wearing fawn-colored trunk hose and a doublet of soft-looking, buttery leather that matched his tall boots, Don Diego stood in the entranceway. Behind him, Maria glimpsed Juana, white-lipped and pale with fright.

"What is happening here?" the imposing figure demanded. Don Diego looked from Maria to Don Gonzalo and Doña Inez, then back again to Maria.

Frozen in place, Maria clutched the waistband of her skirt. Had he come to defend her—or condemn her? Her father and stepmother stood staring at Don Diego as if they didn't know what to make of him. It was suddenly so quiet Maria could hear her heart beating.

Don Diego's glance slid to the bullwhip, then lifted to her father's face. "Why do you beat the girl?" he asked quietly. "What wrong could she have done to merit *this?*"

"Disobedience!" her father snapped, coming to life all of a sudden. "She disobeyed me."

"And me, as well," added Doña Inez. "Do not distress yourself over something so insignificant as the punishment of a worthless *Indio,* Don Diego."

To Maria, she said: "Cover yourself. Have you no shame?"

Maria longed to respond that she had indeed suffered shame last night, when she had been forced to await Don Diego naked in his bed. Knowing it would not help her case to voice that sentiment, she held her tongue, retrieved her blouse from the floor, put it on, and pulled its torn halves together over her breasts.

"Give me the girl," Don Diego demanded in an imperious tone that brooked no argument. "I would have kept her with me last night, but the consumption of too much brandy had dulled my senses. It would be a great waste to mar her beauty with the lash. Give her to me now. I promise she will disobey no more. In the future, I will manage her behavior."

Doña Inez looked stunned, her father gratified. The anger drained from him like water from a leaky waterskin. "You favor the girl, after all?"

"I assure you, Gonzalo, she looks much better to me this morning than she did last night. Thank you for sending her to me. . . . I need a maid to tidy my quarters."

"I *knew* you did!" Doña Inez declared. "That's why I ordered her to await you there and graciously serve you. I told her to sweep all the floors, make up the bed, and attend to your clothing. Unfortunately, she refused to do her duty and thus earned herself a beating."

"Ah, but she *did* do her duty, Doña Inez," Don Diego disputed with a wry grin and a sparkle in his warm, brown eyes. "My quarters are immaculate. However, I still need someone to locate my belongings and settle them in my rooms, so I can be truly comfortable. I assured her last night that this morning would be soon enough to see to these minor details. Didn't she explain this to you?"

Amazed, Maria could only watch and listen as all three of them—her father, stepmother, and Don Diego—behaved as if her only duties were to act as a maidservant. One would think they had all agreed ahead of time not to mention her *true* purpose in being sent to his rooms.

"Maria, why didn't you tell me?" her stepmother peevishly demanded. "Ah, Don Diego! These *Indios* are such a trial. They guard their thoughts so closely one can only assume the worst. You understand, do you not? I thought she had refused to obey me, and we can never permit our inferiors to challenge our authority. *Indios* must obey Spaniards without question. Do you not agree, sir?"

"Of course he agrees!" her father bellowed. "We have had all this fuss for nothing. Maria! Find our guest's belongings and see that they are installed in his quarters. Then dress in something pretty. You offend my eyes with those rags you are wearing. Don Diego must also be offended."

"She *has* pretty clothes. I myself took care of that," Doña Inez said. "If this is another instance of rebellion—"

"I'm sure 'tis not." Don Diego waved the issue aside with one sun-bronzed hand. "You can't beat the girl for guarding her finery when there's work to be done. If punishment is merited, let it be for needlessly soiling a valuable garment, rather than for protecting it from harm."

" 'Twould be an immense relief to me if you assumed her supervision while you are here, Don Diego." Doña Inez sighed.

"Her sole responsibility is to make certain your chambers are kept to your liking, and your meals—other than those we take together—are brought to you as you desire. We are informal here, sharing only the noon meal and sometimes the late evening one, but otherwise going our separate ways. If she displeases you in any fashion, we will, of course, intervene."

"Say no more, Doña Inez. Consider it done. From now on, the girl will answer to me and me only. As for our meals together, I cannot promise to share the noon meal, as I expect to be quite busy during the daylight hours. Often, I will not be here. I will, however, be more than happy to avail myself of your charming company when the sun goes down."

"Not share the noon meal?" Don Gonzalo blinked in astonishment. "Why, what will you be doing, Diego? 'Tis the hottest time of the day from noon until three o'clock. We *never* work the horses then, but only in the cool of the morning or early evening."

"I will be . . . exploring," Don Diego replied with an enigmatic smile. "Sometimes, I may be gone overnight or for several days. Your Ocean of Grass fascinates me, and I'm most anxious to see more of it."

"B-but that's highly dangerous!" her father sputtered. "No one ventures more than a league or two onto the Sea of Grass without a compelling reason. The savages lie in wait. They are quite expert with their bows and arrows. I keep my best cattle and all the horses penned at night, but 'tis nearly impossible to guard the rest. When I do send men out to round them up, I send them forth heavily armed. 'Tis the only way to ensure they will all return."

"Savages could never take me by surprise," Don Diego boasted. It sounded more like a statement of fact than a boast. "El Cid warns me of anyone's approach. Caobo—my hound—does the same. Ah, here he comes now . . ."

The tall, slender, brindle-colored dog burst into the laundry shed and made straight for Don Diego. When the dog reached him, it stood on its hind legs and eagerly greeted him with paws on shoulders and a long swipe of a pink tongue across his beard-stubbled jaw.

"Caobo, down, you rogue!" Laughing, Don Diego pushed the dog away. "Behave yourself or I will send you back to the stable to stay with the horses."

He grinned at Doña Inez's shocked, disapproving expression. "Do not worry, Doña Inez. The cur will not soil your house. He is a very neat, fastidious animal."

"Where did he sleep last night?" Doña Inez eyed the dog with great distaste.

"With me," Don Diego informed her. "Until I find a bed partner who pleases me more, I will allow him to share my blankets, for his presence wards off loneliness."

"A bed partner!" Doña Inez reddened as if the thought of Don Diego having a bed partner would never occur to someone of her delicate sensibilities.

Don Gonzalo guffawed. "Let us hope you find one before the cur gives you fleas," he told Diego.

"Indeed, let us hope so," Don Diego drawled with a sly wink at Maria.

Feeling giddy with relief that she had avoided a beating, Maria was torn between smiling at Don Diego's bold teasing and frowning at him for his presumption. Was she supposed to be flattered to find herself competing with a hound? Unless he commanded her, she never intended to sleep in Don Diego's bed. She was grateful for his interference this morning, but she still intended to sleep as far away from him as she could get.

"May I be excused now to gather your belongings, Don Diego?" She congratulated herself on sounding polite but detached.

"Yes, of course. When you have finished, I would be pleased to break my fast, Maria. The meal need not be elaborate. Whatever is easiest suits me well."

"As you wish, *señor,*" Maria answered.

"After you eat, you must see my horses!" Don Gonzalo crowed. "In my excitement to show you my beautiful mare, La Reina, I could scarcely sleep last night. I am certain she will meet your approval. She rivals any horse you had to leave behind in Spain."

"Then amaze me, if you will, Don Gonzalo. I welcome any distraction from the pounding inside my head."

As the talk turned to horses, Maria gladly fled.

The breaking of Don Diego's fast should have been no inconvenience. Food was ready and waiting in the cook shed. The moment still managed to provide some awkward, difficult moments for Maria. She wanted to thank Don Diego for rescuing her from the lash, but did not know how to do so without giving the impression that gratitude had softened her resistance. Since he had said he would treat her gently and kindly in an effort to win her cooperation in her own seduction, she should have been forewarned. However, she had not realized how charming and solicitous he could be.

In the library, while he sat poring over one of her father's rare books, she served him roasted meat, two coddled eggs, and a bowl of gruel made from crushed corn. Caobo lay at his feet, and under the dog's hopeful scrutiny, she also provided a pewter cup brimming with the sweetly frothed *chocolatl* beverage extracted from cacao beans and laced with tropical spices that Doña Inez horded like a miser. Smiling, Don Diego pointed to the empty chair at the table.

"Come, sit down and join me, Maria. When I eat, you must eat. You brought enough for two, anyway."

Maria stood where she was, at the side of the round wooden table. "I am not permitted to eat the same foods you eat. If my stepmother should hear of this, 'twould be cause for another whipping."

"Not if I have commanded you to join me. Leave Doña Inez to me. I will keep her purring like a kitten." He reached across the table to take her hand. "Come, sit. I insist. It gives me indigestion to eat alone. Would you have me ill? Your company ensures my continued good health."

"You do not need me. You have the company of your dog."

He slanted her a wry glance. " 'Tis not the same thing, and you know it."

"You can join my father, then. He is breaking his fast out in the courtyard. I will take your food there if you wish."

"Ah, Maria, do not flash those fox fire eyes at me in vexation. I prefer *your* company to that of your father, or even my faithful friend, Caobo. Your father almost beat you once today. Hadn't you ought to avoid him until he forgets the unfortunate incident?"

He was reminding her of how much she owed him, and though she still had not told him, she *was* grateful. If he hadn't arrived when he did, she would surely be suffering the torments of hell right now—or be dead. Pulling out the empty chair, she sat down gingerly on the edge of the hard seat.

"Go on." He pushed the plate of roasted meat toward her. "Help yourself."

She looked away. "I cannot." Earlier, she had been hungry, but now her throat felt blocked.

"What is in that cup?" He behaved as if he had not heard her. "It smells delicious."

"Chocolatl." She was surprised he did not know what it was.

"I have never had it. Is it good?"

"I don't know, for I have never had it either, but 'tis considered a great delicacy."

"Then I command you to drink it. It smells too sweet for my tastes. If you like it, I shall ask for it at every meal."

Maria quickly succumbed. *Chocolatl* had been a favorite of little Antonio, and she had always longed to taste the forbidden luxury. Raising the cup to her lips, she took a sip. The froth tickled her nose, and the heady aroma beguiled her, but it was the taste that won her heart. Never had she consumed anything so sweet and rich. She sighed with pleasure.

"Ah," he said. "I wish the thought of my kisses could elicit such a response."

Licking her lips, she ignored his comment about kisses and wrestled with the impulse to drain the entire cup. The drink must be savored, she realized, and slowly licked her lips again, to draw out her pleasure.

His gaze fastened upon her tongue. "Drink some more," he

urged. "Only this time, refrain from licking your lips afterwards."

She cocked an eyebrow at him. It seemed an odd request, but she obeyed, for she craved another mouthful of the *chocolatl's* fragrant sweetness. If she were never permitted to drink it again, she would always remember how luscious it had been. Setting the cup down in front of her, she held the beverage in her mouth a moment before swallowing. It was hot but not too hot, sweet but not too sweet. It was pure enchantment! No wonder the *hidalgos* kept it for themselves.

Concentrating on the exquisite taste, she closed her eyes a moment. When she opened them, Don Diego's face filled her field of vision. He was leaning across the table, so that their noses almost met. Startled by his close proximity, she hadn't the presence of mind to move away but only watched him with a pounding heart. Smiling, he leaned closer yet, encircled the back of her head with his hand to hold her in place, then put his mouth to hers, and gently *licked* the remnants of *chocolatl* from her lips!

His actions fanned a new pleasure, a spreading warmth akin to the sensation the beverage itself had given her. All her senses were suddenly heightened, and her body thrummed with physical awareness. Only his mouth and tongue touched her, but she could feel his heat reaching out to enfold her. When his tongue grazed hers, she nearly leapt from her skin.

A moment later, he released her and, smiling broadly, reached for a bone heavy with meat and dripping juices. At his feet, Caobo whined and eagerly thumped his tail.

"Are you certain you don't want to sample this excellent beef?" he asked, all too casually. "It looks and smells delicious—not sweet like the *chocolatl,* but savory just the same."

His actions left her speechless. She was all the more confounded when he again winked at her before taking a bite of the meat.

"I think I could become greatly attached to *chocolatl,*" he continued, after chewing and swallowing. He cut the remaining meat from the bone and gave the bone itself to Caobo. The dog took it daintily and went off into a corner to relish his prize.

"Especially if I could drink it from your lips, morning and night. Indeed, I would enjoy it even better at night. What about you? What would be your preference?"

No one had ever queried Maria about her preferences on anything; she had not been allowed to have preferences. His remarks were both suggestive and disconcerting. What did he expect in response? No one had ever spoken to her the way he did, as if she might actually *have* opinions worth hearing.

"I . . . I think I should like to drink *chocolatl* at any time of the day or night. 'Tis wonderful."

Her answer delighted him. Wiping his hands on a square of cloth she had provided for just that purpose, he said: "I believe I will tell my hosts I have developed a particular fondness for the drink. That way they won't be surprised at how often you fetch it to my quarters. Whenever you desire some for yourself, you must go and get it."

"May I really?" She could not help smiling or confiding her thoughts. "The bean from which this drink is made is actually quite bitter. 'Tis a miracle something so delicious can be fashioned from it."

"Ah, but 'tis often the case that something sweet derives from something that at first seemed bitter. Trust me, little madonna, I know whereof I speak."

That was the problem; she dared not trust him. A Spaniard could never be trusted. If he thought to charm her with *chocolatl,* he was doomed to disappointment. Half the wondrous beverage still remained in the cup, but she pushed it away with her fingertips. She could not be bought for any price, and certainly not for *this*.

The small gesture did not escape him. "What? Have you finished so soon? I thought you loved it, and here, you have left a great amount to be thrown away."

"I have had enough," she said, rising. "You are right. 'Tis far too rich, especially for one unaccustomed to it. Simple water is enough for me. I need nothing else."

"Maria, I command you to finish it. It would be a shame to let it go to waste."

She stood there, hesitating—torn between her desire to finish the treat and her determination to owe him as little as possible. The thought of being in debt to him terrified her. It would be so much easier to hate him if he stopped being nice to her!

"Go on." He nodded toward the cup. "You know you want it. Why deny yourself? There's no good reason for it."

There is a reason—a very good reason. Don't make me like you, Don Diego. Don't tempt me to stay here to be hurt like my mother. One day soon I will be leaving, and where I am going I will never see you again.

With a trembling hand, she seized the cup, lifted it to her mouth, and quickly drained the contents. She tried to ignore what her mouth found so delightful, but when she had finished, she could not keep from licking the last trace of the delectable *chocolatl* from her lips again. She felt a bit like Caobo, who was gnawing his bone with great satisfaction in the corner.

Watching her, Don Diego grinned. "Tomorrow, when I break my fast, you must bring me another cup. It gives me great joy to watch *you* enjoy something, Maria. Soon, you will feel more comfortable allowing me to give you pleasure."

She shook her head. "Never, *señor*. 'Tis useless what you are doing. You would do better to save your wiles for someone more susceptible to them."

His eyes searched her face, seeing far too much, she feared. "Oh, I think you are susceptible. You simply refuse to admit it. All I need is time, little madonna. In time, you will be mine. I am known for my patience and persistence."

She lifted her chin. "And I am known for my willfulness. If you doubt it, ask Doña Inez."

"Ah, but she has treated you badly. I have already told you not to expect the same from me."

"And I have told you that my expectations do not matter. I am yours to command. Do not ask more from me than obedience, for I have nothing more to give."

"You are wrong, little madonna, and I shall avail myself of every opportunity to convince you of that."

She sought refuge in feigned ignorance of what he meant. "I have finished the *chocolatl*. What more do you desire? Must I eat the beef as well?"

"Not unless you are hungry. As for what I desire, 'tis *you,* little madonna. Just you. Willing and eager in my arms. *Begging* me to make love to you."

His words twisted her heart. Excitement and resentment warred in her. "Tell me what I must say. I will say it, for I am bound to obey you. But what I *feel,* you will *never* control."

He rose to his feet. The table stood between them, but the barrier suddenly seemed insufficient. "Shall we put that to the test? Come here, Maria. Kiss me. Then tell me you feel nothing."

"Are you c-commanding me?"

He nodded. "You can do it quickly, like you drank the *chocolatl,* to avoid enjoying it. But I think you will enjoy it, anyway. Your enjoyment will soon become a craving. We are meant to crave intimacy, my little rebel. Man and woman both seek closeness as they seek the air—because it gives them life. When they come together, they are more alive than you could ever imagine."

"But life is painful, cruel, and disappointing! I want nothing to do with intimacy. It will only give me *more* pain."

He came swiftly 'round the table. "Maria, we have all been hurt! Do you think because I am an *hidalgo,* I have not suffered just as you have?"

"You are not a slave, with no right to your own thoughts or wishes! What can you know of hurt and rejection?"

His hand closed around her arm. With gentle force, he drew her to him. "One need not be a slave or an *Indio* to have suffered the pain of rejection. Kiss me, Maria—or let me kiss you. I will show you that kisses can be even sweeter than *chocolatl.*"

"No! No, don't . . ." she pleaded.

But as he molded himself against her, she could feel her resistance slipping away. His lips brushed her cheek—gentle as a butterfly's wing. Releasing a little sob, she gave up and clung to him. He was strong and solid. Gentle and kind. Beauti-

ful in a rough, masculine way. And he had saved her from the
lash. She could not fight his strength, nor her own inner needs.
She *needed* to be held. Needed gentleness. It had been so long
since anyone had said a kind word to her, smiled at her, teased
her, or offered her anything but scorn and rejection. What would
be the harm of a single kiss?

She turned her face up to his.

He gazed into her eyes for a long, silent moment, then lowered his mouth to hers. He tasted of beef and *chocolatl.* He
smelled of man, leather, and horse. He wrapped his arms around
her, and she imagined his body as a shield against all harm,
hurt, and ugliness. He would protect her from life's sharp edges.
He would deflect all the arrows.

If only she could believe it . . .

His kiss was far sweeter than she had expected—better even
than *chocolatl!* It made her head spin and her knees go weak.
It awakened yearnings and made her body tingle in places that
seemed at once foreign and desperately familiar. She could
easily imagine losing control. She wanted to yield everything
. . . but wondrous as the kiss was, she still felt doubt and
confusion. How could he make her feel this way when she did
not want to feel anything?

Breaking the contact, she gulped air and struggled for nor-
malcy. He laughed softly in her ear, the sound brimming with
masculine triumph.

"Now, tell me you felt nothing, Maria. Deny it if you can.
I will not believe you. I myself felt shattered. Never has a kiss
so shaken me. You have rocked me to my foundations. I can
only wonder what it will be like to join my body to yours in
the final intimacy. We could die of the pleasure, sweetling."

"Don't! Please don't mock me!" Tears sprang to her eyes,
and she pushed him away. "You have had your kiss. Don't
press me for more! I will not give you any more. 'Tis just as
I feared—you have taken far too much as it is!"

In the corner, Caobo lifted his head and watched them, sensing something was wrong.

"Maria! What do you mean? I assure you I never meant to
mock you."

"For you, that kiss meant nothing! You have probably kissed a hundred women—and beguiled a thousand more. But I have known only a mother's kisses, and they were long ago, and chaste and innocent. I am no match for this cruel sport, and well you know it! In your kindness, you are merciless. If I allow you closer, you will surely destroy me. Kiss me no more, Don Diego. The next time, and the time after that, and indeed for all time, I will fight you. I swear I will fight!"

"Maria, stop. What nonsense is this?"

But she would not stop. She *could* not. She struggled and broke free, then dashed from the room. If her father flayed her alive for this, it would only be what she deserved for her foolishness. Anything would be better than allowing herself to care too much for a man who already possessed a power over her she could not understand, much less resist. Why had she kissed him—*why?*

She had known last night, when first she met him, that he threatened her future and her dream of freedom. She had sensed her own vulnerability. How quickly he had toppled her defenses! How quickly she had let him. Fool! *Fool*. Was this how it had started for her mother—with a single kiss? With a shattering embrace? Or simply with her own need for someone to love her?

And someone to love.

Chapter Five

"There she is—La Reina! My pride and joy, the finest horse I own." Don Gonzalo proudly pointed to the animal inside the small wooden enclosure.

Diego stepped closer. All the while his host had been showing off his horses he had made appropriate comments of appreciation, but his thoughts had centered on Maria. He had been wondering where she had gone after she left him, and why she had exploded like a faulty *harquebus* after he had kissed her. He was certain she had enjoyed the kiss as much as he had, but she seemed determined to fight her attraction to him. What more could the girl hope for than to capture the fancy of a member of the aristocracy?

She was, in fact, little more than a slave. Because of her Indian blood, she could never hope to make a good marriage. Obviously, she had been mistreated in the past and ought, therefore, to be glad of a little kindness. He fully intended to protect her from her father's temper and her stepmother's resentment of her beauty . . . so why was she still so wary of him?

He could not understand it. He had never considered himself particularly handsome, but he wasn't ugly, either. The girl fired his blood as no other female ever had, but he had been careful not to abuse his position of power over her. If she would only cooperate, he knew he could give her pleasure. He'd had enough experience with women to trust in his ability to satisfy them. Her own father and stepmother intended for them to be together. Perhaps *that* was the problem; she preferred a whipping to bending to their will.

Shaking his head at her obstinacy, Diego peered into the enclosure at Gonzalo's best horse. He did not expect to see anything spectacular, but he was prepared to compliment his host nonetheless. Don Gonzalo's horses were more than adequate, but in no way compared to El Cid. Only a few were the equal of the mares he had brought with him. Those few— mares also—bore a faint resemblance to El Toreador, and should therefore produce good offspring. However, Gonzalo's only stallion was too thick in the neck and lean in the loin to yield foals of exceptional quality.

This mare, however—

Diego blinked and took a second look. The horse in the corral intently returned his gaze. Head high, nostrils flared, and ears pricked in his direction, she nickered softly, then pranced the length of her pen as if to show off her floating trot. Her black mane and tail streamed out behind her, and her dainty hooves barely skimmed the earth as she spun on a hind foot and trotted back the way she had come.

Apparently frustrated by her confinement, she leapt into the air and executed a perfect *curvet.* When she landed, she kicked out with her hind legs as if to say, "See? I am really something, am I not?"

And she was: A creature full of fire and grace, possessing that indefinable presence that made a man itch to tame her. She was—in a word—beautiful. Just as Maria embodied all of the qualities he had come to consider feminine, La Reina offered a version of perfection among horses. From the tip of her small fine muzzle, which was ebony black like her mane, tail, and lower legs, to the very end of the silky flag she waved so proudly, she exuded good breeding and marvelous conformation. The sheen of her golden coat and her high mettle told him she was at the peak of health. Matched with El Cid, she would produce horses of unmatched quality—or so he hoped.

He readily admitted that the breeding of horses was an imprecise science. His own father had always bred "like to like" and the best of each, but his experiments were not always successful. Sometimes, a promising stallion or mare failed to pass on their best attributes, and the outcome of a glorious match proved disappointing.

Yet Diego would have staked his soul on the certainty that a union between La Reina and El Cid would result in a horse without equal.

"Have you nothing to say?" Don Gonzalo elbowed Diego in the side. "Does she not resemble the illustrious El Toreador?"

"I think . . ." Diego said carefully, "that she surpasses him, if that is possible."

"Hah! I knew it! 'Tis why I have been saving her for a stallion truly worthy of her. The one I have—El Bobo, we call him—will not suffice, so I have kept them apart."

"You call your stallion El Bobo? Is he a dunce then, that his name shows so little respect?"

"No, but I have not much respect for him. As a sire, he is better than most you can find here in the New World, but he is no El Toreador, and even less an El Cid. He produces better than average offspring, especially when crossed with your father's excellent mares, but I could not find it in my heart to give La Reina to him. I feared I would be too disappointed in the outcome if the foal looked more like him than her."

"How did you obtain her? I need not examine her teeth to tell she is younger than the others. She could not have come in the original group my father gave you."

"She did not. She is a granddaughter of El Toreador, not a daughter. Until her death a few years back, her dam was the best of the mares I had from your father. I bred her to a stallion who is dead now, too. He belonged to a friend of mine in Santa Barbola. Shortly after their union, the stallion was gored by a bull and died, so we could not repeat the match. I wept when I heard of the incident. My mare never again produced anything so fine."

"What has been her training?" Diego couldn't take his eyes from the lovely creature. He longed to ride her, and hoped his host would offer him the opportunity.

"She is broken to saddle . . . but she is most temperamental. All my *domadors* fear her. So also, I am ashamed to say, does my *arrendador*. The two do not get on well together. He has tried to teach her the finer points of equitation and the advanced movements, but so far she refuses to learn them."

"Refuses to learn them? But she just performed a *curvet* before our very eyes. She doesn't need to *learn* the advanced movements—she already knows them. Your *arrendador* must strive to properly ask her for them. When he does, she will perform without hesitation."

Don Gonzalo chuckled. "Ah, Diego. . . . You see now why I am so happy you have come! No one in the New World has your expertise. I have searched everywhere for a master horseman who can work with my fiery La Reina to achieve her full potential, but I am surrounded by dolts and dullards who are far more likely to ruin her than to win her submission. From this day onward, she is yours. No one else may lay hands on her."

Diego could not believe his ears. This time, his host wasn't even drunk. If Gonzalo truly meant to *give* him the horse, he would take her back with him when he returned to Spain. A man might live his whole life searching for two horses of the quality of El Cid and this mare, and never be so fortunate as to find them, much less bring them together. First, he would complete the mare's education, *then* he would breed her to El Cid.

"When you say *mine,* Gonzalo, what exactly do you mean?"

"Have I not made myself clear? For as long as you remain at *Dehesa de Oro,* La Reina will belong to you. You may ride her, train her, breed her . . . whatever appeals to you most. Do all three if you like."

"But when I leave here?" Diego persisted. "What will happen to her then?"

Gonzalo thick brows drew together in a frown. "I thought I had made it clear by now that I intend you shall *never* wish to leave. What awaits you in Spain that you cannot find here? Listen, and I will tell you again. This is the land of the future, Diego. Here, there is no one above you. Rather, *you* are above all. Before your arrival, I told my *arrendador* you would be my new Master of Horses. Your reputation preceded you, so he counts himself the most fortunate of men to have the opportunity to learn from an expert reinsman.''

Diego wanted La Reina very much, but the time had come to clarify his own intentions. ''Gonzalo, I am my father's son, and I had thought to inherit *his* legacy, not yours. I thank you for your generosity, but I have been unjustly accused of murder and therefore live only to clear my name and regain all I have so unfairly lost.''

''But the king will never forgive you! And how can you ever prove you are innocent? If you had proof, you would never have come here. There would have been no need. The sooner you make peace with your circumstances, the sooner you will come to appreciate the life I offer. The possibilities—and the riches—are limitless.''

Diego was reminded of what he had told Maria earlier: that something sweet could derive from that which was initially bitter. When it came to himself, he had difficulty believing it. He could never be happy—never know true peace—until his old life had been fully restored to him, and the man responsible for destroying it had been punished.

''What might our king be willing to do in exchange for gold, Gonzalo? What if I should find gold here and take proof of it back to him, so he can send other men to wrest it from the earth? What if I should find an entire city of gold, such as we have all heard exists somewhere on the Sea of Grass?''

Gonzalo snorted derisively. ''Diego, I have spent the better half of my life searching for gold. I have ridden long distances onto the Ocean of Grass and brought Indians back in chains to work in my silver mine. Some I had tortured, but neither fire, the lash, nor disembowelment ever loosened their tongues enough to tell me what I wanted to know: Where can I find gold? Give it up, Diego. Indians are a poor, ignorant people who dress themselves in skins, eat the raw hearts of whatever animals they manage to slay, and can see no value in a yellow metal a civilized man would risk death to obtain. If you desire gold, look to La Reina. The only gold you will be likely to discover can be found in the gleam of her coat. Do not make the mistake of casting her aside in favor of a dream you will never possess. She is dream enough for any man, but especially for a horseman such as yourself.''

Watching the mare cavort in her corral, Diego wanted to agree, but when he thought of his cousin gloating over his downfall and enjoying all that should have been his, he could not so easily cast aside his plans for revenge and the reinstatement of his honor. What kind of man would he be if he refused to fight for what belonged to him?

He must at least fight. 'Twas far too soon to concede victory to Evaristo. Diego blamed himself for not having discovered his cousin's plan in time to stop it. He had been too busy with his passion—horses—to note the warning signs Evaristo had unwittingly displayed: the blatant way his cousin had curried favor with his ailing father, the outrage he had expressed over the loss of the stolen horses, when everyone knew he cared little for horses and spent no more time with them than he absolutely must. The clever way he had led Diego to believe that the thief must be someone they knew. The even *more* clever way he had arranged for Diego to stumble upon the bill of lading with Don Toribio's name on it.

Evaristo had gone so far as to counsel Diego to *not* approach Toribio openly, for the man would only deny it, but to seek him in privacy late at night. In such a setting, his cousin had argued, Toribio would be far more likely to cut a deal for the return of the horses, providing no accusations or embarrassment resulted. Indeed, Evaristo had suggested the very night for the clandestine encounter—and assured Diego that Don Toribio's wife had gone off to visit relatives.

Yes, Evaristo had been so clever, and *he* had been so naive, so involved with his horses that he had not recognized his cousin's inherent wickedness, even after years of evidence that he was a bad seed sprung from the loins of Satan himself.

''Diego, what are you thinking? Have you been listening to

a word I have been saying?'' Gonzalo peered into his face.
''Your body stands beside me, but your thoughts are somewhere
across the sea, I think.''

''Forgive me, Gonzalo, if I seem distracted—or ungrateful
for your kindness, especially for offering me La Reina while
I am here. My father's pastures hold no finer horses than your
mare, and I am honored to have the chance to work with her.
I will think on all you have told me. However, you must realize
that even if I never return to Spain, I cannot remain in your
house forever. Your generosity shames me, for I have naught
to offer in return.''

''Blessed bones of all the saints in heaven! Are you blind
as well as stubborn? You have everything to offer! I have just
told you there is no one in the New World I can trust to properly
train my horses. Only you, Diego, possess the knowledge and
skill to bring out the best in them. My horses are my life, my
greatest accomplishment. I fear it will be my greatest failure
if they never know the hands of a true reinsman. Forget about
the future. The future can wait. For now, think only of the
present. Train my horses, explore a little, if you must—but
only a very little, and go well-armed and well-mounted. Let
the future take care of itself. Enjoy your freedom. My daughter
pleases you, does she not?''

Again, he elbowed Diego in the side. '' 'Tis a pity her dam
wasn't the equal of her sire, though I admit I had little to
do with producing her beauty. That came from her mother.
Sometimes, I look at Maria, and I see her dam all over again—
a female to make a man's blood boil. Until you arrived, I knew
not why I was saving her, but now it gives me great pleasure
to give her to you. Enjoy her, Diego! As I warned you before,
once a man marries he cannot indulge himself between the
thighs of a beautiful woman whenever he wishes. He must sow
his seed in his wife, or she will be angry. If he does spread his
favors elsewhere, he must do it far from home.''

''You honestly do not mind if I use your daughter as you
are suggesting?'' Diego knew that many men regarded women
as mere vessels in which to pour their lust, but he found it

immoral, even obscene, that a man would offer his own daughter, legitimate or not, to a guest in his house.

"Of course not! Why should I mind? The girl is beautiful, but she is still an *Indio*. Her tainted blood dooms her to an unrewarding life. I cannot be responsible for her forever—not that you must now consider yourself her keeper. When you tire of her, you may give her to another. But *you* will have been the first to taste her charms, and the first man to feast upon a woman is a lucky man indeed. If Maria knows what is good for her, she will make every effort to satisfy you . . . and if she does not . . . well, she will suffer for it. The next man to have her may not be as inclined toward kindness as you are."

Diego suddenly had a sour taste in his mouth, as if he had drunk bad wine. Gonzalo made it sound so cold. How could a father be so heartless toward his own flesh and blood?

"I will not mistreat her," he said, though he doubted his host would mind if he did.

"Hah! You may find you have to beat her just to control her. When she looks at you with those fiery eyes of hers, *daring* you to exert your authority, she will goad your temper as surely as she goads mine and her stepmother's. Her mother did not have eyes like that—*her* eyes were gentle—but both Maria and her brothers were born with them. I am inclined to think them an Indian trait."

"Her brothers?" Diego recalled what he had overheard that morning, when Gonzalo hadn't realized he was listening. He had shouted something about "bastard sons" and "betrayal."

Gonzalo waved the question aside. "Forget I mentioned them. They are dead now, anyway. At least, one of them is. I hope the other is, too."

" 'Tis a very harsh sentiment for a man to have toward his own offspring."

"Harsh, yes, but deserved. Let me give you some advice, Diego. If Maria spawns a bastard, take it out and drown it the hour it is born. Let not her pleas dissuade you, or you will only live to regret it."

"You regret Maria?" Diego was astounded.

"I regret her brothers. And often, her, too. There are times when she tugs at my heart, but most times she merely tugs at my temper. To Doña Inez, she is a constant reminder of the affection I once had for another—an *Indio*. Of course, there is also the matter of Antonio."

"I have not heard mention of Antonio."

"Ah, that is a tale for another day! You have only just arrived. You need not hear all our tragedies at once, or you will begin to wonder what sort of place this must be, Diego."

Diego had already asked himself that very question. Indeed, he was still wondering. He shared his host's passion for horses and appreciated all he had been offered, but Gonzalo's streak of cruelty appalled him. In no circumstances could he ever imagine himself taking a bullwhip to a woman. To Evaristo, yes. If he had the chance, he would take a bullwhip and more to his cousin's wicked hide.

But he could not envision any situation in which he would feel compelled to beat Maria—or to drown a helpless infant, his own child, no less. Maria roused his instincts for protection, and if he ever did tire of her he would never pass her on to another man who might mistreat her.

He suddenly realized how responsible for her he had become. She was now his mistress—not in actual fact, perhaps, but in all else. He controlled her future as surely as if he were wed to her. It was a stunning idea, and he experienced a moment of acute, startling denial. *He was not ready for this.* He had not consciously made a decision to keep her, yet somehow her well-being now depended entirely upon him. When he had first made the offer to oversee her behavior, he had not thought ahead to the consequences. Now, he almost wished he could withdraw his offer.

But he could not. 'Twas too late now. He could well imagine what Gonzalo would do to the girl if he said he had changed his mind. Besides, she really was a beauty, and if he could just convince her to give herself willingly ... *eagerly* ...

"Have you any corn?" he inquired of Gonzalo.

"Corn? What do you want with corn?"

"A handful. I need only a handful—to make friends with

La Reina,'' he explained, wishing it could be so easy with Maria.

"She will not be bought with corn!" Don Gonzalo chortled. "Not my high-strung princess."

Nor would Maria be bought with chocolatl. But he would discover something she greatly desired, and once he knew what that something was, he would give it to her, and then she would be his.

He suddenly felt more confident and eager for the chase. He knew how to play this game. He had played it many times and always won. A woman could be no different than a horse; soon, La Reina and Maria would both be his to command.

"The corn, if you please, Gonzalo. I shall start with the corn and continue from there."

On a slope overlooking *Dehesa de Oro*, Maria sat in the tall grass with her arms wrapped around her knees. Helpless to quell her interest in the scene below, she avidly watched her new master talking to her father, as they strolled among the horse and cattle pens, followed closely by the dog, Caobo. Don Diego would have stood out anywhere; his height alone made him noteworthy. He was the tallest, most well-proportioned man at *Dehesa de Oro*—or anywhere else, for that matter. Could a more handsome man exist on the earth?

She did not want to think about him, but all she could think about, it seemed, was Don Diego—and the kiss he had stolen. The mere recollection of that kiss made her tremble, as if struck with cold, despite the sun beating down warmly on her head and shoulders. She *must* stop looking at him and thinking about him; to continue like this was pure folly—a threat to all she had been working so hard to obtain.

Lying back in the grass, Maria tried to concentrate on her newfound freedom and savor it. She had already done all her work—what little there was now to be done—and the remainder of the day belonged to her. She had only to obey her new master, be there when he wanted something, and keep his quarters and his belongings clean and orderly. That was all. Compared to her usual chores, these were small tasks indeed.

No more laboring from long before dawn until long after sunset. She had only to keep track of where Don Diego was and when he might need her, and she could do as she pleased. She must remember he *was* her master and not her friend, and most certainly not her lover. He had promised he would not force her into intimacy unless she invited him, but she would have to be careful that her own desires did not prove to be her undoing.

Doña Inez had already burnt her old sleeping pallet; the smoke from the straw and tattered sheepskin had only just died down. Somehow, she would have to put together a new one and hide it in the west wing in a room away from where Don Diego slept. If she slept anywhere near him, she knew she would be in danger. She could not trust herself to refuse his *chocolatl*-laced kisses. Already, she wanted more of them, a desire that exceeded even her appetite for more of the sweet beverage forbidden to her in the past. Neither *chocolatl* nor kisses were forbidden now; she could have all she wanted of both . . . but the price was far too high!

How she wished for someone to explain these unruly desires! If only she could talk to her mother, whose wisdom had derived from some ancient Indian source unknown to her half-Spanish daughter. Her mother had been a wellspring of peace and serenity—never judging, criticizing, complaining, or bewailing her own fate.

Yet Maria had known when her mother's heart ached with sorrow and longing for her own people. She had many times heard her mother weeping over Don Gonzalo's cruelties. In her childish way, Maria had tried to comfort her, but her mother had only said: "Do not hate him, Maria. Never hate him. We all come from the same source, *Indio* and Spaniard alike. The Spaniards are like men stumbling in darkness, with no light to guide their way. 'Tis why they behave as they do. We must give them love, not hatred in return, that they may walk upright and change their ways."

Maria had never understood. Nor had her brothers, to whom

their mother had urged the same thing. In the end, her mother had given everything to Don Gonzalo, but reaped only a harvest of pain. Returning love for hate now seemed a form of intolerable submission to Maria.

Gazing into the blue sky and searching the heavens for some portion of her mother's wisdom, Maria thought she better understood why Katerina—the Christian name Gonzalo had given her mother—had not fought, or run away. Gonzalo had entrapped her heart, and with it, her will. The ardent young Gonzalo must have told the beautiful young Katerina that he loved and needed her. He must have fed her *chocolatl* to enslave her senses. He had somehow convinced her he truly cared for her, so that she finally surrendered the dream of every captured *Indio:* to escape and return to the Ocean of Grass.

How else could her mother have borne the sacrifice of her freedom?

Maria sat up. She must go and ask Bartolomeo that question. Like her mother, the old *Indio* had been captured a long time ago. At the time of his capture, he had been a man in his prime, condemned to spend the remainder of his days serving the Spanish. Like her mother, he had been lucky not to have been sent to the silver mines, but he was kept at *Dehesa de Oro* to perform the most menial chores, scorned by the other servants and local peasants. Over the years, he must have had many opportunities to escape. What had kept *him* from leaving?

Maria suddenly had to know. Scrambling to her feet, she dashed down the slope and headed for the back side of the long, low building where her father housed his best horses in cold or violent weather. Minutes later, she found Bartolomeo exactly where she had known he would be, engaged in his usual activities. He was busy hauling manure from the horse and cattle pens to the huge manure pile located a league or so downwind of the main house.

For all the years she had known him—which were all the years of her life—picking up and hauling manure had been Bartolomeo's main job. Don Gonzalo wanted no flies bothering his prized animals, so Bartolomeo had to go out each day and remove all the fly-attracting filth in the animal pens. Bartolomeo also had to tend the stinking pile, turning it frequently, so that it heated up and could later be spread on the fields to nourish the vegetables, herbs, and fruits destined for his master's table.

Bartolomeo always smelled of manure, which encouraged the other servants to avoid him, but Maria, like her mother before her, always made certain he had enough to eat and a few primitive comforts in his rude little hut beside the manure pile.

She spotted him now, tending the pile with a huge iron fork, and wondered again why he had not taken advantage of what must have been countless opportunities for escape.

As soon as he saw her he took his fork in one hand, removed the tattered hat from his head, and grinned a gap-toothed welcome. His peasant garments—mere rags—hung from his spare lean frame, and Maria realized she must somehow obtain some new ones for him. His appearance, shabby though it was, delighted her, for he looked pure *Indio*, and could never be mistaken for a Spaniard.

His shaggy black hair—*Indios* never went gray—was parted down the middle and whacked off at the level of his earlobes. His nose was large and flat, as were his lips, and deep grooves bracketed his mouth. Prominent brows shaded his deep-set, black eyes. The Spaniards thought him ugly and stupid, and often made cruel jokes at his expense, but Bartolomeo never showed anger. His expression was serene and ageless, as if he lived mostly inside himself and quite liked the company he kept. He could not speak Spanish—had never learned it—though he understood it well enough to take orders.

Maria suspected he simply refused to speak the tongue of his oppressors, but could have done so had he wished. If that were true, he had only made his life all the lonelier, because in the absence of her mother and brothers, she was now the only person at *Dehesa de Oro* with whom he could converse.

Indeed, the desire to talk to Bartolomeo had originally prompted her to learn the *lengua* of her mother's people in defiance of her father's orders that she be taught only to speak Spanish.

"*Hola*, old friend!" she called out, approaching him.

Never one to waste words, Bartolomeo only nodded and waited patiently for her to state her purpose.

"Bartolomeo," she began, suddenly shy before him. "Old friend, I have come to ask you something."

Her shyness multiplied a hundredfold. She did not know how to proceed. The reason she had sought him out suddenly became less clear to her. The old Indian gazed deep into her eyes . . . endlessly patient, forever waiting, never asking anything for himself. He was apparently willing to haul manure right up to the last moment of his wretched, miserable life.

"Why, Bartolomeo?" she finally whispered, indicating the manure pile with a jerk of her head. "Why do you still do this?"

Chapter Six

She had forgotten and spoken in Spanish, but he answered in his own language—not the question she had asked, but the one she had left unspoken.

"One day, I will return." He inclined his head toward the Sea of Grass. "I will not die here, but out there. They will never find me, or if they do, they will find only the husk. My spirit will be free, never to be captured again."

"But why have you waited so long? How can you bear to be a slave all your life?"

"*You* are here," he said without hesitation, gazing straight at her. "And before you, there was your mother."

"But . . . what are you saying?" She searched his face for some resemblance to her own, for he seemed to be implying more than mere friendship between them. She was shocked he had even mentioned her mother, for Indians never spoke of the dead. It violated one of their customs.

"Your mother is half my spirit," he said simply.

She found it stranger yet that he said "is", not "was," as if she were still alive.

"You are the daughter of my heart." He touched his chest. "You should have been the daughter of my loins. I cannot go until I know you are safe, and someone besides this poor *Indio* watches over you here at *Dehesa de Oro.*''

How foolish is your delusion of helping me! she thought. *You could not have kept me from being beaten this morning. You cannot keep me from being shamed or forced into the bed of a stranger. You are speaking nonsense, old man.*

"Never think I do not watch over you, Maria," he said reproachfully, demonstrating his amazing ability to divine her thoughts. " 'Tis not only this old *Indio* who cares for you, but also the Great One and your mother. With all of us guarding you, you will come to no harm. Still, I would be happy knowing you had another friend in *this* life."

Nonplussed, Maria stared at him. He had never spoken of such things to her. His revelations made her uncomfortable.

"One day, Bartolomeo, I myself mean to run away and find my brother," she told him, hoping it would somehow reassure him. "I would take you with me, but I fear you are too old for the rigors of a long journey. The Ocean of Grass is a limitless place. I myself could become lost and die on it."

"I will show you where to find your brother and your people," he offered. "Even if I am too old or have traveled to the Spirit World by then, still I will show you."

Now, she knew his mind was failing. The dead never returned to assist the living. When her mother died, she had prayed to the god of the *Indios* and to the God of the Spanish, but neither had restored her mother's life, nor given any sign she had gone to a better place. Sometimes, Maria felt the presence of her mother's spirit, but she had never seen it, and no god had ever rescued the oppressed *Indios* or sent the Spanish back across the sea, as she had once begged them to do. She doubted Bartolomeo could deliver on empty promises, and could only interpret them as signs of diminished sanity.

"Do you really know where to find my mother's people?" she asked politely. "After so many years, I would think you had surely forgotten."

"The memory is here," he answered, tapping his head. "And here . . ." He tapped his heart. "To the Spaniards, the Sea of Grass all looks the same. To a man who was born on it, 'tis as familiar as *Dehesa de Oro*. I could never forget the favorite resting places of our people. They move with the seasons and the wanderings of the wooly cows, but like the cows they revisit the same camps, year after year. If anything changes the pattern, they leave a sign saying where they have gone."

"Why have you never told me all this before? You never speak about our people. Indeed, you rarely speak at all."

He gave her a gentle but accusing look. "Because you have never asked, daughter of my beloved."

He was right. She never *had* asked. She was usually too sunk in the misery of her own problems to spend much time with Bartolomeo. "Forgive me, old friend. I see now how I have ignored you. I am ashamed to admit that I . . . I never realized how you felt about my mother."

"We were captured together. That alone should have told you something. I had not yet earned the right to call her my own, but still, we yearned for each other."

"Then you . . ." She couldn't quite say it.

He nodded. "Yes, we had gone off to be alone together. But your father found us and claimed for himself what should have been mine."

"How could you bear it? Did you not want to kill him?"

He smiled. "Do you mean did I wish to become like the Spaniards—full of hate and violence? No—at least, not at first. I considered Don Gonzalo a god, not a man. He therefore deserved your mother. When we first saw him, your mother and I, we did not try to run away. He was riding a great white horse, and we had never seen horses. He made the horse stand on its hind legs and perform many other wonders. We thought him a divine visitor from another world. In awe and trembling, we fell on our knees and buried our faces."

"Then what happened?" Maria stood still as a rock, absorbing the tale. She had heard only a tiny portion of it from her mother, who had not liked to discuss her capture.

"The men who accompanied your father laughed at us. They rode around us, snapping their whips over our heads. They nearly trampled us. Too late I realized they were only men, but I still feared their powers. No *Indio* possessed such marvels as they did: horses, whips, and sticks that killed with a great loud noise. We lived on the land. All we had came from Mother Earth. These men did not dress as we did, or eat the same foods, or live like us. We were afraid, and therefore eager to do whatever they wanted. We worshipped them as gods, and prayed they would spare our lives.''

"But after you came to know them as men—what then?''

"I still believed them to be greater than myself. They had the right to tell me what to do. My place was to obey without question.''

"And you still believe that?''

He shrugged. "They possess a knowledge of things I will never understand. Perhaps their minds are larger than mine.''

"What do they know that you could not learn if you had the chance? If they were only willing to teach you, you could master their weapons and discover how to ride and train horses. In your youth, you could have done so.''

He eyed her sadly. "You say that because you are one of them, Maria. You share their blood. But I cannot imagine understanding the same things they do—the bird tracks, for instance.''

"The bird tracks?''

"The scratching that means something to so many of them when they see it.''

"Their writing! Oh, Bartolomeo, there is no great mystery to that. I myself can do it. I can *read* the scratching, and I have practiced drawing the same signs in the dust. 'Tis easy. When Antonio was alive I stayed with him at his lessons, in case he should need anything. I learned the way of the scratching long before he did. He died before he understood his letters, and I rescued his precious books from the fire where Doña Inez had thrown all his things. I still have the books, hidden where no one will ever find them. Sometimes, I take them out and study them. The books tell amazing stories about men the Spanish never wish to forget.''

Bartolomeo tilted his head, considering. "A great wonder . . . and not so different perhaps from the signs our people leave when they wish to tell others where they have gone. I can read them easily, but the Spanish cannot.''

"There! You see? They are no greater than we are. They are only different. But how can you bring yourself to do the same miserable work each day of your life? How can you endure the constant stench of manure without complaint?''

She wrinkled her nose against the noxious fumes that assaulted her nose this very moment. The odor from the aging pile was less objectionable than the smell of freshly dropped excrement, but it was still overripe and offensive.

Bartolomeo leaned on his fork and inhaled deeply. "To me, 'tis sweet, the scent of Mother Earth. Therefore, I relish it. I do not find my work displeasing—only my captivity. Each day, as I move among the animals, I am filled with awe and gratitude that I share their lives. No other *Indio* is permitted so near the horses or cattle—only me, Bartolomeo. For that, I humbly thank the Great One.''

" 'Tis unnatural, your love for the labor you are forced to perform. Are you not lonely?''

Grinning, he shook his head. "How can I be lonely? In my heart, I talk to the animals. They answer in sighs and snorts. I know each of them better than the Spaniards do. They tell me which grasses they prefer, and when they like to sleep, play, and drink. Each has its favorite spot for dropping manure and making water. I know the leaders and the followers, which are given to fighting and those who will not fight no matter how much they are provoked. I study their ways as I once studied the ways of the wooly cows. In my youth, I yearned to slay cows and take their flesh and skins, but these creatures are my friends. I have learned much from the Spaniards. An *Indio* would never think of keeping the source of his meat so close at hand, as the Spaniards do with their cattle. Nor would he ever think of taming and riding a horse.''

"When I leave here, I will take horses with me," Maria recklessly confided. "If I find our people, I will teach them the way of the horse. Horses will change their lives forever.''

"You are not afraid of a tall, snorting stallion?" The old *Indio's* brows rose in amazement. "When such a grand beast

flies across the earth, his beauty surpasses that of an eagle
soaring high into the heavens. In his eyes, I see the mark of
the Great One, and I bow my head and tremble. The Spaniards
tame horses, but they do not own them. The spirit of the horse
is free. Knowing this sweetens my own captivity, and I can
bear it more easily.''

Maria succumbed to impulse. "Bartolomeo, I *will* take you
with me! Together, we will give our people the gift of the
horse. Then no one can ever capture or enslave us again."

A radiant look stole over the old man's face. "Yes ... yes,
perhaps, it will be that way!"

The light faded almost as quickly as it had come. "Or perhaps
not. If you take me with you, they will surely catch you. You
are right, Maria. The rigors of such a journey would be too
much for me. You must go without me. If you have horses,
and you are not afraid, you will find our people. 'Tis as I said.
If my body cannot accompany you, I will send my spirit to
show you the way."

More nonsense.

She knew he would never see the Ocean of Grass again,
except for the portion that hemmed *Dehesa de Oro*. Perhaps
he meant to walk out on the grasslands when death approached.
By the time the *vaqueros* found him, it would be too late to
punish him; he would be gone from this life.

She must leave him to his delusions. "Thank you, Bartolomeo. I am glad I spoke with you today. 'Tis a great pleasure
to hear my mother's tongue. It makes me feel close to her."

"She is with you always, Maria. When you leave here, she
will accompany you."

And still more nonsense.

Loathe to hurt his feelings, Maria only nodded. "Good-bye,
old friend. My new master is probably looking for me."

"Your new master?"

"The new Master of Horses."

"Ah! The Spaniard who brought the new mares and the
proud stallion that allows no one near him."

"I had not heard that about his stallion. Is he a rogue then?
The stallion, I mean."

Bartolomeo again revealed the gaps where his teeth should have been. "No—not a rogue. There is no evil in him. But someone has abused him, and now he trusts no one but the man who brought him. Everyone fears the horse, as much— or more—than La Reina. I will keep watch to see what comes of this."

"So will I, Bartolomeo. My father has given me to the new Master of Horses, and I . . . well, that is why I sought you out. Because I am . . . was . . . confused. I needed someone to talk to."

"And are you now at peace?"

She smiled, and the lie came easily. "Oh, yes! I feel much better now."

"The Great One sees all, Maria. He does not abandon us. Remember that."

She wished she could be as certain as he was; his serenity and faith amazed her. Bartolomeo should have despaired long ago. Instead, he behaved as if joy had been his constant companion. Sorrow had burned a hole in his heart, but he had managed to survive by closing his mind to the pain. With a wave of her hand, she left him to his manure pile.

On the way back to the house, she again had to pass the stable and corrals. Hoping to avoid a chance meeting with her father or Don Diego, she maintained her distance, but as she crossed the open space behind the hub of activity, a lone horseman suddenly came around the side of a building and headed straight toward her.

She had nowhere to hide and could only stand there, breathing like a bellows, as she watched him come. It was Don Diego . . . riding La Reina.

Normally, the mare fought her rider, seeking to dislodge him, as she did with Maria. But with *this* rider the traitorous horse stepped daintily, her neck proudly arched, her eyes soft, her mouth gently chewing at the iron bit between her teeth. She looked *happy* to carry Don Diego, and to surrender her entire body to his service.

Don Diego appeared enraptured. He did not even see Maria; all his attention was focused on the animal beneath him. A foolish grin lit his face, and as he drew closer she could hear him crooning: "Ah, my beauty! You are indeed a queen—a shining example of royalty among horses. You scarcely trot . . . you float. Oh, what a grand time we shall have together!"

Oblivious to his surroundings, he stroked the mare's neck and continued his outrageous compliments until he nearly ran over Maria. Only when she leapt out of his way with a cry of fear did he come to his senses. Halting the horse, he gazed at her in surprise.

"Maria! Where did you come from? I almost trampled you."

"I have been watching you ride toward me for quite some time. You were so intent on your horse you never noticed."

He noticed *now*—and flashed her a sheepish smile. "I confess I was thinking only of La Reina, not of you or anyone else. I did forget my surroundings. This mare is better than I had dared anticipate. Not even El Cid—my stallion—is so sensitive, and I myself trained him. La Reina knows only the rudiments, but one day, she will do it all and do it gladly."

Maria envied his easy mastery of the horse. "My father's men fear her, but I have always thought she was misunderstood."

He eyed her with new respect. "You are right. She has lacked understanding . . . but look what she will do with scarcely any urging!"

The mare suddenly spun on her haunches and pranced across the plain as if she had done this a hundred times before. Don Diego sat straight and tall, doing little that Maria could see. His body moved with La Reina's—no bouncing, no jolting, no thumping—as Maria always did when *she* tried to ride. La Reina simply floated, first at a high-stepping trot, then slowing to a walk, then moving to a trot again . . . and finally into the canter. The only difference was that, for *him,* she was not running away or leaping about crazily, but working smoothly and easily, stopping, starting, backing, and moving sideways with no more control than Don Diego's finger on a loose rein.

Maria had many times watched her father's *arrendador* and *domadors* work horses. Only the best-trained animals could be trusted not to seize the bit and go wherever they pleased. To ride a horse on a loose rein was the ultimate goal of all the training done by the Spaniards, yet it remained a feat achieved only by the best horsemen, on horses destined to be ridden by the richest *hidalgos*.

La Reina had never before exhibited such obedience to a rider. To date, only the *arrendador*, Miguel, had managed to remain seated on the mare for any length of time. He, too, rode with a loose rein, but La Reina did not float for him. Rather, she seemed tense and unhappy, and often bolted. Now, in the hands of the new Master of Horses, she seemed to be dancing. Maria could tell the mare was delighted to carry a man who so obviously understood her.

Maria wished she could copy what she was witnessing. She yearned to discover how Don Diego managed to sit so still, yet communicate his wishes.

"How are you controlling her?" she demanded, as he trotted back to her, his face split in a wide grin.

"I am not controlling her. I cannot *make* this mare do anything. She is doing it all because she wants to."

"But you are telling her what to do!"

He laughed. "No, I am only asking her inside my head and gently giving her the signals. Then she does it on her own."

"What signals? How can you first ask her inside your—"

Before she could finish the question, there came a great shout. "Diego! Diego, come back here!"

Her father lumbered around the corner of the nearest building, very near the spot Maria had first seen Diego appear. Even at a distance, she could tell he was winded and frustrated by his own inability to walk faster.

"Diego," he complained loudly. "I cannot watch you ride when you take it into your head to leave me in the dust. Do you expect me to run after you?"

Several men trailed her father, among them the *arrendador*, Miguel. "Stay there!" Don Diego shouted over his shoulder. "I will return in a moment."

He smiled down at her. "Save your questions for tonight when we are alone, little madonna. Conversation is an excellent prelude to bed sport. I am *eager* to answer your inquiries."

"Forget my questions, Don Diego. Tonight, my only plans are to sleep—unless, of course, you *command* me otherwise."

"Ah, Maria . . . can you not be more like this lovely mare here? I have only just made her acquaintance, but already she responds to me as if to a lover. There is no resistance. She offers enthusiasm to proceed to the next step! I hardly have to ask her at all. I only have to picture in my mind what I want, and she hastens to give it to me."

"Then take *her* to bed, Don Diego. I assure you I will not mind at all."

She spun on her heel and quickly walked away from him, only to hear his laughter echoing behind her.

That night, Maria made it a point to make up her bed in the library. Don Diego inspected her little pallet of fresh straw, covered over with an old woolen blanket, and pronounced it fit only for Caobo. Again, he invited her to share the comfort of his wide, soft bed, but she refused, and he finally retreated, grumbling about her stubbornness.

All night she tossed and turned, unable to sleep in the crackly new straw. The memory of his kisses tormented her, keeping her awake. When morning came, she laid out fresh clothing, fetched warm wash water, and put together a simple meal, this time with no *chocolatl.* Her exasperated master noticed the lack as soon as he sat down at the table.

"Maria, where is my *chocolatl?* I mean, your *chocolatl?*"

"I have already broken my fast, Don Diego. I have no need of *chocolatl,* this morning or *any* morning."

"Perhaps not, but I have need of watching you drink it. Go and get some at once. Please," he added, "I am not commanding you. I am only asking you to fetch it."

"Then I refuse," she calmly stated. "If the choice is mine, I will not do it."

They both knew she was not talking about *chocolatl.*

"Maria," he sighed. "You are beginning to try my patience."

He was beginning to try hers, but she said nothing.

"Very well, go without it. However, I do have one other request. No—this time, 'tis a command. Put a flower in your hair—a red one, to match your skirt. I am delighted to see you have finally abandoned your old rags, but you need a flower in your hair to complete the picture. Flowers in pots hold little appeal for me. I prefer to see them framing your lovely face."

She flushed and nodded. *"Sì, señor.* Is there anything else you desire?"

Too late she realized what she had asked and bit her tongue. She knew quite well what else he desired. He grinned.

"Yes, but since you already know the answer to that question, I will not belabor the point. I will only bid you to prepare a few things for me take along on a small journey."

Her heart leapt and then abruptly plummeted. She wanted him to depart—but knew she would miss him. No one else would notice if she wore flowers in her hair, or urge her to drink *chocolatl.* "You are leaving *Dehesa de Oro?"*

"Does the news please or sadden you? Either way, 'tis only for a few days, I would think. Your father and I will leave the day after tomorrow. Now that I have seen his horses, he cannot wait to show me his silver mine at San Martin. On my long journey here, it seems I missed the place altogether."

"You did not miss much. San Martin is smaller than *Dehesa de Oro."*

She had gone there once with her father, Doña Inez, and little Antonio. It was a two-day journey by cart, but much less on horseback. Aside from the mine itself, only a few peasants lived there. Don Diego and Doña Inez had been showing their son the source of their wealth. Naturally, they had not allowed him to examine the starving Indians who labored deep in the bowels of the earth every day until the day they died, but Maria had gotten a good look at them. Their dull faces and lifeless eyes had seared their images on her heart.

The mine was a terrible place, filled with the stench of human suffering and the whistle of the whips that kept the *Indios* working, even when they were so ill and malnourished they could scarcely remain on their feet.

She paused in her musings to discover Don Diego watching

her with a quizzically raised eyebrow. "Your father is very proud of the scientific manner in which he makes the earth yield her riches. He claims it is the best-producing mine in the New World."

"If he says so, I am sure you can believe him."

"You disapprove of mining?"

She turned away from his discerning gaze. "I have no opinion on the matter. My father does as he pleases."

Actually, she *hated* what her father did to the Indians there. He claimed to be saving their souls by rescuing them from heathen practices and reforming them through honest labor, but the Indians never lasted long in the mines. From time to time he had to send men out into the wilderness to capture more *Indios,* and his men often complained that the once-numerous savages were becoming difficult to find.

Not long ago, the mine overseer had come to *Dehesa de Oro* to discuss the possibility of allowing the captured Indians to breed and produce children. As it was, males and females were confined to separate cages when their work was done. Despite frequent use by the guards, the females rarely gave birth, and when they did the babes usually died.

What Maria had overheard had given her hope that conditions at the mine might one day improve, if for no other reason than to encourage a higher rate of survival among the children of the slaves.

"I can understand why you might disapprove of mining," Don Diego continued. "But surely 'tis not as bad as your expression suggests. Yesterday, I witnessed how your father cherishes his animals—down to the lowliest beast of burden. He understands that even an animal cannot work well if it does not eat properly or suffers mistreatment."

She saw no sense in arguing. If Don Diego went to the mine he would see for himself how things were, and he would probably think nothing was wrong with it. Her father could obtain new slaves any time he wanted them, but horses and cattle—even oxen and asses—had to be bred and raised and trained, or else brought all the way from Spain. A prime horse was not easily replaced, but the Ocean of Grass could provide an endless source of human fodder for the mines.

"I will go and prepare for your journey. Is there anything else?"

"The flower," he reminded her. "The flower for your hair."

"*Sì, señor,* I will get a flower." Her hand flew to her unbound hair, which she had combed until it gleamed and crackled with life. She had not done it to win his admiration, she told herself, but she did enjoy hearing his compliments.

"Oh, Maria . . . one more thing. Must you call me *señor?*"

She stiffened and looked away. "What else shall I call you? Sometimes, I may say Don Diego, but 'tis more proper for me to use *señor.*"

Mischief danced in his eyes. "Why not *querido mío?* I still intend to be your love, Maria."

He would not give up. If she were fortunate, he would stay a long time at the mine, giving her the opportunity to build up her resistance to him.

"Why not *pestifero* or *pestilencia?* I assure you that you will never mean more to me than some foul, bothersome thing."

He laughed. "Think of me while I am gone, Maria. Perhaps you will change your mind."

She shook her head. "No, *señor,* never."

She refused to be like her mother or even Bartolomeo, sacrificing her own happiness and freedom for the sake of love.

Chapter Seven

Maria somehow managed to avoid Don Diego for the next couple of days, until—at last—he left with her father, both of them riding horses, not taking the cart, as she had expected her father, at least, to do. After they had gone—disappearing in a cloud of dust, *vaqueros,* horses, and Diego's dog—she realized that Don Diego had hardly said a word to her since he had suggested she call him *querido mío.*

He had been busy with the horses, spending hours with La Reina, because he had chosen the mare to be his mount for the trip. She had heard him explaining to her father that El Cid was still recovering from the long journey which had sapped his great strength and stamina. This decision had ruined Maria's plans for his absence, during which time she had hoped to improve her riding skills. It would have been the perfect opportunity, as she expected to have plenty of time on her hands and no one watching her, particularly at night.

No sooner had Don Diego and her father ridden away from *Dehesa de Oro* than Doña Inez sent for her. "You will not lie about while your master is gone, Worthless One. You may have charmed him, but you have not charmed me. There are chores to be done. After you do them, you may spend an hour on your knees before The Sorrowful Mother, begging her forgiveness for all your shortcomings.''

Maria lacked the will to resist; a few short days of kindness had dimmed her fighting spirit. Don Diego was having a very bad effect on her. Feeling vulnerable and alone, she returned to her old tasks and could not stop herself from longing for his return. Indeed, her longing was so bad that each day she put a flower in her hair in the hope he might come home early and see it.

He did not come home early. He came home late—a full eight days after his departure. When he arrived he did not look happy and failed to even notice her, much less the red poppy she wore in her hair. Her father, on the other hand, was as jovial as she had ever seen him. To spare himself the walk from the corral, he dismounted by the house, all the while laughing and talking with his *vaqueros*.

His mood was contagious, affecting everyone but Diego. The *vaqueros* murmured among themselves, sharing some ribald joke that set all of them—save Diego—to shamelessly guffawing, until Doña Inez suddenly appeared.

"What is all this commotion? Gonzalo, where have you been? You had me worried. I was beginning to think the savages must have broken free of their cages and slain all of you in your sleep. Come inside at once, and tell me the news.''

"There is no news, Inez. The mine is exactly as it has always been—short of laborers. I will have to organize a hunt for more workers soon. Indeed, 'tis my Christian duty. Before I send new ones down into the mine, I will first convert them, so their labor will be pleasing to God, as well as to me.''

"Naturally," Maria's stepmother snapped, "but what took you so long?''

Don Gonzalo turned to Don Diego and rolled his eyes heavenward. "Details! Always there are details. I do not go to the mine often enough, so when I am there I must deal with a mountain of petty problems and decisions. Tell her how busy we have been, Diego! She will never believe me otherwise.''

'' 'Tis true, Doña Inez, we were busy beyond my wildest imagining.'' Cynicism laced Diego's comment, and Maria noticed that he failed to crack a smile. He slid off La Reina, took down her reins, and quietly handed them to a *vaquero*.

"I will come to the corrals soon to check on her," he said to the man, whose name was Ignacio.

"I know how to care for her, *señor,*" Ignacio responded.

La Reina whinnied a protest as she was led away, and Ignacio jerked on her reins.

"Cease pulling on her mouth!" Don Diego shouted, his face dark and angry. "You are undoing all my good work."

Without a comment to Maria or anyone else, he stomped past her and into the house, with Caobo slinking silently along behind him.

Unable to conceal his ire a moment longer, Diego stormed through the house toward the west wing. As soon as he reached the privacy of his quarters, he tore off his leather gloves and half his garments. He felt filthy . . . defiled. He could not wait to cleanse himself.

He went straight to the table where water and a basin awaited him, and sought relief from his misery in thorough ablutions. To his great disgust, no matter how hard he scrubbed his face and body, he still felt soiled beyond redemption. If it were at all possible, he would leave *Dehesa de Oro* and never again return. Eight days alone with Don Gonzalo had turned his stomach; the man had no morals, no kindness, and no compassion for any human being he considered beneath himself.

The mine itself had been bad enough. Day and night, stone turned in the great crushers, cracking ore, and one had to live with this sound, as well as the rumble of hooves across stone floors—hundreds of hooves pounding ore-mud with copperas and quicksilver to accrete an amalgam of precious metal. Raw billets of the stuff were then purged in huge furnace beds until molten metal could at last be poured into bars of silver weighing thirty marks.

The sounds and stench of the place had thoroughly revolted Diego, but what made the whole process even more hellish was the cost to human and animal life—especially human life.

Diego knew he was not a saint—far from it. But he could never take pleasure in suffering the way Don Gonzalo did. The Indians at his silver mine lived and died in abject misery and poverty, while the prison guards had been selected from the lowest class of men Diego had ever had the misfortune to meet. They wielded their whips with inordinate relish, amusing themselves by testing how much pain a man could endure before giving up all hope and dying.

Gonzalo made no effort to hide these conditions. Indeed, he spent most of his time defending the necessity of "keeping the *Indios* in their places," which to him meant terrified and groveling. But what offended Diego most of all was his host's blatant sexual excesses with the youngest and prettiest of the female slaves—that, and the fact that Gonzalo expected *him* to join in his degradations.

On their second night at San Martin, Gonzalo had drunk heavily, then summoned a prison guard to fetch the choicest of the young females at the mine. Both men and women were sent below to work in the sultry darkness, for the women were often as strong as the men—but the youngest and fairest were kept above ground to cook for the others and remove the filth from the overcrowded cages. Three of these young women had been brought to Gonzalo, who had then invited Diego to join him in "teaching them the fine points of how best to serve their Spanish masters."

Diego had politely declined. The look of terror in the eyes of the three girls—two of them younger than Maria—had convinced him he wanted nothing to do with the night's revelry. Instead, he sought his bed in an adjoining room. Sleep, however, had proved impossible. Diego could not understand a word of the girls' frightened babble, but their shrieks, pleas, and sobbing needed no translation. When the sobs became cries of agony, Diego had gone to see for himself exactly what was happening next door.

To walk into Gonzalo's chamber had truly been a descent into the jaws of hell. It was worse than going into the mine. At some point Gonzalo had invited the prison overseer, his *vaqueros,* and a couple of the highest ranking guards to join him. By the time Diego arrived on the scene, all were naked, and two of the girls were bleeding. The third had fainted, and lay sprawled on the floor beneath two men.

When Gonzalo saw him, he shoved one of the girls in Diego's direction and urged him to "take his turn at her." Diego had lost no time in seizing a heavy, wrought iron candlestick and threatening any man who did not immediately stop what he was doing. Sensing his mood, the normally docile and quiet Caobo had assisted him by snarling, baring his teeth, and raising his hackles.

Surprised by his anger, Gonzalo had ordered the overseer to take the women, including the unconscious one, back to their cages, so that the other women could minister to them. When everyone had left but Gonzalo, his drunken host had apologized, blaming his rowdy behavior on drinking too much, as well as having Doña Inez for a wife.

"My only opportunity for sexual release is when I come to San Martin," he had whined. " 'Tis not usually this bad. The women enjoy my attentions, and afterward I give them little gifts. Things just went too far this time. I assure you, it will not happen again."

After that, Gonzalo had been on his best behavior—he was charming, solicitous, and eager to please—but Diego found it difficult to forgive him. On the day they left the mine, he had insisted on seeing the women to make certain they were all right. Two had already been sent to work below ground. The third was dead. She had never regained consciousness after what the guards and *vaqueros* had done to her.

"What does it matter, Diego? They are only *Indios,*" Gonzalo had said. "There are more where they came from. Remember, those girls are heathen savages. I regret what happened, but truly, it was only accidental. I never meant for them to be harmed."

"What about your *vaqueros,* the guards and the overseer? What excuse do you make for them? Did *they* mean no harm?"

"Ah, Diego, rush not to judge them. In this remote outpost, their lives are harsh and meager. The *Indios* would as soon slit their throats as look at them. The bloodlust went to their heads, is all. Perhaps they should be faulted for that, but certainly, 'tis understandable. Anyway, they have promised they will never do it again, either.''

"And you believe them? If I were you, Gonzalo, I would send them into the cages alone with the Indians. Let the savages determine their punishment."

"Diego, Diego . . . You are still a newcomer to the New World. You do not yet understand how things are here. Wait awhile. You will soon see that 'tis us against them. Where the *Indios* are concerned, we can afford no compassion—and I say that as a man who once loved an *Indio.*''

Diego greatly doubted that Gonzalo had ever truly cared for Maria's mother. Having seen this side of him, he could hardly stand to be in his company. His own father had often been cold and distant, but to Diego's knowledge he had never been malicious or needlessly cruel to those beneath him. Not like Don Gonzalo. Diego felt tainted by their association and was determined to put distance between them.

Tomorrow or the next day, he promised himself, he would take El Cid, who should now be rested, and go out to explore the Ocean of Grass. The sooner he found gold, the sooner he could leave here. He must remember his own goals and not be distracted by the temptations Gonzalo had placed in his path.

Completing his ablutions, Diego finally felt better—not exonerated from guilt for his own part in the death of the Indian girl—but better. He would always blame himself for not having interfered sooner. What he should have done was stop Gonzalo at the very beginning, but he had not thought it his place to tell his host how to live his own life. Now, he realized he should have shamed him into better behavior.

Combing his fingers through his damp hair, Diego turned from the table and discovered Maria standing silently in the corner near the door. She looked . . . uncertain? Perhaps frightened was a better word. He had not even said hello to her— had not so much as noticed her. Thoughts of his own uncleanliness had occupied his mind. Now, another unpleasant thought intruded: If Maria knew what had happened at the mine, she would hate her father—and him.

No wonder she refused to trust him or yield to his passion! A young Indian woman risked her life in the hands of a Spaniard. If he decided to be cruel or kill her, no one would intervene. No one would even care.

Maria was so beautiful ... so innocent and untouched. If Don Gonzalo were not her father, she would be in the exact same position as the girl who had died. Her own father considered her his property to dispose of according to whim. She had no more protection than the girls at the mine. She was entirely at Gonzalo's mercy—rather, *his* mercy—now.

"Maria ..." he murmured. "How good to see you! Come here, little one. Let me hold you a moment."

For once, she made no issue of the request and simply did as invited. She walked into his arms and allowed him to hold her tightly. He rested his chin on her shining hair.

"I have missed you," he whispered, feeling cleansed and renewed by her presence. "Did you miss me?"

"I ... I thought of you," she admitted. "I thought of you often, Don Diego."

The fact that she called him by his given name, rather than *señor,* did not escape him. At any other time he would have pressed his advantage. Now, he was simply too glad to be holding her to say anything that might send her away.

"You were right, Maria. The mine is a wretched place. I could not wait to leave there and return to *Dehesa de Oro*—and you. Most of all, I wanted to see you."

"Then you will not be going there again any time soon? You will stay here for a while?" She lifted her face to gaze up into his eyes, and he was pleased to see that she seemed genuinely happy to have him back and distressed by the idea of his departing again in the near future.

"I will never go there again if I can avoid it. 'Tis too depressing. But I do have plans to go exploring soon."

Soon, but not right away, he told himself, instantly changing his mind about leaving the following day. He did not want to go anywhere when Maria was softening toward him.

"Why must you go exploring? What do you seek?" she asked, frowning.

"Gold. I seek gold, Maria."

It was the wrong answer. He knew it as soon as the words left his mouth, for she leapt back from him as if scalded, her eyes filled with accusation.

"Maria, what is it? Surely, you do not object to me searching for gold. The sooner I find gold, the sooner I can leave here. And when I go—if you are willing—I will take you with me."

"I should have known! Indeed, I *did* know. Spaniards always seek gold," she said with a toss of her shining black hair. "They kill for gold, even more than for silver."

He reached out his hand, but she backed further away. "Maria, if I find gold and establish a gold mine, I will not run it as your father runs his silver mine at San Martin."

Maria's eyes flashed. The fox fire glittered in them, and she again tossed her head in derision. "Will you not, *señor?* Who will you send down into the mine to bring up the gold? The peasants work the land, but they balk at mining, and *hidalgos* have never been known to do their own labor. You will therefore send *Indios,* as my father does. And if they refuse to work for you, you will beat and starve them until they no longer resist."

"I am a much kinder man than your father! I will never do as he does."

Her lower lip trembled. He wanted desperately to kiss her and soothe away her fear, but her eyes warned him to keep his distance. "I do not believe you, *señor.* If you should find gold, you will do exactly as my father does. You have only to say the word 'gold', and your eyes shine with the fire of greed. The lust for the yellow metal is in you. It *lives* inside you and possesses you. You are its slave, and it is your master."

"That does not mean I will be cruel or violent in my efforts to secure it. . . . Maria, listen to me!"

He had no idea how they had reached this impasse. One minute, she was melting in his arms, almost confessing that she had missed him, and the next, she was glaring at him, her eyes shimmering with tears of betrayal and anger.

"Maria, listen," he softly entreated.

But she would not. Her lovely face was adamant. "You are

like all the rest of the Spanish. Do not claim you are different. A man who lusts for gold lusts for nothing else.''

"What foolishness! I have already told you, I lust only for *you*—not gold. I want you in my arms and in my bed. While I was gone, I could think of little else but you. I could hardly wait to return so I might see you again.''

"You should have stayed at the silver mine. 'Tis where men like you belong. Never forget I am half *Indio*. You may cage my body as my father cages the *Indios* at his silver mine, but you cannot cage my heart, *señor*. My heart is my own, and I will never freely give it to an *hidalgo*.''

"Then why did you walk into my arms a moment ago? I never commanded you. You came of your own free will. You *chose* to come.''

"I forgot for a moment that you are a Spaniard! I was glad to see you, and so I came. I will not forget again. Your lust for gold reminded me of who and what you are.''

"I am a man first, Maria—and only then a Spaniard. 'Tis the man you missed. 'Tis the man who longs to hold and kiss you now.''

Before she could flee, he moved quickly to recapture her in his arms. He pulled her toward him, so he could feel the soft contours of her femininity against the hard planes of his own body. The contact wildly excited him, and the disdain in her eyes challenged him to *prove* that she felt the same attraction as he did, and ought not to fight it.

She held herself rigidly, but he rubbed his body against hers, allowing her—*forcing* her—to acknowledge the changes she caused in him. Her eyes widened, and she tried to lean back, but he held her still and, with only a minimum of restraint, thrust his pelvis against her.

"You see what you do to me, Maria?'' The question came out hoarsely, and he had to resist his own instinct to toss her onto the bed and fall on top of her.

For the briefest moment, she seemed to relax and yield to him—or perhaps he only imagined it. In the next, she stiffened and resisted all the more. Her black hair swirled about them as she turned her head to avoid his lips. "Are you preparing to rape me, *señor?*"

Madre de Dios! She used words like a sword. Jumping back, he broke the contact between them. Was he no better than Don Gonzalo and his *vaqueros,* or the prison guards? How easy it would be to lose control with her! How tempting to take what he wanted and damn the consequences. She believed the worst of him, anyway; why keep struggling to show her the best?

"No, damn your eyes! I'll not rape you, though you seem intent on provoking me to it."

He shoved her away with such force that she fell backward against the bed and sprawled on top of it, offering another view to convince a man to forsake all his good intentions.

"Pull your skirts down!" he shouted. "Close your legs, and stop looking at me as if you fear I'll attack you. I am not your sire, and I will neither beat nor rape you. I may, however, destruct before your very eyes if you continue to flaunt yourself in my direction."

She immediately sat up and began rearranging her rumpled clothing, her face rosy and mutinous, her eyes glittering.

"Remove that silly blossom from your hair! Don't put one there again until you *intend* I shall notice it and take it as a sign that you welcome my admiration for your damnable beauty."

She stood up, yanked the scarlet blossom from her hair, and flung it through the open window. "May I leave now?" Her tone was icy. "Or have you further instructions regarding my behavior? I humbly await your next order."

The slight tremor in her voice was his only satisfaction. In every other aspect—posture, facial expression, and gleam of eye—she managed to portray bored indifference. She had spent a lifetime, it seemed, perfecting that Indian passivity and stoicism that so infuriated the Spanish. He would have preferred for her to run at him screaming, intent on pummeling him with her small fists.

"Yes. Prepare my things for another journey. I am leaving again tomorrow."

"I cannot have everything ready by tomorrow. I can brush

the mud from your boots and beat the dust from your garments, but 'tis too late in the day for any washing that might be required.''

''Then I will leave the day after tomorrow—or whenever suits you! Be gone from my sight, and do not make me have to look at you before I go, or I cannot promise I will not rape you, after all, monster that I am!''

She bolted from the room, and Diego watched her go in a flood of shame. He hardly recognized himself anymore. This was *not* his normal behavior. He thought back to the moment when he had first seen her and invited her into his arms; she had come so willingly and trustingly! Then it had all gone wrong.

He had been a heartbeat away from obtaining all he desired, and now he might never get that close again. He might as well go exploring. He certainly could not give up his plan to search for gold just because she did not approve. However, she was right about one thing: If he did find gold, he *would* have to use Indian labor to mine and transport it. He would either have to capture the Indians himself or borrow some from Don Gonzalo. There was no way around it.

He must not allow his feelings—no, his *lust*, he corrected himself—for a little *Indio* girl to influence his plans. Why had he ever promised to refrain from touching her unless she wanted it in the first place? He ought to put an end to this foolishness, call her back, and *command* her to remove all her garments and go to bed with him. Then he would be done with all this maneuvering around the issue. Once he made her body sing with delight, she would more readily accept her position and begin devoting herself entirely to his pleasure. Why had he ever thought he could make her like and desire him for himself alone? He was Spanish, and she was *Indio*. They had nothing common and could never mate as equals. They were *not* equals. She understood that better than he did. If she *never* gave him enthusiasm and eagerness between the sheets, he would have to be satisfied with possessing the most luscious female body he had ever seen, and not bother himself with what was going on behind her beautiful fox fire eyes.

Frustrated and angry, he flopped on the bed and lay looking up at the underside of the tile roof overhead. After a few moments, he realized that what he needed now was horses. It made no difference that he had just spent two days in the saddle. Don Gonzalo had insisted on going more slowly than the distance warranted and stopping often to rest, but Diego needed to clear his head and lift his spirits. The only way he knew how to do that was to go out and work with a horse.

Grooming the animals gave him a sense of peace, and when he was training a horse—or only riding it—he escaped to a world where sorrow, injustice, and every other unpleasantness ceased to exist. He never thought of himself as a master of horses, but more as their teacher and friend, leading them along the path to the full realization of their potential.

'Twas the same he had offered Maria . . . but she had rejected the idea. Rolling off the bed, Diego resolved to seek solace among the horses and forget about finding it in the company of a woman, most particularly a little half-*Indio* with shining black hair, fox fire eyes, and a distrust of Spaniards that was as wide and deep as the ocean. From now on, he would stick to horses.

Maria had Don Diego's things packed by late afternoon of the following day. She had assembled enough food supplies, water, and grain to merit taking along a pack horse. He could stay away from *Dehesa de Oro* for a long time. Indeed, she was hoping he might stay away forever.

Since he was taking his stallion instead of La Reina, she should have plenty of opportunity to practice riding the mare and might then be able to make her escape before he returned— or soon enough thereafter so as to avoid being alone with him. She wanted no more painful, confusing encounters, wherein her mind said one thing and her body another. The man had too much power over her. Even when she fought him, she wanted him. The thought of surrendering was always in her head. He was the biggest threat to her future freedom she had yet discovered. She knew she had to leave soon, or she would

not leave at all. She would spend the rest of her life cherishing
the few crumbs he tossed her way and greatly regretting lost
opportunities.

She must leave soon. As soon as possible.

In the meantime, she avoided him, which—luckily—he had
ordered her to do. She saw him only once that day, and then
only long enough to tell him he could depart the next morning
if he wished. That night she went to bed happy, secure in the
knowledge that she no longer needed to fear the Master of
Horses, for he would soon be gone. Even the prospect of being
at the mercy of her stepmother again did not scare her as much
it normally would have. She consoled herself with the promise
of her own escape before too many more days had passed.

One good thing had resulted from Don Diego's presence at
Dehesa de Oro: La Reina was much calmer and less inclined
toward disobedience. Maria had heard the men talking about
it, and she hoped she herself might benefit from the improvement in the horse's attitude. Possibly by as early as tomorrow
night, she would know if the fiery mare were going to be easier
to handle or still the same old hellion.

Excitement made it difficult to sleep, but eventually, she
dozed off—only to be awakened by loud noises outside the
house.

She sat up in the blackness of the library and struggled to
make sense of the sounds she was hearing. Men were shouting,
horses whinnying. A *harquebus* went off, reverberating through
the thick walls of the house. Maria smelled smoke—and the
sharp tang of gunpowder.

"Diego! Come quickly!" her father shouted outside the window. "The *Indios* are attacking."

Indios.

A wild hope fluttered in Maria's breast. For years after
Lorenzo's death and Santelmo's escape to the Ocean of Grass,
Maria had nurtured the tiny hope that her remaining brother
would return and rescue her from their father. With the passing
years that hope had died, and she had come to resent being left
behind. Her brothers should never have abandoned her; though
small and weak, she would have tried hard not to delay them.

It had been cruel of them to forget about her; she had never forgiven them for it.

Perhaps Santelmo had come for her now! He might have obtained horses, learned to ride, and now returned to rescue his long lost sister from the cruelty of the Spanish. Oh, pray God he had come for her! She would make him take Bartolomeo, too. Scrambling off her pallet, Maria dressed hurriedly and raced from the library.

Chapter Eight

Diego lost no time responding to Gonzalo's summons. He had not been sleeping, anyway; he had been lying fully clothed on his bed, thinking about Maria, and debating whether or not he should break his word, go to the library, and awaken her with kisses. Part of him welcomed the interruption, for he hated debates about honor. There was no in-between ground; a man was either honorable, or he was not.

By the time he and Caobo reached the center of the uproar, it had shifted to the stable area. Empty corrals revealed the reason for the attack. The Indians had come to steal horses, and had made off with a good many—including La Reina and El Bobo—but not, *a Dios gracias,* El Cid. Diego's stallion would have trampled any man who tried to put a lead rope on him. For once, Diego was glad that a disgruntled and vengeful stable worker at his father's farm had once beat El Cid as a colt and thus made him wary of all humans but those with whom he had already established a trusting relationship. At the time, that had been Diego.

The Indians had not gotten the stallion, but the tragedy was still bad enough. The thieves—save for one dead one—had already disappeared, taking a half dozen of Don Gonzalo's most valuable horses, along with two of Diego's mares.

In the light of the torches held by several *vaqueros,* all of whom looked deadly serious and angry. Gonzalo was livid. Hair standing on end, belly protruding grotesquely over the waist band of baggy white trousers, Diego's host appeared in danger of expiring from a fit of red-faced fury.

"There now, do you see?" he demanded as soon as he found breath to express himself coherently. "They have stolen my finest horses, and two of your mares. Now, do you comprehend the magnitude of our problem? You think I should show mercy to the savages and treat them kindly? Brutality is the only way to deal with them! Keep them starving. Make them suffer. Only then will they respect us. We are fortunate they did not slay us all in our beds. They came in so quietly, sneaking past my guards. Your dog did not even hear them! 'Twas as if they knew the place and exactly where to go to find my best horses. As *Dios* is my witness, they will pay for this!"

"Do you know who did it?" Diego calmly questioned. "From what tribe did the dead man come?"

"What difference does *that* make? One tribe is the same as another. It could have been my own bastard son who led them here. I care not which ones did it. I will punish them all. When it grows light, we will ride out and find the nearest encampment of savages. I will skin the entire lot of them! Slavery is too good for these lowly vermin. They can roast over hot coals, instead. I will chop them into pieces so small even the crows won't be able to find them. The only way to prevent others from stealing our horses is to punish every savage we can lay our hands on and leave their dead bodies where other savages will be sure to find them."

"I agree we must go after the horses," Diego interrupted. "I will help all I can with that. But what you do to the Indians is your own business. I want no part of torture, bloodshed, or mass slaughter."

"Have not the stomach for it, eh, Diego? What if they had made off with El Cid? You would sing a different tune then."

"Perhaps. Make no mistake, Gonzalo. I am as furious as

you. I despise horse thieves. But I will not punish the innocent along with the guilty. If you doubt it, give me the man whom you know for certain took La Reina, then stand back and watch what I do with *him.*"

"Done! That man will be yours alone. Devise something terrible, for La Reina is my best horse. Her loss cannot be tolerated. . . . Maria! Come see what your blood kin have done to me." He indicated the empty corrals with a sweep of his hand.

For the first time that night, Diego saw her, a slender wraith hovering near the edge of the commotion. Head held high, she stepped into the torchlight. Completely clothed, she looked much as she did in the daylight—except for her hair. It tumbled in wild disarray down her back and around her shoulders, framing her pale face with midnight shadow.

"Father," she said. "Did you . . . or anyone . . . take time to identify the *Indios* who did this? They are not *all* to blame."

"Pah! Another tenderhearted peacemaker. Diego shares your sympathies. I know not why he should, since he lost two horses that required great trouble and expense to bring here. No one recognized them, Daughter. How could we? All *Indios* look the same. Perhaps, if *you* examined the dead savage . . . I know your mother went behind my back and taught you much about Indian ways. You might be able to identify his tribe."

"I . . . I have forgotten most of the things my mother taught me. I doubt I could," Maria protested.

Studying her, Diego wondered if she told the truth. Her presence out here in the darkness struck him as unusual; neither Doña Inez nor any of the servant women had ventured outside to join the men in fighting off the Indians. Yet Maria was here. Could she possibly have had some part in this?

"I am sorry the *Indios* took your horses, Father," she said earnestly, as if to dispel the notion. "Especially your favorite mare. And you too, Don Diego. Knowing the value of the animals—how much they mean to you—I regret your loss."

"Do not worry, Daughter. We will find them and bring them all back. The savages will not get away with this. And when I am finished with them, they will never dare try it again. I thought the lesson had been taught the last time, when I took my eldest son's life for his treachery. It seems I was wrong.''

Gonzalo's threats sickened Diego. He refused to take part in a bloodbath against all Indians. The horses must be retrieved, and he approved of punishing the guilty, but the rest, the women and children . . .

''Gonzalo, are you certain there is no one among your men— or among your servants—who could at least identify the tribe of the dead man, so we know which one is responsible?''

''No, no . . .'' Gonzalo shook his head. ''No . . . wait! There *is* old Bartolomeo. He is the only *Indio* I still keep at *Dehesa de Oro.* Everyone else balks at performing his chores. Miguel! Go and fetch him. Maria, you will have to translate.'' Gonzalo turned apologetically to Diego. ''For many years, that old man has lived among us, but he still has not mastered our language. If anyone can identify the dead savage, he can.''

As the *arrendador* headed off into the darkness, Diego turned his attention to Maria. She seemed unhappy that her father had thought of the old Indian.

Gazing worriedly at Don Gonzalo, she said: ''I hope I do not disappoint you, but I remember little of the language of the *Indios.* When I was a child, you forbade me to speak it and ordered my mother not to teach it to me.''

''She taught it to you, anyway. Behind my back. You cannot fool me, Maria. The two of you put your heads together and jabbered away like birds. You only quit when you saw me coming. You have not forgotten it. A language learned in childhood remains in a person's head forever. You will translate whatever old Bartolomeo has to say or wish you could.''

''*Sí, Padre.*'' Looking unhappier by the moment, Maria stepped back from her father.

Miguel soon reappeared, accompanied by an old man shuffling along behind him. Diego could smell the new arrival; he stank of horse manure and the accumulation of years of filth. Gonzalo wrinkled his nose and swore an oath.

''*Dios!* He is so rank he makes my eyes water! Come here, old man—but not too near. Do not pretend you cannot understand, or I will fetch a lash to awaken your faculties. You have a job to do. Tell him, Maria. He must go with us to look at the dead *Indio*. Diego, you are coming, too, are you not?''

''Of course.'' Diego lacked enthusiasm for the task, but he still hoped to focus his host's anger on a single tribe, the one responsible, rather than allowing him to spread his vengeance on all Indians. Once the tribe was identified, he would attempt to narrow the search even further. With any luck, only the guilty parties would suffer—as they deserved.

They walked a short distance onto the dimly lit plain, where a full moon played a game of hide-and-seek behind a bank of silvery clouds. The dead *Indio* lay on his side where he had fallen after attempting to flee on foot. A lance had cut him down, piercing right through him, but Diego did not ask who had done it, or where they had gotten the weapon. He himself usually carried a sword, and he had brought a crossbow and a *pistola de arzon,* but no *harquebus,* on the long journey from Spain to *Dehesa de Oro.* He assumed that Gonzalo's *vaqueros* knew how to defend their patron's land and had been properly armed for the purpose.

When the old Indian saw the body and the darkly stained grass around it, he wailed and sank to his knees beside it. Diego had to restrain Caobo from sniffing at the body. Maria touched the Indian's shoulder and murmured something, but Diego could not hear what she was saying.

''Does he recognize the fellow's tribe from what he is wearing?'' Gonzalo demanded. ''Considering he is almost naked, I cannot see how he possibly could.''

It was true. The dead man wore only an animal skin stretched across his loins and held in place by leather thongs. Feathers protruded from his long, greasy looking hair, and a necklace of assorted animal teeth and claws dangled from his neck. What he lacked in garments, he made up for in ornamental paint. Black and white pigment streaked his body in no apparent pattern, except for a white circle around one eye.

To the old Indian, however, his dress, hairstyle, and ornamentation apparently meant a great deal.

''*Abrache,*'' he said, lifting his gaze to Maria.

The word had no meaning to Diego, but Maria blanched.

She obviously knew what the word meant and dreaded giving the news to her father.

"Well?" Gonzalo regarded her impatiently.

"He comes from . . . the same tribe as my mother."

"Blood of the saints! I *knew* it. 'Tis why they understood our habits so well. Santelmo must have led them here. Once again, he is after my horses and knows exactly which ones to take. I keep my favorites in the same corrals where I kept them when he was a boy. Those same corrals are now empty. At first, I thought it must be a coincidence. 'Tis difficult to believe he still lives after all this time, but who else could have done it? Who but my own flesh and blood would know *Dehesa de Oro* so well?"

The *vaqueros* withdrew, muttering among themselves, and the old Indian remained in a cowed—or grieving—position. Only Maria stood straight as a lance, staring down at the dead man as if she expected him to leap to his feet and run away.

"Padre!" she finally said. "Can you have him turned so the light hits his face? Perhaps this man is Santelmo. It has been a long time, but I think I would recognize him."

"Bring the torches closer!" Bending down, Gonzalo himself yanked the lance from the Indian's body and tossed it aside. Then he seized the dead man's shoulder and flipped him over onto his back. "There! Is it Santelmo? I see nothing familiar in his ugly, *Indio* features."

Miguel held a torch near the Indian's face. Maria shook her head and sighed. She sounded half-relieved, half-disappointed. " 'Tis not Santelmo. This man is a stranger."

"Bury him then, before he fouls the air. Bartolomeo may dig his resting place—or burn him. By tomorrow morning, when I pass this way in search of the thieves, I want no reminders that he ever existed. . . . Miguel! Remove his necklace first. I will take it with me. When the *Indios* see it, they will know why I have come, bringing death to all who gaze upon it."

Miguel normally obeyed Gonzalo without question. He had been delighted to join his *patrón* in raping the young girls at the mine. But this time, the *arrendador* balked. "*Señor,* make Bartolomeo do it. I had rather not touch him. These savages are known to carry heathenish diseases that are foreign to us. Handling his necklace alone could bring misfortune.''

What a coward! Diego thought. The man had not minded touching those young girls. Reaching down, he grabbed hold of the necklace and tore it from the dead man's neck. The slender thong snapped in two, but the teeth and claws did not scatter, for they had been tied on individually. Holding the bauble aloft, he examined it in the light of the *arrendador's* torch.

Miguel's eyes widened with fear. The tips of his long, luxurious mustache quivered, and he would have retreated to a safer distance if he could have done so without being obvious. Diego saw nothing to rouse his own fears. The workmanship in the necklace was crude by Spanish standards, but most impressive when one considered that Indians possessed no tools like those belonging to Spanish craftsman.

Each tooth and claw had been carefully selected and arranged by size, from the largest in the center to the smallest at either end. Each piece had then been polished until it gleamed like the finest gold and ivory-inlaid crucifix. Diego did not find it strange or heathenish that a man would wear items representing his success in the hunt. Spaniards regularly wore the cross, the symbol of a deity who had died for them, much the same way as these animals had surrendered their lives for this hunter.

Perhaps, Diego mused, the Spanish and the *Indios* were not so different, after all.

''Imagine wearing such a pagan thing!'' Don Gonzalo took the necklace from him. ''I told you these *Indios* are little better than animals, and this necklace is proof of it.''

''May I see it, Father?'' Maria offered her palm.

''No! Miguel is right. It might be tainted and is probably the handwork of the devil. The savages may worship these teeth and claws as false idols. Who knows? These people are the servants of Lucifer. Torture is the only way to save their souls. I wish Fray Leonido were here to grant God's blessing before we ride out tomorrow. We shall have to be satisfied with Doña Inez rattling her beads. I just wish I had a few more days to recover from our trip to San Martin. Mounting a horse again so soon after our last trip will not be easy.''

Diego scanned the eastern sky. It was growing lighter as they spoke. ''Dawn is not far away,'' he pointed out. ''If we are going to leave at first light, we had better hurry. We do not want to give the thieves too great an advantage. The longer we wait, the more difficult it will be to find them.''

Diego refrained from saying it, but he hoped to catch up to them *before* they reached their encampment. That way, there would be less bloodshed, unless Gonzalo insisted on punishing the entire tribe.

''Madre de Dios! I am tired before I start.'' Scratching his bare belly with his free hand, Gonzalo turned away. ''Prepare for our departure, Diego, but I must steal another hour or two of sleep before I can ride again. . . . Miguel! Wake me when all is ready. Remember to take plenty of weapons and gunpowder. A *pistola de arzon* in a leather holster for each man. Forget the *harquebus.* 'Tis too heavy and difficult to manage. Diego, you must wear armor to protect yourself from arrows. I have some that will fit you. I always wear a breastplate and an armored hat when I go north into the wilderness. 'Tis best to take no chances.''

As Gonzalo retreated in the direction of the house, Diego tried to imagine his host in typical Spanish armor. He pitied the poor horse who would have to carry him, in addition to the cumbersome saddle in which Gonzalo usually rode. Gonzalo and his *vaqueros* used large, heavy saddles with round knobs on the pommels, where a man could secure a rope if he caught a steer with his *lazo.* The use of a *lazo* was a custom unique to the New World. Diego hoped to master the art of *lazo*-tossing one of these days, but thus far he had not had time to learn the skill. He had been too busy.

Well, he had wanted to explore the Ocean of Grass, and this was his opportunity. Only he had not intended to take Gonzalo with him, much less a bunch of *vaqueros.* However, recovering La Reina and the other horses was now his first priority. The thought of La Reina, especially, being in the hands of ignorant savages made his blood run cold. What if they meant to eat her instead of ride her?

He wanted to ask Maria if that was a possibility, but since he had ordered her to keep her distance, he was reluctant to initiate conversation. If she *had* taken part in the theft—or even if she had not—he would be far better off never speaking to her again!

Looking around, he saw that she had melted into the shadows and was following her father at a slight distance. Assuming she had done as he had ordered and packed for him, he would not have much to do to prepare for this distasteful adventure. It would be done already. He made up his mind to avoid her before his departure. The thieves deserved to be punished, but he did not want to look in her eyes and witness her fear that there might be a terrible massacre of her mother's people. He would try to prevent it, but short of turning his *pistola* on Don Gonzalo himself, he might be unable to stop it. The *vaqueros* would give him no support; Gonzalo had chosen his *vaqueros* as he had chosen his guards at the mine—because they hated and feared Indians.

Could he shoot a Spaniard in order to save an *Indio?* Diego doubted it. Much as he disapproved of the way Gonzalo lived his life, he was still indebted to the man and could not yet desert him.

Diego stopped to groom El Cid and feed him some corn to fortify him for the journey, then headed for the house. When he entered the west wing, he was relieved not to encounter Maria. He could tell she had been there, however, because the tallow dips had all been lit. He found a portion of his belongings piled neatly in the center of his bed, along with spare bedding, several water gourds, and a sack of dried food obviously meant to be taken with him.

He sorted through the items, rejecting some, and adding a few others, for he did not know how long he would be gone on this chase. Maria had not touched any of his weapons, and he grimly gathered them together as Caobo lay still, watching him. Suddenly, the dog lifted his head from his paws and looked toward the door. Maria stood there, her arms laden with an armored breastplate and hat. She also held a long lance, and attempted to maneuver it through the doorway.

"My father sent these things to you. If you have need of anything else, I will go and fetch it."

She kept her lashes lowered, and he longed to see the expression in her fox fire eyes. What was she thinking?

"Thank you for assembling my things, Maria. You did a good job. Here . . . let me take that armor. It must be heavy."

"Take the lance," she urged, "before I drop it. I dislike holding it, anyway."

He took the lance first and leaned it upright against the wall. Then he took the armor. It was much too heavy for her. He dreaded wearing it, especially now, with the heat of the season increasing each day. He set the armor on the bed alongside his other supplies.

Half-expecting her to be gone when he turned around, he was surprised to find her still standing in the room, her gaze leveled at the floor. Slowly, almost reluctantly, she raised her eyes to look at him.

"*Señor* . . . Don Diego, I have something to ask you. And something to . . . to promise you."

He folded his arms across his chest and waited. Curiosity burned in him, but he did not dare press her. He sensed she was gathering her courage.

"Don Diego, if you can stop my father from slaughtering my mother's people and my brother, then when you return I will . . . I will be everything you wish me to be. I will give you anything you want."

She spoke precisely, as if she had planned each word but found it agonizing to say them. He did not pretend ignorance of what she was talking about. Toying with her would have wounded her dignity and demeaned the offer, which he believed to be sincere. She was simply too innocent to realize it would never work; gratitude was a poor substitute for honest passion or affection. It could never yield the ecstasy he dreamed of sharing with her.

"Maria, the thieves must be caught and the horses returned

to *Dehesa de Oro.* I am committed to that. You cannot expect me to do less, no matter what you offer.''

''I understand,'' she said, ''but I do not think my brother stole the horses. If my father finds Santelmo, he will give him no chance to explain or defend himself. I know my father. When this vengeful mood possesses him, he will slay any *Indio* who crosses his path.''

''Why do you deny it was your brother who stole the horses? Whoever it was must have known *Dehesa de Oro.* That old *Indio* confirmed that the dead man belonged to your mother's people.''

''Santelmo would have come for *me,* not just for the horses!'' Maria struck her breast with her fist for emphasis. ''That is how I know he did not steal them. He cannot have forgotten the little sister he left behind when he and my eldest brother first escaped. He would not have returned to *Dehesa de Oro* and made no attempt to see or speak to me.''

Two spots of hectic color bloomed in Maria's cheeks. Diego mentally scolded himself for having suspected her of complicity in the theft. 'Twas obvious she preferred to believe that her brother had never come, rather than accept that he cared more for horses than he did for her.

''Perhaps he did not look for you because he feared getting caught. You were in the house, not out by the corrals.''

''Then he would have left some sign,'' she said haughtily. '' 'Tis what *Indios* do to keep one another informed of their movements. They leave signs no white man would ever notice.''

''And you found no such signs?''

''When it grows light I will look again, but no, I saw no signs.''

''And you have practice in reading Indian signs. Am I to believe your mother taught you?''

Despair shone in her eyes. ''I do not know. Perhaps she did. I do not remember. But I think my own brother would have left something!''

She looked so anguished and disappointed. His heart went out to her. He could not refrain from going to her and slipping his arms around her slender waist. She allowed him to hold her and even clung to him a little bit.

"Don Diego, do not let my father kill my brother and all my mother's people. *Please.* I beg you. If you help me in this, I will hold nothing back from you. I will give you all you demand."

Sighing, he rested his chin on her fragrant hair. "Maria, make no promises you cannot keep. A part of you would still resent the sacrifice you were forced to make. And that small part would prevent you from the wholehearted eagerness I so much desire."

"But I *am* eager!" She leaned back to look up at him. "Part of me *wants* to surrender to your kisses. Indeed, I must fight to restrain myself. But if you do this for me, I will fight no longer. You will see how eager I can be."

Taking his face in her hands, she stood on tiptoe to press her lips to his. The tender contact went to his head like the strongest brandy. For one breathless moment, he held her to him and shamelessly reveled in his desire for her, taking all she gave and urging her to give more. She responded by opening her mouth and allowing him to plunder it with his tongue. When his hand moved to her breast, she gasped, and the small sound restored his sanity.

Thrusting her away from his overheated body, he held her by the shoulders and looked down into her bedazzled eyes.

"Maria, stop. Do not do this. You will only be sorry if we go much further. I have no wish to betray your trust in me, so I must tell you that I myself intend to punish the man who took La Reina. I pray it was not your brother, but if it was I intend to bring back his head mounted on that lance you just brought me."

The threat jolted her to her senses. "You would do that, *señor?* You would actually do that?"

The horror in her eyes was worse than he had imagined, but he had to tell her the truth. Here in this place, surrounded by a sea of grass, a fine horse was a man's greatest treasure. The thief must be punished, or others would soon come to take the rest of the horses. She *must* understand the magnitude of the crime. He did not possess her father's streak of cruelty, but he did agree with the necessity of keeping the Indians on foot and making them think twice about ever again stealing horses.

"I don't *want* to, Maria, but I must. I will try to prevent a mass slaughter, but I cannot promise that your father and his men will listen to me. In any case, I have already agreed to punish the man who stole La Reina, and I will not go back on my word."

"I heard you make that promise, but I thought . . . I hoped, you would reconsider if I offered to give you what you want from me. Is a horse's life greater than a man's? 'Tis only an animal, after all!"

"In this land, there are many Indians, but few Spanish and even fewer horses. We cannot allow the Indians to become equal to us, Maria. I am a Spaniard, and so—in part—are you. Your father gave you to me, and I will protect you. From your own brother, if need be."

"My brother would never hurt me, as you do!" She struggled to free herself from his grip, and he despised himself for what he had just done to her.

He had deliberately and knowingly turned her against him. He had aroused not her passion, but her hatred. Now, even if he succeeded in averting a bloodbath, she would always consider him the enemy—if not as bad as her father, then worse, worse because he had given her hope and then crushed it.

"Maria, try not to hate me. Try to understand."

Tears shimmered in her eyes, and her mouth trembled, but she fixed him with a cold, distant gaze that shriveled his heart and soul. "For you, *señor,* I feel nothing. Nothing at all. Forget what I told you a moment ago. 'Twas all a lie. I have no feelings at all for you—neither hate nor passion. If the *Indios* should manage to kill you on this journey, I will not shed a single tear. Either for you or for my father. *Adiós, señor.*"

He released her at last and watched as she fled from the room. "*Adiós,* Maria," he whispered after she had gone.

Standing alone in the empty room, he knew he had never felt so alone . . . not even when his father had rejected him. Somehow, this seemed worse.

It *was* worse, for he had never intended to spend the rest of his life with his father. His father was old; he would soon die. But Maria was young, and filled with life and beauty. She could have enriched his lonely existence until he himself grew old and died.

Not now, though . . . he had destroyed any chance he might have had with her.

Chapter Nine

Maria knew not how she survived the first few days after Don Diego rode out with her father and most of his *vaqueros*. Once again, Doña Inez kept her so busy that she sometimes trembled from fatigue and exhaustion. She had no time to seek out Bartolomeo and find out if he had discovered any signs left by the horse thieves.

Her days were a blur of activity and her nights plagued with troubling dreams. In them, she witnessed scenes of violence involving her father, Don Diego, and the Indians. She was always helpless to stop the bloodshed or prevent the Indians, even the children, from being slain.

She had no one to talk to, and loneliness weighed on her more heavily than in the past. Twice, she initiated conversations with Juana, who made no effort to hide her unhappiness that her *vaquero* had gone with Don Gonzalo.

The girl rebuffed her in a startling and hurtful manner. " 'Tis *your* fault they had to leave," she said. "Your *Indio* relatives are a pestilence on us all. They deserve to die for stealing our *patrón's* horses. You probably told them which ones to take."

"I did no such thing!" The young woman's hostility amazed Maria. "I had no *idea* they were coming."

Of all the peasants employed at *Dehesa de Oro,* Juana had always seemed the one most likely to become her friend. Slightly older and on the plain side, with a crooked nose and protruding front teeth, she sometimes smiled at Maria behind Doña Inez's back, and once she had made a face as if to ridicule her. She worked almost as hard as Maria, so the two had no time to pursue a relationship, but Maria kept hoping. Now, she realized they would never be friends, and she mourned the lost opportunity.

A week passed with no word from the men. Not knowing what was happening drove Doña Inez into a frenzy. She piled work onto Maria, seeking her out in the west wing where she often fled to escape, demanding that she do more and more.

"Lazy, good-for-nothing wretch!" her stepmother screamed at her on the tenth morning after the men had set out. "I have been looking for you for hours. Until your father and Don Diego return, you will go back to sleeping in the cook shed, so I know where you are when I want you."

She launched into a long list of chores she wanted done by nightfall. Half of them were things Juana normally did. Lost in her own misery and worry, Maria had been unusually docile and accommodating, but something suddenly snapped inside her, and she turned on Doña Inez with a snarl of outrage.

"*You* are the useless and worthless one, Doña Inez! Until Don Diego himself orders me to return to the cook shed, I will continue sleeping in the west wing. I am a human being, not a beast of burden, and I refuse to obey you any longer."

Doña Inez sucked in a deep breath. Her cheeks puffed out like a toad's. "Why, you ungrateful little savage! How dare you speak so to me! All these years I have had to put up with you. You have been a trial from the very beginning. Why, you caused the death of my poor Antonio, my little jewel—"

"I did *not* cause his death! I only made a mistake. My sorrow over it was great. I have paid dearly for my error, and I am sick of your whining and ordering me about as if I were a slave in this household."

"You *are* a slave—a worthless *Indio!* I have every right to order you about. When your father hears of your insolence, he will beat you as he should have done that day when Don Diego took your part and put a stop to it."

"Let him beat me," Maria recklessly challenged. "I care not what he does. Let him beat me until I die. If I am never to be free of you both, then I prefer death to living in the same household where I must see you every day."

"I will tell him all this, and let him deal with you. You think Don Diego will protect you now, but he will not, Worthless One. He is one of *us*—an *hidalgo*. There is a point past which you can never hope to push him. 'Twas *my* idea to give you to him. Do you think I would have done so if I did not have perfect confidence that his loyalties lie with the aristocracy? No. I would not have risked it. No matter how much he relishes bedding you, he will never marry you nor give your children his name. I will find a wife for him with similar bloodlines. Then you will see how quickly he casts you off—or keeps you hidden from polite society. He will make no sacrifices for *you,* girl. You are doomed to the same disappointments as your mother. Accept your place and be glad of it, for your only other choice is the silver mine."

Maria violently shook her head. She refused to accept that she would never know any other life but this one. She had been willing to sacrifice everything to spare the Indians, but Don Diego's unwillingness to protect them had released her from any form of debt to him. She owed him nothing now. Her stepmother thought to enlighten her, but Maria already knew that Don Diego was a loyal *hidalgo* who would never betray his own best interests.

"I shall remain in the west wing of the house until my master's return," she told Doña Inez. "You commanded me to serve Don Diego, and I will continue to do so. His quarters are my sole responsibility. All other chores you must delegate to Juana and the rest of the servants."

"You will regret this! I have borne your rebellion one time too many. When the men return you will be severely punished—as much or more so than the wretched savages who stole our horses. I pray they find your brother, Santelmo, and the tribe from which your mother came, and that they destroy them in the name of *Dios* and all that is right and just.''

''Killing helpless *Indios* is not right and just! Nor can it be pleasing to the God you worship, and especially not to His Sorrowful Mother. *Cristo* did not preach hatred, but love for one another.''

''You presume to lecture *me* on the dictates of my faith? Now you are a blasphemer and a heretic! When Fray Leonido hears of this, he will haul you away to face the Inquisitor. What I have failed to accomplish, *he* will achieve for me. You will rue this day, Maria. The torments devised for blasphemers are far worse than anything you can imagine.''

Fear clenched Maria's insides. She had heard tales of the dreaded Inquisitor. Her stepmother's boasts were not idle. She had perhaps gone too far in provoking her.

''If I have said anything to offend The Sorrowful Mother, I will go now to beg her forgiveness. I will spend three hours on my knees in the chapel—but I will *not* obey *you* any longer, Doña Inez. I belong to Don Diego now. Him alone will I serve.''

''Three hours on your knees will not save you!'' the pinch-faced woman spat out. ''I will not forget a word of this incredible exchange. 'Tis all committed to memory.''

Brushing past her stepmother, Maria headed for the little chapel off the courtyard. There, she dropped to her knees on the stone floor before the flower-draped statue of The Sorrowful Mother. And there she remained until hours later, when the clatter of hooves and shouts of arriving men told her that Don Diego and her father had finally returned.

Diego knew that their arrival would cause a great commotion at *Dehesa de Oro*. It started while they were still a couple of leagues away. A servant came out of the house and spotted them, returning without the horses they had sought and indeed with fewer horses than they had taken with them. Four of their bedraggled party of twelve were wounded, including Gonzalo, and three were dead. They had brought back the bodies of the dead *vaqueros,* while the wounded struggled to remain mounted on their horses long enough to reach the ranch.

"We are almost there, Gonzalo." Diego edged El Cid closer to Gonzalo's limping horse.

"Good, for I am losing strength," Gonzalo moaned, hunching over the knob on his big saddle. "I may be dying. The savages have killed me. My own son probably shot the arrows that pierced my thigh and shoulder. Too bad I was not wearing the armor I insisted on taking. The wounds will fester, and then I will die."

"They will not fester. We got the arrows out quickly and purified the wounds soon after. Do not tell me you don't remember—you bellowed loud enough to wake the dead."

Gonzalo lifted his head and gave Diego a look of annoyance. "If you are making a joke, Diego, I am not amused. Your efforts to save me hurt like the fires of hell. At least, now, I know how the savages will suffer when I finally send them into eternity."

"You swore they would not fight, Gonzalo. You claimed they would fall on their knees and worship us, making themselves easy victims," Diego reminded him. " 'Twas I who questioned the wisdom of not posting guards around our campsite and preparing ourselves for a possible ambush. Now, I realize I should have stood guard myself. We removed our armor and lay down to sleep like gullible children."

"I was not expecting an ambush, because they have never fought back before! This was the first time. They have *always* been docile as sheep, and fallen on their knees in awe at the sight of men riding horses. I cannot imagine what got into them. They stole horses right from under our noses. What surprises me even more is that we have not seen a single one of those horses we were hoping to find."

"It surprises and worries me," Diego conceded. "We do not even know for certain that the Indians who attacked us are the same ones who stole the horses."

"They *are* the same ones. They sought to prevent us from following them, and the attack was how they achieved their objective. Here we are, limping home like beaten dogs with our tails tucked between our legs.''

"As soon as we reach *Dehesa de Oro,* I will assemble more supplies and head out again, Gonzalo. And this time, I am not coming back until I have retrieved all our horses."

"By the time you resume the search, they will be long gone, my friend. They will have returned to their hidden villages where you will never find them. You will only get lost and die in the wilderness."

"By the blood of *Cristo,* I will find them!" Diego swore. "I am roused to anger now. I will search the entire continent, if I must, but I will find them and take back our horses. 'Tis imperative. With a stallion and a small band of mares, they can begin breeding and raising their own horses. 'Tis the very thing you have feared all these years, Gonzalo. Now, I see why. They can be cunning and vicious."

"Perhaps I should thank *Dios* I will not be alive to see it." Gonzalo sighed and clutched the saddle apple with both hands to avoid toppling from his horse. "I may not make it as far as my own house."

"You will make it," Diego gruffly insisted. "Doña Inez is already coming for you. Look there. She is running toward us with a portion of skirt held high in each hand. *Madre!* I would not have thought she could run so fast."

"And I would not have thought I could be so happy to lay eyes on my shrew of a wife. Well, the woman has always claimed to know something about healing. If she does not, I am in grave trouble. So also are my wounded men."

Diego could hear her now, screaming her husband's name. Other women were running toward the bodies of the dead *vaqueros,* slung across the horses Miguel herded ahead of them. Diego wondered where he would get more men to take with him. All the able-bodied *vaqueros* at *Dehesa de Oro* would be needed to guard the place from attack and keep the ranch running smoothly. This next journey would be a long one. Fortunately, he did not need many men; the fewer he took with him, the faster he could travel. With guns and fast horses, the Spaniards still had the advantage over the Indians. This time, he would go carefully and take no chances. Arrogance and carelessness had led to their downfall, but Diego had learned his lesson. The next time he met the savages, they would not find him sleeping.

He needed someone to guide the party—someone who spoke the language of the *Indios* and had some idea where their villages were located. None of the *vaqueros* met these requirements. If he were fortunate enough to capture a lone *Indio* out on the plain, he needed a linguist who could make sense of his babbling. Maria could do that, but she could not, of course, find Indian villages. She had spent all her life at *Dehesa de Oro*.

Diego suddenly remembered the old Indian, Bartolomeo. The fellow might not remember much, but he would be better than nothing. He might recall landmarks and watering places. Finding water on the vast grasslands was a challenge. If Bartolomeo did no more than that, it would be worth taking him along. He would secure the old Indian's cooperation by promising leniency toward the women and children of the thieves. Without Gonzalo along, there would be no bloodbaths; only the actual wrongdoers would be punished.

As the women of *Dehesa de Oro* descended upon them, Diego had no more time to plan the search. He had all he could manage answering the questions and accusations of Doña Inez. The next several hours were a whirlwind of confusion and complaint. The activity did not diminish until the dead men had all been buried and the wounded made comfortable.

Doña Inez proved less of a healer than Don Gonzalo had hoped, but Maria somehow managed to bring order from the chaos. She found a stout old peasant woman named Dorotea who had experience dealing with wounds and fevers. By nightfall, Gonzalo was resting more or less sedately in his own bed, and the other wounded men lay in a makeshift infirmary in the quarters of the *vaqueros,* with Dorotea in charge. Diego was finally able to seek the comfort of his own quarters and the solace of hot food taken in privacy and served by the woman whose company he had been longing to have all to himself.

The day had taken its toll on Maria. She looked wan and

tired from her labors as she poured wine into a goblet for him, then set it on the table in the library where she had laid out his meal. As she turned to leave, he caught her arm.

"Maria, wait. Sit and rest a moment. Eat with me. You must be as hungry and exhausted as I am."

She lifted her lashes to give him a long, assessing glance. "You are right, *señor*. I *am* weary—too weary to eat. Before I can sleep, I must still unpack your things and put them away."

"There's no need for that. I will be leaving soon, and taking you with me. Tomorrow—not tonight—you must pack some things for yourself."

Her eyes widened. The flickering tallow dip on the table cast a warm glow on her pale features and heightened the color in her bloodless lips. She suddenly looked alert and wary.

"What do you mean—you are taking me with you?"

"You and the old Indian, Bartolomeo. I am taking you both—him, because I need a guide to help me find water, good grass for the horses, and the Indian villages—and you because I need someone to translate my conversations with him and any other Indians we may chance to meet."

"Even after this, you are not giving up?" Her smooth forehead wrinkled into a frown. "Men have been killed and wounded, including my own father. His survival is greatly in doubt, yet you still intend to go after the horse thieves?"

He nodded. "Does that surprise you? More than ever, 'tis necessary I regain the horses and teach the Indians a lesson. Your father claims the Indians have never before been so bold as to launch an attack on Spaniards. An occasional stray arrow has found its mark, but there have been no battles worth mentioning. We cannot allow this challenge to go unanswered, or *Dehesa de Oro* itself will be threatened."

Maria made no response. He was not surprised, for his logic could not be refuted.

"As soon as possible, we will depart," he continued. "Each day of delay means the Indians can put more distance between us. My hope is that the horses will slow them down, not enable them to go faster. As yet, your relatives cannot know much about horses. They will have difficulty managing the animals and keeping them together.''

"You cannot prove 'twas my relatives who did it. Did you see the horses when you were attacked? If not, *señor,* you are only guessing that your attackers were the same Indians who stole La Reina."

Diego shook his head. "True, I did not see them, but it stands to reason they were the exact same men. Your father believes so. We were attacked at dawn as we lay sleeping. 'Tis a miracle we were not all killed. We had no time to muster a defense or even put on our armor. If not for Caobo sounding the alarm they would have cut all our throats, and we would never have known what was happening. We owe our lives to my dog, who gave us the opportunity to fight back."

At the mention of his name, Caobo, who lay at his feet, thumped his tail and gazed adoringly up at him. Diego selected a choice hunk of meat from the platter on the table and fed the hound from his own fingers. Thoroughly awake now, the dog rose and tried to see over the edge of the table. His nose told him more meat remained, and he wanted it.

"No, Caobo," Diego admonished. "Get down. Hero or not, I will not allow you to become a nuisance, begging at meals."

Caobo obediently collapsed at his feet, and Diego glanced at Maria. She had not moved from the spot where she stood beside the table. Her expression was unfathomable.

"Maria, we saw no horses," he repeated. "But there were many *Indios.* The horses were probably up ahead of us, and the Indians had dropped back under cover of darkness to discourage us from venturing further into their territory. 'Tis the most likely explanation for the attack. If that was their goal, they succeeded in it. We could not press on with so many of us dead or wounded. We had to turn round and come home."

"So the Indians won the encounter," she said softly, but it was impossible to tell if she were elated or simply stating a fact. Her features remained impassive. Only her eyes, as usual, glittered.

"Yes, they won it. But the next time, *I* will be the victor. I have sworn to your father I will not return here without the horses."

"And you want my help and Bartolomeo's."

"I'll not be giving either of you *pistolas,* but yes, I will expect you to translate, and Bartolomeo must help us find water and good grass."

"The Ocean of Grass is *filled* with grass," she said mockingly.

"Some of it is more like a desert," he disputed. "And very desolate with no water in sight. We did not have to go too far north to encounter such land. We entered upon a dry region, then changed our minds and altered our direction because we did not think the Indians would take the horses there. Forage would be too hard to find."

"I will go and tell Bartolomeo to prepare himself." Maria started to turn away, then stopped. "But how will you keep him alive on this journey? He cannot possibly walk such a long distance, but as an *Indio* he is not permitted to ride a horse. Nor am I," she added bitterly.

"Your father has other beasts of burden," Diego said. "I recall seeing a couple of asses in the corrals. We will fit them out with saddles, and you can ride as we do. It will take some practice to get the hang of it, but you will soon learn."

A glimmer of pleasure lit her eyes. He saw it before she quickly lowered her lashes. "May I be excused now to seek out the old *Indio?*"

Diego paused before giving his permission. He studied her face and her slender figure, but found no more clues to her thoughts. Did she dread accompanying him on this mission? Or did she see it as an opportunity to explore the homeland of her people—perhaps even to escape?

He suddenly realized he would have to keep a close watch on her, in case she conceived the idea of locating her brother before he did. She could not get very far on an ass, but perhaps she did not know that.

"You may go now," he finally said. "No, wait—Maria, have you ever before ridden an ass?"

"No, *señor*, I have never ridden one, but believe me, I have had plenty of experience with asses. So has Bartolomeo."

Did she mean what he thought she did?

A smile hovered about her lips, but she did not raise her eyes to meet his gaze. He did not know what to think. She was one surprise after another.

"Go," he said. "Deliver your news, and then get some sleep. It will not take me long to eat. As soon as I am finished this room will be yours again, at least for tonight. For one last night, you will have a roof over your head. Enjoy it while it lasts, Maria. You will soon be sleeping in the open, exposed to all the elements."

"That does not scare me, *señor*. I am half-*Indio*, remember?"

How could he forget?

They were ready to leave just before noon of the following day, and Maria could hardly conceal her elation. She was leaving *Dehesa de Oro*, and taking Bartolomeo with her! It was almost too daunting to think about the possibility of escaping the search party and finding the Indians on her own; she could not picture herself attempting it unless Bartolomeo were able to accompany her. Still, the idea was there, simmering in the back of her mind, and flooding her with excitement.

In the meantime, she enjoyed their departure, especially the look on Doña Inez's face when she found out that Don Diego valued her abilities enough to insist she go along on the trip. Her stepmother did not utter a word of protest, and Maria concluded that she must be as glad to be rid of her as Maria was glad to be leaving. Perhaps Doña Inez was simply too preoccupied with her husband's injuries to care what happened to her now.

It was a clear, hot day, with the sun beating down fiercely. Miguel, Ignacio, and two other *vaqueros* sat ready and waiting on their horses. They were bringing two packhorses, but could spare no more men for the party. Men were needed to manage the ranch, and with the losses they had already suffered they were severely shorthanded. Doña Inez had already sent a rider

to Santa Barbola to hire more *vaqueros* to replace the ones
who had died.

To Maria, this was a prime example of Spanish arrogance and
shortsightedness. There were plenty of peasants and common
laborers at *Dehesa de Oro,* but they were not deemed worthy
enough to be taught the fine art of reinsmanship or the handling
of weapons. Instead of training peasants, her father and Miguel
usually sent to Santa Barbola when they needed riders for
the round up and branding of cattle or other tasks involving
horsemen. So determined were the Spanish to keep their inferiors afoot that they put themselves to great trouble and expense
rather than compromise their standards.

This time, their arrogance would surely work to her advantage, Maria thought. She had only to outwit five men, and she
and Bartolomeo would be free. A moment would present itself
during this journey when all the men would be sleeping or
occupied, and she and the old *Indio* could escape. She was
counting on it.

But first, she had to master riding a cantankerous, lop-eared
ass, whose soft, brown eyes gave no hint of his stubborn nature.
He had refused to stand still while she tied her belongings in
a bedroll behind the saddle. Now, when she hiked up her skirts
and attempted to climb aboard him, he spun around in circles
so fast that she could not get her leg over his back.

Miguel and the other *vaqueros* burst out laughing at her
futile efforts. Bartolomeo finally came over and offered to hold
the animal. While the old man held him, he crooned in the
animal's ear and rubbed the arch of his neck. Thus calmed, the
little ass blew through his nostrils and calmly allowed Maria
to mount him. Once she was safely aboard, with her skirt
bunched around her legs to cover them, she discovered that all
her hard work of riding La Reina had not gone to waste.

When Bartolomeo turned her loose, she managed to sit
through the animal's contortions as he sought to dislodge her.
Indeed, he only succeeded in dislodging the floppy brimmed
straw hat she had worn to ward off the hot rays of the sun.

She could not control his direction, however, and he set off
across the grasslands braying at the top of his lungs. Hanging

onto the reins, she resigned herself to being the butt of everyone's humor—and to leading the party on their quest—when she heard Don Diego's shout.

"Turn him, Maria! Pull hard on your right rein and turn him in a small circle until he gives up."

Don Diego never had to pull hard on a horse's reins, Maria thought resentfully. She had no desire to again travel in small circles, but soon realized she had better try the tactic or she would not be able to stop the animal. If they came to the edge of a cliff, he would go right over it.

She pulled hard on the right rein until he bent his body around her leg and came to an abrupt standstill that almost unseated her. Riding up to her on El Cid, Don Diego instructed: "Now, you must not let him stop whenever he wants. Keep him going until *you* say he can stop. Go on—kick him. Kick him hard with both feet."

Maria kicked, but her leather sandals did not have the same effect as a *vaquero's* heavy boots with spurs on them. The ass took a step, brayed in protest, and dug in his heels.

Don Diego laughed so hard he doubled over in the saddle. "You are doing fine," he lied. "Just fine. Keep at it, Maria. But do not allow him to get away with anything—and keep your seat at all costs."

She resolved at that moment to never fall off in front of him. She would "keep her seat" and master the ass if it was the last thing she ever did.

"Fall in behind me and Miguel. You and Bartolomeo will ride in the middle with two of us in front and three behind. 'Tis the safest place for you both. You and Bartolomeo are the only ones without arms."

Maria saw that Don Diego was already perspiring beneath his armored hat. Beneath his breastplate, he was surely soaking wet. He wore a quilted, buff leather doublet under his armor, leathern and baize trunk hose, and his usual tall, cuffed, thigh boots. He carried a long sword at his side, a lance in his hand, and a *pistola* in a leather holster fastened to his saddle. He was so handsome he made her heart ache, but she did not envy him his heavy, protective gear. As the day progressed he would only become more uncomfortable in the heat, while she could endure it better in her light garments. Apparently, there were *some* advantages to being a woman and an *Indio*.

The ass seemed disposed to follow the stallion, so Maria simply sat there and allowed him to indulge his own whim. Don Diego rode back to collect the others, and when they were all together he raised an arm and signaled them to fall in behind him. Bartolomeo joined Maria in the center of the party and gave her a gap-toothed grin. He, too, wore a hat, adorned with a feather, and his rags had been replaced by a peasant's shirt, trousers, and sandals.

The old *Indio* was having no difficulty riding his own ass; this one was older and gentler. He kept his long ears back, as if listening for his rider's next instructions. Hemmed in by Diego and the *vaqueros,* the asses had no choice but to go along with the horses. They had to trot to keep up with the long-legged strides of their taller companions. Maria gritted her teeth against the bumping motion and grabbed hold of the hair on the ass's thick neck to keep her balance.

The journey suddenly seemed much less exciting. She tried her best to sit squarely in the middle of the ass's bouncing back as he carried her away from *Dehesa de Oro.* She also tried to make plans, but *Madre de Dios!* How could she think about escaping or finding her brother when it required all of her concentration just to keep from landing in the dust?

Chapter Ten

That evening, Maria made a simple meal from the provisions they had brought along with them. After everyone had eaten and the *vaqueros* had retired to their bedrolls, Don Diego summoned her and Bartolomeo. He sat on a folded blanket in front of the small fire made from dried animal dung that Bartolomeo had diligently collected. Leaning back against his saddle, propped on the ground behind him, he motioned for them to sit down in the knee-high grass. He appeared to be deep in thought, giving Maria and Bartolomeo ample opportunity to finish their last evening chores before complying.

There was no water nearby, and no trees. Serrated foothills rose in the far distance, but nightfall had obliterated their shadowy outlines. Maria was intensely aware of the sky overhead, dominating the solitary landscape. She felt no fear, but had overheard Ignacio muttering to Pedro, one of the *vaqueros* who happened to be Juana's man, that he dreaded each step that took them further north into the land of the savages.

Ignacio, Pedro, Miguel, and Fernandez—the fourth *vaquero* —were already stretched out on the ground on the opposite side of the dying fire, their heads pillowed on their saddles, their hats covering their faces. Diego had volunteered for the first watch, and his *pistola* and lance lay close at hand. He had removed his armor. His dark hair, matted down by the armored hat, clung to his forehead in thick waves and curls. Gazing into the distance, he paid no attention as they approached.

Nearby, the hobbled horses and the two asses munched grass contentedly, side by side. With the camp chores now completed, Maria was eager to lie back against her own saddle, gaze up at the stars, and allow her sore muscles some much needed rest. She ached in places she had never realized it was possible to ache, and she hoped there was no more work for either her or Bartolomeo to do this night.

Kneeling down on the grass, she sat back on her haunches. Bartolomeo did the same. With growing impatience, she waited for Don Diego to state his reasons for summoning them.

The dim firelight cast the hollows of his face in dark shadow. Finally noticing them, he watched her silently for a moment before speaking. At last, he said: "Maria, ask the old man if he knows of any rivers near here."

Turning to Bartolomeo, she obediently posed the question. Bartolomeo answered with a swift nod of his head and gave his answer, which she translated for Diego.

"He says yes, there are many rivers further to the north. The *Indios* know all of them. In which one are you interested?"

Don Diego sighed. "I do not know which one. That is the problem. I just wondered if there was one that might run north and south, instead of east and west."

Maria queried Bartolomeo, received his reply, and again translated. "He says most of them do run east and west. However, some angle to the north or south in places. One in particular could be said to run north and south, but it lies many days journey from here."

"All right then, ask him which one he would be most likely to follow if he were fleeing from your father."

Maria blinked at the question.

"He says he would follow the River of Trees, so named because many trees grow along its banks. He uses a different word to name them, but I think he means poplar trees."

"Would such a river have shallow places where one could safely lead horses across it?"

Bartolomeo answered yes, then added that if he were fleeing north, taking horses with him, he would try to follow the River of Trees for a good part of the way.

"Tell him I want him to guide us to that river. I assume he knows how to get there."

The old man told Maria he did, that he had not forgotten the way, to which Diego responded: "Tomorrow, we will alter our direction and go wherever he tells us. How many days does he think it will take us to reach this River of Trees?"

Bartolomeo only shrugged his shoulders. When pressed, he replied: "Ten sunrises. Perhaps more. Since we are riding instead of walking, it may be less."

Miguel suddenly tossed aside the hat covering his face and sat up on the opposite side of the fire. "Don Diego, what plans are you making without us? We are here to find stolen horses, not explore the wilderness. We should go back to where we fought the Indians and take up their trail from there."

"That trail will be cold by now." Diego stretched his arms over his head. " 'Tis a waste of time to return to that spot. We must try to guess where the Indians have taken the horses, and then attempt to waylay them."

"You cannot expect this old *Indio* to show us the way! Years have passed since he was captured, and his memory may be faulty. Even if we find this so-called River of Trees, the thieves may not be there with our horses."

" 'Tis a chance we must take," Diego responded. "We have little choice. The horses need grass and water. It only stands to reason the Indians will follow a river and avoid harsh, dry country. Once we find the river, we can search the banks for hoofprints. If we find some, we will know we are headed in the right direction."

"I wish Don Gonzalo were here. He would say otherwise."

"Well, he is not here, is he? When he was in charge, we got ambushed and never even saw the horses. So, now we will do things my way."

"You risk lives with this foolishness!" Miguel glared at him from across the fire. "We know this land better than you do. You should listen to us, not to a smelly, old *Indio*."

"You have appointed yourself the leader of the others?" Diego asked calmly, but his hand moved to his leather holster.

"I was their leader long before you arrived, Don Diego. Just because you are the new Master of Horses does not make you an expert on what we should do to find our horses. I say we should capture the first *Indio* we see and torture him until he tells us something useful. Perhaps we should begin with Bartolomeo. Why don't you ask him if he remembers how to find the village of his people?"

Diego nodded to Maria. "Go ahead. Ask him. Let us see what he says."

Maria swallowed hard. She wanted no harm to come to her old friend. Diego would not hurt him, but the others might. They shared her father's views on Indians. From Bartolomeo's expression, she knew he understood the exchange. Still, she asked the question, and the old man gave a careful answer.

"Well?" Don Diego demanded.

"He says there is no single village. Rather, there are many camping places to which my mother's tribe returns year after year, as they follow the woolly cows. I could have told you this myself, Don Diego. He is an old man. Let him sleep now, or he will be unable to guide us tomorrow."

"One more question." Diego held up his hand. "This River of Trees—will it take us to the place where your mother's people used to camp at this time of year?"

Maria repeated Diego's question, but hesitated to give Bartolomeo's answer. She did not want to reveal any more than she must about the habits of her mother's people. For once, she wished Bartolomeo practiced deceit, but the old man seemed unable to lie. Despite all he had suffered at the hands of the Spanish, he believed he owed them perfect honesty.

"Well?" Diego again prompted. "You might as well tell me the truth, Maria. I intend to spend the rest of our lives out here, if necessary, searching for those horses. As I told your father, I will not give up until I find them."

"That is no threat for me, Don Diego, but yes, he says the

river will lead us to one of their encampments. Whether or not they will be there, he cannot and will not promise."

"Hah!" Miguel barked. "Hold a burning brand to the soles of his feet, and then ask him again. 'Tis the only way to be certain he does not deceive us. They will be there, and he well knows it."

"There is no deceit in him," Maria protested.

She gazed across the smoldering embers of the fire at the *arrendador*. Miguel was considered a good-looking *vaquero*, with his flashing black eyes and well-groomed mustache, but she suddenly found him ugly and dangerous. Until now, she had never really gotten to know him; he had simply been her father's best reinsman. She suddenly realized that he was cut from the same bolt of cloth as her father, and she greatly disliked him.

" 'Tis understandable why you stoop to defending an *Indio*," Miguel drawled, once again lounging against his saddle. "You are a *colorada* yourself, even if you are Don Gonzalo's daughter."

"A *colorada*?" Diego's eyes narrowed. "I have never heard that term used to describe Maria or anyone else. What do you mean by it? You had better not be insulting her, Miguel. She belongs to me, and I defend what's mine."

"Here in the *Nueva Vizacaya*, it means a red-skin. But 'tis more a statement of fact than an insult."

In the blink of an eye, Diego yanked his *pistola* from its leather holster and pointed it at the *arrendador*. "Apologize, Miguel, or I will shoot the tips off your mustache. I may take part of your face along with them."

Maria rushed to push Bartolomeo out of the way. Whether he was defending her or not, Don Diego had never looked so menacing. It was easy to believe he was a murderer—he looked like one now. He probably *had* murdered a man in Spain.

Miguel never moved a muscle, except to incline his head in Maria's direction. "Forgive me, girl, for simply stating the truth. You have no objection to being called a *colorada*, do you? If so, I will refrain from using the term."

Maria drew a deep breath. "I would prefer to be called Maria. That is my name, after all."

"Then Maria it will be," Miguel snarled.

Diego sighted down the muzzle of his *pistola.* "No, you will call her *Señorita* Maria, and be mindful of whom you are addressing. She is the daughter of your *patrón,* and the mistress of your new Master of Horses. I should not have to remind you of this."

"Why do you set such store on a female whose own father treats her with a lack of respect? Never mind. I will not belabor the point. Put away your *pistola,* Don Diego. If I were you, I would not waste my precious gunpowder on one of your own countrymen. I would save it instead for the *Indios.*"

Lip curled in disdain, Miguel resumed his prone position and covered his face with his hat. Don Diego watched him, his mouth drawn tight in anger.

"Maria, fetch your things and bring them over here next to mine. You will sleep beside me tonight and every night, as you have been doing at *Dehesa de Oro.* I want you close, where I can protect you against *Indios* and all other marauders, be they animals or Spaniards." Maria knew better than to challenge him over sleeping arrangements.

Miguel's boldness had astonished her. The *arrendador* seemed to think *he* should have been appointed leader of this expedition. His hostility surpassed mere resentment of Don Diego's authority; she sensed he was jealous of her relationship with the Master of Horses—the one he assumed she had. Perhaps, she mused, as she fetched her saddle and sleeping blanket, he had been hoping her father would give her to him one day. Don Gonzalo had always set great store on Miguel, and treated him almost like a son, but Miguel was not an *hidalgo.* Indeed, her father had often complained of his limitations in training horses.

No sooner had she spread her blanket and settled herself beside Don Diego than he hooked an arm around her waist, hauled her to him, and arranged his own blanket over the top of them. Her heart beat a frantic pace as she waited to see what he would do next. Surely, he did not intend to make love to her right in front of Miguel and the others!

She lay on her side, facing away from him, and he cuddled close to her, fitting his body around hers and even throwing a leg over her legs, as if staking ownership. Nuzzling her ear, he whispered: "Relax, little madonna. Be still. You need not fear for your virtue. I have no intention of claiming your maidenhead this night. But we must prove to Miguel that you truly do belong to me, or he is likely to view you as fair game for his own base desires."

"Miguel and the others are my father's own men," she whispered back. "They would never touch me without his permission."

"That is where you are wrong, Maria. Out here, anything can happen. When civilization no longer exists, men forget to be civilized. They revert to their animal instincts."

Trapped against his body and acutely aware of his warmth and strength, Maria wrestled with the awakening of her own animal instincts. She doubted she could sleep in this position, where every little movement they made could each be felt by the other.

His hand rose to her face and gently smoothed her hair back from her forehead and cheek. "Sleep, little one. I know you are tired, and tomorrow will be another long day."

She tried to ignore the press of his nether regions against her backside, but all she succeeded in doing was imagining that part of him more vividly. Fortunately, having wrapped himself around her like a cocoon, he soon surrendered to his own fatigue. Not until he began breathing deeply was she able to relax.

Just before sleep claimed her, she roused long enough to wonder who was now keeping watch. As if to answer the question, a furry body suddenly brushed against her arm, and a long tongue swiped across her outstretched hand. Caobo circled twice and flopped down on his stomach, then lifted his muzzle, nose quivering, as he took in the scents on the breeze.

"*Señorita* Maria . . ." came Miguel's voice, low and seductive in the darkness of the star-spangled night. "If you are still awake, mark how our great leader has failed to keep the first watch."

Maria pretended to be sleeping, yet she, too, worried about Don Diego's carelessness. For all his brave boasts, he had succumbed to exhaustion like everyone else. In the morning, when he realized what he had done, he would be angry with himself. His desire to demonstrate that she belonged to him had apparently overridden his caution. She wished that Miguel had not witnessed this weakness in Diego. The *arrendador* seemed the type to try and use it against him.

The murmur of another voice reached her ear, and she strained to identify its source: Pedro!

"For all his fancy tricks with horses, he will only get us killed out here. *Dios!* I wish I were home with Juana."

"If you are so scared, get up and take the watch he has abandoned," hissed Miguel. "Wake me in a short while, and I will take over for you. He is a fool! From now on, we will pay him lip service but make our own arrangements for safety and security."

"Enough!" Diego stirred behind her. "I am not sleeping. I am only lying here listening. I wondered how you regarded me. Now, I know. I also know I can trust none of you, and changes must be made before we go any further."

"I said nothing disrespectful!" The voice belonged to Ignacio, his tone ripe with indignation.

"Nor did I," Fernandez hastened to add. "We are loyal to the *patrón,* and therefore, Don Diego, to you."

"Good. I am glad to hear it." Don Diego sat up, but kept his hand on Maria's shoulder. "As for you, Miguel and Pedro, you may both return to *Dehesa de Oro* in the morning. I would rather continue this adventure alone then worry about your loyalty or lack of it."

"No!" Miguel shouted. "You will not send us away. We will not go. Don Gonzalo would have my head if I returned to the ranch without La Reina, and no one else will employ me as *arrendador* once I have lost his confidence. A man cannot survive without the favor of his *patrón.*"

"What are we to do, then?" Diego asked in a silky-soft voice. "Have you any suggestions?"

"I pledge to you my loyalty and faithfulness," came the grudging reply.

"On your honor as a gentleman?"

"On my honor, and by the blood of *Cristo.*"

"And you, Pedro?" Diego pressed. "What will you do?"

"I will do the same," Pedro answered. "On my honor and by the salvation of my immortal soul."

"You will not argue when I give an order, nor plot behind my back to relieve me of my command of this mission?"

"We have given our oaths, Don Diego. You can ask no more of us," Miguel growled. " 'Tis you alone who will lead this expedition. However, I advise you to take into account that you are still a stranger among us. You know little about the New World, and we are entitled to our own opinions."

"Perhaps I will solicit them occasionally." Diego gently kneaded Maria's shoulder. She held her breath, listening intently and marveling at Don Diego's sagacity.

"I may ask your opinion, but when I make them the decisions will all be mine, *señors,*" Diego continued. "And once they are made, there will be no complaints or bickering among you. We are greatly outnumbered, and have no one but ourselves to rely on when trouble comes, as it surely will. I would have you with me, not against me. So long as you give me your respect—and give it also to Maria—we will do well together. Have we reached an understanding?"

"Sí, señor."

When each of the men had offered the appropriate response, Diego arranged himself comfortably with his *pistola* in one hand and his other still on Maria's shoulder.

"Sleep now, all of you. I will choose who takes the next watch, and I will awaken him when his time comes."

Silence fell, and Maria adjusted her position so she could feel Diego's thigh against the small of her back. His touch gave her comfort and reassurance that no evil would visit her during the night.

That was well done, Don Diego, she told herself before drifting off to sleep. *That was very well done.*

* * *

The days of their journey soon began to assume a pattern. They rose with the sun, broke camp, caught and saddled the horses, assembled the loads on the packhorses, and tried to cover as many leagues as possible before the heat of the day made travel a misery.

At noon they rested for an hour, watered all the animals and allowed them to graze, then once again mounted and rode northeast toward the River of Trees. When the sun reached a certain level over the western horizon, they searched for a new campsite. As soon as they found one, they split up—two or sometimes three of the men going off to hunt game for their supper, and the remainder setting up camp and gathering fuel for the cook fire.

Diego decreed they must use few supplies, for game was plentiful in this region, and they must save what they had for emergencies. Bartolomeo warned them that they must cross a dry, desolate stretch of land before they came to the river. The deer were small, fleet and wary, but no match for a man with a gun or crossbow, so they dined frequently on venison.

Bartolomeo snared rabbits and an occasional fowl, which he insisted upon cooking whole with the feathers still on it. He delighted in catching rodents and lizards, which nobody else would eat. Maria made note of his methods, because she knew that if she had to escape without him, she would need to know how to survive on her own. Her mother had taught her about edible roots, plants, and berries, but she had forgotten most of it. While the others looked down their noses at Bartolomeo's offerings, Maria gingerly partook of them and experimented with her own modest efforts at procuring food.

The biggest problem was finding water, yet Bartolomeo always seemed to know the location of the next freshet or stream meandering across the flatlands. The others took his skills for granted, but Maria shamelessly begged the old man to reveal his secrets, and soon, she too, could study the surrounding terrain and make a reasonably good guess at where they might find water and how long it would take to reach it.

Occasionally, fierce thunderstorms swept down upon them from the distant, high sierras toward which they were traveling. Buffeted by thunder and lightning, and pelted by heavy rains, they emerged from these downpours with a sense of gratitude for the sunshine that usually caused complaints.

No matter what the weather, Maria relished the vastness of the territory and the endless vistas of sky and grass. The grass often grew as tall as her knees when she sat in the saddle. With each passing day, her riding skills were improving. She learned to follow the motion of the animal beneath her and not tire herself by gripping too hard with her legs. Riding was a matter of finding one's balance, not exerting one's strength. Even Don Diego seemed surprised by her progress.

"You are doing much better than I thought you would," he said one hot afternoon, as they stopped to make camp. "If I did not know better, I would swear you had prior experience."

He slanted her a curious look, but she managed to maintain her composure. "Where would I have gotten experience, *señor?* My father never permitted me near the horses."

"I know. 'Tis why I am so amazed at how quickly you have adapted to riding that cantankerous creature. Bartolomeo has not your ease of sitting still in the saddle—though you both seem to have a natural talent."

Bartolomeo's ass offered fewer challenges than her own. However, she conceded that the old *Indio* was doing well. As for herself, she knew that if she had *not* practiced riding La Reina, she would still be thumping about like a sack of grain and falling off with great frequency.

"Thank you, *señor,* for the kind words, but I am still unable to sit as you do—so that Gaspar and I appear to be one."

"Gaspar?"

She nodded. " 'Tis the name I have given him."

"Gaspar, eh? It suits him. As for my skills, they take years to acquire, but you should be pleased with yourself for acquiring the rudiments so quickly. I cannot help but wonder what you would do on the back of a real horse with three good gaits."

The horse and I would gallop away from here so fast that

you would never catch me. Give me your stallion—or La Reina—and you will never see me again.

"I would probably fall off," she said demurely. "That is, if I could find the courage to get on a horse in the first place. They are too high off the ground for my tastes."

Don Diego laughed. " 'Tis a good thing, then, that your riding is confined to Gaspar. If you fall off him, you have not far to go to reach the ground."

"I prefer the ground best of all," she assured him, turning her head to hide the lie in her eyes.

More than ever, she yearned to ride horses—not just to escape—but for the sheer pleasure of flying across the plain, with the wind in her face and a wild joy in her heart. Riding a horse must be the ultimate freedom; no wonder the *Indios* had risked so much to obtain horses! It was wrong of the Spaniards to try to keep this delight—and necessity—to themselves.

That night they camped in a narrow pass between steep, rocky hills. Water trickling down from some lofty promontory provided the last liquid they would see for several days.

"Let the animals drink all they want, tonight and tomorrow morning," Don Diego announced. "And be sure to fill all our water gourds and skins to the brim. We will need every drop we can carry."

Maria watched as Diego wiped the sweat from his stallion with a dampened square of soft fabric. His hands moved so tenderly over the horse's silver-white hide that she could not help wondering what it would feel like to have him caress *her* with the same tenderness. The image of his hands moving across her body inflamed her cheeks; her entire face felt as if the sun had burned it raw. She gave herself a mental shake and tried to concentrate on her task—gathering dried brush to feed the evening cook fire.

The trickle of water had once nurtured greenery in this barren place, but the plants had long since died and left behind only skeletons. Already, she had a small pile of brush. It would not be long before she found enough to keep the fire going half the night. A fire kept wolves and other curious or hungry predators away from their campsites. Maria no longer feared these beasts, for she slept each night now in the circle of Don Diego's arms. He never touched her intimately, but he kept her near. His restraint was admirable; it was also beginning to wear on her nerves. At times, her shameful desires kept her awake. She lay in the darkness listening to Don Diego breathe. Occasionally, she could even feel his heart beat. She had to fight the impulse to turn around, press herself against him, and hungrily seek his kisses and caresses.

Only the knowledge that one of the others was standing guard kept her from yielding to the temptation. Either the same knowledge subdued *his* passion, or he no longer wanted her. Her own vanity insisted that he continue to desire her, despite the number of times she had rejected his advances.

If only she could escape *now,* while she still had the will to do so, but it was not yet time! La Reina was the horse she wanted, and they had not yet found La Reina or any sign of the Indians. They had not yet reached the River of Trees.

She would know when the time was right. Until then, she knew she should be glad of Don Diego's restraint. And she must use every available opportunity to hone her survival skills in preparation for the day when she would need them.

With that idea in mind, Maria looked around for Bartolomeo. At this hour, before the sun set, the old *Indio* usually spent his time hunting small animals or searching for tubers to augment their evening meal. They had taken no game today, so Bartolomeo had probably gone off on his own to see what he could find to eat. Maria suddenly realized she should have gone with him.

"Did you see where the old *Indio* went?" she asked Pedro, who was rummaging through the supplies spread out on the ground near the pack horses.

"He is probably looking for grubs or a juicy fat snake to eat for supper. The last I saw him, he was headed up there." Pedro pointed toward the steep side of the pass.

"He climbed up there?" Maria studied the steep rocky ascent. It must have been a difficult climb for an old man, but Bartolomeo never seemed to worry about his age.

Pedro nodded. "If you are going to follow him, be careful you do not start a rock slide."

Maria looked at Don Diego, but he was busy picking out his stallion's feet and paying no attention to her. "Pedro, the brush to start the fire is over there. I want to make certain Bartolomeo is all right. I will not be gone long. Tell Don Diego where I am, if he asks."

"Tell him yourself before you go," Pedro muttered. "I have my own chores to do."

"Then do not disturb yourself," Maria said, stung by his cold attitude.

None of the *vaqueros* had challenged Don Diego since that first night, but they had not gone out of their way to be nice to him either—or to her. They mostly ignored her, even when she waited on them at mealtimes, helped to gather up their blankets, or watered their horses. She had done these things out of habit, because she was accustomed to being useful, and indeed, they all seemed to expect it of her, even Don Diego. She wished now that she had been less eager to offer her services. She had behaved in the manner of a slave, and that was exactly the way they all thought of her.

Turning on her heel, Maria hiked up her skirt and began to climb the steep rocky slope. It was hard going, and her skirt hampered her, but she reached the top without causing a rock slide. The view delighted her. She found herself standing on a promontory that was much like a flat tabletop. One could walk across it from one side to the other and peer over the edge to see what lay below.

Bartolomeo was doing just that. He stood at the very lip of the promontory. If he took one more step, he would fall. Maria almost called out to him, but stopped herself just in time. She feared startling him. Just then, he turned around, and the expression on his weathered face startled her.

Never had she expected to witness such a joyful transformation: Bartolomeo glowed with happiness. An inner radiance lit his face, and his eyes looked dazzled.

"Bartolomeo? What is it? What have you seen?"

"Come!" He motioned her toward him. "See for yourself what these old eyes of mine have never dared hope to witness again in my lifetime."

Chapter Eleven

Diego finished grooming El Cid, put on his leather hobbles, and fed him a small amount of corn to replace the grass the horse would not be eating tonight. He did not much care for the rocky place where they were camping, but since it had water, and this was their last chance to replenish their supply before they crossed the dry region on their way to the river, he knew he should not complain.

Still, it made him uneasy to think of bedding down in this narrow enclosure, and he dreaded passing through this maze of high plateaus and odd-shaped rock formations in the morning. Such territory invited ambush, and problems for the horses—everything from picking up stones in their hooves to stepping in crevasses and possibly breaking a leg.

Besides, he had become attached to broad vistas and unhampered views of the sky. Cramped confines now made him feel constrained and out of sorts. Nor was he anxious to sleep on solid rock instead of grass.

Diego wondered where Maria had set up their bedding. He led El Cid into a corner of the pass away from the other horses and turned him loose. Watching for Maria's slender figure, he felt a jolt of alarm when he failed to spot her. Bartolomeo was also missing, and already, dark shadows filled the canyon. The last rays of the setting sun did not reach down into this desolate place.

The old Indian's absence did not bother him too much—Bartolomeo often went food gathering and exploring for small game, but Diego did not like the thought of Maria wandering this treacherous terrain. He, at least, had sturdy boots to protect his feet. She had only sandals—and she lacked Bartolomeo's uncanny ability to avoid getting lost, no matter the surroundings.

"Miguel! Pedro!" he called sharply to the two nearest *vaqueros*. "Have you seen Maria and Bartolomeo?"

Miguel only shrugged, showing no interest, but Pedro stopped what he was doing and approached him. *"Señorita* Maria climbed the side of the pass to look for the *Indio*. I warned her to be careful."

"She went up there?" Diego pointed to the steep slope which looked difficult, if not impossible, to climb.

"Sí, señor."

"Why did you let her go?" Worry gave way to anger.

"Because she is not my responsibility. You have made that very clear to us, *señor."*

"If she is hurt or lost—"

"It will not be our fault. We have done nothing wrong."

"Get out of my way, then," Diego snapped. "If I am not back with her by dark, make some torches and come after us. Otherwise, we will break our necks on the descent."

"Sí, señor."

"Woolly cows!" Maria exclaimed. "Hundreds of them—no, thousands! More than I can count. Oh, Bartolomeo, they are indeed wondrous to behold!"

Her old friend sighed with pleasure. "Yes. Yes, look at them. They fill my hunter's heart with such gladness it makes my chest hurt."

"Sit down and rest a moment. We will watch them for a few moments. There is time before it grows dark."

Bartolomeo squatted on the ground. "Now, I can die happy,"

he said. "I have seen them once more. I was worried because we had not yet spotted any on this journey—yet here they are, waiting for us to find them."

Maria sat down cross-legged and feasted her eyes on the scene below. To her right were the tall formations through which they must pass to find the river. To her left was the crimson sky of sunset. And directly below, on the plain spread out in front of them, was a tremendous-size herd of the huge lumbering beasts she had heard so much about but never seen at close range: the woolly cows.

They did not look much like cows—at least, nothing like her father's Castilian cattle. These creatures had huge heads, and beards like billy goats. Dark brown in color, they were woolly about the shoulders, forequarters, and heads, but had humped backs, black horns, and meager tails with a swatch of hair at the tips.

She could not imagine how a man could hunt and kill them on foot, yet her mother's people had subsisted almost entirely on the meat and robes from these magnificent creatures since the dawn of time.

"Tell me how you once hunted the woolly cows," she urged Bartolomeo. "Do they run as fast as cattle?"

"Ah! They run faster. But they have the same instincts as your father's cattle. They like to stay together, and where the leaders go, the rest will follow. When they are frightened, they will run right over a cliff, the entire herd. That is how we often caught them. We drove them ahead of us to some place like this one. When they plunged over the edge to the rocks below, they died quickly or were so injured that we could go among them and stab them with our spears."

"What a great waste of meat! How could you use so much at one time?"

"We could not. We knew it was wasteful, but without weapons like the Spaniards have and no horses to chase them, we had no other choice. Sometimes, we covered ourselves in skins and were able to creep close to the herd, but if we wounded a bull and did not kill it on the first thrust of the spear or with an arrow, it would turn on us. To go among a herd on foot requires great courage. Often, a man does not return alive."

"With a horse, a man could go safely into the herd and kill one," Maria said. "He could slay a single cow, feast on its meat until it was gone, and then follow the herd when they moved to a new location. Never would he have to go without meat and hides. Horses would change everything for him."

"Yes, horses would change everything." Bartolomeo nodded, never taking his eyes from the herd.

"Maria! There you are," a familiar voice cried. "And you, Bartolomeo. 'Tis getting dark. What are you doing up here?"

Maria breathed a sigh of relief that she and Bartolomeo had been speaking their own language. She would not have wanted Don Diego to overhear their conversation about horses.

"Come and see what we have found." She rose and pointed to the plain below. "There is still enough light."

Don Diego look unhappy as he approached. "I was worried about you, Maria. You should not go off alone in this rough country."

"I am not afraid. This country is my homeland."

"Nonsense. You were born at *Dehesa de Oro* and have always known a gentler way of life."

"Gentler?" She snorted in derision. "My life has been far from gentle, *señor*. To me, this is a far kinder place than the one where I was born."

Her exhilaration at seeing the woolly cows abruptly faded. She had hoped he understood her situation by now, but his own heritage had obviously blinded him to the suffering of those around him.

"Well, what has made you lose track of the time like this?" he said, coming abreast of them. Then he, too, spotted the great herd grazing on the plain below. "*Madre de Dios!* Woolly cows—what the missionaries call buffalo."

Watching him marvel as she and Bartolomeo had done renewed Maria's excitement. "Did you ever expect to see so many in one place?"

"No," he replied. "As God is my witness, I thought the accounts describing such a phenomenon were exaggerated. Ask

154   *Katharine Kincaid*

Bartolomeo if there is any way to get down there safely. If so, I would like to kill and butcher one before we go any further. We could use the meat.''

The answer to the question displeased Diego. Bartolomeo related that he was sure he could find a way, but it would mean several days delay or more. They would have to return the way they had come and go around the escarpment on which they now stood. When they completed the adventure, they would still have to come back and traverse the hazardous area to reach the River of Trees.

''It will take too long,'' Diego sadly conceded. ''Right now, we cannot spare the time.''

''Tell him we will see more woolly cows before we are finished,'' Bartolomeo sympathized. ''There will be many along the River of Trees. Water is as necessary to them as it is to us. The Master of Horses must not despair.''

Maria translated, and after that, they returned to the others. No one got much sleep that night. All night long, Maria heard first one, then another, man stirring. As usual, Don Diego stretched out beside her, but she knew from his frequent movements that he was either unable to find comfort or eagerly anticipating the dawn.

In the end, they all slept late—past the time of their usual rising. Ignacio, who was on watch, dozed off, and even the rays of the sun did not wake them. When they finally awoke, they discovered why: Dark, heavy clouds hid the sun altogether. Diego was furious.

''Hurry! We must get moving,'' he barked at everyone. ''I am denying myself the pleasure of buffalo hunting in order to attain our goal, and here we are starting off late, anyway. Ignacio, if you fall asleep again while you are on watch, I will devise some terrible punishment. While you slept, we could have been attacked.''

They were soon threading their way through the intricate turns of the pass behind Bartolomeo. He was the only one who had any idea where they were going. Maria rode behind Don Diego, with the four *vaqueros* bringing up the rear. Toward noon, the wind rose and whistled down the pass, while darkness enshrouded it. The storm broke soon after. Lightning bolts stabbed all around them. Thunder boomed and bounced off rock on every side, making the horses shy and the asses bray in fear. Rain poured down in a deluge so heavy it was impossible to see the trail.

Bartolomeo found shelter for himself and the four *vaqueros* beneath a ledge of rock, but there was no room for Maria and Don Diego to crowd in among them.

"We will go ahead and look for something," Don Diego shouted over the storm's fury.

Grabbing Maria's reins, he led her away through the downpour. It seemed so odd to be soaked to the skin in the very heart of what was supposed to be hot, dry country. Maria had been wet before on this journey, her garments molding to her body like a second skin, but she had never been this cold, nor this fearful of the elements.

Each crack of thunder prickled her chilled flesh; each bolt of lightning made her cringe. She expected at any moment to be struck. To add to the misery, the footing was terrible. Thus far, Gaspar had been remarkably surefooted, stopping at nothing, but now, he slipped and slid on the loose stones and balked, pulling so hard on his reins that he almost unseated Don Diego.

Maria closed her eyes against the dash of water in her face and prayed it would soon be over. All at once, the rain ceased to batter her. Opening her eyes, she saw that Don Diego had led her beneath a shelf of rock that was just wide enough to shelter her, Don Diego, their mounts, and Caobo, who immediately shook himself and sprayed water in all directions.

El Cid lowered his head and tossed his wet mane, then blew through his nostrils in appreciation at being out of the storm. When Don Diego dismounted, water poured from his armored hat. Giving her a rueful grin, he removed it. Then he noticed her chattering teeth, and his grin became a grimace. Quickly, he removed his armor breastplate and set it against the wall. Then he lifted her down from the saddle and enfolded her in his arms, against his strong hard body. Grateful for his warmth and substance, Maria melted into him. He was as wet as she, but somehow, crushed against his leather doublet, she felt warmer and drier.

They remained thus, neither speaking, until the rain and thunder died down, and they could make themselves heard again.

"Are you still cold?" Don Diego leaned back and tilted up her face.

"A little," she admitted, "but not as bad as before."

"We must think of a way to warm you."

"A fire?" she asked hopefully, though she knew it would be impossible to find dry fuel.

"You know I cannot light one here—unless perhaps 'tis a fire *inside* you." He put his hands on her hips and drew her closer. "Will you let me kiss you, Maria? I cannot promise it will be as effective as a cup of steaming hot *chocolatl,* but I hope it might help. If it does not, one of the pack horses carries a kilderkin of brandy. As soon as we can return to the others, I will give you some. We will all drink a mouthful to warm our chilled bones."

"The storm has eased, but the rain shows no sign of stopping. It may be a long time before we can warm ourselves with brandy," she told him. Already she felt warmer, but she withheld that information.

"That leaves only kissing." He raised his hand to her face and wiped away the wetness on her cheekbones, then tilted up her chin with his fingertips.

She held her breath and tried not to think of all the reasons why she should stop this, at once. There were, she realized, plenty, but she also had reasons to continue. On this journey, he had been letting his beard grow, and she yearned to see how it felt. Whenever he got close to her, strange yearnings filled her, and she wanted to be closer still.

"One kiss only," she bargained.

"Only one? One will hardly be enough to warm you."

"I disagree. One will do it."

She outlined his mouth with her own fingers, testing the texture of the hair on his upper lip. It was soft and wet. He suddenly opened his mouth and grabbed her finger, closing his teeth on it, but not biting hard enough to hurt. The playful gesture made her laugh.

"The inside of your mouth is warm," she said. "My finger no longer feels cold."

He sucked on her fingertip for a moment, then abruptly released it. "That is what I should like to do with other parts of your body," he whispered.

The suggestion brought a flush of heat to her cheeks. Seeing her response, he smiled. "What? Are you warming already? I have yet to kiss you. But I will, now."

Slowly, ever so slowly, he lowered his mouth to hers. The kiss began gently. His new mustache tickled. Then, as he increased the pressure, she forgot about his beard and mustache, forgot, even, that she ought not to be kissing him. She no longer recalled her surroundings or that it was raining and he was a Spaniard, while she was an *Indio*. She never once thought about escaping or taking horses to her people. It all disappeared. There remained only the wonderful reality of his mouth on her mouth.

He kissed her, and she kissed him back, molding herself to the hard planes of his body and relishing the differences between them. His hands moved down her back, caressing her waist, cupping her bottom. She did not resist, for they brought warmth, comfort, and pleasure. Moaning, she pressed against him, silently yielding to his unspoken demands.

"Maria . . . oh, Maria!" he murmured, momentarily breaking the contact. " 'Tis torture, what you do to me!' "

She wanted to tell him it was torture for her, too. Conflicting desires were tearing her apart. Fortunately, circumstances prevented them from acting upon wayward impulses. They were alone, but not that far from the others. Before his mouth could find hers again, she gently clapped a hand over his lips.

"*Señor,* I think I hear the others coming. The rain has stopped, and you have had your kiss. We should resume our journey now."

"It has not completely stopped," he complained. "Besides, I do not hear them coming."

No sooner had he said the words than they both heard Miguel. "Don Diego! Where are you?"

"Here!" Diego replied. He released a long sigh. "Unfortunately, we are here."

A moment later, the rest of the party rode into view—looking as sodden and miserable as Maria had felt before Don Diego's kiss heated her blood.

"The worst of the storm has passed, and I think we should keep going," the *arrendador* said. "The old *Indio* has been making hand gestures, trying to tell us something. He seems to think 'tis unsafe for us to remain here."

"Unsafe?" Diego turned to Maria. "Ask him what's wrong. Why should it be unsafe?"

Bartolomeo explained that after a heavy rain, places like this were subject to sudden, violent flooding from water cascading down from the higher elevations. He suggested they keep going and try to find a less dangerous trail.

Diego immediately agreed. "I was going to stop for a drink of brandy, but any delay might be unwise. We had better do as he says. He knows this country better than we do."

They continued their trek through the long, narrow pass. The rain diminished, but never did stop. Maria worried they would be forced to spend another night in the bottom of the crevice. But late in the afternoon, the trail began to rise upward. Don Diego rode ahead of her to help Bartolomeo. His ass was balking at the steep, rocky ascent.

Half way up the incline, they spotted a natural indentation in the rock, a place that promised shelter for the night. Looking eager to explore it, Miguel rode past Maria and urged his horse up the treacherous trail. Leading Bartolomeo's ass, Don Diego reached it first, disappeared from sight for a few moments, then returned to shout down to the rest of them.

" 'Tis almost like a cave up here! It will be a fine place to camp, safe from flooding or any other disturbance. Come along, all of you! There is enough debris lying about to build a fire. Maria, can you make it on your own?"

Gaspar had been giving her no trouble, so Maria nodded that she could, and Don Diego disappeared from sight. However, as she nudged the little fellow's sides, encouraging him to follow Miguel's horse, he suddenly balked. He planted his feet on the loose stones and refused to go another step.

Pedro passed her, and then Ignacio and Fernandez. Fernandez paused a moment to inquire: "Do you need help?"

"I doubt it," Maria said. "Perhaps, if he sees everyone leaving him, he will find the energy to carry me up there before nightfall."

"The next time you see a stick, grab it. When he gets stubborn, you must beat him. If you want, I can get out my *lazo* to use as a whip." His hand dropped to the coil of rope tied to the side of his saddle.

"No, thank you." Beating was the way of the Spanish; she refused to make it her way, too. "Tell Don Diego not to worry about me. I will be along shortly."

"All right, if you insist, but you are spoiling the animal. His defiance should be met with instant punishment."

After he had left her, Maria kicked Gaspar harder, but he still refused to budge. She decided to get down and lead him. The harder she pulled on his reins, the more he resisted. He simply sat back on his haunches and ignored all her efforts. Disgusted, Maria went behind him and tried to shove him forward. Nothing seemed to work.

Hands on hips, she paused to consider the problem—and heard a distant, muffled roar that seemed to be coming nearer. At first, she had no idea what it might be; she had never heard anything like it.

As the whooshing sound approached, filling the pass with the echo of gurgling fury, she suddenly realized what it was: water!

A huge quantity of water was bearing down upon her, swirling through the pass, uprooting huge rocks and boulders, and tumbling them over and over in the flood. She could see it now, rushing toward her with a vengeance. She knew she must move, but her arms and legs refused to function. She stood staring at the wall of water, and knew that death had arrived.

"Maria!" Diego hollered above the roar. "Maria, get up here!"

She looked up to see him stumbling down the incline toward her, running as fast as he could go, but it was a long way, and he would never reach her in time to save her. Gaspar suddenly realized his own peril. He gave a great, startled bray and jumped into the air, knocking her to one side as he galloped away— not *up* the steep incline to safety, but into the very path of the onslaught.

"Stop!" she screamed. "Gaspar, come back!"

"Maria, grab my hand! I will pull you to safety!" Diego had thrown himself down on his stomach atop a huge boulder halfway up the incline. Leaning out over the edge of it, he extended his hand to her. Beside him, Caobo whined and whimpered, as if he wished to help. To reach Diego's hand, she had to climb a short distance, and the water was bearing down on her, sweeping everything ahead of it.

She attacked the incline with all the strength and agility she possessed. Rocks skittered from beneath her sandals. She fell to her hands and knees. Clawing at the incline, she struggled to climb faster. She had just managed to grasp Diego's hand when the water hit. Black, cold, and wet, it slammed her against the rocks. Mercifully, consciousness deserted her.

Her next sensation was one of pain and stiffness. She could scarcely move any part of her body. She felt as if she had been pummeled from head to foot, then tossed aside to die. She wondered if she *had* died, and gone to the hell Doña Inez had threatened would be her final destination. The pain suggested she was doomed to suffer forever.

"Maria, can you hear me? Maria, wake up. You are safe and have broken no bones. 'Tis a miracle for which I give humble thanks. Only you must wake up now. I cannot let you sleep. I must know if your wits have deserted you. Wake up, little one. Tell me you are going to live."

Why couldn't he let her sleep? It was cruel of Don Diego to call her back to the world of the living. Death seemed preferable to opening her eyes. She moaned and sought to drift off again, but he would have none of it.

"A sound. You made a sound!" he hollered in her ear. "Can you still speak? Show me you have not lost your faculties, Maria. Give me a sign that you know where you are and who is speaking to you."

"Leave me alone," she mumbled. "I want to sleep."

"No! Sleep would be the worst thing for you. You are wet, cold, and badly bruised. You can sleep when I am finished tending you. Here, you must drink this. It will revive you."

"No," she protested, but he lifted her head and held a goblet to her mouth. Made of metal, the vessel felt cool on her lips, but a burning liquid scalded her tongue. She coughed and spluttered, trying to catch her breath.

"There now," Don Diego crooned. "Good girl. 'Tis the brandy I brought. Drink all of it, please."

She had no choice. The brandy burned all the way down to her stomach, but it did revive her. "What ... happened?" she managed to ask.

"You were caught in a sudden flood," Diego reminded her, his face very close to her own. Firelight illuminated it, but all around them, darkness had gathered. "The water almost carried you away, but I refused to let go of you. Somehow, I managed to pull you out. I did not know if I could do it, but I did, *a Dios gracias.*"

"Thank you," she said. "I am grateful, but I hurt too much right now to *feel* grateful. Is everyone else safe?"

He nodded. "All but Gaspar. We have not seen hide nor hair of him, and 'tis too dark to go searching. Tomorrow will be soon enough to find out if he survived. I am afraid the water may have dashed him against the walls of the pass."

"Dios! I am so sorry. He was not a bad beast, but something got into him and he would not listen to me."

"He probably sensed something amiss without knowing what it was—or how much it could hurt him. Rest now, Maria ... unless you are hungry. Are you? The others have eaten already, but I will find something for us."

"No." Maria shook her head and winced at the pain. "You go ahead. I can eat nothing."

Bartolomeo's face appeared over Don Diego's left shoulder.

162   *Katharine Kincaid*

The old *Indio* grinned down at her. "I knew you were not dead," he said. "A little flood could never kill you. You are much too strong."

She felt like disputing that, for every tiny movement revealed a new ache. In the end, she said nothing. The effort of talking—and thinking—exhausted her. All she wanted to do was sleep beside Don Diego and forget the entire experience. If her poor little Gaspar was dead, what would she do now? Would she have to walk? Her questions would have to wait until morning; oblivion beckoned too strongly.

Chapter Twelve

By the next morning, Maria had almost recovered. She was black and blue all over, but the stiffness and pain were not quite so bad—especially after Bartolomeo finished with her. He had risen before anyone and busied himself making a fire and brewing something in a cookpot, using mysterious ingredients from a small leather pouch he wore around his neck. While Maria drank the hot, bitter concoction, he chanted words that had no meaning, even to her.

When Miguel and the others awoke, they complained to Don Diego. "He is doing pagan, *Indio* things. You should forbid him," Miguel grumbled.

"If they help Maria, I care not what he does. We must get moving again. We cannot stay here. The flood has passed, and there is no more water except what we brought with us, and that will soon run out."

Maria had already realized she could not delay the party. She hastened to assure everyone that she was able to travel. "I am better, today. Bartolomeo's remedy has helped me. 'Tis only made of herbs. There is nothing to fear from it."

"Are you certain you are ready to ride again?" Diego paused in gathering up his weapons and bedding.

"Of course I can ride. Have you found Gaspar?"

He shook his head. "Not yet. I was thinking of taking you up in front of me on El Cid, until you are stronger. That will do fine for today. After that, if we fail to find him, we will have to think of something else."

"What else?" Miguel demanded. "We have only a pack horse to put her on, and her father would never approve."

Don Diego gave the *vaquero* a sharp glance. "It may be necessary. If I say she will ride one of the pack horses, she will do so, and you will make no criticism."

"She knows not how to ride! She will only ruin the horse—or fall off and get hurt again."

"Riding an ass differs little from riding a horse," Don Diego countered. "What she does not know, I will teach her."

Maria thrilled to hear him say such a thing—actual lessons from the Master of Horses!

"You will be sorry if you do teach her," Miguel grumbled. "Don Gonzalo would whip any man who suggested teaching an *Indio* how to ride a horse. There are things *Indios*—and even females—should never be taught, or they will begin to think themselves equal to us. The subtleties of riding horses is one of them."

"What are the others?" Don Diego drawled. "Reading and writing? Handling weapons? Someday, Miguel, even Don Gonzalo will have to allow Indians to learn the secrets of horsemanship. He may discover he needs them as workers, not just at the silver mine, but to round up his cattle. It will happen in our lifetime. If it does not, we will never tame the grasslands and expand the Spanish empire. Now that I have seen with my own eyes the immensity of these lands, I see also the necessity of changing the way things are done here. There are too few men to do all that must be done on horseback. We need more *arrendadores* like yourself. We must therefore begin to teach others—if not Indians, then who?"

Miguel exchanged angry glances with the other *vaqueros*. Don Diego's words had upset all of them. "I do not know, *señor*, but I believe Don Gonzalo will never approve of such changes. Say these things to him, and he will send you away. He will not keep you as his Master of Horses."

Don Diego only grinned. "Can you teach La Reina the *curvet* and the *levade?* If so, why haven't you? Your *patrón* will not send me away, Miguel. He wants me for what I know. You, too, would be foolish to make an enemy of me, for then I will never teach you these things, either."

Resentment flared in Miguel's black eyes. But after a moment, he asked: "When we return to *Dehesa de Oro,* will you demonstrate some of your training methods? I admit I would like to learn them."

"Perhaps. It depends on the rest of this journey. Thus far, you have done little but find fault. Do a better job of holding your tongue, and I will consider it."

"I will try, *señor,*" Miguel meekly answered, but Maria could see he was steaming.

She wondered how long the *arrendador* would remain loyal to Don Diego. He was like a bull challenging a newcomer to his pasture, testing his strength before engaging him in battle.

Later, when they still had not found Gaspar, Don Diego took her up on El Cid. Maria watched carefully how he handled the stallion. His hands were always light and gentle, never moving more than the width of a fist in any direction. His reins were the loosest of anyone's. He could have bridled El Cid using strands of her hair for reins, and he never would have broken one.

The intimacy of their position soon began to distract her. She resorted to questions to keep from thinking about it. "How is it you can ride so powerful an animal as this stallion with so much slack in your reins, Don Diego? Whenever I wanted Gaspar to stop or turn, I had to pull hard on the reins, and often, he just ignored me."

"Gaspar was never properly rein-trained," Don Diego explained. " 'Tis not the iron in his mouth that controls El Cid. I first taught him to obey my wishes through the use of a training halter called a *jaquima.*"

"A *jaquima?* What is that?"

"It consists of two strings of plain leather, tied over the

poll of the horse and positioned so they hang down along his cheekbones. Their purpose is to hold a hard noseband of plaited rawhide in place over the animal's nose.''

''What good does that do? Is it the noseband, then, that controls him?''

Don Diego's chuckle was a warm rumble at her back. ''How curious you are! No, 'tis not the noseband alone that does it. 'Tis the knot of prickly horsehair securing the noseband. The knot must be centered and hanging loose beneath the horse's chin. When the reins are engaged—if the horse is pulling or going too fast, for example—the knot rises and chafes his tender skin. He quickly learns that he prefers his rider to keep the reins loose, rather than tight.''

''Then how do you turn him? If you wish to go to the right, for example.''

''It can be done with the use of the leg as well as the rein. However, for a horse to be properly rein-trained, one need only use reins of the same coarse, prickly material as the knot. Hair from a horse's tail, or better yet, a cow tail, are plaited to make this prickly sort of rope. To turn the horse, the rider must bring the horse's head around by means of a sideward and downward pull of the reins, so the knot will *not* chafe him. At the same time, he brings his outside rein to rest on the neck of the horse, so the horse wants to move away from it. Using this method, one can soon turn a horse with no more pressure than touching his neck with the outside rein.''

''Amazing!'' Maria committed the information to memory. No one had ever explained any part of horse training to her, and she found it fascinating as well as useful for the future.

''My father has a half dozen *domadors* who can easily take a young horse to this point,'' Diego continued. ''But they must work the horses daily, until their responses become a matter of reflex. Only then will they pass the youngsters along to an *arrendador,* like Miguel, who will complete the animal's education. The *arrendador* bits the horse, gives him leather reins, and teaches him about the spur—always bringing him along so he never thinks of fighting his rider. He learns to stand still on command and to give instant obedience to the slightest pressure. This results in starts, stops, and variations of speed and direction that seem effortless."

The enthusiasm with which he described these things impressed Maria almost as much as the revelations themselves. She realized that Don Diego truly loved his work and was delighted to talk about it. He went on to describe how the best horses, those with the most ability and natural talent, such as El Cid and La Reina, were kept in training long after others were put to their daily labors.

Only the most agile horses learned the advanced movements such as the *curvet*—a great leap into the air—and the *levade*, where they stood on their hind legs, pawing the air with their forefeet. Stallions with tremendous strength and conditioning could do the *levade* while advancing forward, a technique originally developed for use in battle.

"El Cid can do this, as well as many other maneuvers suitable for parades and tournaments. He will also stand calm in the face of exploding firearms, but he has yet to learn the intricacies of aiding a rider in the use of the *lazo*. I myself must first master the technique."

"Will you show me sometime how he does the *curvet* and the *levade?*" Maria asked wistfully, for she longed to witness such remarkable feats of horsemanship.

"If you wish." He gave her waist a quick squeeze. "But I do not make him perform the movements very often, for they require a certain level of conditioning. When I know such movements will be called for, I take care to exercise him carefully. To avoid injury, he must first be prepared."

" 'Tis all a matter of preparation, isn't it? From what you have told me, I can see that one thing builds upon another. What a person witnesses at the end is *not* where one begins."

"Maria, you have just taken all the wisdom of horse training and reduced it to one, essential truth. Whenever I try to teach others my methods, I sometimes find myself struggling to impart this notion of careful preparation—but men, in their impatience, often reject it. These, I know, will never become horsemen, much less trainers of horses."

"Patience is something the *Indio* learns early in life, *señor*.

My mother taught me that the mysteries of nature only reveal themselves when one cultivates patience and an attitude of quiet watching and waiting.''

"Your mother must have been very wise."

Maria nodded. "In some things, yes . . . in others, no."

"Well, we all have our limitations. Though I am a Master of Horses, I have never used a *lazo* or done much work with cattle. If I am to succeed in this country, I will have to learn new skills—or perhaps not, since I do not intend to remain here for very long."

Gold. He was thinking of gold, Maria knew, and she fell silent, subdued by the reminder.

Not long thereafter, they found Gaspar: dead, waterlogged, and covered with flies. He had been overtaken by the flood and tossed about in the turbulence until he drowned. Now, his body was wedged tightly between two big boulders, and everything he had been carrying was ruined.

Maria could not hide her tears. He was only a little ass— not as valuable as a horse—but still, she had come to love him. He had not deserved to die in such a violent manner.

"Tomorrow, if you feel well enough, I will put you on one of the packhorses," Don Diego said. "Until you gain confidence that you can handle the horse on your own, I will lead you behind El Cid."

His announcement drew scowls from the *vaqueros,* especially Miguel, but no one said anything, and they continued onward. The remainder of the day was uneventful. The next day, Maria mounted the horse. He was called El Blanco, for he was light-colored like El Cid but neither as pretty nor as smooth-gaited. In the absence of a spare saddle, Don Diego tied a thick saddle blanket around the horse's midsection and rigged up a pair of stirrups.

Still, Maria found riding El Blanco difficult. El Cid's walk and trot had been easy to sit, or perhaps she had been spoiled by the security of having Don Diego's arm around her. El Blanco bounced her around as Gaspar had done when she had first mounted him. Once again, she had to adjust—no easy feat for her sore, bruised muscles.

She managed not to complain, either that day or the next. On the day following, they emerged from the maze of rock formations to find themselves facing a plain that tipped gently downward toward the distant gleam of a river.

"There!" Bartolomeo pointed triumphantly. "The River of Trees."

Maria thought there was no need to translate, until Miguel growled. "Is this it? Where are the trees? I see no trees along its length."

Bartolomeo explained that trees did indeed grow at other places along the river banks. According to him, it was a long river with plenty of grass for the horses on either side.

Don Diego demanded a moment of silence. "We should thank *Dios* we have come safely this far. Now, if we can only find our horses and punish the horse thieves, we will know He is truly watching over us."

Maria prayed that *Dios* was watching over the Indians, especially her brother. Stealing was wrong, but surely, *Dios* understood how much the Indians needed horses!

That evening they camped beside the river and played in its shallows, driving off waterfowl, who took to the skies in a great protest of flapping wings and excited cries. The water was irresistible, and the *vaqueros* waded into it with glee, splashing one another, dipping their hats in it, and dumping the contents over one another's heads.

Even the horses frolicked along the broad sandy banks, happy to drink their fill after such long abstinence. Moving upstream with Bartolomeo, Maria washed herself as best she could without totally submerging or removing any clothing. Of all of them, only Don Diego seemed unaffected by the river. Keeping one eye on the ground, he strolled quietly along the bank, searching for hoofprints made by horses other than those they had brought with them. He did not return for supper until it was too dark to see any longer.

That night they dined on fresh fish Bartolomeo had caught— spearing them with a sharpened stick taken from a thorny bush growing beside the river. Maria had tried to help him spear the elusive quarry, but she needed far more practice. She was amazed that the old Indian had not lost his skill, considering how long it had been since he had last speared fish in a river.

She learned much from the experience, not only about fishing, but about cooking their catch whole on stones nestled in hot coals. Bartolomeo promised her that tomorrow they would dig edible tubers to add to their meal. Along the river, tubers were plentiful. Maria fell asleep that night to the murmur of water, while Don Diego took the first watch.

She awoke to the crack of gunfire, and an outbreak of pandemonium. It was just barely light, and Caobo was barking and Pedro screaming: *"Indios!* They are attacking us!"

Diego and the *vaqueros* fumbled for their *pistolas,* and more gunfire followed. Maria could not decide whether to flee or remain where she was. Lifting her head, she spotted small, naked figures running away from their encampment. They looked like women, and Don Diego soon realized it, too.

"Hold your fire! Stop shooting! They are only females."

"They are still *Indios!"* Miguel fired another shot at the fleeing women.

Maria saw one tumble and fall, and her heart lurched. Rising, she could see several bodies strewn across the plain. The acrid scent of gunpowder stung her eyes and made them water as she inhaled the smoke from the discharges. It was suddenly quiet. The Indians were far off now, running for their lives. Some were only small children. Holding them by the hand, women dragged them along behind them.

"Maria, get Bartolomeo and come with me. We will examine the fallen. Perhaps we can identify their tribe."

Without a backward glance, Don Diego strode off across the plain toward the bodies. Bartolomeo was already hurrying toward her, so Maria simply motioned for him to follow. The other *vaqueros,* in various states of undress, joined them. Soon, they were looking down at the first body—that of a young woman.

"Madre de Dios! She is still alive." Don Diego sank to his knees beside her and gently turned her over. She was bleeding profusely from a wound in the center of her back. The ball had exited her front and made a terrible jagged hole. She looked

up at them, her eyes wide with fear and confusion. As they watched, she struggled to breathe properly.

She had long black hair and small, up-tilted breasts with brown nipples. Except for a short hide skirt, she was naked, without so much as a feather or amulet to identify her tribe.

"What is she? Tell him to ask her before she dies on us," Diego coldly ordered Maria. "Or *you* ask her. You speak their language."

"What tribe?" Bartolomeo demanded, bending over the woman. "To what tribe do you belong?"

She did not seem to understand. She made a sound, but Maria did not recognize it. "Tell us your name," Maria urged, falling to her own knees beside the woman. "Can you tell us your name?"

The woman looked at her and said something, but Maria did not recognize the dialect. "I cannot understand what she's saying!" she wailed. "This language is unknown to me."

"She is not one of our people," Bartolomeo confirmed. "Look, she still has her digging stick in hand, and over there is a reed basket. She and the others must have come to dig tubers along the river."

Maria translated Bartolomeo's observations. While she was still speaking, the woman gurgled and stopped breathing. The light faded from her eyes, and she lay staring at nothing.

Don Diego quickly made the sign of the cross. "She is gone," he said dully, with regret instead of coldness. "We have killed her, but she is no horse thief, nor even from the same tribe."

"She is still an *Indio,*" Miguel spat. "Her life is worth nothing. If we had not killed her, she would have tried to kill us."

Don Diego raised his head to look at the *arrendador,* and there was such fury on his face that Maria felt frightened. "With what?" he asked. "A digging stick? Do you honestly believe she meant to attack and slay us with only a digging stick?"

Miguel made no answer, but his scowl deepened.

"Go and check the others," Don Diego ordered. "See if anyone else survived our careless shooting."

No one else had. Four naked women and a child lay dead on the plain.

"We will bury them before we break camp," he announced. "Ignacio, you will keep watch in case the Indians return. If they do, hold your fire! Give me a chance to explain what happened here. Not that there *is* any rational explanation. Pedro, you should have waited to sound the alarm until you could see them more clearly."

Pedro glared defensively back at him. "I saw figures coming toward me through the darkness. How could I have waited? I thought we were going to be attacked. 'Tis why you have us stand watch, is it not? So no one can sneak up on us like they did the last time."

"Yes," Don Diego sighed. "But these were only women and children coming to dig tubers. They were not after us or the horses."

He headed for the river, walking like a stiff old man. Maria would have liked to comfort him, but she needed comfort herself. These were not her mother's people, but they were Indians and completely innocent of any wrongdoing. What made it worse was the knowledge that before they were finished, more Indians would surely die.

Gathering up her skirts, she ran after Don Diego. When she reached him, she grabbed his arm. "Wait, *señor!* Stop."

He turned to look at her. "What do you want, Maria—an apology? There is nothing I can say."

"Let us turn back," she begged. "We can return to *Dehesa de Oro* and tell my father the horses are gone forever."

His brow lifted in shock. "Turn back? Maria, this changes nothing! I grieve for those poor souls who lost their lives this morning, but my resolve is as strong as ever. If they are not to have died in vain, we must find the horses and the guilty Indians. These senseless deaths are as much *their* fault as ours. If not for them, we would not be out here, shooting at women and children. Nor would your own father be lying wounded at

Dehesa de Oro, a victim of savages who *did* intend to slay us."

"No good will come of this adventure," she bitterly insisted. "What good has come of it so far?"

But even as she asked the question, she knew the answer. She was learning how to ride properly, and had discovered some of the secrets of horse training. Soon, she would be ready to escape, and when she left she would take El Blanco and the other horses with her—including El Cid, if he would follow the others. She and Bartolomeo would leave these greedy, heartless Spaniards to die in the wilderness, or else learn to survive as the Indians did, by digging tubers and catching fish. In all likelihood, they would starve first.

"Go see to your horse," Don Diego ordered. "Currycomb him and pick out his feet. After that, if we are still busy burying Indians, you can start on the other horses, except for El Cid."

She didn't dare refuse; his face and eyes had hardened. There was no softness left in him; her appeals would only fall on deaf ears. *Dios!* How she hated this side of him, when he retreated into Spanish arrogance and shut her out entirely!

"Sí, señor," she answered, adopting a tone and demeanor of servility. She must *never* forget the differences between them, because they only resurfaced again to remind her that trusting him would be a great mistake. Giving him her heart would be a disaster.

For the next several days, Maria avoided speaking to Don Diego. They followed the river, and the land was gentle, making for easy riding. As he saw that she *could* handle El Blanco, he allowed her to ride unassisted, except for a curt correction, when she did something wrong. The *vaqueros* muttered among themselves and watched her disapprovingly. In their eyes, she also saw something else—something ugly and disturbing.

They had begun to lust after her. She knew this, because she often caught one or the other of them staring when she shook out her hair, or washed in the river, or went off alone in search of privacy.

Being the only female among six men presented challenges. Thus far, on their journey, she had tried to be discreet and take care of personal needs under cover of darkness, when no one could see her. But here, on this broad, flat plain, it became more difficult. The moon was now full and the nights almost as bright as daylight. Her only recourse was to hide among the horses, when she needed to be alone. Still, she often sensed someone watching—not Don Diego, for he seemed intent on avoiding her, too—but Miguel or one of the others.

At such times, she could only hope that being the daughter of their *patrón* would protect her. It had always protected her at *Dehesa de Oro,* but she was well aware that out here, only Don Diego stood between her and the *vaqueros.* If they chose to do so, the men could overwhelm Diego and kill him, then do whatever they wished with her. When they tired of their sport, they could kill both her and Bartolomeo, return to *Dehesa de Oro,* and blame everything on the *Indios.*

These were bleak thoughts to be thinking, but Maria felt terribly alone these days. In her solitude, she imagined that anything was possible. Traveling through this land of plenty, where food was abundant and hardships infrequent, gave her plenty to think about—and it gave the men lots to think about, too. They covered long distances, and each day, as her riding skills improved, the *vaqueros* seemed more angered by her progress.

"You really think you are somebody—riding a horse you should not be allowed near," Miguel said to her one afternoon behind Don Diego's back. "Just wait till we return to *Dehesa de Oro.* I will tell your father what went on out here. He will remind you of who and what you are—or your stepmother will."

"My father gave me to Don Diego. I am his responsibility now."

"Hah! He should have given you to me instead. I would have made certain you did not feel free to rise above your station. If something should happen to the new Master of Horses, I will be next in line to have you."

His words echoed her own unspoken fears, and Maria shivered, though the sun was hot. To get away from him, she kicked El Blanco into a fast trot and hurried to catch up to Don Diego. He had ridden on ahead to search for hoofprints.

She was greatly relieved when they encountered buffalo the following afternoon, placidly grazing beside the river. The herd was smaller than the one Maria had first seen, but big enough to cause a ripple of excitement among the men and horses. As they neared the herd, El Blanco started prancing and snorting, as did the other horses and Bartolomeo's ass.

"Fresh meat on the hoof!" Miguel cried. "I assume we have your leave to shoot them, *señor.*"

Don Diego was already reaching for his own weapon—not his *pistola,* but the longer weapon Maria had yet to see him use. His eyes shone with eagerness to match Miguel's. "It will take a *harquebus* to bring one down. I will shoot only one animal. That's more meat than we can use before it spoils."

"Only one!" Miguel snorted. "I say we take at least one to a man. There are more than enough. Why should only you have the pleasure of hunting?"

"All right, one to a man!" Diego agreed. "María, stay here with Bartolomeo. Ignacio, leave the packhorse with them."

Ignacio handed the packhorse's lead line to Bartolomeo and quickly joined the others. Excitement gripped all of them. Maria had seen nothing like it. The men were united as they had never been before now.

"*Caballeros,* let's go get ourselves some woolly cows!" Don Diego cried, and El Cid surged forward.

The others hesitated only a moment, then followed at a flat-out gallop. El Blanco did not like being left behind. Nor did the packhorse and Bartolomeo's ass, who brayed loudly.

"I cannot hold him!" Maria wailed, hauling back on the reins.

El Blanco ignored her. Taking the bit between his teeth, he shot out beneath her. She had just enough presence of mind to grab hold of his mane to maintain her seat. From the corner of her eye she saw the packhorse break free from Bartolomeo. Bartolomeo's ass started bucking. It was enough to unseat the old *Indio,* who was thrown off him and landed in a heap in the grass.

Maria could not see if he was hurt. Never before, except for a few times on La Reina, had she ridden at such speed. She knew from experience that she could easily fall off. This time, she was determined to remain aboard. El Blanco only wanted to reach his companions; he picked Ignacio's horse as his object.

Ignacio was riding straight toward the center of the herd of buffalo. When the buffalo saw the men on horseback bearing down on them, they began to run in circles. The *vaqueros,* accustomed to cattle, spread out to contain them, but the woolly cows would not be contained. Maria suddenly found herself right in the midst of them.

It was impossible to turn El Blanco. Buffalo surrounded them on every side. The horse became frantic. Dozens of buffalo now separated him from the rest of the horses. He whirled about, snorting with terror, then reared and pawed the air. Maria clung to his mane, too afraid to even scream. She knew if she fell into the midst of these churning bodies, she would be crushed. Their scent filled her nostrils, heavy and earthy. Huge bodies brushed against her legs, pinning them to El Blanco's side.

That alone kept her from falling, but she was at the mercy of El Blanco's instincts—the greatest of which was flight. He raced alongside the fleeing buffalo, neck outstretched, white mane flying. Long strands of hair whipped her face and eyes, blinding her. Maria could only pray he would not go down among the woolly hulks surrounding them on every side. Once again, she faced certain death. *Madre de Dios!* Where was Don Diego?

Take advantage of this offer to enjoy Zebra's newest line of historical romance novels....Splendor Romances (formerly Lovegrams Historical Romances)- Take our introductory shipment of 4 romance novels -Absolutely Free! (a $19.96 value)

Now you'll be able to savor today's best romance novels without even leaving your home with our convenient and inexpensive home subscription service. Here's what you get for joining:

* 4 BRAND NEW bestselling Splendor Romances delivered to your doorstep every month
* 20% off every title (or almost $4.00 off) with your home subscription
* FREE home delivery
* A FREE monthly newsletter, *Zebra/Pinnacle Romance News* filled with author interviews, member benefits, book previews and more!
* No risks or obligations...you're free to cancel whenever you wish...no questions asked

To get started with your own home subscription, simply complete and return the card provided. You'll receive your FREE introductory shipment of 4 Splendor Romances and then you'll begin to receive monthly shipments of new Zebra Splendor titles. Each shipment will be yours to examine for 1(days and then if you decide to keep the books, you'll pay the preferred home subscriber's price of just $4.00 per title. That's $16 for all 4 books with FREE home delivery! And if you want us to stop sending books, just say the word...it's that simple.

4 FREE books are waiting for you!
Just mail in the certificate below!

If the certificate is missing below, write to:
Splendor Romances, Zebra Home Subscription Service, Inc.,
P.O. Box 5214, Clifton, New Jersey 07015-5214
or call TOLL-FREE 1-888-345-BOOK

FREE BOOK CERTIFICATE

Yes! Please send me 4 Splendor Romances (formerly Zebra Lovegram Historical Romances), ABSOLUTELY FREE! After my introductory shipment, I will be able to preview 4 new Splendor Romances each month FREE for 10 days. Then if I decide to keep them, I will pay the money-saving preferred publisher's price of just $4.00 each... a total of $16.00. That's 20% off the regular publisher's price and there's never any additional charge for shipping and handling. I may return any shipment within 10 days and owe nothing, and I may cancel my subscription at any time. The 4 FREE books will be mine to keep in any case.

Name _____

Address _____ Apt. _____

City _____ State _____ Zip _____

Telephone ( ) _____

Signature _____
(If under 18, parent or guardian must sign.)

Terms and prices subject to change. Orders subject to acceptance by Zebra Home Subscription Service, Inc. .
Zebra Home Subscription Service, Inc. reserves the right to reject or cancel any subscription.

SP0699

SPLENDOR ROMANCES

ZEBRA HOME SUBSCRIPTION SERVICE, INC.

120 BRIGHTON ROAD

P.O. BOX 5214

CLIFTON, NEW JERSEY 07015-5214

Chapter Thirteen

Diego glimpsed a flash of red skirt, white blouse, and streaming black hair in the sea of brown bodies. His heart leapt into his throat. He knew at once what had happened: Maria's horse had taken off with her and unwittingly carried her right into the middle of the stampeding herd.

Her skirt billowed out in the wind, and he could see her bare legs gripping El Blanco's heaving sides. Without a saddle, not being an experienced rider, she was more likely to tumble off than remain on the horse's back. If El Blanco stopped suddenly or got jostled too hard by the fleeing buffalo, she would fall into that river of bodies and be stomped to death in a matter of moments.

How was he to save her? Too many buffalo separated them. None of the *vaqueros* were near her, either, nor did they seem to notice her predicament. He heard a boom, and a fat cow dropped like a stone. The rest only ran faster. Beneath him, El Cid lengthened his strides to keep up. Diego had his own *harquebus* primed and ready, but there was no sense wasting a shot to kill a buffalo when he might need it to help Maria.

He suddenly had an idea. The herd was running alongside the river, but if he could turn it and head the huge beasts into the water, it might slow them down—even bring them to a halt. They would have to resort to swimming, and they could not possibly swim as fast as they could run.

Bending low over the stallion's neck, he urged him to greater speed and passed the leaders of the herd. He drove El Cid hard, putting distance between himself and the buffalo. Then he leaned back, set the stallion down on his haunches, spun him around, lifted the heavy *harquebus* and fired into the faces of the leaders. One of them crumpled and fell, while the others swerved toward the river. Diego rode shouting after them. He could hear Caobo barking madly, but could not see the dog in the chaos. It was a wonder the staghound had not been trampled. He suddenly spotted Ignacio off to the side, and enlisted his aid.

"Turn them! Help me turn them into the river!"

The man looked stunned by his actions—and no wonder! No other horse but El Cid could have met the challenge of facing down a herd of maddened animals while his rider shot over his head. After a moment of hesitation, Ignacio shoved his own weapon into its leather holder and grabbed the coil of rope fastened to his saddle. Giving it a snap to uncoil it, he whirled it over the heads of the buffalo and rode shouting after his quarry, driving them ahead of him toward the water.

The entire herd plunged into the river, carrying Maria with them. Those in front immediately slowed down, while those behind clambered over the top of them. Calves ran bawling beside their mothers, splashing through the shallows and hurling themselves into deeper water. In the space of several heartbeats the stampede was over, and Maria still clung to El Blanco's neck as the water rose up his sides.

Diego plunged into the river after her. Confused, their momentum broken, the buffalo circled, holding their noses out of the water and snorting. They had lost all sense of direction, but still presented the danger of collision.

"Hold on, Maria! I am coming!" Diego cried.

El Blanco suddenly noticed El Cid, and determinedly headed toward him. Maria's face was as white as her blouse, her eyes wide open and staring. She did not seem to see him.

"Maria!" He hooked an arm around her waist and dragged her to him through the water.

She came alive suddenly, crying out and clinging to him. As he set her in front of him, she wrapped her arms around his neck. He turned El Cid to leave the river. Reins dragging, El Blanco followed, too happy to be reunited with another horse to even consider running away.

"I was so afraid," Maria sobbed against Diego's chest. "I knew if I fell I would die. It was like the flood, only worse. This time, I was conscious and *knew* what was happening."

" 'Tis over now, and you did well, Maria—remarkably well. You had no saddle, and yet you kept your seat."

"I was too frozen with fear to fall off! Besides, I wanted to impress you . . ." She started laughing through her tears. "I wanted to impress the Master of Horses."

"Well, you succeeded. I *am* impressed. Not even an experienced *vaquero* could have done any better. Relax, now. After a supper of fresh buffalo meat, you will forget this ever happened."

"If I never see another woolly cow in my lifetime, I will rejoice," she asserted. "They are horrid beasts—stupid and ill-smelling!"

Now, Diego had to laugh. "Do you mean to say the *Indio* in you does not love them? I thought your mother's people survived on buffalo."

"Oh, they do! They revere them as sacred. But I have seen enough for one day. Take me far away from them, please, Diego."

"I will, Maria." He hugged her close to him. "Do not worry. I will."

They gorged themselves on roasted buffalo steaks that night, all except for Bartolomeo. He chose to eat raw parts of the animal that no one else would dream of touching. Though limping and sore from his own mishap, the old Indian could hardly wait to cut the liver from the nearest dead cow. He ate it while it was still hot and steaming. Then he gobbled raw entrails, drawing the greasy guts through his few remaining teeth, as if to strip out the last, delicious flavor.

He wanted to teach Maria about the choicest morsels to be found in a newly killed buffalo, and he was offended when she refused to taste the blood and milk he drew from a slashed cow udder and offered to her with ill-concealed delight. Only Caobo seemed to share his tastes. The others were revolted and complained to Don Diego, but he told them to leave the old man alone. Just this once, Bartolomeo ought to be allowed to relive the joys of his youth, long ago before his capture. Otherwise, the things he most relished would only go to waste.

"You have no desire to try his delicacies?" Diego teased Maria later, out of earshot of the drowsy, stuffed *vaqueros* lounging on the opposite side of the fire.

She shook her head. "I guess I am not as much of an *Indio* as I thought I was. I remember my mother telling me how much she missed the feasts her people had when they killed the woolly cows. She especially enjoyed the curdled milk they sometimes found in the belly of a calf."

"It sounds as if they had orgies, not feasts." Don Diego shuddered, the motion exaggerated in the light from the popping fire. It flared up occasionally as fat dripped into it from the second round of roasting buffalo steaks.

"You are right. They were pure orgies," she conceded. "Indians always eat heartily during times of plenty. They must store up fat against the times of famine. The further north one goes, the harsher the winters become—or so my mother once told me."

"How does an Indian hunt buffalo without the advantage of a horse or a *harquebus?*"

"They have their methods." She shared Bartolomeo's memories of stampeding buffalo over high cliffs. "I think they also set fires, to force the animals to depart from their normal routes and travel where the *Indios* want them to go . . . perhaps into a river, like you drove them today. Did you notice how they floundered about in the water? A man could easily kill them with a bow and arrow or a spear."

A new thought suddenly occurred to her—one she chose not

to share with Don Diego. El Blanco had been slowed down by the water, too. Perhaps this was how the Indians could first learn to ride and train horses—if they took them into water! In a river or stream, the horses could not so easily buck or run away. And if the Indians fell off, little harm would be done.

"I think your mother's people must have more courage than I do," Don Diego snorted. "The very thought of entering a herd on foot—in water or not—makes my blood run cold. It's dangerous enough when one is mounted."

"You see now why they dared to steal horses," Maria could not resist saying.

"Yes, I see. But that still does not excuse them, nor convince me to abandon the idea of retrieving our stolen animals."

"I was afraid it would not. I just wanted you to understand better why—"

"You will never persuade me, Maria. Your father and I have been sorely wronged, and I will not rest until I have my revenge for it."

"But what about the wrongs done to my mother's people? The Spaniards believe that because I am the daughter of an *Indio,* my life is worth little, yet you have saved me twice now—no, three times, if you count the time my father wanted to beat me. If you truly share the sentiments of your countrymen, including my own father, why did you bother?"

"Maria, you know why. You do not have to ask." Diego reached out his hand to smooth the hair back from her face. The gesture was fast becoming familiar to her. He seemed to enjoy touching her—even in small ways—but what he really wanted was to touch her more intimately. Hadn't he earned that right, by now? she wondered, feeling churlish for punishing both him and herself.

"Thank you for saving my life," she said. "Think not that I am ungrateful, but—"

"But you still refuse to share my bed," he finished for her. "Do you not?"

She nodded, and was suddenly quite miserable.

"And I still refuse to command you. What a sorry pair we

are! Both of us so stubborn. 'Tis amazing how well we are matched.''

Maria did not want to think about it, much less talk about it. "I am very tired, *señor*. And I have eaten enough. Have I permission to go to sleep now?''

"Yes," he sighed, shaking his head. " 'Tis obvious our conversation distresses you. Retreat, if you must. But one day you will stop fighting me, Maria. I feel it in my bones. The hour of your surrender is drawing near, and for me it cannot come fast enough.''

She lacked the strength to deny it. At this very moment, she wanted nothing more than to curl up in his arms and feel safe, warm, and comfortable. She longed for his kisses and caresses—wished she could lose herself in the wonder of loving him. But she could not . . . not now, not ever. Despite all that had happened, nothing had changed between them: They were as far apart as they had ever been.

"Sleep well, *señor*. I will see you tomorrow.''

"Sleep well, Maria.''

Another three days passed, and they came to a place where steep, rocky hills hugged the opposite shore. On their side of the river, tall, graceful poplar trees bent over the water. The river was exceptionally clear here, and Maria could see tiny silvery fish darting among the multicolored pebbles and stones on the river bottom.

It was an ideal campsite. They still had several hours of daylight, but Don Diego called for a halt. After dismounting and taking care of his horse, he left Maria and the others and trudged upstream. Maria knew he was once again searching for hoofprints, but this time, he had not gone far when he suddenly gave a great shout.

"Here! Here, they are! I have found hoofprints, and several of the horses are even shod. The mark of their iron shoes cannot be mistaken.''

Everyone but Maria and Bartolomeo rushed to view the

discovery. They knelt, pointed, and conferred together, eyes alight, hands gesturing.

Then Miguel arrogantly announced: "This set of prints belongs to La Reina. I would recognize them anywhere. Her feet are more dainty than the others."

Don Diego instantly agreed with him. "She was shod, was she not?"

Miguel nodded. "She always wears down her shoes in the exact same way. Look here. The fronts of the shoes show a clearer imprint than the backs—meaning the backs are worn down. By now, she must need new shoes altogether."

"Without doubt," Don Diego said. "Now, look over here. Do any of Don Gonzalo's mares toe out slightly?"

"Yes. Margarita, an old roan-colored mare."

"Then these must belong to her. Apparently, the horses were brought here to drink from the river, but their tracks lead away from it." Diego followed them into the tall grass. "Here, they fade away and become lost—but tomorrow, we will set off in this direction and see if we can follow them by the trail of droppings the horses will have left behind."

"Here are some droppings!" Fernandez cried, a short distance away.

Everyone ran to study the droppings. "They are not too hard and dry." Diego pushed at them with the tip of his sword. "The horses must have passed here fairly recently. Caobo! Leave the droppings alone."

He pushed the dog to one side, preventing him from burying his slender muzzle in the manure. Maria knew that Bartolomeo could identify the time lapse quite accurately, for he knew manure better than anyone, except, perhaps, Caobo. However, no one thought to ask for his opinion, so she did not volunteer it. Nor did she point out the imprint of a man's bare foot that she herself discovered on the soft ground a short time later. Instead, she quietly obliterated it.

For the remainder of the afternoon, while Don Diego busied himself with writing materials and a leather-bound book he had brought along in his pack, the *vaqueros* indulged their high spirits. After they set up camp, they placed bets on how soon they might catch up to the stolen horses. Then they began to amuse themselves by tossing pebbles to scare away the fish Maria and Bartolomeo were once again trying to spear for the evening meal.

"Old man!" Miguel called out in a mocking tone. "Have you caught one yet? If not, you will have to move faster."

Bending down, he picked up a handful of stones and sent one skimming across the top of the water. Glancing down at his palm, he selected another missile, frowned, and held it up to slanting rays of the late afternoon sun.

"If you toss another stone our way, you can go hungry tonight," Maria scolded. "Or else, you can plan on roasting more buffalo steaks. The meat has started to spoil, but 'tis all we have. Perhaps you prefer spoiled meat to fresh fish."

They had brought along a portion of meat from the buffalo they had slain, but after three days in the sun, it was no longer appetizing.

"*Madre de Dios!*" Miguel suddenly exclaimed. "Look here! I think I have found gold."

"Gold? Where? Let me see it!" Pedro cried.

The *vaqueros'* excitement exceeded their elation when Don Diego had found hoofprints. They converged upon Miguel and crowded around him, begging to see the gold nugget.

Proudly, he held it aloft. " 'Tis gold, is it not? I found it in the riverbed. Perhaps there is more." He bit on the nugget, and his grin widened. " 'Tis surely gold! Look at it."

He held it out in the palm of his hand, but refused to allow Pedro or anyone else to take it. " 'Tis mine! You can feast your eyes upon it but you cannot have it."

"I will look in the river then. Perhaps there is more." Pedro rushed to the water's edge, scooped up a handful of stones, and began pawing through them. "I will find my own gold! Where there's one piece, there's bound to be another."

"Give it to me," Don Diego demanded, striding up to the *arrendador*. At the onset of the commotion, he had set aside his work and risen to his feet, leaving everything piled at the base of a tall tree.

"I will tell you whether 'tis real or not," he offered.

Miguel made a fist around the nugget, clutched it to his chest, and scowled at Don Diego. "If it has value, I want it back. I found it, and it belongs to me."

"I only want to see it. When I first came to the New World, before I started on the journey to *Dehesa de Oro,* I had a chance to examine some raw gold at Santa Barbola. I can tell you whether this is the real thing, or only an imposter."

Miguel reluctantly handed it over. " 'Tis a known fact that gold can be found in streambeds. The rain washes it down from the mountainsides. This may have come from those cliffs on the other side of the river. There could be an entire mountain of gold over there. We have only to find it, and we will all be rich men."

"We would have to get it out of the mountain first," Don Diego said drily. "And that would be easier said than done."

While he was studying the nugget, Pedro, Fernandez, and Ignacio scrabbled in the shallows, searching for more nuggets.

"I found one, too!" Ignacio hollered. "Not as big as Miguel's, but the color is purer."

In the end, Don Diego examined both of them and pronounced them to be real. He then returned the nuggets to their eager owners. "I regret I cannot tell you the value of the individual pieces, but they are worth something. Guard them well, *señors,* until you have a chance to see how much you can get for them."

"Tomorrow, we will cross the river and scale those cliffs," Miguel announced. "If we are fortunate, we will find an entire vein of gold. I only wish we had brought the proper tools to search for it. I say we agree now to share in whatever we discover—except that I should have a slightly larger portion, since I found the first nugget."

"Just a moment," Don Diego interrupted, frowning. "We are here to find horses, not gold. I am as eager as anyone to search those cliffs, but if gold is hidden there we need not fear its sudden disappearance. We cannot afford the time to search for it now. We have just discovered the first sign of our horses, and must hurry to catch up to them."

Miguel threw up his hands in protest. "Let the horses go!

We have found something far more important—*gold,* Don
Diego. Gold can buy all the horses we could ever want or need,
the finest horses in all Spain. We can import them by the
dozens.''

'' 'Tis not that simple,'' Don Diego insisted, his frown deep-
ening. "Horses often die on the journey from Spain to the New
World. And what about the importance of keeping the Indians
afoot? The best horses are already here—La Reina and the
others will produce horses of exceptional quality, especially
when crossed with my stallion. Do not be a fool, Miguel. The
gold nuggets may not have come from the cliffs across the
river. Perhaps they washed down from mountainsides far
upstream. We could search for years and never locate the mother
lode.''

"You do not intend for *us* to be the ones to find it!'' Miguel
accused. "You plan to return here later by yourself and look
for it. You and Don Gonzalo will put together a work party of
Indios to come here with beasts of burden to haul away the
treasure and tools to hack away at the rock.''

"If I decide to do that, I will bring all of you with me,''
Don Diego promised. "Tools and beasts of burden will be
needed—and so will workers. It takes time and money to organize such a great effort so far from *Dehesa de Oro,* but I will
make certain you get your fair share.''

"You will not decide my fair share! Nor will you dictate to
any of us. If you want the horses so much, go ahead without
us. We will stay here and search for the gold. What about the
rest of you? Will you go with him or stay here with me?''

Miguel swung around to face the others, but Don Diego
lifted his sword and pressed the tip of it into the *arrendador's*
back.

"Enough!'' he spat, his eyes glittering.

Maria cringed at the prospect of violence. Miguel had finally
driven Don Diego too far. Growling low in his throat, Caobo
crouched and showed the *arrendador* his teeth, as if adding
his own slender weight to the argument.

"We have already established that I am the leader of this
expedition,'' Diego said. "I say we will keep going until we

find the horses. Once they are safely ours again, we can debate how best to search for gold.''

Miguel arched his back to avoid the press of the sword tip, but his face was still rebellious and angry. ''Do you intend to use that sword on an unarmed man, Don Diego? If not, then put it away. I am not an *hidalgo,* so I am inexperienced with swords, but I will gladly fight you to decide this issue. Name some other weapon—*pistolas* or daggers.''

''You have been spoiling for a fight all along, Miguel. If I whip you in a fair fight—hand to hand, no weapons—will you finally cease testing me?''

''You will not whip me,'' Miguel boasted. ''You are the sort who slays an enemy while he sleeps in his bed. You lack the courage to face a man openly.''

A crimson flush spread like a stain across Don Diego's jaw. ''You have been listening to too much gossip, Miguel. But your sources are wrong. I never killed a man while he slept in his bed. Confronting my enemies face-to-face has always been—and will always be—much more to my liking. We are all necessary to the success of this mission, so there will be no needless shedding of blood, either yours or mine.''

He tossed his sword on the ground. ''Turn 'round and face me. Let us settle this conflict, once and for all. If I can pin you to the ground for the count of ten, you must bow to my wishes. If you can pin me instead, I will bow to yours. Maria, you will do the counting. Caobo, stay back.''

The dog dropped to his belly, paws outstretched in front of him. Maria knew he would stay there, for he worshipped Don Diego like a god. As Miguel slowly turned to face him, the other men surrounded the two adversaries. Bartolomeo watched from a distance. Maria remained where she was. She had never heard Don Diego deny he had killed a man in Spain, but she had no doubt he was telling the truth. In the beginning, she had hated almost everything about him, but since then he had proven himself to be a man of honor and principle.

On many things, their views differed, but he had always remained true to his word. If he lost this fight, her own fate and Bartolomeo's would be in the hands of Miguel and the others. Miguel would never allow them to live—not now. From all the stories she had heard, men would kill even their best friends to obtain gold.

"I will do the counting," she said. "As soon as one or the other of you is pinned to the ground, I will begin."

"This is foolishness!" Pedro objected. "No matter who wins this confrontation, I intend to remain here and search for gold. Never again will I have such an opportunity."

"Then I will fight each of you individually," said Don Diego.

"We outnumber you!" Ignacio snorted. "Unless you mean to kill every one of us, you cannot prevent us from doing what we please."

"Are you honorable men or not?" Don Diego demanded. "You gave me your word to obey without question. You swore on the blood of *Cristo* and the salvation of your immortal souls."

"But that was before we discovered gold! This changes everything," Ignacio insisted.

"It changes nothing. Fight me now. I am ready. Fight me all together or only one at a time. I care not which. There can be only one leader, and I will be it, or die trying."

Bending at the knee, Don Diego motioned for them to come after him. Maria could see he was determined. He *would* die before he conceded. There would be no more bargaining.

The others watched him uncertainly. They had spent their entire lives obeying the aristocracy and cultivating their favor. Without a *patrón*, a man was destitute. Don Diego represented their *patrón*. He was the voice of authority. To go against him meant they could not return to *Dehesa de Oro* unless they killed him—along with all witnesses—and lied about what had happened out here. If they did *not* find gold, where would they be? Could they even trust one another to keep these things secret?

Their faces revealed their thoughts—and it was Miguel who finally backed down. "Don Diego is right," he said. "We gave him our word. Besides, the gold will still be here when we return with the horses."

"You do not speak for me!" Pedro cried. "And what about Ignacio and Fernandez? I say we should settle this now."

"Pedro, old friend," Miguel cajoled. "Think of what you are doing. Will you give up Juana? If you become an outlaw, you will never see her again. And you, Fernandez. You have a wife and children. Don Gonzalo will turn them out into the wilderness. We have too much to lose, *señors*. Especially when we cannot be certain those cliffs contain gold."

"If it does, 'tis ours!" Pedro shook his fist for emphasis. "We cannot let it go to the *hidalgos*. They get everything while we do all the work. 'Tis neither fair nor just. Juana and I should have the chance to live like royalty, too."

"Bide your time, Pedro," Miguel cautioned. "Don Diego will not see us cheated, will you, *señor?*"

"I give you my word—as an *hidalgo*," Don Diego said, straightening. "If ever gold is found in this place or anywhere near it, all of you will be richly rewarded."

"How do we know that Don Gonzalo himself would not prefer us to look for gold, instead of horses?" Pedro demanded, still not convinced. "Why else did the *conquistadors* first settle this land, if not for gold? 'Tis what all men want."

"First, the horses, *then* the gold," Don Diego replied. "Your *patrón* would agree. Any thinking man would want both, and there is no reason why both cannot be obtained. If you doubt we can find this place again, I assure you we can. I have been mapping it as we go along—marking landmarks in my book and taking notes of all we encounter. Maria, fetch my book over by the tree. I will show you."

Maria ran to get the leather-bound book. When she handed it to Don Diego, the men did not crowd around to see it, as he no doubt expected. "See here," he said, opening the book and pointing to a particular page. "I have written down a description of this campsite and how we got here. There are notes for the entire journey."

"None of us can read," Pedro complained. "So what good will your descriptions be to us?"

"If you cannot read, then you had better not kill me or Bartolomeo," Diego pointed out in a reasonable tone. "We are the only ones who know where we are or how we got here."

"I have been keeping track in my head," Miguel growled. "I do not need to write it down to remember it."

"How fortunate you have such an excellent memory," Don Diego drawled. "So much of this land looks the same. I have even been noting the location of the stars at night, like mariners do, so that day or night, I can chart my course and find my way home again."

Miguel only glared at him, and Maria wondered what they would all think if they learned that Don Diego was not the only one who could read his black book. They hated him because of who he was, and what he knew. They were also afraid to lose the benefits of his knowledge and experience.

"The hour grows late." Don Diego tucked the book under one arm. "It will soon be dark, and I am hungry. Are we eating fish tonight, Maria—or spoiled meat?"

"Fish, I hope. There is still time enough to spear some."

She beckoned Bartolomeo to return with her to the river. It looked as if the crisis had passed.

That night, long after dark, she could hear the men murmuring among themselves, while Don Diego steadfastly ignored them. They kept their voices low, but she could tell that they continued to disagree over what should be done.

That night, Don Diego slept with his *pistola* in his hand and spent most of the night in watchfulness. He got little sleep. Nor did she. All night long, she tossed and turned, expecting the *vaqueros* to turn on them. But the night passed without incident, and the next morning, they all rode away together from the pleasant campsite along the river.

Don Diego ordered the men to spread out and keep watch for droppings, and they spent the day riding from one pile of manure to the next—following the trail of Indians and horses.

Chapter Fourteen

Two nights passed, and Diego exhausted himself trying to remain awake each night to guard against attack by his own men. As the third night approached, he decided that the men were not going to attack. Though they continued to grumble among themselves, they had apparently made their peace with the decision to first retrieve the horses and only then search for gold. Little did they realize he was as eager as they were to find gold—even more eager.

He was a horseman first, though, he reminded himself as he rubbed down El Cid before turning him out to graze for the night. After a lifetime of putting the welfare of horses above his own needs and comforts, he could never turn his back on them now and allow the savages to have them. But if he did not soon get some sleep, he might lose the trail altogether.

Today had been unusually frustrating. After riding through a patch of grass so tall it hid everything, including wildlife and horse droppings, they had come to a flat, arid, stony place which contained no signs of horses or any other life. They spent hours crisscrossing the area in a futile attempt to decide in which direction to go from there. In the end, Bartolomeo had somehow led them to a sandy embankment where they had once again spotted hoofprints.

Diego did not know what they would have done without the old *Indio*. Bartolomeo's instincts were guiding them more than Diego wanted the men to know. He *was* trying to keep track of landmarks in his book, and studying the location of major constellations in the sky overhead, but landmarks were sometimes few and far between, and sometimes he forgot to notice them. These days, he was too tired and preoccupied to write them down while they were still fresh in his mind.

He no longer trusted his own accuracy. If something happened to Bartolomeo and he had to retrace their steps, it would not be easy to recognize landmarks seen from a different direction. It would be better to follow the stars, but he was no expert in that field, either. Star positions changed with the time of year, and he had never really been a mariner. To him, the sky in the New World seemed different from the sky he recalled at sea.

He hated the precariousness of his position. Not only was he a stranger in a strange land, but he could trust neither his own skills nor those of his companions—except for Bartolomeo. And tired as he was, he doubted he could defend Maria, if the need arose. He had to sleep!

He ate his portion of meat from a couple of rabbits the old Indian had snared and roasted, fed Caobo some scraps, and lay down near Maria beneath a canopy of brilliant stars. Tonight, the men were quieter than usual; perhaps, they, too, suffered from fatigue. He hoped they were through complaining or plotting against him, and would let him sleep. Ignacio was due to stand the first watch, and Pedro the second. Diego planned to take the dangerous hours directly before dawn.

"Maria," he murmured, before he allowed his eyes to close. "If you hear anything—anything at all—wake me, will you? Caobo may be off hunting. We have had little to give him lately, and he has had to search for his own food."

"Of course," she answered. "Do not worry. I may not be as good as Caobo, but I awaken at the slightest sound."

"Gracias." Clutching his *pistola,* just in case, he surrendered

to the need to sleep. The next thing he knew, Maria was shaking him by the shoulder.

"Don Diego, wake up! The *vaqueros* are gone. They have taken all the horses except for El Cid and Bartolomeo's ass."

Diego leapt to his feet so fast he invited dizziness. As his vision cleared, he saw it was true. The *vaqueros* had deserted them, taking everything, including the supplies and most of the gunpowder. Caobo lay sprawled on his side, tail thumping, as if wondering what all the fuss was about. The dog had only learned to warn of arrivals, not departures.

The *vaqueros* had left only a single water gourd and a few items they could not have stolen without disturbing those they were leaving behind. By now, Bartolomeo had awakened. The old man was sitting up, holding his head in his hands, and grimacing, as if in pain.

"Ask him if he heard anything during the night," Diego instructed. "How could this have happened without one of us noticing?"

While Diego searched the ground for hoofprints showing where the *vaqueros* had gone, Maria went to the solitary figure and conferred with him a moment, then quickly returned.

"He says he heard nothing, but he has a large lump on his head and a bad headache. So do I, *señor*. And I keep seeing two objects where I know only one should be."

"What? You should have told me you were injured! Let me see your head. Those vermin," he muttered when he discovered a prominent swelling on the back of her head beneath her silky hair. "They give vermin a bad name."

He wondered why the *vaqueros* had not bashed *him* over the head with some heavy object; he had probably been sleeping so soundly they had not thought it necessary.

"I will kill them for this," he promised. "I will go after them on El Cid and kill them."

"No, *señor!*" Maria grasped his hands, her eyes anxious. "Please, you must not leave us alone out here. They only returned to search for the gold—but they took all the weapons with them."

"No, I still have my *pistola*. If they had tried to take that, I *would* have awakened."

"Will a single *pistola* be enough to keep them from killing you? They are more heavily armed than you, *señor*. If they see you coming, they will surely kill you."

He already knew this—and resented being helpless and outnumbered; he could do nothing, it seemed, until the odds improved. With both Maria and Bartolomeo injured . . .

"Perhaps you had better sit down," he urged, suddenly worried, "before you fall down."

He reached for her arm to steady her.

"I will be all right." She brushed away his hand. "I am more worried about Bartolomeo. He is an old man. For him, a sharp blow to the head could be fatal."

"Then you must both rest. Today, we will do nothing but lounge about camp and tend your injuries."

"You will not leave us?" Fear flashed in Maria's eyes.

"I will not go after Miguel and the others. But if all of our food is gone, I will have to see about finding some. And I must look for water. A single gourd will not last long. El Cid and the ass need water, too. On a single gourd of water, we cannot even return to the River of Trees. No doubt Miguel and the others are well aware of this."

"They planned this well." Maria agreed. She suddenly sagged against him. "Ah! Now, I feel sick to my stomach."

"I told you to sit down!" Diego gently pulled her to the ground. "Leave everything to me. I will check on Bartolomeo and make you both comfortable. Then I will see if I can locate a source of water."

Maria wrapped her arms around her upraised knees and rested her head on them. She looked pale and weak. "I hope you can, *señor*. For I am not ready to travel today."

Diego spent the remainder of the day searching for food and water. He spotted antelope gamboling in the distance, but they raced away before he got into shooting range. That night, they did not go hungry. Bartolomeo roused himself long enough to dig some tubers and catch a type of rodent that lived in the ground not far from their campsite. He made a small fire and roasted his offerings whole, but neither Maria nor Diego could bring themselves to even taste the rodent. They sat across the fire from the old Indian and watched him smack his lips with relish as he ate.

"He seems to be feeling better." Diego dug into a blackened tuber that was actually not too bad, considering its blandness and need for salt. Sadly, the *vaqueros* had taken the salt with them.

"I think so," she responded, picking listlessly at her own tuber. "When I asked him, he told me he was still suffering a bit of dizziness and occasional twinges of pain in his head."

"And what about you?"

"I will be better tomorrow. Tonight, I cannot eat. Do you want my tuber?" She held it out to him.

"You must eat. You have had nothing all day."

"Tomorrow, if we have food, I will eat." She set the tuber down next to him.

"Drink some water, at least," he urged.

Again, she shook her head. "My stomach wants nothing in it. Give my portion to your stallion, or Bartolomeo's ass. They are the ones who must be thirsty."

"I daresay they are, but they will derive some moisture from the dew that coats the grass at night. Tomorrow, when I ride El Cid, I will let him go wherever he wishes. If there is water around, he will find it."

"We will not resume looking for the *Indios* and the horses?"

"Not until we find water and can figure out how to carry it with us. You must ask Bartolomeo if he knows of a way to transport water in the absence of gourds or waterskins."

"He will tell us we need the stomach or bladder of a large animal. They can be blown up and filled with water, then tied off to make a reliable container."

"Wonderful. All I need do is find a large animal, kill it using only my *pistola* and remove its body parts. Losing my *harquebus* is a great hardship, Maria. Without it, we cannot hunt properly."

"We will not starve, Don Diego. Bartolomeo told me tonight

that tomorrow he will begin looking for grubs. He says they make a very acceptable meal.''

"I cannot eat grubs! Tell him I will stick with tubers.''

"So will I—if tubers remain available. I know how to search for them now. Bartolomeo has taught me a great deal. Some things I learned from my mother, but hearing about them and actually doing them are two different things.''

"Out here, everything seems different.'' Diego sighed. "The sky, for example. Until I started sleeping out in the open, I never noticed how much activity goes on overhead.''

"I never noticed either, but you are correct. Last night, before I fell asleep, I lay and watched the stars for a long time.'' Maria lifted her eyes and gazed at the star-spangled heavens. "I saw many falling stars. And in the north, the edges of the sky were strangely bright. I have never witnessed such a phenomenon, and it frightened me a little. If you had not been sleeping so soundly, I would have awakened you to see it for yourself.''

She looked at him, and the glint of fox fire lit her eyes. She was truly lovely, he thought, and completely unaware of it.

"It was probably nothing,'' he assured her, smiling. "Once, when I was a child, my father told me he saw a huge star fall to the earth. Its light was so bright it seemed like day in the middle of the night. The horses bucked in fear, the dogs howled, and the cattle stampeded and broke free of their pens. All the humans ran outside to see what was happening. It was enough to make them race back to their beds, jump inside them, and cover their heads. Everyone believed the world was coming to an end. In the morning, they were much surprised to find themselves still alive.''

" 'Tis a good story, but I hope I myself never witness such a phenomenon. My mother placed great significance on celestial happenings. All Indians do. They believe that falling stars and rings around the moon have special meaning, if we can only figure out what it is. The sky tells us about changes in the weather, and even helps us keep track of where we are when the land all looks the same.''

Diego peered at her in surprise. "You can read the stars as the mariners do? Why did you never mention it?''

She smiled. "You never asked . . . and besides, 'tis not I who can read them, but the *Indios*. I never did learn the trick, but my mother once told me that all Indians can read the sky the same as you *hidalgos* read the writing in books."

"That is amazing! Who first taught them these things? In my country, only the most educated men can name the constellations and tell you where they appear in the sky at different times of the year. 'Tis considered a science. Some men spend their entire lives carefully studying it."

"The *Indios* have their wise men, too, Don Diego. Each generation passes down what it has learned to the next. Because I was raised Spanish, my knowledge is limited. I know only a few things my mother or Bartolomeo taught me. However, I know many Spanish things the *Indios* will never understand."

"Such as?" Diego prompted, fascinated by her views on life. She had a foot in each world, yet belonged to neither, and it gave her a unique perspective.

"Such as the realization that a man on a horse is not a god or supernatural being. Controlling a horse is a matter of training the animal, not divine intervention. 'Tis the same with the use of weapons. The *Indios* are awed by what they cannot understand, but if they were taught—"

"They would then become dangerous to those they outnumber—us, their enemies. Maria, someone has taught the horse thieves that *any* man can learn to control horses. If it was not your brother, Santelmo, who do you think it could be?"

"I know not." She glanced away from him. "But I pray it was *not* Santelmo. If you kill him, I will never be able to forgive you, Don Diego. It makes no difference that I owe you my life. He is my brother. We share the same blood. Spilling *his* blood is the same as spilling *mine*. And I will hate you for it."

"Maria . . ." He placed his hand over hers where it lay on the ground between them. "I wish we could remove this conflict between us. I wish we could be only ourselves—a man and a woman, as God created us. We could be so happy together! So . . . complete."

"I know." Gently, she removed her hand from beneath his.

"But we must accept what *is,* Don Diego, not what we wish things could be."

He wanted to grab her then—tilt her back in the grass, lift her skirt, and join his body to hers. He wanted to hear her cries of pleasure and vows of fidelity. Wanted to make her sigh, laugh, cry, and tremble. She had bewitched him, and he was almost willing to promise her anything to win her consent to explore the joys of lovemaking with him. *Almost.* He could not bring himself to lie to her. Lies would destroy any chance he might still have with her. She hated lies worse than anything. She could never trust a Spaniard because she had experienced only sorrow and betrayal from them, starting with her own father.

He thought he understood how she felt—he knew her well— but she still did not know him. She continued to associate him with *all* Spaniards. What more could he possibly do to win her trust and admiration?

"You should get some rest now," he gently chided. "I never meant to keep you awake so long talking. Look! Bartolomeo has finished stuffing himself and has gone to sleep."

"What about you? When will you sleep?"

"When Caobo returns from hunting," he told her. "My dog has no fondness for tubers, and Bartolomeo did not offer to share his rodent. So Caobo went off to catch his own meal."

"He is a good dog," she murmured. "I like him. Knowing he is standing guard at night makes me feel safer."

"Yes, but he is unreliable. He keeps going off alone at night. And he never warned me about Miguel and the others."

"He is not to blame," she defended. "He had no idea he was supposed to warn you about Miguel. As for going off alone, he must see to his own needs, since you neglect them. You Spaniards are too quick to place blame. Neither dogs nor humans can be expected to starve without making protest."

Her bitterness prompted a response. "I have never beaten that dog, Maria—nor would I be out here hunting down *Indios* if they had not started this enmity between us."

"They did *not* start it! The Spaniards trespassed on *their* lands and sought to enslave them, not the other way around."

Diego threw up his hands in exasperation. "You are right, of course. Why are we arguing? Leave me to my watch, and get some rest, Maria."

"I will, *señor. Buenas noches.*"

While she made up her bed, Diego rose and walked out onto the plain. He had to get away from the temptation she presented. Never had a woman—or a man, for that matter—so attracted and challenged him. He could never seem to win her approval, nor banish the feeling that he had somehow failed her. Again and again she drew near, like a wary deer expecting a trap, only to leap away at the last moment, certain he meant to harm her.

He wondered if he were losing his sanity, wanting her so much and denying himself the pleasure of taking her. Once he had bedded her, he would no longer be a slave to her smiles and frowns—falling over his own feet to gain the first and avoid the latter. Bedding her would purge his system of unhealthy desires. He was beginning to believe what many men claimed: Unless a man regularly released his seed in the body of a female, he would slowly sicken and die. A man's seed was meant to be planted in a woman, not retained in his own body to weaken and bedevil him.

He walked for a long time, keeping watch over Maria and Bartolomeo as they slept beneath the stars. Deep in thought, he failed to notice anything different in the sky until he suddenly looked up and witnessed the strange light Maria had mentioned. The northern sky was abnormally bright—so bright he could not understand how he had failed to notice it before this. Could the northern plain be burning, illuminating the heavens above it?

He recalled Maria telling him how the Indians sometimes hunted buffalo by using grass fires to herd the animals in a particular direction. He decided to awaken her and Bartolomeo, so the old *Indio* could tell him what he thought, but they were both sleeping so soundly that, mindful of their injuries, he changed his mind.

Sitting down beside Maria, he watched the sky and waited

for further developments. As the night passed the light intensified, as if it were approaching at a very slow pace.

An hour or so before dawn, Caobo returned, slinking through
the grass to join Diego and press his trembling body against
his side.

The dog's fear alarmed Diego. Caobo had never behaved
like this before; being a staghound, he had courage to spare.
But tonight, the dog whimpered and nosed Diego's hand for
comfort. Diego did not know what to think. He rose and went
to check on El Cid and the ass. Like the dog, they seemed
disturbed. Facing the north, they stood motionless, ears pricked
to detect the slightest sound, nostrils flared to drink in the
scents.

In the north, along the horizon, a ball of intense white light
suddenly appeared, as if the sun were rising! The light blinded
Diego; he raised his hand to shield his eyes. In the distance,
wolves began to howl. The hair on Caobo's neck stood straight
up, and he, too, howled. Braying loudly, the ass stumbled about
in his hobbles. Poised as if he might suddenly explode, El Cid
remained motionless.

Bending down, Diego quickly released the stallion's leathers
and tossed the hobbles aside. He started to do the same for the
ass, but the animal contorted his body in a vain effort to buck,
kick, or run away.

Diego heard a shrill, feminine cry . . . a scream of pure terror
that sliced through his heart.

Spinning around, he saw Bartolomeo kneeling and Maria
standing, both of them staring at the sky. The whole plain was
bright as noontide. A hot wind blasted Diego. Rain gusted in
his face, and he smelled something burning. A low rumble,
like gathering thunder, reverberated through the soles of his
feet. He wanted to run and hide, but there was no place to go.
No place offered protection. In his own rising panic, he could
feel his wits scattering.

Save Maria.

The thought grounded him and kept him from bolting. Thunder cracked. As the ball of white light bore down upon them,

El Cid reared and pawed the air, came down, and galloped away, with Caobo running hard on his heels.

Diego ran shouting toward Maria. Calling her name, he warned her not to look into the light or she would be blinded. She raced in his direction, and they met in a shower of light, sparks, and thunder that threw them both to the ground and flattened the grass all around them. Summoning all his strength, Diego rolled over and tried to protect her with his own body, while beneath them, the earth creaked, shuddered, and groaned.

He did not dare look up, but heard an explosion and sensed a white-hot flare of light above them. There came a shattering roar and the universe trembled ... followed by an abrupt, profound silence.

Several moments passed before Diego gained enough courage to open his eyes. It was utterly dark, as one might imagine the inside of a grave: No sound. No light. A stillness beyond comprehension.

Diego moved only because Maria did. Pushing at his chest, she gasped and coughed. "Diego ... what was it? What has happened?"

He shook his head, then realized she could not see the motion in the impenetrable darkness. "Who can say? A priest might call it the Last Day—the Day of Judgment—except we are still here. We are not dead."

"Are you certain? Perhaps we *are* dead, but do not know it."

He realized he was crushing her soft contours beneath the weight of his body. "We are not dead," he announced with certainty. "We are still flesh and blood, not spirit. I know this, because my body can still respond to your body."

He levered himself off of her. The stirring of lust seemed an obscenity following the spiritual cataclysm they had just experienced. "Are you all right?"

"Yes. I am shaking, but I am not hurt."

Still trembling himself, he took her hand to pull her up beside him as he strained to pierce the blackness with mere eyesight.

"It must have been a falling star—a big one, passing closer

to the earth than anyone has ever yet witnessed. It may have hit the earth. We will never know, I suppose. But it was awesome.''

''It could not have struck the earth, or it would have destroyed it. It was too big—too fiery. And now 'tis so dark. Hold me, Diego. I know it has passed, but I cannot conquer my fear.''

Clinging together in the all-encompassing darkness, Diego kissed her hair. '' 'Tis over now,'' he soothed. ''We must check on Bartolomeo and the animals.''

''Bartolomeo! Oh, how could I have forgotten him?'' She pulled away from Diego. ''Bartolomeo! Where are you? Answer me, and we will come to you.''

There was no response. Nothing disturbed the deep, black silence. ''You spoke in our language. Try speaking in his,'' Diego urged. ''Perhaps, he did not understand.''

She tried again. Still, no response.

''Where is he?'' She swung back toward Diego. ''Do you think he is dead?''

''We will have to wait until dawn to find out. 'Tis too dark to rekindle the fire.''

''And what about Caobo, El Cid, and the ass? What has become of them?''

''We will know soon enough, Maria. Try to remain calm. Come here. Let me hold you until it grows light again.''

This time, she came weeping into his arms. ''I never knew the heavens could be this horrible! But then I have never been this far north. I was so afraid. I could not understand what was happening.''

''A falling star,'' he repeated. ''It could only have been a falling star.''

''Maybe it was more—an omen warning us to turn back! Do you think we are being punished for coming this far north?''

''Maria, stop it. That is superstitious nonsense. You must not allow fear to banish common sense.''

He managed to control the tremor in his own voice as he sought to reassure her. But he could not help wondering if it were true. They had ventured beyond the boundaries of the known world; they had invaded territory few men besides *Indios* had ever seen. He knew less than she did about this land; she *could* be right.

Dawn would reveal the truth. If the land had changed—or Bartolomeo and all the animals were dead—it might be a warning or even a punishment. Such circumstances would render it difficult, if not impossible, for them to return to *Dehesa de Oro*. Without a guide, horses, water, or food, they would die out here, wandering in the wilderness until their strength deserted them.

"It will be all right," he murmured, stroking her hair. "You will see—it will be all right."

He wished he himself could believe it.

Chapter Fifteen

By the time the sun rose in the east, Maria had regained a measure of calm. She reminded herself that she was not given to outbursts of panic or fear. Her mother had taught her perseverance, along with patience, and she would not now embrace the tactics of Doña Inez, who made a great issue out of every incident, both large and small.

Still, it was daunting to discover that they were completely alone on the vast plain. El Cid and Caobo had disappeared, while Bartolomeo and his ass were both dead. At first, the old *Indio* had appeared only to be kneeling there, where Maria had last seen him, facing north, with an expression of great amazement, awe, and yes, happiness upon his weathered face.

When she and Don Diego went up to him and touched his shoulder, he toppled over, and they knew he was dead. On closer inspection, they saw that his eyes were wide open, the lashes and brows singed away, and the inner eye covered with a strange sort of film, such as Maria had never before seen.

"They are like the eyes of a blind man I once saw in Spain," Don Diego muttered, crossing himself as if to ward off evil. "This is indeed an incredible happening."

Maria brushed away tears and choked back a sob. "He was

my friend and a fine, good man! He did not deserve the suffering
he endured at the hands of the Spanish, and now he is dead.''

"Forgive me, little one, if I seem unfeeling." Diego grasped
Maria's shoulders and gently turned her away from the body
of her friend. "I am still grappling with the shock of what we
witnessed. At least, Bartolomeo died out here on the Ocean of
Grass, where he was born. He would be happy about that,
would he not?''

Maria nodded. Diego's understanding of Bartolomeo's feelings pleased her. Her own father always seemed to think he
was doing the Indians a favor by enslaving them, claiming he
was introducing them to modern society and religion. He never
realized that Indians had feelings of their own and wanted
nothing to do with modern society.

"During all the years of his captivity, Bartolomeo wanted
nothing more of life than to one day return to the Ocean of
Grass," she murmured. "Now, he will not have to go back to
the manure pile where he spent most of his life. Out here, his
spirit can fly free at last.''

"Come," Don Diego said. "We will gather stones to cover
him and protect his body from the wolves.''

They spent the better part of the morning burying Bartolomeo
and then butchered the ass for its meat, hide, bladder, and
stomach. The poor beast had died of a broken neck trying to
fight his hobbles, which had prevented him from fleeing along
with El Cid and Caobo.

By the time they finished, it was late in the day. They collected dried buffalo dung to make a fire to roast a portion of
the ass's meat. Maria used some of its blood to make a kind
of pudding to go with the meat, and rendered some of its fat
into a liquid they could drink instead of using the last of their
precious water. Without a means of transportation, they would
have to carry whatever they could and set off in the morning
in search of water.

"Caobo will return to us," Diego assured her that night as
they ate their meal before a fire which he had moved some
distance away from Bartolomeo's grave and the remains of the
ass. "If he still lives, the dog will find us. At this very moment,

he is probably sniffing the wind for our roasting meat. The scent will draw him to us as quickly as a rope tied around his neck.''

"And El Cid? What of your stallion? Do you think he will return, also?''

Don Diego's eyes looked bleak. " 'Tis much harder to predict his actions. By now, he desperately needs water. He will look for water first—and then grass. His next desire will be for companionship—of his own kind, not the human sort. If he thinks of me at all, it will be to wonder why I do not suddenly appear, bringing him a handful of corn. He has not the nature of a dog, to follow his nose and seek out his master. Caobo is accustomed to leaving and returning in his own good time. El Cid is not. His search for other horses will either lead him to La Reina or back to the *vaqueros,* for there are no other horses out here.''

"Perhaps he will wander alone forever. You may never see him again. I grieve for your loss, for I know how much that stallion means to you.''

Diego's eyes shone with a suspicious sheen. Having never witnessed a man's tears, Maria was deeply touched.

"I brought him a long way to lose him now, Maria, but I am not giving up hope. We will try to track him as best we can without Bartolomeo, for he will eventually lead us to water. I hope we can recover him before we encounter Indians. On foot, we are helpless. We should avoid firing my *pistola,* as I must save my ammunition in case of attack—all the more so since flight on horseback is no longer a possibility.''

"We could keep searching for the Indians with the idea of stealing back horses,'' she suggested. "Then we would once again be mounted and better able to search for El Cid.''

The idea made sense to her. They could sneak up on the Indians, mount a couple of horses, and herd the rest away before the *Indios* discovered them. No one would get hurt. If Don Diego first regained El Cid, however, he would want to ride shooting into the midst of the horse thieves. In that case, men would die.

"No, we will look first for El Cid, and pray he will lead us to water. If he has not broken his neck like Bartolomeo's ass, he will do just that. If he is lying dead somewhere, I hope we do *not* find him. I would prefer thinking of him running free in a place where there is more grass than he could ever eat."

"If he had all the grass in the world, he would still want a mate." She bit down on her wayward tongue. Why had she mentioned such a thing, when it would only give Diego pain?

Diego set down the dagger he had been using to cut slices of meat. He gave her a long look that heated her blood and stirred something to life within her. "Yes, he will be as lonely as I am without you to share my blankets, Maria."

It was yet another reference to all they did *not* share, because of her stubbornness.

"Forgive me, *señor,*" she finally said. "I should not have mentioned that about your stallion. I am sure he will be happy. Of *course* he will be happy."

"Maria." Don Diego sighed and leaned back against his saddle. "After all we have endured together, can you not call me Diego—at long last? There is no one to hear you resort to such a shocking informality. Neither is there anyone to see you, judge you, or keep you from doing anything you wish to do. We are completely alone now. We may die alone out here, without ever again setting eyes on another human being. Before I die, I should like to hear my name on your lips. Not *Don Diego,* but simply Diego."

"Diego . . ." she whispered. The sound of the name that often echoed in her dreams at night entranced her.

"What? I cannot hear you, Maria. You will have to say it louder."

"Diego!" she shouted, then sat back, grinning. "There! I have said it. Are you now satisfied?"

"Not quite." He slanted her another look that made her heart thump. "There are other pleasures I should like to experience before I die."

Sensing his intent, she moved first, widening the space between them. He regarded her silently for a moment, his disappointment obvious in his shadowed eyes and in the downward slant of his mouth.

She waited, *wanting* him to come after her. Her instinct to resist was so ingrained that she did not know how to tell him she now welcomed his pursuit, and indeed was growing desperate for it.

He suddenly looked too weary to make the effort.

Picking up his dagger, he wiped it on the grass and resheathed it in its leather casing. He avoided looking at her. "I am going to bed now, Maria. Tomorrow will be another hard day. We might as well sleep at the same time. We have little left to lose but our lives. If the savages want them, they can easily take them. I will be able to shoot only one anyway, before the rest overwhelm us, and I can do that as well if I sleep as if I do not. Weary as I am, I will not be able to stay awake tonight no matter how hard I try."

"Sí, señor. . . . I mean Don Diego . . . Diego."

"Well . . . a bit of progress," he drawled mockingly. "Give me another five years and perhaps I can persuade you to curl up beside me voluntarily, without having to force the issue. Give me twenty, and I might manage a kiss. Give me fifty, and . . . oh, forget it. 'Tis doubtful I will live another fifty years, especially out here."

His sarcasm stung. She had no answer for it except to move Bartolomeo's saddle closer to his. She lay down near him as if she had intended to curl up beside him. He steadfastly ignored the gesture; it was not enough to satisfy him. She could not blame him for being disappointed. It was not enough to satisfy her, either, but after spending most of the previous night in a state of terror, she, too, was exhausted.

They soon slept, and neither of them awoke until the morning sun bathed them in a radiant heat that promised to become unbearable. Before setting out, they ate as much as they could of the ass's meat, then loaded themselves down like pack animals. Diego gazed mournfully at the saddles—his and Bartolomeo's—which would have to be left behind. They were much too heavy to carry.

"We will take only the bridles," he told Maria. "With those, we can still ride bareback. Are you ready? Can you comfortably carry all you are taking?"

Maria nodded. "I am fit and strong . . . Diego. I have worked all my life. Have no fear I cannot keep up with you."

By mid-afternoon, they were both stumbling in the heat. Maria's mouth was drier than the pile of buffalo bones she saw baking in the sun. She wondered how long it had been since they had last spotted a fresh hoofprint or a pile of manure to indicate El Cid's passage.

"Stop," Diego commanded. He thrust the water gourd in her direction. "Drink. You seem ready to collapse."

"I am fine," she lied. "I need only a swallow of water."

The single swallow only made her thirst more ravenous, but she handed the water gourd back to Don Diego without comment. When he refused to take a drink himself, she protested. "You, too! You must drink some, too."

"I do not need it," he insisted. Beneath his metal helmet, the sweat poured down his face. His bronzed skin was pale.

"Drink, or I refuse to go another step," she declared, throwing down her burdens. "This heat is worse than anything we have yet experienced. Without water, *you* will soon collapse."

Diego grinned. "Now, I see why your stepmother laments your stubborn, rebellious nature. All right, I will allow myself a swallow if you will take one more."

She waited until he was finished before she argued. "That is enough for both of us. Who knows how long it will be until we find more water? We must conserve what we have."

Diego studied the barren horizon. "I hope El Cid's instincts are right. The grass is sparse here and the land hotter and drier. Little grows, except for those strange spiny plants over there. They are the sort that appear only in deserts."

"Spiny plants?" Maria squinted in the direction he was pointing. "My mother once told me how the *Indios* could always find water even where there was nothing but trees and plants with prickles on them. She said they cut the plants down and suck the moisture to be found in their hearts."

A short time later, they did just that. Don Diego employed his sword to cleave a large spiny plant in two, and they were able to refresh themselves on the astringent moisture that oozed from its center.

Not as good as water, Maria thought, her mouth puckering, but better than nothing. It relieved her thirst and gave her a brighter outlook on their situation. Best of all, among a stand of the prickly plants, they found more hoofprints from a single shod horse, indicating they were going in the right direction.

"He will lead us to water," Don Diego repeated. "Though I shudder to think of the damage being done to his hide from the spines on these plants."

"Unless he went crashing through them, probably very little. He is no fool. Like us, he will be careful."

They camped that night near a rocky butte and knew that on the morrow they would have to do some climbing. Maria sensed they were nearing a source of water. Scrubby vegetation clung to fissures in the rock. If nothing else, when it rained, water must sluice down the sides of the butte from the higher elevations. The vegetation was still dry, however, indicating no recent rainfall.

"Look!" Diego exclaimed, while searching for fuel for their evening fire. "El Cid must have stopped to graze here on these tender green leaves."

He had found some green scrub growing part way up the side of the butte. Some of the leaves had been stripped away, and the damage appeared fresh. "What do you think?" he asked, turning to her.

She smiled at his enthusiasm. It lit his rugged features like the light cast from a tallow dip. "If Bartolomeo were here, he could say for certain, but yes, I think you may be right."

They dined that night on meat she had roasted the night before. They made their beds on the incline of the butte and gazed up at a sky once again filled with stars. Maria could hardly move, and all her muscles ached, but she nonetheless felt a brimming satisfaction. They had survived their first day alone in the wilderness.

If they were to survive others, she would have to summon all the skills she had learned from Bartolomeo. These included snaring small game, finding water, and digging tubers and other edible plants. She and Don Diego were finally equals, facing the needs of each day standing shoulder to shoulder. All the things separating them no longer seemed to matter.

Neither she nor Don Diego could rely on anyone else; they had only each other. And *she* was better equipped to keep them alive than he was. His skill with horses, weapons, and the knowledge to be found in books would not help much when they had none of these things. If they found another river, it would be up to her to catch the fish in it. If they found the Indians, or the Indians found them, her ability to communicate might be the only thing to save them.

A single *pistola* could only do so much.

Don Diego's hand suddenly brushed hers. He entwined his fingers through her fingers. "What are you thinking, little one?"

She lacked the nerve to reveal her true thoughts. He was a man, after all, and might not appreciate hearing how much he needed a lowly woman. "I was just gazing at the stars and hoping that none of them fall on us tonight."

"They will not fall on us," he stated, as if he knew it for a fact. "Or if they do, the impact will be far away—not like last night."

" 'Tis a whole different feeling, tonight," she agreed. "The night wind is so sweet. And no odd light illuminates the horizon."

"The new moon is rising," he noted. "Last night, I saw no moon."

"Nor did I. The howling of the wolves seems normal, too." She listened for a moment to the wind and the wolves, the peculiar night music of the Ocean of Grass.

" 'Tis beautiful," he murmured. "I could almost believe we are the only two people alive on the earth, this night." He squeezed her hand. "It would not bother me if that were true, Maria. We would learn to live somehow."

"We could do it." She turned on her side to face him. "My mother's people have done it. They have lived more or less peacefully on this land since time before memory."

He, too, lay on his side, facing her. "But what sort of lives, Maria? I cannot imagine they are comfortable or happy. You cannot imagine it, either, can you? I have no desire to eat grubs, though I suspect I may be forced to do so before this is over. I see all this emptiness, and all I can think of is how I would like to fill it with horses and cattle. 'Tis a land made for grazing animals—when they eat down the grass in one place, they can move to another. There are broad stretches of desert-like land, but always there is grass growing somewhere. If forced to spend my life here, I would set about building my own empire—much like your father has done, except I see myself as enjoying it more, and showing far more compassion to those with whom I share this Eden.''

"Always you have the need to conquer and tame!" Maria exclaimed. " 'Tis almost a sickness within you—one that does not allow for compassion. Why can you not enjoy the land as you find it? Why must you seek to change everything?''

"Because I am a man, Maria, and that is what men do—conquer and tame and make things their own.''

As you would do with me, Maria thought, withdrawing her hand from his.

Nothing had changed; she was a fool if she believed otherwise. He still sought to dominate and change *her,* to bind her to him so she would *never* be free and must share in his dreams and ambitions, at the expense of her own.

He again grasped her hand and held it firmly. "As a woman, what would you do, Maria? Tell me, so I may understand what it is that keeps driving us apart.''

She thought for a moment. "I would . . . I would *respect* what I found in a strange place and . . . and attempt to understand it before I assumed it must be changed. I would try to see the good in it before I unwittingly destroyed it. I would not always assume that *my* way is the only good and right way. I would be open to . . . to new possibilities. I would hope to learn, not merely to condemn, or even to teach. I would try to cherish the beauty I found before I sought to replace it with some *new* beauty.''

"*Madre de Dios!* You ask much of a man, little one.'' He again lay back and locked his hands behind his head to pillow it. "Do you ask the same of yourself, Maria, when it comes to me? Are you willing to give *me* the same respect you demand

I give others? Or do you judge and condemn me outright because I was born a Spaniard?''

His questions gave her food for thought. She had no immediate answers, but suspected that she did indeed blame him for being both a man and a Spaniard. In truth, she constantly expected the worst from him, even when he demonstrated the best. He was *not* like her father, or any other man she had ever known. He was capable of gentleness as well as strength.

Trust. 'Twas so hard to trust! To open herself to disappointment in case she should prove to be wrong. She fell asleep pondering the dilemma, and awoke to find herself wrapped in Don Diego's arms, pressed intimately against him and immediately aware of all the possibilities inherent in their position. She managed to extricate herself from his embrace before he, too, awoke, but all that day, as they climbed the butte in the hot sunshine, she thought about what he had said. She *was* being unfair, and demanding more of him than she herself was willing to give. It was a sobering—disturbing—thought.

Something had shifted between them.

Diego did not know what it was or why it had happened or how, but he sensed it and was wildly exhilarated—and simultaneously dismayed. Now, when he had nothing to offer her, when he himself was reduced to nothing, she had begun watching him with new eyes. Eyes of sensual awareness and desire. Eyes of acceptance. Eyes that told him his advances would not now be rejected, as they had so often been rejected in the past.

He could not understand it. When he had possessed the power to change her life entirely, to protect and shield her from her father's cruelty, when he had been a man other men envied, when he rode a fine horse and could provide all manner of material comforts, she had been unwilling to give him so much as a smile for his efforts. Now, when he did nothing, and could provide little—even water, a necessity of life—her mouth softened whenever she looked at him. Her fox fire eyes welcomed him. Beckoned him. Teased and tormented him.

For the love of *Dios!* Did she not realize how precarious their situation was? Without a horse he felt naked, vulnerable, powerless ... even unworthy. He counted himself a mere shadow of a man.

He probably could have taken her last night—or even this morning. *He* had been aware of the intimacy of their position long before she had awakened and discovered it—from neck to knee their bodies had been pressed together—but something restrained him, and he feared taking advantage.

Never in his life had he felt so useless and inept! Nothing but his *pistola* and a small quantity of gunpowder stood between them and death. Whenever he thought about it, he became sick with fear. He had *always* had at least his horse to buttress his own opinion of himself. Even back in Spain, when he had been threatened with the king's wrath and the vengefulness of Don Toribio's relatives, he had never felt this helpless. As long as he could take his horses with him, he had known he could manage anywhere and make a new life for himself. But here ... alone in this wilderness ... with so little to sustain him ... and unable to impress Maria with his resourcefulness ... he had begun to doubt himself.

She had known the trick of cutting open the spiny plants to drink their moisture, not he. *She* knew the language of the Indians. *She* could catch fish, using only a sharpened stick or spear. *She* could find edible tubers. He still had his strength and brawn, but she had the clear advantage in knowledge. In all his lifetime, he had never felt so uncertain.

His father's doubts about him had severely undermined his self-confidence, but at least he had always had the security of knowing his father was wrong. It was a sudden, devastating shock to realize that out here, even his *father* would be less of a man than he had always been. In this huge, dangerous, humbling land, his own father would be greatly diminished. So would his cousin, Evaristo. For that matter, so would the King of Spain!

None of these men could begin to imagine the challenges this land presented. He himself had not been able to imagine them . . . and now, here he was, his life depending on a small, slender woman. If something happened to Maria . . .

His self-confidence was further shaken when, shortly after noon, she stopped and studied some holes in the rocky ground with great interest.

"What is it?" he asked, trudging back to her. "Have you found something?"

"Small animals live in these holes," she said excitedly. "Have we time to stop so I can try to catch one for our supper?"

How on earth did she expect to catch one?

"We should not stop yet," he said, asserting his authority. "Besides, if rodents live in those burrows, I am not yet hungry enough to eat one."

The light left her lovely eyes. "We should not disdain any food we might run across, Diego, for we will surely need it."

"You are right," he grudgingly agreed. "Stop, if you wish."

While she busied herself fashioning a snare from a length of braided horsehair taken from a bridle, Diego suddenly spotted a hare hopping past some rocks. He fumbled for his *pistola,* whipped it out, cocked it, and shot the creature on the spot. Maria jumped at the noise and dropped the snare. When she saw the bloodied animal—minus its head—crumpled against the rocks, she released a long sigh.

"There was no need to waste a shot, Diego. We could have used the snare to catch that rabbit."

"This was quicker." Diego blew away the smoke from his *pistola.* He would not allow her to destroy his pleasure and satisfaction at having secured their next meal. "Let us quickly clean and gut the animal, then go a bit further. I did not want to stop yet, anyway."

"All right, let us do it."

A short time later, they were once again on their way. ascending a steep rocky path going up the side of the butte. Suddenly, Maria again stopped and cocked her head, as if listening intently. "Diego, do you hear it?" she asked.

"Hear what?" He strode back to her, paused, and stood silently, his ears straining.

"Water!" she cried, and darted past him. "I am sure I hear the sound of falling water."

He had not heard a thing, but he dutifully followed her, hoping she was right. They climbed quickly and soon arrived at a spot where water trickled down between the boulders above and formed a miniature wading pool surrounded by sparse greenery. The leaves of some of the plants were stripped and shorn, as though an animal had eaten them. Diego looked around in rising excitement.

He did not see El Cid, but dared to hope that the stallion was nearby. Tilting back his head, he gave a short, sharp whistle, a signal he had trained El Cid to recognize and respond to. If the stallion were within hearing distance, he would come running, anticipating some reward.

"Maria, you are a marvel!" he exclaimed, while he was waiting.

She was already on her hands and knees, scooping up water in her palms and shamelessly slurping it. With water running down her chin, she grinned at him triumphantly. "I hardly dared hope I would find some. Come and drink, Diego. 'Tis the best water I have ever tasted."

"Any water would taste good right now." He knelt beside the little pool, cupped his own hands, and dipped them into the sparkling liquid. After drinking deeply, he splashed her, and she retreated, laughing.

"Water!" she crowed. "We have found water! And we have a nice fat hare for supper. Can life be any better than this?"

Yes, Diego thought, watching her. *Tonight, when I take you in my arms and teach you about being a woman, then it will be perfect, all a man could possibly need.*

Tonight, he would put an end to all the teasing, rejection, uncertainty, and torture. Tonight, he would finally make her his.

They played in the little pool, splashing each other, alternately drinking more water and dipping it up to spill over their heads and overheated bodies. This continued until Diego suddenly realized that they ought not to waste the precious resource. The trickle from above was only a small one and might soon run out, before they had even filled the water gourd or the stomach and bladder of the ass.

As he was lecturing Maria on the value of conservation, they both heard the muted thunder of hoofbeats. Jumping to his feet, Diego sprinted up the path that led to the top of the butte. He met El Cid, coming down—mane and tail streaming, nostrils flared to scent him, eyes searching for the treat he was accustomed to receiving when he responded to Diego's signal.

Diego had no treat to give him. When the big, white horse skidded to a halt in front of him, he threw his arms around the stallion's neck and hugged him. No words could pass the huge lump in his throat.

It was Maria, coming up behind him, who spoke: "The most noble of horses has returned to his beloved master. And no sight on earth could be more beautiful to behold."

Diego could only nod in agreement. This fleet-footed, powerful animal did not need him; he needed it. He was humbly grateful for the stallion's loyalty to his training. Diego had known and commanded horses all his life, but he had never fully comprehended how miraculous it was that these magnificent animals chose to obey and serve him. El Cid and all the rest of his species were a precious gift from God to mankind. Men ought never to forget it or take them for granted or resort to cruelty in their care or training. If he had been cruel, El Cid would never have answered his summons. He would have run the other way and never looked back.

"I am so happy you are reunited!" Maria clapped her hands with joy, and the stallion lifted his head and pricked his ears in her direction.

Diego quickly grabbed the short rope hanging from his braided halter. It was his custom to turn horses out wearing just such a combination—a halter with a shortened rope attached that was unlikely to catch upon anything.

"Welcome back, old comrade," he murmured soothingly. "Do not be afraid of Maria. She, too, is your friend."

Together, he and Maria led the stallion back toward the pool.

Chapter Sixteen

That night they fed El Cid every green thing they could find. Maria was delighted when he consented to eat from her fingers and allowed her to get close to him and gently stroke his neck. Diego warned her that the horse had once bitten and broken a man's finger for being so bold, but she was determined to overcome the stallion's distrust, so that he would accept her as he did Diego.

After they fed him Diego reapplied his hobbles and turned his attention to bathing in the little pool. Maria tended the roasting meat while he did so, but could not help noticing the care he was taking to get himself as clean as possible. He removed all his upper garments as well as his boots, and stood beneath the trickling water to wet his hair and upper body.

She wished she had thought to replenish their water supply before he used up all the water—or dirtied it. Seeing her squinting at him in the gathering darkness, he called out: "In case you are wondering, I have already filled the gourd and our new containers. Cease staring at me so disapprovingly and instead, come join me."

His hands went to the waist of his trunk hose, and he started to peel them downward. Shocked, she spun back to the fire and their supper. Did he actually intend to stand naked in her presence, as if it were perfectly normal?

"Maria, this feels wonderful! Come on. There's room enough for two beneath this delightful spill of water. I will scrub you, and you can scrub me."

"I have to tend the meat, or it will burn! Anyway, we have no soap. You will have to use sand for your scrubbing, like the *Indios* do, and it will hardly be the pleasant experience you are imagining."

"If the experience involves you, it will be pleasant. Sand or soap—makes no difference to me."

"In the cooler night air, you will take a chill," she scolded, still refusing to look at him. "You had better get out of there."

"A chill! After the day's heat, I would welcome a chill. 'Tis glorious to once again feel clean. Get over here, Maria. You can keep your eyes closed if you must. Only come and bathe with me."

The thought was tempting—but also terrifying. She knew where bathing with him would lead. She was suddenly shy and afraid to reveal her own body, not to mention feeling nervous about seeing all of his body. She *had* seen him, of course, and he had seen her—but that was a long time ago, so long she had half forgotten that first night they had met.

Besides, playing naked in a pool was different: a brazen, wanton thing to do. She could manage a few heated kisses, perhaps even a caress or two, if she could keep her misgivings from overwhelming her, as they so often did. But to boldly remove all her garments and cavort with him in the light of a rising moon . . . well, that was beyond her. She had never done such a thing.

She jumped when he suddenly touched her shoulder.

"Relax, little one." He chuckled in her ear. "For the sake of your modesty, I have made myself decent. Why this shyness? I have already seen you, and you have seen me. At least, now, we are better acquainted. Here." Reaching around her, he took the stick she had been using to poke the meat and test its doneness.

"Let me tend the meat, while you go and bathe. I will not even look at you."

"Do you promise?" She glanced over her shoulder at him. He was decent, but barely. He held the skin of the rabbit he had killed in front of his manly parts.

He noted where she was looking and grinned—a boyish, mischievous grin. "I thought you might like me better if I wore a skin, instead of Spanish clothing. Do I look like an *Indio*, now? What do you think?"

Jerking her head around, she fought laughter. Oh, he was wicked! Wicked and fun. "Perhaps I will go and bathe, after all. If the meat burns, you are responsible. 'Tis all we have to eat tonight, so you had better keep your eye on it—and not on me, while I am bathing."

Dios! She sounded prim and proper, almost like Doña Inez, or some other Spanish lady who spent most of her time cultivating piety and condemning all human pleasures.

Diego squatted in front of the little cook fire, and she quickly rose and went to the pool. Once there, she stripped off her garments, bathed and scrubbed herself with a handful of sand, then struggled back into her clothing, for she had nothing else to wear. Her belongings had all been lost when Gaspar got carried away in the flood.

Finger-combing her wet hair, she returned to Don Diego at the cook fire, all the while trying not to gawk at his bare buttocks as he bent over the meat.

At her approach, he looked up. "There, now. You feel better, do you not?" He sounded smug.

She nodded.

His eyes roamed over her approvingly. "You certainly look better—cleaner and more refreshed. Too bad you lack clean clothing. Of course, you could always remove your garments, wash them, and allow them to dry tonight while we are sleeping."

The thought *had* crossed her mind that she would love to wash her soiled and tattered skirt and blouse. Her garments had not had a washing since Diego pulled her from the raging waters of the flood that had taken Gaspar and all her belongings.

"My clothing probably would not be dry by morning," she pointed out, kneeling down beside him. "Your efforts to see me naked again are all for naught, Diego. I will not oblige you. However, in the morning I might wash my garments while they are still on me and allow the sun to dry them as we continue our search for the horses and the *Indios*."

He flashed her another wicked grin. "I approve of that plan. Seeing you in wet clothing will be almost as good as seeing you naked. You could wear rags and still be beautiful, Maria. Indeed, I *have* seen you in rags and thought you were as lovely as any highborn princess."

Self-conscious beneath his admiring scrutiny, she pushed her damp hair back from her temples. "Since I lost my comb my hair is impossibly tangled, and without my hat, my nose is burned from the sun. I do not *feel* lovely, *señor*—Diego—but thank you for telling me I am."

His brow furrowed. "You lost all that when the water carried away poor Gaspar?"

"I lost everything he was carrying. Do you not remember?"

"Of course, I remember! But . . . you have never once complained of your losses, so I myself forgot about them. Is that why you have taken to braiding your hair and tying the end with a bit of leather?"

"It was the only thing I could do with it to keep it from becoming a nest fit for rodents."

"Dios! I wondered why you were doing it. I missed seeing your hair floating about your shoulders like some black, silky cloud. I should have realized you no longer had a comb to tame it. From now on, you must use mine."

"May I use it now?" she asked, blushing, her cheeks burning like hot coals.

"After we eat," he said. "The meat is done."

She wondered how he was going to eat and still shield his manly parts from her gaze. He solved the problem by setting aside the rabbit skin and laying his doublet over his lap as they ate. The meat was delicious, and they savored every bite— even sucking the tender marrow from the bones.

"Caobo would relish these," she said, indicating the little pile of bones with a nod.

It was fully dark now, except for the glow of the smoldering fire and the light of the moon.

"Yes," Diego said. "I miss him. I thought he would be the first to return to us—and instead, it was El Cid we found. I wonder if he encountered a pack of wolves and they ran him off their territory, or even killed him."

"We must not allow ourselves to think sad thoughts." Maria voiced a truth she had learned long ago, one that often quelled her own despair. "If we do, we will only become miserable and fail to notice the beauty surrounding us."

"And is that how you have survived all these years, living under the rule of your father and stepmother?"

"Yes," she confided, but did not mention that she had fed her spirit with the hope of escape and taking horses to the Indians. "Whenever I am angry, unhappy, or bitter, I can still find joy in the blue of the sky, the green of the grass, or even the scent of a horse."

"The scent of a horse?" One corner of his lips curved upward. "And here I thought I was the only one who enjoyed such a simple, rustic pleasure."

"Being an Indian and a female, I was not allowed near the horses, but I could still smell them and watch them and take pleasure in their grace and beauty."

"The way I take pleasure in watching you. You need not explain. I understand perfectly. Maria . . ." He held out his hand to her. "Will you come and sit between my legs and let me comb your hair for you?"

He held up a silver-toothed comb, which she already knew was engraved with fruits and flowers and must have come from Spain. Only a rich man would own such a tool for his own personal grooming; the first time she had seen it she had admired and coveted it. It was remarkable it had survived the rigors of the journey thus far.

"I can comb it myself," she demurred. "You need not bother yourself with my tangled hair."

"I would *prefer* doing it—'tis no bother."

She rose then and went to sit in front of him as he faced sideways to the fire. He pulled her back between his legs, his bare knees rising one on each side of her. Then he began to comb her hair, using long gentle strokes, starting at her scalp and ending at the tips of her waist-length tresses.

If she were a cat, she would have purred.

As it was, she could not stop herself from reveling in the sensation of his touch. Leaning back against him, she allowed him to bring his arms around her and comb her hair as she had often done it—a small handful at a time, held out in front of her, where she could see it.

"I have never combed a woman's hair before," he murmured against her neck. He nuzzled and kissed her in the crook of her neck and shoulder.

The intimacy made her shiver.

"I have never before had anyone comb my hair—except my mother, when I was a child. I cannot remember it being this pleasurable."

"Pleasure is what I seek to give you, Maria, if you will only allow it."

By now, she was so relaxed she could deny him nothing. His hand lightly brushed her breast and then closed upon it. She arched her back and grew still and breathless, focusing upon this new sensation. Through the fabric of her blouse, he stroked and squeezed her. Setting down the comb, he gently grasped her other breast, so that he held them both now and cupped her fullness. She moaned softly in her throat, her body coming alive as his hands moved over her.

She could find no words to stop him as he pulled down her bodice and exposed her upper body. While he toyed with her breasts, he kissed and nuzzled her neck, whispering sweet compliments that further eroded her resistance.

"How beautiful you are, Maria! How I have longed to do just this. To hold and touch you. To caress your tenderness. Your breasts are exquisite—so soft and full. So very womanly."

He kept one hand on her breasts, while the other roamed

lower. Pulling up her skirt, he reached beneath it. "Please don't ask me to stop, Maria."

She could no more fight him than keep a star from falling. The little voice that had always urged caution—warning her away from him—was strangely silent. Perhaps it had given up, or simply bowed to the inevitable. She wore no undergarments such as Doña Inez used to armor herself against any possible invasion. Her stepmother had not provided any to go with her new clothing. Maria preferred comfort over propriety, any-way—it was the single advantage she could claim to being half savage.

Except at her womanly time, she avoided wearing undergar-ments, and for some reason, on this journey her womanly time had not arrived when it usually did. Perhaps the scarcity of food and water had somehow affected her normal functioning. Whatever the reason, she was glad there were no awkward barriers to slow Don Diego in his quest to explore her body.

He gently touched her female passage, as if to give her the chance to get used to him touching her there . . . and she did need time to accustom herself to the heat the action generated. As his fingers began to move, exploring, she stiffened against the shocking intimacy.

He took her earlobe between his lips and nibbled it, then whispered: " 'Tis all right, Maria. I swear I will not hurt you. Let me touch as you as I will. You must learn the language of lovers, the silent communication a man and woman may use to tease and excite each other."

As he spoke, he pushed against her from behind. She had once overheard Juana giggling with another maidservant, exclaiming about the size of "Pedro's man-root, that great old-thing he likes to poke me with." She thought of Diego poking her, and her stomach muscles clenched in delicious anticipation—but he felt so huge! Would he tear her asunder?

As his fingers caressed and stroked her, she forgot to worry. She could only marvel at these new sensations—these marvel-ous delights she had never before experienced. He was so gentle! Yet demanding, too. He would not allow her to squirm away from him or protect her modesty. He even pressed a finger into her, stretching and manipulating her tender tissues, which resulted in a kind of pleasure-pain.

He paid particular attention to a secret nubbin of flesh that she had never realized was so sensitive. A pressure began to build within her, and she wanted to clench and unclench the muscles of her female passage. But it was all so strange and new! She did not know what was right or wrong, and questioned what she was supposed to be feeling.

"Ah, Maria! You are almost ready for me. Relax and let the feelings come, my love."

Diego turned her then, bending her backward, and kissing her—fusing their mouths together while he maneuvered her body so that she lay half beneath him. He lay on his side, where he could kiss and caress her at the same time. Now, as he kissed her, he also stroked her between her legs, and she wrapped her arms around his neck and surrendered to the building heat that threatened to consume her.

She wanted this man. Wanted to become a woman. *His* woman. His lover. She had fought it for so long—her own desires and his. Now, there was only one desire, to possess and be possessed. To join with this man who had teased and tempted her, saved her life on more than one occasion, taught her to ride a horse, and to relish her own femininity.

Madre de Dios! She wanted him inside her. Now. This very instant.

She clawed his back and raised her hips off the ground. She writhed against his busy fingers. She entwined her tongue with his and silently urged him—begged him—to take her.

"Soon, little one, soon!" he promised.

He seized one of her hands and pushed it downward between them. The doublet was gone from his lap. It lay bunched and crushed beneath her hip. Nothing covered him now, and he wordlessly offered himself for her to explore. With a trembling hand she discovered the exact size, feel, and shape of him.

He groaned at her touch. Then he was moving over her. "Maria, I can wait no longer! Forgive me, little one. If I hurt you, I will make it up to you later. But now . . . now, I must have you!"

He poised over her a moment, his face and shoulders blocking out the sky and moon. Then he plunged into her. She felt a sharp, searing pain—an exquisite agony as something tore apart inside her. She gasped and pushed him away, never having suspected how much their joining would hurt. He thrust deeper still, but she cried out and begged him to stop.

"Open to me, Maria! Do not fight it. Soon, you will feel the pleasure, too."

She could not believe it. This was terrible—not at all as she had expected! His caresses had promised so much. How could it have turned to pain so quickly?

He remained still for only a moment before the urge to move seemed to overwhelm him. He thrust once. Then twice. A frenzy overcame him, and he plunged and bucked like a stallion, driving himself into her, withdrawing, and then driving again . . . and again . . . and again.

At first, she held herself still and rigid, enduring rather than enjoying, resisting the pain, pressure . . . and pleasure. Yes, there *was* pleasure—a glimmer of it—and a need to squeeze and hold him! Could she do it? Could she fight through the pain to reach the pleasure?

The next time he thrust inside her, she thrust back, meeting him halfway. "Yes!" he urged. "Yes, Maria! Follow me. I will show you the way."

She caught his rhythm and surrendered everything. Gave him the eagerness and enthusiasm he wanted. And in return . . . *rapture!* Quite unexpectedly, her body shuddered with it. She trembled with ecstasy as wave after wave of intense pleasure flowed through her body. She clasped and held him, squeezing her inner muscles in a spasm of delight. He groaned her name and stiffened in a last, final contortion, flooding her with his seed.

Long moments passed. So spent was their energy that they could not move. He finally rolled to one side. "Forgive me, Maria. I did not mean to go so quickly, or cause you pain. I know it was your first time. You feared it for so long, dreading what you thought it might be. But I had to *show* you. . ."

He sounded anxious and worried. She had expected triumph,

not solicitude. If she loved him for nothing else, she would have loved him for that.

"Hush," she said. "It was wonderful. You need not apologize. After the pain, there came . . . a wondrous release."

He leaned over her. "Really? You felt it? You truly felt it?"

Even now, he was less triumphant than genuinely pleased; *her* pleasure seemed to matter more to him than his own, which had been apparent. Her love for him deepened. What manner of man was he—this Spaniard—to even worry about a woman's pleasure?

"Yes," she admitted. "Was I not supposed to feel it? Am I not normal? Should I be weeping now, as so many women do afterwards?"

"No! Oh, no. Of course, you should not be weeping. You came willingly each step of the way, so what need is there for tears? Still, a woman's first time is often painful, or so I have been told. I have not deflowered enough virgins to have learned this all on my own."

"That reminds me," she said, smiling. "I have no flower in my hair." The opportunity to tease him was too good to let pass. "You said you would never touch me unless I tucked a blossom into my hair to signal my readiness."

"What—no blossom? *Cristo!* I forgot. Now, you *will* hate me, won't you?"

"No, Diego," she whispered. "I wish I could. I *should*. But somehow, I cannot." She reached for him and drew him down to her. "Diego, I . . . I . . ."

"What?" he murmured. "Say it, Maria. Say what you feel."

" 'Tis not what I *want* to feel! You have forced me to it. Not to the lovemaking, no. In the end, I did come willingly to that. But to the *loving* . . . to this sweet, aching possessiveness I feel for you—Diego, it scares me so! What if I now lose you?"

"You will not lose me, Maria." He took her hand and kissed her fingertips. "You belong to me, now. You are mine, and I am yours. Your father gave you to me, so you have been mine for a long time, but that is not the way I wanted you. I wanted you to want *me* in return."

"*Dios* help me, I *do* want you!" she cried, clutching at him. "That is what frightens me so. Now, I no longer belong to me anymore!"

"We belong to each other, my little love." In the waning light and warmth from the fire, he gazed down at her with great tenderness. "What can be so wrong or fearful about that? 'Tis meant to be. I knew when I first saw you, sleeping naked in my bed, that it was meant to be. What exists between us, Maria, is rare and special. Your father does not enter into it. I will protect and shield you always. No one will ever hurt you again. I will not allow it."

Now, her tears started. They gathered in her eyes and spilled unchecked down her cheeks. She wanted so much to believe him!

"I love you, Diego." She sniffed and swiped at her tears. "But I am half-*Indio*, and you are a Spaniard. My father and stepmother intend you should marry a Spaniard."

"Hush." He placed his hand over her mouth. "Out here, we are Diego and Maria, two people who love each other— not Spaniard and *Indio*, the conqueror and the conquered. We will find a way to circumvent your father's plans for me. We will chart our own course, Maria."

"But what about—?"

Again, his hand covered her mouth, preventing her from voicing yet another objection. In her head, she voiced them anyway: *What if we have children? And what about my intention to help the Indians by giving them horses? Do you still insist on searching for gold and using Indian slaves to mine it?*

She foresaw so many objections—so many stumbling blocks to their happiness.

"We will deal with one problem at a time," he told her. "Right now, our first problem is survival. After that, 'tis finding the Indians and regaining the horses they stole. I will not kill your people if I can avoid it, Maria—especially your brother assuming he is involved—but I will warn them. They cannot take my horses—or your father's—and not expect reprisals. This one time, for *your* sake, I will overlook their crimes. But if they dare come to steal from me again—"

"They will not! If we find them, I myself will talk to them. I will urge them to avoid *Dehesa de Oro* and go somewhere else to steal horses."

Realizing what she had just said, she abruptly shut her mouth. Now, it would come: their first fight after becoming lovers. He would say the Indians should not be allowed to have horses, either his or anyone else's.

"You think they *should* have horses," he said flatly.

"Diego, you have seen what it is like out here. You *know* now why they want horses."

"Yes, I know," he sighed. "But they cannot have mine or your father's. Horses are. . . . Maria, they *belong* to the white man! We are the only ones who know how to ride or train them."

More tears trickled down her cheeks. She wanted to say, "See? I told you so. It can never work out between us," but she said nothing. Their dilemma must now be apparent, and he would regret having taken this step.

"Maria, forget the damn horses!" He pressed against her, allowing her to feel the full weight of his body. "I will not allow horses or anything else to come between us. We will deal with these things one at a time. Promise me you will try. We may never find the Indians or the horses. It may never be an issue. We could die of hunger or thirst out here. Why are we even discussing this?"

He was right. They could both die tomorrow. They could wander the Ocean of Grass for a long, long time, and never encounter another human being, much less a valuable horse. Why waste the precious time they had together arguing about it?

"Love me again, Diego. Keep me from thinking. Tonight, I want only to feel. To feel you inside me, over me, under me, all around me—"

"Gladly, little one. From now on, I will keep you so busy loving me that you will have no time to think or argue."

He kissed her again, and she was once again lost to sensation, with no thought in her head but to please and be pleased by him.

* * *

One day melted into another, and Diego remained true to his word. He kept her so busy loving him that there was no room in her mind for worry or doubt. They retraced their steps back to where they had last spotted signs of the stolen horses and resumed their search, though the trail was now fainter and interruptions more frequent.

Diego took her up in front of him on El Cid, but their close proximity to each other meant they could not keep their hands to themselves. Time and again, his hands would start roaming her body, or she would wriggle against his lap, and they would soon have to stop, tumble off the stallion, and seek release from the mutual fever that raged inside them.

They had gone for so long *without* touching each other! Now, they could barely go a half day without indulging themselves. They wasted so much time dressing and undressing that Diego laughingly suggested they would do better to ride naked. If it were not for the certainty of being burned by the sun, Maria would have agreed.

They experimented with all sorts of positions, even attempting to join their bodies while on horseback, an effort which did not succeed, except to provoke laughter and teasing. They were so intent on sensual pleasure that they often forgot to hunt or eat or keep watch for water. They hungered and thirsted more for each other than they did for food and drink. Still, Maria managed to snare small game and find enough tubers to ensure they did not starve.

Once, Diego got close enough to a small deer, crippled in one leg, to shoot it, and then they feasted. One night it rained, soaking them as they lay naked in each other's arms. Completely nude, they got up and ran around, trying to fill water containers and entrap water in Maria's skirt, so that El Cid could drink his fill.

Another night, they stayed awake all night talking, sharing important moments from their past. Maria was relieved to learn the whole story of the murder that had driven Don Diego to seek refuge in the New World. He did not mention his plans for regaining his inheritance and exposing his wicked cousin, Evaristo, so Maria hoped his desire for revenge was dying— driven away by the power of her kisses.

She knew she held him enthralled, as he did her, and all these questions and concerns seemed far away and unreal. Life revolved around the eternal hunt for food, water, and sexual release, all of which they managed with magnificent success— particularly the latter. Not even the lack of shelter overly concerned them. Maria knew they would eventually have to think about it, but for now, there was only Diego, and a happiness she had waited all her life to find.

It was fortunate they had so much to occupy them, for the goal of locating the horses proved amazingly elusive. Twice, they stumbled across evidence of human encampment, including horses, but their quarry remained somewhere far ahead of them. Wherever the Indians were going, they kept moving— at a faster pace than Maria and Diego, which was only natural, since they were probably not stopping so often.

Then came the morning when Maria awoke—naked, as usual—to find something sharp as a knife blade pressed to her throat. A short distance away, six short, dirty, half-naked men held a struggling Diego, and behind him, a dozen others were trying to get a *lazo* around a rearing El Cid.

They had not found the Indians. The Indians had found them.

Chapter Seventeen

"We are friends! We come in peace." Struggling to contain her fear, Maria searched the faces of their captors for anyone who looked like Santelmo.

None did. However, it had been years since she had last seen her brother, and he might have changed as much as she had. When the two men holding her realized she spoke their language, they exchanged glances of amazement and uncertainty. But those engaged in subduing Diego never paused in their efforts. One of them lifted a large rock and raised it high over Diego's head. There was no doubt the man intended to drop it and crush Diego's skull.

"No!" Maria screamed. "Don't kill him! I am an *Indio,* and we have only come here to find my brother."

The man holding her grunted and shouted something to the others. In her panic, Maria had trouble understanding what he was saying, but it sounded like: "Stop! Do not kill him yet."

As her captors released her, she scrambled to her feet. The man threatening Diego reluctantly lowered the rock, but his five comrades hung onto their prize. They looked pleased to have captured a Spaniard, and eager to finish him off. Grabbing her skirt to cover her nakedness, Maria confronted them.

"We are not your enemies! Let him go," she pleaded, "and tell your friends to leave the horse alone. The stallion is hobbled. See? His legs are restrained. He cannot flee, but in his struggles he may hurt himself—or one of *you* will get hurt."

The Indians muttered among themselves, making guttural sounds and gestures, only half of which Maria understood. They spoke too rapidly for her to follow. Although she knew their language she had only conversed with Bartolomeo, and he had had a slower, more deliberate manner of speaking. As they debated whether or not to heed her advice, these men sounded like a flock of chattering water fowl.

At last, pointing to El Cid's hobbles, his captors backed away from the horse and eased the pressure on the three *lazos* they had managed to get around his neck. The stallion immediately stopped fighting. All his muscles quivered as he faced them, head held high, ears erect. He appeared to be wondering what sort of men these were, and if they meant to harm him.

"Who are you?" one of the Indians demanded.

Maria saw that he had the same wild, black hair as the others and a badly scarred face, and wore only a scrap of deerskin to conceal his private parts. He also had the same burning black eyes—fox fire eyes!—she had always been accused of having. Indeed, every *Indio* there had eyes like hers, and excitement leapt in her heart. These men *had* to have come from her mother's people.

"I am one of *you,*" she responded, straightening and eyeing them proudly. "My mother was an *Indio* captured by the Spanish many years ago. Perhaps you know of my brother, Santelmo, who fled the Spanish and attempted to return to you? I do not know if he made it—or even if he is still alive, but we have come here in search of him."

"Santelmo? Santelmo!" Again, the men chattered among themselves.

"Maria! What are they saying?" Diego called out to her. "What did you tell them?"

By now he was on his feet, but two men still held him by the arms. He had stopped struggling when the Indians started listening, but she could tell he was wary and ready to fight.

"I told them about my brother, and explained how we came here looking for him. I made no mention of the stolen horses. When we are so outnumbered, it would be foolish to state our true purpose."

"Good girl! So far, you have said all the right things to keep us alive. . . . Where did they learn about *lazos?* Are they from your mother's tribe?"

Maria nodded. "I think so. Mark their eyes, Diego. They have my eyes."

"Dios!" he exploded. "You are right. They have fox fire eyes—and I thought you were the only one in the world to have them."

The two men holding Diego abruptly released him. Giving them a look of annoyance, he rubbed his arms, while one of them grumbled: "Do not try to escape, Spaniard. You are now our prisoner. Because of the girl we will allow you to live, but if you run away we will come after you and slay you."

"What is he saying?" Diego questioned, and Maria saw frustration as well as anger in his face.

She translated the warning, then added: "You must be careful not to offend them, Diego. My mother once told me it was not unusual among her people for a captured enemy to be taken home to the women for torture. I do not think they will harm me, but as a Spaniard you are feared and hated. The wives and mothers of any *Indio* killed or enslaved by my father or other Spaniards will want their revenge."

"My *pistola!*" Diego suddenly cried, as an Indian pawing through their belongings lifted the weapon with obvious glee.

"Let him have it," Maria counseled. "All we possess belongs to them now—including El Cid. There are twenty of them, and only two of us," she reminded him.

"Not El Cid!" Diego's eyes locked with hers. "Not my horse, Maria. I cannot allow these ignorant savages to claim my horse."

Her heart went out to him. For the first time in his life he was discovering how it felt to be entirely at the mercy of other men—to possibly be a slave, if he even managed to survive. In the blink of an eye he had gone from conqueror to conquered.

She had long wished to see a proud Spaniard humbled and brought low, but now, she derived no enjoyment from the moment. Instead, she wept inside for Diego.

"Your horse or your life, Diego. That is the choice."

"I would sooner cut out my own heart!" he snapped.

"They will cut it out for you," she retorted, "and their rage may then turn on me. For now, behave as if you are pleased to share your wealth with them, at least until we discover if these are the Indians we seek. Whether they are or not, there will be time enough later to plot your escape."

"*My* escape?" His gaze held hers. "What do you mean—*my* escape? I have no intention of leaving here without you."

She had no time to answer, for the Indians were gathering all their things and motioning for her and Diego to follow the scar-faced, bandy-legged leader who had first spoken to her. They barely gave them time to dress before they were prodding them with sharpened sticks to encourage them to move faster.

"Tell your Spaniard to bring the horse," the leader ordered. "Be sure he knows the animal belongs to us now. We will use him to cover our mares, and then we will have *more* horses."

"Mares? You have horses?"

The Indian proudly nodded. "And if your Spaniard tries to run away and take the stallion with him, we will shoot him with his own *pistola.*"

"But how do you even know about horses and *pistolas?*"

"We know," the *Indio* said, his black eyes fiery. "No longer are we a poor, helpless race. We have a *cacique* who has opened our eyes and taught us much. He once lived among the Spanish and knows all their ways."

"His name. What is his name?"

"You have already spoken it."

"*Santelmo!*"

"Yes." The leader nodded. "It is for him to say if you are his sister. If indeed you are, why have you given yourself to an enemy? For many days now, we have been following you. We have seen how you behave with one another. Have you no shame? We can understand how he might have compelled you to lie with him, but your own eagerness to yield to his wishes surprises us. This we do not understand. Until you spoke to us, we had planned to capture you both and take him back to the women for torture and you to be a slave. We may still do that. Santelmo will make the decision.''

''Maria, tell me what he is saying.''

While she and the Indian had been talking, Diego had come to stand beside her. He bristled with protectiveness and jealousy, and she feared what he might do—or try to do—if he understood their conversation.

''I will tell you later,'' she said. ''For now, you must fetch El Cid. They are taking us to their *cacique.*''

''Their *cacique!* That is a Spanish term. It means a nobleman, or a *patrón*. How do they even know it?''

''They know many things that would surprise you, Diego. These are not the poor primitive savages you expected to find.'' Excitement and elation swept Maria. Soon, she would see her brother!

''Then who *are* these people?''

''Patience, Diego. Soon, we will know.''

But it did not happen soon. Four days passed before their party arrived in the vicinity of the main body of the Indians. The Indians refused to allow her or Diego to ride El Cid, and with everyone on foot, they made slow progress. Maria only knew they were nearing the others when the leader of the group finally chose to tell her.

''Tomorrow, you will see our *cacique.*'' It was almost the first thing he had said to her—other than terse commands— since their capture. ''By this time tomorrow, unless our *cacique* says otherwise, your Spaniard will be in the hands of the women, and your own fate will be decided.''

Maria knew better than to argue. For four days they had been silently but closely guarded. All her attempts at conversation had been met with silence. Even she and Diego were not permitted to speak to each other. Maria had only to look at Diego to see that his ire was growing. Patience did not come easily to a man accustomed to giving orders to others. Maria knew how much he resented his helplessness, but there was nothing she could do to assist him. At night, the Indians bound them hand and foot, or staked them out spread-eagled on the ground. They could not have run away or overpowered their captors had they tried.

The region in which they camped this last night before joining the tribe differed greatly from the grassy, often arid plain. They had been traveling in the direction of a ridge of high sierras, and had now reached the foothills of those rugged mountains. Here, the vegetation included stands of *sotol* palms and prickly *tuna* at the lower elevations, while cedars and dwarf oaks speared the sky on the heights. The air was cooler, and carried the scent of the cedars.

It was a different sort of wilderness—one uniquely suited to support human beings. Water spilled down from the mountain to form many little streams and rivulets. Rabbits and other small game abounded. Black-horned antelope watched them curiously from a safe distance, and high up on a rocky promontory, a solitary black bear gazed down at them.

They dined that night on partridge, a small, blue-gray fowl. Thousands existed in this place. Roasted whole, the meat of the bird was excellent, but Maria had little appetite, so anxious was she over the outcome of the following day.

"Tomorrow, we will join the main body of the Indians," she managed to whisper to Diego, as they sat across from each other at the cook fire.

" 'Tis about time," Diego grumbled. "I was afraid we were going to spend the rest of our lives trudging on foot across these uninhabited plains."

They are inhabited, Maria wanted to argue, *by my people,* but there was no point arguing with an opinionated Spaniard. Besides, the leader of the Indians was watching them intently, as if suspecting them of plotting escape. Beneath the curved-up brim of Diego's metal hat, his glowing eyes beamed disapproval. The man had appropriated Diego's armor and wore it even at night, so proud was he of his new acquisitions.

"Maria," Diego whispered, his tone urgent. "Listen to me.

This may be our last opportunity to speak before we reach the Indians.''

Maria feigned great interest in the remains of her partridge. "Take care. The leader sees everything, Diego. He is watching us now.''

"Old Scar-Face?" Diego lifted a tiny meaty bone to his mouth and paused before eating to whisper: "He does like to spy on us, does he not?''

Scar-Face. It was a good name for the leader. He did indeed have a wicked-looking scar that ran from browline to jawline. Someone had slashed him to the bone, nearly destroying the eye on that side of his face.

"What do you wish to tell me, Diego? Say it quickly, before he comes over here and stops us.''

"If your brother is not among the Indians tomorrow, give me some signal. Cough, or something. I will then leap onto El Cid's back, trample any Indians in my path to you, and grab you up in front of me. Before they realize what is happening, we will escape.''

"Diego, they will only shoot us with your *pistola*.''

"They have no experience with the weapon. I saw them studying it the other day. They are afraid to shoot it, or else they would have done so by now. We could probably have escaped any time we chose these last few days, but I wanted to see where they would lead us—and learn about the fate of La Reina and the other horses, assuming they have them in their possession.''

"Scar-Face claims they do have other horses and weapons. I have had no chance to tell you this. Whether or not La Reina is among them, I cannot say, but—''

"If they have horses, of course, she is! Where else would they have gotten horses, except from your father? My only fear is that by now they may have slain and eaten her.''

"No, they understand how horses should be used, Diego. They intend for El Cid to cover their mares and produce more horses.''

"That is a relief—of a sort. Fortunately, they fear El Cid. 'Tis a great advantage that only I myself can handle him. I will

be leading him tomorrow, and once I am on his back, I know
a few tricks to—''

"Hush! Scar-Face is coming. Do not worry. I will cough if
I think we must flee.''

That night the Indians again bound them, but they were up
early the next morning and on their way again. Deeper into the
foothills they went, and now began to encounter sentinels.
Several times, Maria spotted a single Indian watching their
approach from some high, lonely place. Scar-Face waved to
each of these men, who then disappeared, racing off to tell
others of their arrival.

Shortly after noon, after climbing a steep, rocky pass, they
finally spotted the Indian village. It lay in a pretty, green valley
nestled in the embrace of towering hills, which sheltered it
from the ever-present wind. Maria could see at once that these
people were different from the Indians who dwelled in the
south. The southern Indians had long planted maize, cultivated
fields of vegetables and squash, and built solid permanent
homes. These mountain dwellers were a far rougher lot: a small,
dark people who lived in buffalo hide shelters and open brush
arbors.

Men, women, and children—the latter mostly naked, while
the former wore only minimal hide garments to guard their
modesty—raced toward them, laughing and shouting. Some of
the women were naked, too, their breasts bobbing as they
converged upon Maria, Diego, and El Cid. Barking dogs accompanied them, and among the dogs was Caobo!

The brindle-colored staghound headed straight for Diego and
flung himself at his master in an ecstasy of welcome. A short
sharp whistle stopped him in his tracks. Tongue lolling in a
dog-smile, Caobo glanced over his shoulder at another man—
taller than the surrounding Indians—striding purposefully
toward them. The man said something, and the dog trotted back
toward him, tail wagging. Midway, he paused and again faced
Diego, as if undecided about where he owed his loyalty.

"Caobo!" Diego shouted, and the dog bounded toward him,
only to be brought up short a second time by the piercing
whistle.

"Traitor!" Diego muttered. "My own dog has chosen to obey another master."

Maria had no time to console him, for she was studying the man who had whistled. He was almost as tall as Diego, his body broad-shouldered and well-made. She had last seen Santelmo as a slender youth, but here was a man in the fullness of his prime. His face looked familiar, but there was little of the boy she had known in the harsh, blunt features of this toughened warrior.

If this man *was* her brother, he had gained strength and confidence, and now exuded an air of authority that made him stand out from all the others. Scar-Face immediately went to him, and they stood conferring together, while the people gathered around, gawking, pointing, and chattering. They did not press too close to El Cid. Their amazement and awe of the stallion extended also to Diego.

Maria took this as a good sign; these short, black-haired, black-eyed people had obviously had rare opportunity to see a Spaniard or his horse, which meant they might not be so eager for revenge.

Diego, she saw, paid little attention to the Indians. His eyes looked past them, over their heads, and she knew he was searching for horses. El Cid seemed to be looking for them, too. His nostrils quivered as he drank the wind and deciphered its contents, then whinnied once, loud and plaintively. There came a distant, responding whinny, but Maria could still see no horses. El Cid began to prance and pull at his lead rope.

Diego calmed him with a word and a hand over his nose. As he did so, Scar-Face and the tall Indian stepped closer.

"I am Santelmo," the man announced, the light in his black eyes flaring. "What is your name?"

He spoke in Spanish, and Maria no longer had any doubt she had encountered her long-lost brother. To prove who she was, she responded in the language of the Indians.

"I am Maria Encanta. My father is a Spaniard, Don Gonzalo. My mother, an *Indio*, was called Katerina."

"Then you are my sister, grown to womanhood now." His black eyes sparkled with disapproval. "The willing slave of a Spaniard."

"Yes, and you are my brother—my blood kin who abandoned and forgot me. I waited for you, Santelmo. All these years, I waited for you to come and rescue me. When you finally came, you stole horses but made no effort to contact me. All these years, I dreamed of bringing you horses, but I did not know where you were or even if you were still alive."

Santelmo's unrepentant glance went to the stallion. "I see you have brought me a fine stallion, along with a Spaniard ripe for disembowelment and torture. The women will enjoy testing his courage."

"That Spaniard has many times saved my life! Before that, he prevented our father from beating me. He is not like Don Gonzalo, or any other Spaniards you have known. He is also a Master of Horses—an *arrendador* without equal. Not only has he taught me to ride, but he has shared many things about training horses."

Santelmo's brows rose in astonishment. "He has taught *you*—a woman and an *Indio*? What manner of man is he, to break the laws the Spaniards cherish?"

"He is just and fair-minded," Maria defended. "At first, because of his heritage, I wanted nothing to do with him, but now—"

"Now, he has softened your woman's heart and enslaved you with your own feelings for him." Santelmo's lip curled derisively. "What he could not gain by force, he won by seduction."

"Yes! And I am glad of it and proud to be his woman. He will never abandon me as *you* have done."

This silenced her brother, though he still looked doubtful. "If you trust a Spaniard as our mother once did, you make a grave mistake, Maria."

"I have made many mistakes, such as longing for my brother to rescue me from the cruelty of our father and stepmother. If you had come for me, there would have been no need for me to give my heart to a Spaniard."

A look of sad weariness stole across her brother's face. "I had to choose between you and the horses, little sister. I could not figure out how to safely take both. It had to be one or the other. More I could not manage without getting caught. In the end, I decided in favor of the horses. They will change our lives, as nothing else can. Even the elders have come to realize that the Spaniards are not gods simply because they can control a horse. Nor are horses gods. They are animals like any other. We can learn their ways as we know the ways of the woolly cows. One day, we will have enough horses for all men—and women—to ride. Then we need no longer fear our enemies or starve when the great herds leave us. We can follow them and always be assured of meat.''

His thoughts so clearly echoed her own that Maria could not help smiling—or forgiving him. She could understand why he had chosen horses over his own sister. ''Now that you have horses, you must still learn to manage them. I have brought you a Master of Horses. There could be no better man to teach you all you wish to learn.''

''Yes, but *will* he teach us, or will he seek to enslave us, like others of his race have done before him?''

They both turned to look at Diego. He watched them impatiently, his handsome features twisted by a frown.

''I think I can make him so happy he will want to stay forever among the Indians, teaching and helping us,'' Maria whispered. ''If I am enslaved, so is he. Diego loves me, my brother, as I do him.''

''He is a *Spaniard*. You dare not forget that!''

''Leave this matter in *my* hands, Santelmo. His name is Diego. Welcome him now, and remember what our mother taught us—patience makes all things possible.''

''In the case of Spaniards, I strongly doubt it. You bring a venomous serpent into our midst. 'Tis not like finding a dog alone on the plain and befriending it.''

''The dog! Was it you who found him? He belongs to Diego. We had despaired of ever seeing him again.''

''He is *my* dog now. I have made him mine, and I will make the stallion mine, too.''

''The stallion is loyal only to Diego. No one else can get near him.''

"*You* were near him, and he did nothing."

"He has grown accustomed to me. He knows I will not hurt him."

"Then he can grow accustomed to me."

"Seek not to rush things, Santelmo! If you do, Diego will never cooperate. Give us both time, my brother, and I think you will be pleased with the results."

Santelmo sighed. "You push me hard, little sister. My own wife was planning to roast your Spaniard's entrails over hot coals tonight. Long before you got here, our sentinels warned us of your arrival—and she had planned for *you* to ease her own burden of work."

"I will still do that," Maria offered. "You will not regret our reunion. I promise you that."

"We shall see. Especially about your Spaniard. 'Tis hard for me to believe I can ever befriend him, but for your sake I am willing to try."

" 'Tis all I ask, Santelmo. Now, come, and I will introduce you."

In the Valley of Green Grass, as the Indians called it, Maria soon discovered that each family had its own hide-covered dwelling, a brush-covered arbor, and/or a wattled hut in which to live. To her great relief and pleasure, she and Diego were given their own quarters, furnished with the best the Indians had to offer.

Even Diego was impressed as he inspected the conical hide dwelling made of skins stretched across cedar poles. "Compared to how we have been living, this is a royal palace," he said to her, smiling, as women filed in and out of the structure, bearing gifts from their own meager stores of tools and household implements.

"They are sharing all they have with us," Maria told him. "See how generous they are!"

She nodded toward the growing pile of items in the center of the lodge, some of which mystified her. She had never tanned

a hide or prepared the leather-like staple made from berries
and pounded buffalo meat which the Indians treasured. Nor
had she fashioned containers from hide, clay, or rushes, nor
put up and taken down a dwelling. Yet she was determined to
master this new life and make a place for herself and Diego
among the tribe. For now, he seemed content to do the same.

There was indeed a horse in the encampment—one of his
own mares. The remainder of the stolen horses were hidden at
a different place, which Santelmo described as a kind of natural
enclosure where water and grass could be found but the horses
could not wander away or hurt themselves. Her brother had
promised to show them the place in the near future.

He had also confided that his plan to learn to ride and then
teach others was proceeding at a snail's pace. The horse he
had selected for this purpose—Diego's mare—seemed quiet
and gentle until someone climbed on her back. Then she tossed
the unsuspecting rider to the ground. Santelmo wanted to know
what he was doing wrong, but Maria had not yet approached
Diego with the idea that he should teach the Indians the secrets
of good horsemanship. She was too afraid of provoking an
argument.

Now, seeing how much he liked their new accomodations,
she decided to press the matter. "Diego, we must repay my
brother and his people for their generosity. Instead of killing
us, they are treating us as family. That surely deserves some
display of gratitude on our part."

Diego's glance turned wary. "Where is this conversation
leading, Maria? Naturally, I am pleased we have not been slain,
but my objective remains the same. I want the return of my
horses, and those of your father. There can be no compromise
on that. If Santelmo agrees to hand them over without a fight,
I will agree to abandon all thought of retaliation. I will even
agree to give him my dog, since your brother has usurped
Caobo's loyalty, anyway. At least, I know the dog will be well
taken care of—a fact which does not apply to the horses.
Santelmo is too ignorant to properly care for horses."

"Diego, you cannot just walk up to my brother and demand

the return of your precious horses. He will never surrender them without a fight—and that is what I am trying to avoid.''

Diego's mouth hardened. He gazed down at the pile of gifts, to which the women were still making additions. ''A fight is inevitable, Maria. Surely, you see that. But first, I will try to gain your brother's confidence—and then to reason with him. I will explain to him how important horses *are* to the Spanish. He may kill me for it, but other Spaniards will come along. He must be made to understand that when Spaniards see horses among the Indians, they will consider it their duty to retrieve those horses and punish the Indians who have them. Any Indian possessing horses will become a hunted man, chased by angry Spaniards. They will seek to kill him and enslave his offspring.''

''Horses will enable the Indians to evade their enemies! 'Tis why they *want* them, Diego.''

''Indians lack the capability to ride and train horses. Has your brother learned to ride La Reina yet? Or even my gentle old mare?''

''There has not been time enough for him to learn. What he does not know, *you* could teach him, Diego, much as you have taught me. . . . I have told him you are a Master of Horses and promised that you will teach him.''

''*What?*'' Diego stared at her, incredulous. ''How could you be so presumptuous, Maria? You have no right to promise anything on my behalf—especially that which contradicts my own will and beliefs.''

''I did not want him to kill you, that's why! His hatred of Spaniards rivals your contempt for *Indios*. I did it because I thought you had come to care for me and would do it for *my* sake, if for no other reason.''

She wondered now if he truly did care for her, or if it had really only been a dream. The kisses, the caresses, the sweet intimacies must have meant nothing to him, so cold and angry did he now appear.

''Have you been manipulating me, Maria?'' His tone was low and dangerous, vibrating with hurt and fury. ''Was it all a pretense on your part?''

''A pretense on *my* part!''

"You thought if you gave yourself to me and spread your thighs with eagerness, you could make me forget I am a Spaniard. You could use me to achieve your own ends."

"I never did!" she denied, but even as she said it she knew it was a lie. She *had* thought to enslave him—to make him so happy that he would consent to remain here forever among the Indians, teaching them all he knew.

"It will never work, Maria. I cannot change my colors overnight. I am sorry if you thought otherwise, but I am who I am. I cannot become something different so you can derive some advantage from it. . . . I have sympathy for the plight of your people, and I abhor your father's cruelty towards them. But I will not be party to some quiet revolution that will change the course of history. I did not come here to bring the horse to the Indian, but to take the horse away from him, before he learns how to make proper use of it. You can do nothing to influence me in this matter. Nor can your brother."

Maria stood frozen to the spot, her heart shattering. It was too late now for him to think he could *stop* the Indian from having the horse; he could not. The revolution had already begun. Once a man realized what was possible and how it could affect his life, the seed was planted. In time, it would grow to fruition. The tender shoot might be trampled or uprooted, but it would only spring up again, as persistent as a weed in Doña Inez's carefully tended garden.

Despite her diligence, Doña Inez could never uproot all the weeds—and neither could the Spaniards keep the horse from the Indian.

"You are wrong, Don Diego. So very wrong."

He lifted a brow in inquiry. "Wrong, Maria? Explain yourself."

She shook her head, at a loss for words. "Do not ask me to explain. I lack your great intellect and gift for words. But I say you are wrong, and one day you will know it. You cannot own the wind, sun, rain, moon, or stars. These wondrous mysteries belong to all of us. So does the horse. He is my dream, too. His beauty, strength, and power can be put to *my* service, as well as yours. The Indian knows that now, and you can never take that knowledge away from him.''

''No, but I can take the horse away—and *keep* it away from him. And I will, Maria. Understand that. I *will*.''

He turned on his heel and left her standing alone in their new home, contemplating this terrible rift between them.

Chapter Eighteen

Diego stood on the fringes of the laughing, chattering women and children and watched Maria among them, as they all made a game of finding and digging tubers. They had descended from their stronghold in the Valley of Green Grass and come here this dewy morning in order to look for the staple which augmented their primary diet of meat.

Diego and a few other men, including Santelmo, had the pleasant duty of guarding them. Several times over the past ten days, signs of a rival Indian band had been spotted. Once, when Santelmo had taken Diego and Maria to see the horses hidden inside a long canyon, they had stumbled across the remains of a cook fire. Another time, a hunting party had spotted another hunting party tracking the same game.

Both incidents had caused a great commotion, with the men feverishly assembling their primitive weapons, and the women keeping their children closer and instructing them on what to do in case of an attack. If not for their fear of attack, Diego could almost believe that these simple people led lives of idyllic comradery and loyalty to one another. Everyone shared the intense work load involved in survival, but seemed to enjoy life while they did so.

Their existence was extremely perilous, but they gave little thought to the future. The needs of the present preoccupied them. The men spent nearly all their time hunting, no easy task on foot. Small game was abundant, but could not meet all the needs of the people, while the larger game, such as buffalo, refused to stand still in one place to be killed. Sentinels spent countless hours perched on lofty promontories, searching the plain below for any sign of distant movement that might indicate the presence of woolly cows.

Once, the entire encampment had hastily packed their belongings and set out to find the buffalo, sighted the day before, only to be disappointed when the animals had disappeared by the time they arrived where the herd had first been seen. The women had repacked all their belongings and grudgingly returned to the Valley of the Green Grass. The women themselves—and dogs pulling conveyances loaded down with goods—were the only beasts of burden. Diego marveled at their strength and perseverance in moving loads a man would find difficult to carry for any distance.

Caobo was being trained to this work and took to it eagerly, with Santelmo's little daughter urging him onward and exclaiming over his progress. By now, Diego could easily identify Santelmo's daughter as well as the *cacique's* young wife, with whom Maria had struck up a friendship. The daughter was called Grasshopper, for her tendency to leap about from place to place, rarely remaining long in one position or sitting quietly, but always examining everything with great curiosity, including Diego himself. He often turned around to discover her behind him, grinning shyly, her black eyes alight with fox fire, as she watched his every move.

Santelmo's pretty wife was named Blue Water, for reasons Diego had yet to discover. She seemed hardly more than a child herself, but had enthusiastically embraced the responsibility of teaching Maria all she needed to know to become a resourceful wife. With markedly less enthusiasm, Santelmo had been doing the same for Diego, silently and patiently showing him how to string a bow and fashion arrows, made from seasoned ash or dogwood collected sometime in the past.

In the relatively short time since their arrival among the Indians, Diego had developed an enormous respect for the knowledge and inventiveness of a people who possessed little more than fire and flint but somehow managed to survive and even prosper in conditions where most white men would soon die of hunger and exposure. Their mastery over nature and their exuberant happiness in the face of daily hardship seemed to him incredible. He found it fascinating to observe them and watch Maria adapt to their ways.

At the moment, Maria and Blue Water were boisterously competing to see who could locate the best and largest tubers, then dig them up the fastest. Convulsed in laughter, they had engaged the other women in the competition, and little Grasshopper was hopping about on the plain trying to help her mother win. Santelmo exchanged a look of amused indulgence with Diego, and Diego suddenly realized that he genuinely liked Maria's brother.

Of course, he had not liked Santelmo's insistence upon turning El Cid loose among the other horses in the hidden canyon— nor had he approved of leaving all the horses there alone, even though the canyon seemed safe enough to ensure that the animals would still be there when they returned.

"We will come back when you are ready to show me how best to ride and train a horse," the *cacique* had loftily informed him on the day they had finally gone there, taking El Cid and Diego's mare with them. "Until then, we will leave the horses alone together to breed and produce more horses."

"You ought not to do that," Diego had argued. "El Cid and El Bobo will fight for control of the mares. They will destroy each other in their zeal to prove who should be the master."

Santelmo had only shrugged. "Let them fight. The strongest will win, and that is the one I want to sire all my new horses."

"They are not your horses," Diego had recklessly pointed out. "They belong to me and your father."

Santelmo had been adamant. "Not any more. Now, they are mine. Replace your blindfold, Spaniard. Without me or one of the others, you will not be able to find this place again. Nor will I bring you here—until you agree to teach me. Maria, do the same. Replace your blindfold. I will not risk what I have gained on your foolish woman's heart. In your blind affection for this man, you may well betray me.''

"I will not betray you, Santelmo." Maria had lifted her blindfold, made from a strip of rawhide, as was Diego's. "It was always my intention you should one day have horses. If ever the opportunity arose, I myself meant to bring them to you.''

Diego had glanced at her in surprise, only then realizing that she had been planning all along to escape from *Dehesa de Oro* and take horses with her, as her own brothers had tried to do. She had gazed steadily back at him.

"Now you know the worst about me, Diego," she had said, showing no repentance. "Before you ever came to the New World, I dreamed of how I might flee from my father's house and bring horses to my mother's people. I am here now, and here I will stay. I pray you will stay with me.''

He had stared at her, speechless, hardly knowing how to respond. In that moment, she had seemed to be an entirely different woman. No longer was she the embittered, frightened, young girl he had first encountered in his bed at Don Gonzalo's house.

She had truly changed. These days—rather, these nights— she came to him warmly and freely, giving of herself as he had always dreamed she would, holding nothing in reserve, eagerly exploring all the delights of the flesh. Now, he understood that it was all part of her evolving plan to entice him into this new life and make him forget he had ever lived another life or thought like a Spaniard.

Yet it was *he* who had brought her here! Somehow, she had turned it all to her own advantage, and now expected him to join her in living as a savage, a prospect that both attracted and unnerved him. At times, he found himself actually considering it, but at other times he violently rejected the notion. As much as he had grown to admire and respect these people, he was not one of them and never would be.

Their language was still largely incomprehensible. With Santelmo and Maria, he could speak Spanish, but with the rest, he was reduced to hand signals and gestures that barely conveyed the simplest thoughts. Even more importantly, his expectations were different. Living in a hide dwelling was fine during the hot season, but when the cold winds of winter scoured the landscape, he wanted thick walls around him and more room than the little structure afforded.

He missed variety and seasoning in his diet, and was not yet ready to abandon all the comforts of civilization. His boots were wearing out, for example, and he dreaded the prospect of going barefoot. The hide footgear the Indians used looked comfortable enough, but he had no idea how to go about making some, and neither did Maria. True, the stars at night were glorious, and the sunsets a grand spectacle—giving him a peace of mind and contentment he had rarely experienced before now—but he often yearned for more to drink than mere water, and wished he had brought along some books to feed his thirst for knowledge.

No one here could read, much less write. He tried to picture himself and Maria having children here in this wilderness, and his blood ran cold with the thought that his offspring might know no more than what the savages could teach them. What of mathematics and science? Philosophy and religion? His children would grow up never seeing a ship, a church, or even a house or carriage! It was unthinkable.

And yet, as he watched Maria and Blue Water laughing and digging together, looking so free and happy, he wondered how he could bear to tear her away from *her* heritage and force her to return to a civilization where she could never be anything more than a slave. Horses would narrow the gap between the Indian and the Spaniard, but they would never close it entirely . . . and he could not conceive of giving up his own plans to indulge *her* dream for the future.

What was he to do? He would never leave here without El Cid and La Reina, even if he could somehow bring himself to abandon Maria to the life she obviously preferred . . . and how could he ever surrender *her?* The mere thought of doing so made him feel ill, as if he had eaten something potentially fatal.

Maria came running up to him just then, her face alight with triumph. "I won, Diego! I won. See how many tubers I found—and how large they are."

She held open the neck of her gathering bag, and he dutifully peered inside. "I guess I know what I will be eating for the next fortnight," he teased.

"These are not meant as a replacement for meat, but as an accompaniment," she scolded. "But, oh Diego! Is it not wonderful how the land provides all we need to be comfortable and happy?"

"Yes," he said, nodding, loathe to see the light fade from her eyes if he did not agree. " 'Tis wonderful, Maria."

Hypocrite, he inwardly castigated himself. *Coward! Tell her what you really feel.*

The little party left the plain then, and headed back toward their stronghold. Santelmo led the way, with Diego at his heels, the women and children in the middle, and several men bringing up the rear. They walked in a long, straggling line, with the children often breaking away to run and examine something of interest. There was no sign of danger, and no one noticed anything strange or unusual—until Diego himself noticed how quiet it had suddenly become.

They had entered the foothills and begun climbing a narrow, steep path that rose upward from the plain. He stopped and turned around, wondering why the laughter and chatter of the women and children had dissipated. Perhaps, he speculated, the wall of rock on one side had muted the sounds. To quell his sense of uneasiness, he decided to wait until Maria caught up with him. The trail he had just ascended twisted and turned, so he knew it might be several moments before she trudged into view. He suddenly wished Caobo were with them, but all the dogs had been left behind to help guard the village and the elders.

Behind him, Santelmo's voice intruded upon his growing concern: "What is it, Spaniard? Why have you stopped?"

"I was wondering why I no longer hear them. 'Tis unnaturally silent all of a sudden."

"You are right. Come! We will see where they are."

Santelmo passed Diego at a run, his hide-clad feet slipping

and sliding on the loose gravel underfoot. Diego sprinted after him. They had gone only a short distance when something— or someone—dropped on them from above. Diego saw only a blur of movement, and his skull exploded. A blinding white light obliterated his vision, he heard a cracking sound, and then . . . nothing.

His next conscious thought was one of pain. He was sure his head had been split in two. He managed to lift a hand to the throbbing spot, and it came away wet. He struggled to open his eyes and examine his hand, but the appendage wavered in front of him. All he could see was a red smear on his fingers. He groaned and tried to concentrate—to understand what had happened to him.

Slowly, memory returned. He had been running to look for Maria. *Maria!* Something dire had befallen her. He lurched to his knees and then to his feet, his vision still blurred. The world spun around him. Nearby lay Santelmo, crumpled against a rock, his own head bloodied. Diego staggered over to him and knelt down.

"Santelmo, wake up!" He shook the man's shoulder. "Santelmo, we have been attacked. Struck down like dogs. We must go after the women and children. Santelmo, get up!"

Maria's brother stirred and opened his eyes. He stared at Diego as if suspecting him of having dealt the felling blow. Diego repeated his pleas, adding: "Blue Water and Grasshopper. They were coming along behind us. Remember? They were digging tubers on the plain."

Comprehension dawned in the Indian's eyes. "And Maria. She was with them."

A dagger twisted in Diego's heart. "Something has happened to them. I feel it in my soul."

"Stolen," Santelmo muttered. "They have all been stolen by a rival band of *Abrache.*"

"How do you know this?" Diego helped Santelmo rise to his feet.

"Men need wives! So they take other men's wives, along with their children. I know this because they leave the men alive if they can, in hopes we will not bother to send a war party after them. We will only go raiding to replace our losses. If they had killed us instead, our blood kin would hunt them down and slay them in return.''

"You steal wives back and forth from each other?" Diego could scarcely believe it. "That . . . that is barbaric."

" 'Tis the way of things out here on the Sea of Grass, Spaniard. Wives grow old and die. They bleed to death in childbirth. Or they drown in a river crossing. For whatever reason a man loses a wife, he must quickly find another. Where else is he to get one except from his enemies? We raid each other all the time, but this time caught me unaware. Come, I will show you the truth of the matter.''

Staggering a bit, Santelmo retraced their steps down the path. They found scattered tubers and Maria's gathering skin, but no sign of the women and children. Then they found the men who had been guarding the rear of the line. They, too, had been clubbed on the head and knocked unconscious, but not slain or scalped, as they would have been had their enemies intended more than a quest for women.

"What do we do now?" Diego bent to help Santelmo revive one of the guards, who happened to be Scar-Face. "We cannot overlook this. I want Maria back. I will strangle any man who dares to put his hands on her.''

Santelmo gave him a long assessing look. "You truly care for my sister, do you not, Spaniard?"

Diego only snorted in answer, but the question severely rattled him. Yes, he cared for her. He could not *live* without her—damn her fox fire eyes! From this moment on, he had but one purpose: to get her back. His need to see her smile and hear her laughter was stronger than his need to breathe. The thought of Maria in another man's arms, forced to endure his caresses and his invasion of her body, filled him with such horror and dread that he feared he might burst from the force of his emotions. The splitting pain in his head in no way compared with the pain in his heart.

"When do we leave to rescue them?" he growled. "We must go quickly before the trail turns cold.''

"As soon as we revive these men and fetch some others to

accompany us. I wish to take the *pistola*, too, as well as bows, arrows, and spears. If we can avoid it, we must kill no one—only retrieve the women and children. There must be no blood spilled between us, or the killings and attacks will never end. We are already sworn enemies with other bands. I would not be sworn enemies with this one.''

''If a hair on Maria's head has been harmed, I cannot promise I will not kill the man who did it.''

''I know how you feel, Spaniard. I feel the same about Blue Water and Grasshopper. My wife was a mere child when I first took her from a neighboring tribe. I watched her grow in beauty. When she finally became a woman, I knew I had to possess her as a wife. No other could please me half so well, nor could another child take the place of Grasshopper. They each own a piece of my heart. We will recover them, have no fear. Now, let us help these men, so we can leave as soon as possible.''

They were soon on their way—not fast enough to suit Diego, but with hours to spare before nightfall. The trail was easy to follow. Fallen tubers marked the way. Santelmo insisted that Blue Water was doing it deliberately, for they had not discovered *her* gathering bag, meaning she still had it with her.

The children had apparently delayed the party. It was a child they found first, sitting alone on the plain, looking frightened and forlorn. The little boy was Scar-Face's son, and the fierce-looking warrior eagerly embraced the lad. Later, he questioned him, but Diego could not understand what was said.

''Are the rest of the women and children all right?'' he asked Santelmo. ''What did the boy say?''

''Some of them are hurt.'' Santelmo was scowling. ''They resisted capture, and were roughly treated. The boy is too small to recall details, but he remembers seeing blood. His own mother has a hurt arm. A couple of the others have injuries as well—one in the leg and another in the head.''

Diego's gloom deepened. Maria would not give up without a fight. She might be one of those hurt. The men briefly discussed what to do about the child, for they feared being slowed down by him. Scar-Face refused to leave his son behind to make his own way back to the encampment. He also objected to the idea of returning with him to safety.

Horses would have solved the problem for everyone, Diego realized, allowing Scar-Face to take the boy up on an animal and proceed along with the others. In the end, Scar-Face decided to carry the child and continue the search. Diego felt so guilty about the inconvenience that he offered to take turns holding the boy, which Scar-Face stonily accepted.

Diego discovered how difficult it was to half-run, half-walk, while carrying a heavy weight, at the peculiar ground-eating pace the Indians adopted whenever they wanted to go some place in a hurry. He could barely keep up when he was *not* carrying the child. When he was, he lagged far behind the others who had no time to worry about an out-of-breath Spaniard.

Horses had made him soft, he grudgingly conceded, and he resolved to practice run-walking every morning to toughen his body and remain fit. The image of Don Gonzalo—fat and dissipated from rich living—taunted him. Gonzalo could never measure up to the strength, stamina, and determination of the average *Indio,* yet he considered himself far above them!

It was laughable, really, how arrogant the Spanish were. Few Spaniards of Diego's acquaintance could match this grueling pace. It pricked him even more when Scar-Face came running back to him, snatched the boy from his arms, and dashed away again, leaving Diego huffing and puffing to catch up. Horses would have solved *this* problem, too, he thought with annoyance.

Night fell before they found them. When it became impossible to follow the trail in the darkness, the Indians lay down where they were and slept like dead men. They posted no guards, and Diego sat up, peering into the blackness and listening to the wind blow, for half the night. Exhaustion eventually forced him to sleep, and he awoke with a start when Santelmo nudged him in the ribs with his foot.

"Get up, Spaniard," he hissed. "We know where they are, now, and we intend to ambush them, just as they did us. Will you stay here and look after Scar-Face's son, or do you insist on accompanying us?''

''I will accompany you, of course!'' Diego scrambled to his feet.

''You would do better to stay here.'' Santelmo's frown was just visible in the early predawn light. ''If you get hurt, I will have to answer to my sister, and she will not be pleased.''

''If you are so worried, give me my *pistola*,'' Diego retorted. ''You know not how to use it, anyway. 'Tis better I should have it.''

Santelmo shook his head and patted the weapon, which he wore at his waist tucked inside the thong that secured his breech clout. ''I will not have to use the *pistola* to get the good of it. When they see it, they will be afraid. Most *Indios* know the damage a *pistola* can do. This much the Spaniards have taught all of us.''

''Here.'' He thrust a sharpened stick into Diego's hand. Then he bent, picked up a rock near Diego's feet, and handed him that, too. ''If you need weapons, use these. I would give you a bow and some arrows, but I doubt you have developed any skill with *our* weapons.''

Diego resolved to teach himself how to use a bow or convince one of the Indians to help him. He could never ask Santelmo— not unless he agreed to teach him about horses in exchange. A stick and a rock seemed poor weapons indeed, he thought, hefting the stick in his hand and testing its weight for use as a spear. He longed for his sword, or a real spear. Since he had neither, he knew he had to be content with what he had. He just hoped he would not be outmaneuvered by an expert in one of the weapons he had previously disdained.

They set out at a brisk pace, run-walking through a rosy mist rising from the damp grass. Santelmo led the way, displaying a confidence that made Diego wonder if he had scouted ahead in the darkness to plan their approach.

A short time later, just as the eastern sky brightened and they were almost at the crest of a little rise in the undulating landscape, Santelmo called a halt and motioned everyone to the ground. Diego promptly dropped to his stomach, while beside him, Scar-Face set down his son and pushed him downward, signaling him to be silent.

Below them, lying on the plain, Diego could see huddled shapes—the objects of their search! He looked around for a guard and spotted only one man, sitting up with a spear in his hand. However, he was resting his head on his upraised knees, as if dozing. They were in luck!

Santelmo motioned for everyone but the child to follow him. Dropping to his knees, he began slithering down the hillside on his stomach. Diego did the same. At the bottom of the rise they regrouped, and Maria's brother silently assigned each of them a target. It was obvious he had carefully studied the situation and determined that there were almost as many of them as there were of the enemy. Plus, they had the advantage of surprise.

The most difficult part would be making certain that each man attacked a *man,* and not a sleeping woman or child. Diego had to quell his own desire to immediately identify Maria and single her out for protection. The success of Santelmo's plan depended upon every man doing as he had been told.

Santelmo waited to give the go-ahead signal until a bar of brilliant white light along the eastern horizon heralded the arrival of the sun. When the signal came, Diego half-crawled, half-slid through the tall grass, heading straight for the man assigned to him. It was one of the nearest. Santelmo apparently doubted he could reach one of the further targets without being discovered. Diego shared his doubts. When he reached his target, he rose up on his knees—rock in hand—and struck the man's head as hard he could. The resulting thud was absurdly loud. A moment later, other thuds and muted cries erupted on either side of him.

Not far away, Santelmo struck a man with the edge of his hand, using it like a rock, to render him unconscious. Diego marveled that he had such strength, and did not break his hand in the process. There was no time to savor the moment. A cry of alarm went up, and those who had not yet been incapacitated found their weapons and scrambled to their feet.

Someone leapt on Diego from behind. He fought to remove

a powerful arm clamped across his windpipe, cutting off his air. He tried rolling over on top of his assailant, but the man only squeezed harder. Diego suddenly realized he was fighting for his life. This was not supposed to be happening!

Santelmo had said not to kill anyone or hurt them seriously, but the man strangling Diego ignored the rules of the game. He had but one intention—to kill him! Or break his neck.

Diego fought with a strength born of desperation. He needed air! None could pass the restriction in his throat. He could feel his strength waning. Darkness closed in around him. He wrapped his arms around the man's neck, hoping to flip him over his own head and break his hold. The strategy failed, and the press of a knee against the small of Diego's back became a new agony—a new threat.

His assailant was bending him backward. If he did not succumb to strangulation, the pressure would snap his spine. Nothing Diego did made a particle of difference. Just as he lost consciousness, the awful pressure eased.

Too late! screamed his air-deprived lungs. *Too late. Deliverance has come too late.*

Chapter Nineteen

Awakened by the screams of the children and the sounds of fighting men, Maria quickly realized what was happening: They were being rescued!

Rolling over and jumping to her feet, she spotted Santelmo's warriors—and Santelmo himself—subduing their captors. From the look of things, the surprise attack was going to be successful. Most of their captors now lay unconscious, including the man who had told her he was her new husband and she must obey him from now on. Those still fighting were far outnumbered, and would soon be overwhelmed.

Only one of the enemy seemed to have the upper hand: the powerfully built leader of the band. He had a stranglehold on another tall, well-built man—*Diego!*

Diego's face was turning blue from lack of air. "Santelmo! Santelmo, help me! Diego is being killed!"

Maria flung herself on the leader's back and clawed at his ears and eyes, but he paid no attention. Maria could not see his face, but she recalled the way he had looked when she had first laid eyes on him—lips drawn back from his teeth, eyes smoldering, as he gazed down at a quivering Blue Water.

"Ha! This is a pretty one. She will be mine."

He had then spotted Maria. His eyes had lit up even more, but before he could open his mouth, another man had claimed her. "Then I will have this one. Her beauty outshines all the others."

The leader had grunted, his disappointment obvious . . . and now this monster was killing Diego!

"Santelmo!" Maria shrieked. "Help me!"

"Get away!" her brother shouted, and Maria realized she was shielding the leader with her own body.

She leapt to one side, and Santelmo gave the man a mighty whack with Diego's *pistola,* felling him like a tree struck by lightning. Maria dropped to her knees beside Diego's limp body. By now he had lost consciousness. She could not even tell if he were alive.

"No! You cannot die!" She clawed at his leather doublet. The garment fit him snugly, and seemed to be obscuring his breathing. When she failed to loosen it, her panic mounted.

"Diego, wake up, I beg you!"

She slapped his cheeks and then tried to shake him. Her mind spun; what more could she do? She could not bear to lose him, not her Spaniard, the man she had come to love as much—or more—than her own life.

"Get out of the way. Let me help him." Santelmo pushed her to one side and knelt in her place. He, too, tugged at the neckline of Diego's doublet, but the leather held stubbornly. Abandoning the effort, he tilted back Diego's head, stuck a finger in his mouth to open it, leaned over, and blew his own breath down Diego's throat.

Maria could not believe such a tactic would work. She held her own breath. Once, twice, three times, Santelmo blew down Diego's throat. Then he rolled him onto his side and clapped him sharply between the shoulder blades.

"Wake up, Spaniard. I grow tired of breathing for you. Your life is hardly worth this much effort."

Diego coughed—a wondrous sound. Maria clapped her hands in joy as he took a deep, shaky breath, slowly awakening from the unnatural sleep. Santelmo helped him to sit up, while around them familiar faces gathered. The rival Indians were all conquered now and lying motionless on the plain.

"Get him on his feet, my sister," Santelmo instructed. "We must quit this place before we have to fight again. We will take their weapons, but these wife stealers will be angry when they awaken. They may try and come after us."

"Diego and I will not delay you," Maria promised. "Now, that he is breathing again, he will quickly recover his strength. Thank you, my brother. I will tell him what you did. Perhaps it will change his mind about helping us."

"I desire only one kind of help from him, Maria. After this, if he still refuses I will send him back to his own kind. He will be no good to us, except as another mouth to feed."

"We can feed ourselves!" she protested.

"Yes, but the meat and tubers you claim can go to feed our own people or you alone. I did not mean you must accompany him, my sister. You are always welcome among us. I will find you a new husband, and—"

"No!" she snapped, as Diego stirred and gazed up at them, rubbing his throat and gulping air as he drew deep, shuddering breaths. "I want no other husband but this one. He is the only man I can ever love."

Santelmo sighed. "I should have let him die, then, for he will only bring you grief in the end. Wait and see. He will still refuse to teach us, or be one of us. If you doubt it, ask him now in Spanish. Use his own language so he can understand what we are saying."

Maria grasped Diego's hand. "Diego, can you get up and walk now? We must leave before our enemies regain consciousness. And on the way back to the Valley of Green Grass, I must tell you something and ask a favor of you as well."

Diego swallowed, grimacing as he did so. "I . . . I . . . can walk," he rasped. "G-give me a moment. I will soon be fine."

"Walk first," she urged. "Then worry about talking. What have to say can wait until you are feeling better."

She helped him to his feet. He stood, swaying but determined, pulling slightly away from her rather than lean on her. " 'Tis

just my . . . throat. The rest of me is . . . unharmed. *You*. How
are you?''

The fear in his eyes reminded her of the fear that must have
been in her own eyes just moments ago. "I am well, Diego. I
was not hurt or injured in the attack. Nor were Blue Water and
little Grasshopper. See? Here, they come.''

She indicated the arrival of her friend and her friend's daughter with a smile, then frowned as she thought of the women
who had suffered injuries. "But I wish we had horses to carry
some of the others. One has a badly swollen ankle and should
not be walking on it. Another has a broken wrist.''

Diego nodded. "Horses. Yes . . . we all need horses,'' he
croaked.

His comment ignited a spark of hope. Perhaps he had already
had a change of heart! When he realized who had saved him
and breathed life back into his body, he would have to relent
and agree to teach her brother.

"Come, Diego. Let us go home now.'' She took his arm to
walk with him.

He said nothing, only allowed himself to be led away.

"All right, Maria. You win. I will teach your brother about
horses.''

The words filled Maria with elation and joy. She lay entwined
in Diego's arms in the privacy of their hide dwelling, where
they had already joined their bodies once this night. She hugged
him hard and searched for words to thank him.

"Diego, you will not regret it! You will soon see that 'tis
only right the Indians have horses. They have a natural way
with animals and will never abuse them. Nor do they intend
to use horses to make war on the Spanish. My brother wants
only to be left alone. He would be happy if he never had to
see another Spaniard—excepting *you*, of course. Horses will
give him the ability to avoid the Spanish altogether. The Ocean
of Grass is a huge place, with plenty of room for the Indian
to disappear on it. Now, they will be able to—''

"Hush, Maria." Diego stopped her babble with a passionate kiss, then pressed her down with his naked body.

Maria eagerly wrapped her arms around his neck. She relished the idea of another joining, for she could never get enough of Diego's loving. Tonight, when he had promised to teach Santelmo about horses, she felt especially close to him. Nothing separated them any more. He had taken the first step toward a permanent bond with her people. Stroking his hair, she smiled into his eyes as he leaned over her.

"I love you, Diego," she whispered.

The noise from the festivities outside almost obliterated the declaration. The Indians were celebrating the return of the women and children with feasting and dancing. There had been injuries, yes, but no lives had been lost. They had cause for celebration. The light from the great fire the men had built illuminated one wall of the structure, and the shadows of the dancers made weird patterns against the reddish glow.

"I love you," she repeated, counting the moment as the happiest of her entire life.

"Maria, my sweet, listen to me," Diego entreated, and she knew from the tone of his voice that what he had to say was serious—and she might not like it.

"I must explain something to you," he continued, his voice still raspy but distinct. "I have said I will teach Santelmo. I will also make him a gift of my own mares in exchange for saving my life. But I intend to keep El Cid and to return your father's horses to him—not right away, but soon, when I get the chance. La Reina is not mine to give, nor are the others. 'Tis not right that your brother lays claim to all of them. I still do not approve of his theft of the horses."

"But you see now how much the Indians need them!"

"Of course I see how much horses are needed. 'Tis just as the Spanish have always feared, and what you yourself have argued—horses will change the lives of the Indians. Once they know how to ride, train, and breed horses, nothing will be the same. They can go wherever they please and kill Spaniards if they so desire. I tremble to think of my part in this endeavor. Indeed, I will be making it all possible. I am going to help

them, Maria, but I come to it reluctantly. I intend to teach
Santelmo all he wishes to learn and give El Cid time to breed
the mares I am giving your brother. However, when I leave
here, as I surely must one day, I will take La Reina and the
rest of your father's horses with me. I will also take you . . .
if you will come willingly.''

"Oh, Diego! How quickly you turn joy to sorrow!" Tears
gathered in Maria's eyes as she considered all he had just said.
He still meant to return to his life as an *hidalgo*!

"Maria, my love, *will* you come with me? . . . Or will you
tell your brother what I have just told you, and thereby prevent
me from doing what I know to be right?"

If he had stabbed her in the breast with a dagger and twisted
it, he could not have hurt her more—or posed questions more
difficult to answer.

"Diego, I could never do anything to harm you," she finally
said, blinking back tears. "I will say nothing of this to my
brother—at least, for now. I will only tell him you have agreed
to teach him and remain with us a while in order to do that.
As for the rest . . ."

She shook her head. Her tears spilled over and ran in rivulets
down her cheeks. "I can make no promises. Here, among the
Indians, I am happy. In my father's house, I was miserable
To go back to that—"

"You will not be going back to that! We will build our own
house. Start a new life. Breed our own horses and cattle."

"That takes gold, Diego. A vast quantity of gold—or silver.'

"We can find a way to obtain all we need. I will search for
gold, and—"

"And use Indians to mine it!"

"I will *hire* Indians to mine it, not enslave them as you
father does."

"Hiring them *will* enslave them, for they will then become
dependent upon you. And what do you think my father will
say when he discovers you have taught my brother to ride and
even given him horses? He will kill you for it, Diego! 'Ti
breaking Spanish law. When you are dead, other Spaniards will
sing his praises for properly punishing you."

"Maria, I will not have my children—*our* children—growing up ignorant, knowing nothing beyond the world of the *Indios*. Running about naked on the plains, subject to attack by rival bands, broiling in the summer's heat, freezing in the winter winds, worrying about the source of their next meal. There are some advantages to civilization, my love."

"And many disadvantages! Especially for half-*Indios* and quarter-*Indios,* or whatever our children will be. Diego, we can be so happy among my brother's people! *Here* is where we can make a new life. Will you not consider it?"

"Will you not consider what I have asked of you—to return with me, to *trust* me, to give me a chance to prove that I am different? Our lives will not be the same as what you knew before you met me."

Maria bit her lip against the sobs rising in her throat. " 'Tis not *you,* Diego. 'Tis the world we live in I do not trust. I dare not trust it! You speak of educating and protecting our children. In *your* world, if something happened to you, they would become slaves and I along with them. That is what you are asking me to risk; can you not see that?"

"Trust me to protect you, Maria." Rolling onto his side, he gathered her into his arms. "Trust me to know what's best for you and any children we might have together. I mean to give you a good life—and a safe one."

"My mother trusted my father!" she wailed, unable to stop herself. "And I vowed I would never do the same—trust a Spaniard! Her whole life was a warning that I must never fall in love with one, for it can never work out happily."

"Maria, Maria . . ."

He held her then, saying nothing, allowing her to weep and wrestle with her doubts and fears. In his arms, she felt safe and protected, as if anything were possible. But she knew how she would feel when she left his embrace—exposed and vulnerable. She especially knew how she would feel if she ever again returned to civilization. She *had* to make him stay here!

Fortunately, he would not be leaving tomorrow or the next day. She still had time to change his mind. She had tonight to love and pleasure him, and make him realize he could not live without the gifts she alone could give him.

She took his face in her hands and kissed him. Then she began to caress him, touching him in ways she had already learned excited and teased him.

"Maria ..." This time, her name was a moan wrenched from the depths of his being.

Yes, it might work! It had to work.

But before things could go any further, someone outside called her name. "Maria! Where are you? Bring Diego, and come join the feasting and dancing."

It was her brother, come to fetch them to the festivities. Santelmo was probably wondering whether or not Diego had agreed to teach him.

"I would rather stay here," Diego complained in a low tone, as she quickly rose and made herself presentable.

His desire to be alone with her pleased her. But it would not hurt him one bit to learn he could not have her to himself whenever he wanted. She was not, after all, his slave. She *did* have choices, and he must take them into consideration.

"No, we cannot stay here," she said. "But later, we can be alone again ..."

"Later," he grumbled. "I want you alone *now*, not later."

"Patience, Diego. You must learn to have patience." Filled with a new resolve to use every means at her disposal to change his mind, she assured her brother that they would be right out to join him.

Santelmo was delighted to learn of Diego's capitulation, and immediately declared himself ready to become his blood brother and to share all he had with him.

"What does this involve?" Diego whispered to Maria as they awaited the preparations for the ceremony.

Looking wary and apprehensive, Diego watched her brother sharpen a flint between two stones.

"I have never witnessed this ritual, but I suspect that your blood must now mingle with my brother's blood. He mus intend to use a sharpened flint to cut you both, when a dagger or a knife could do it more quickly and cleanly. Horses are not the only things we can give them, Diego. There is much else we can teach them, which will make their lives easier. My brother has probably forgotten most of what he learned in my father's house, or he would not resort to a flint when he ought to be using a knife.''

''My dagger went the way of my *pistola,*'' Diego muttered. ''I have deeply mourned its loss, never more so than now.''

Santelmo stopped sharpening his flint and tested its edge with his thumb. Satisfied, he grinned and held up his hand, palm flattened, indicating that Diego should join him and do the same. Despite his reservations, Diego did so without hesitation. While the other Indians sat in a ring around them, silently watching, Santelmo quickly slashed first his own palm, then Diego's.

As blood spurted from the wounds, Santelmo pressed his hand against Diego's, so that their blood ran together and became indistinguishable. After a few moments, Santelmo withdrew his hand, wrapped it in a piece of hide to staunch the flow of blood, and offered Diego a similar bandage.

''Now, we are brothers!'' Santelmo grandly announced in the Indian language, so that everyone present could understand. ''From this day forward, all I own belongs to this man, and all he owns belongs to me.''

He repeated the declaration in Spanish for Diego. ''Now, we will exchange gifts. Wait here, while I fetch something for you, my brother.''

''Does this mean that *his* horses are now mine?'' Diego whispered to Maria, his face brightening, as Santelmo strode off into the darkness.

''And yours are now his,'' she answered. ''Do not excite yourself, Diego. He will take nothing belonging to you unless his need is so great that he cannot avoid it. Moreover, he will defend what you own as if it were indeed his.''

No sooner had she finished speaking than Indians around the circle rose and began approaching Diego to give him objects she quickly recognized. Silently, out of respect for Santelmo, they returned Diego's *pistola,* dagger, breast shield, iron helmet, and other items they had taken.

Diego's surprise and pleasure were obvious.

"Now, you must give them gifts in return," Maria whispered. "Especially since we were given so much when we first arrived here."

"I should have known." Diego sighed.

Within moments, all his belongings were once again in the hands of his new friends, but now he sat among them as an equal—accepted as one of them. Despite her earlier disappointment, Maria's heart swelled with joy and pride. Even Scar-Face was grinning, and Santelmo, who had just returned to the circle, was beaming.

"Tomorrow, we will go to the Canyon of Horses. I must begin learning about horses at once," he told the gathering. "However, the Spaniard will not wear a blindfold, for our blood is one now, and we trust each other."

Maria's joy faded a little as she translated this for Diego. After tomorrow, he would be able to get the horses any time he wanted. He could claim La Reina and the others whenever the notion took him. Diego's eyes widened as she told him this and softly added, so her brother could not hear: "You are free to leave whenever you wish now, Diego. No one will stop you. You have what you wanted."

"I am not going yet, Maria. First, I will fulfill my promise—as I explained to you earlier this night. And until I know I have *you,* I do *not* have all I want."

Santelmo interrupted their quiet exchange. "This is for you, my brother," he said in Spanish. He dug into a small pouch and extracted an object. Placing it in the center of his uninjured palm, he offered it to Diego.

When she saw what it was, Maria gasped. The object glittered in the light from the fire, as if it had captured the very essence of the flames and contained the fire's energy within it. The size of a small rock, it was a chunk of purest gold, at least three times the size of the nuggets the *vaqueros* had found.

"*Madre de Dios!*" Diego exclaimed, taking the gold from her brother's hand. "Where did you get this?"

Santelmo merely shrugged. "In a streambed far to the north of here. Gold has no value to an *Indio,* but the Spanish part of me would not allow me to leave it lying there."

Diego held the chunk of gold up to the light, so that everyone could see it and marvel at its rich color. "The lode from which this came must be pure, indeed. Surely, you know that white men would torture and kill you to gain the knowledge of where you found this. Your father's own *vaqueros* deserted us in order to search for gold."

Santelmo's eyes bored into Diego's. "My brother would not torture or kill me."

"No, he would not," Diego agreed, shaking his head. "I owe you my life, and I will never betray you for the sake of gaining gold."

Only for the sake of gaining horses, Maria thought, suddenly miserable.

"If I thought more gold could be found where this piece was located, I would take you there," Santelmo said. "I would even help you dig the gold from the heart of the mountain, or wherever else it came from. I know how you Spaniards value the yellow metal."

"But you think this is all there was?" Diego hefted the chunk in his hand, as if assessing its weight.

"I *know* that is all there was. I searched the area well. I combed the stream bed. Climbed the nearest hills. Looked everywhere. For I thought if I had enough gold, I could convince Spaniards—perhaps even *hidalgos*—to sell horses to me, but I could find only this chunk. There *is* no mother lode of gold, Don Diego. . . . There are only fragments such as this one. Many *Indios* have them, but they cannot tell you where they come from. When I finally realized this, I abandoned all hope of ever buying horses, and knew I would have to steal them instead."

Diego rubbed the chunk of gold with his thumb, bringing up its color. "I cannot believe there is no mother lode somewhere. Before I came to the New World, I read accounts of whole cities of gold, waiting somewhere on The Ocean of Grass for the Spanish to discover them."

Santelmo laughed. "I have trudged the entire length of the plains, and I have never seen such a sight! I know *Indios* who have gone further north than I have, as well as east and west, and they can report no such discovery. The Ocean of Grass is filled with riches—all we need to survive and enjoy life can be found here—but there are no great quantities of gold. Forget gold, my brother. Live among us, and be happy. Enjoy the company of your woman. Hunt with us, ride with us, and teach us about horses. Life is good here on the plains. With horses, it will be even better. Stay with us, my brother, and be free. All you could ever want is here. You need only open your eyes to see it."

"I will think about what you have said," Diego answered. "Thank you for the gold. If I ever do return to your father and the Spanish, this nugget alone will grant me a measure of freedom to break away from the rest and live my own life."

" 'Tis not enough to make you secure," Santelmo said, "nor to surround you with the usual wealth of an *hidalgo.*"

"True, but this chunk of gold is better than nothing. It would give me a start toward establishing my own small empire."

"Your empire?" Santelmo frowned. "Only a Spaniard would think in terms of building an empire—and then only an *hidalgo.*"

" 'Tis what I am, Santelmo—an *hidalgo.* I cannot change overnight. You and Maria have shown me a new world, have offered me new opportunities. Now, I must decide whether or not I can accept them. At the moment, I still think not."

Silence fell after that. A short time later, they all retired for the night. Early the next morning, Santelmo roused them to go to the Canyon of Horses. They remained there all day, with Diego patiently teaching Santelmo—and Maria—the best methods for handling horses and persuading the animals to behave as they desired.

Thus began a pattern for the days to follow. When it came time to teach Santelmo and the other men how to safely ride, Diego followed Maria's advice and had the Indians work the horses in water. When the men fell off they did not get hurt, nor did the horses. Amid much laughter, the men remounted.

Diego frequently declared his astonishment at how rapidly the Indians mastered the skill of riding. One afternoon, he gave them a demonstration of advanced equitation, as he called it, putting El Cid through his paces and greatly impressing the Indians. Some of them wondered aloud if perhaps Diego might not be a god, after all, considering his ability to make a horse do things that they had never imagined a horse could do— such as rear up and advance forward on his hind legs.

Diego opened their eyes to new possibilities, and seemed to truly enjoy instructing the men and watching them succeed. Nowhere could he have had more eager and enthusiastic students. Maria rejoiced in the satisfaction she saw on his face as he taught her brother and the others.

While his days were joyful and fulfilling, she made certain his nights were equally so. Giving Diego pleasure gave *her* pleasure, and the days and nights unfolded in a haze of happiness that, to her, was *true* gold, while the chunk of yellow metal that Diego kept hidden away in their dwelling was only a poor imposter, capable of bringing nothing but misery.

Later, she would scold herself for never having realized how precious and fleeting this time really was. When it abruptly ended, she was caught totally unprepared.

Laughing and talking together, she, Diego, and Santelmo returned one evening from the Canyon of Horses to discover that Blue Water and little Grasshopper were missing from the encampment. They had gone out that morning with the other women and children to search for late ripening berries or thorny tree beans they could dry and save for winter. The party had split up. When they gathered together to return, Santelmo's wife and daughter were not among them.

The women had conducted a brief, futile search, then returned to the camp to get help. They had found but a single clue, and it was an ominous one: Near Blue Water's dropped gathering skin, they had discovered an iron horseshoe.

"White men have taken my wife and daughter!" Santelmo exploded, flinging the horseshoe to the ground in front of him. "I must go after them!"

Diego remained calm. "We will both go after them—on horseback. We will find them more quickly that way."

"I am going, too," Maria quietly announced. "If they have been harmed 'tis a good idea to have another woman with you to help care for them."

"If they have been harmed, I will kill the men who took them! My warriors will ride with me, and we will—"

"Wait a minute. Stop," Diego said. "You and I and Maria can ride the best. The others are still learning, and may be more hindrance than help. At best, they will delay us. Let the others follow on foot if you wish, but we will take the three fastest horses. A large army is unnecessary. A small one can move more quickly and without attracting notice."

"All right—but hurry! It will soon be dark." Santelmo set off at a run in the direction of the Canyon of Horses.

Diego started to follow, then stopped and turned to Maria. She almost ran into him, and tripped over Caobo, who took turns these days following first one man, then the other.

"My *pistola!*" Diego cried. "We should not go without it. I fear we may need it . . . and have someone restrain this dog. 'Tis better if he does not accompany us."

"To whom did you give the *pistola* that night when you and Santelmo became blood brothers?" Maria anxiously questioned. "Tell me, and I will go and get it."

"Scar-Face, I think. Yes, I am certain I gave it to Scar-Face."

"Go and get the horses, while I fetch the *pistola*," Maria told him. "I will meet you at the entrance to the Canyon of Horses."

Chapter Twenty

Darkness overtook them before they found Blue Water and little Grasshopper. The next morning was overcast, and at first, they had difficulty following the trail. A sandy area finally revealed the clear imprint of tracks from four horses—one of them missing a shoe. Now, they at least knew they were headed in the proper direction.

In their haste they had brought no supplies, except for a partially filled water skin Scar-Face had thrust into Maria's hands, along with Diego's *pistola*. Maria wondered what they would do for food if they were forced to follow the trail all way the back to *Dehesa de Oro*.

Diego had expressed no opinion regarding the identity of the men who had taken Blue Water and Grasshopper, but she blamed her father's *vaqueros*. Who else could it possibly be? she asked herself, as she encouraged her already tired mare to keep up with El Cid and La Reina.

They were a long way from the spot where the *vaqueros* had abandoned her and Diego, but perhaps the men's search or gold had led them here to explore the region's high sierras. Or perhaps they had given up that quest and resumed their earch for the horses. Maybe they were looking for her and

Diego! Whatever the reason, they were now headed south—presumably returning to civilization.

Maria feared for Blue Water's safety. She knew how the *vaqueros* would look at her—as hardly human, and therefore unworthy of respect or protection. They would use her roughly, without any regard for her feelings or indeed, for her health and well-being. These men had been a long time without a woman's company, and Maria easily recalled the lusty looks she herself had occasionally received from them. Only Diego's presence had kept her safe, and without Santelmo at her side Blue Water had no chance of surviving this encounter unscathed. Maria just hoped little Grasshopper would be left alone. She was only a child, after all.

Late that same afternoon, they came upon Santelmo's daughter—naked and dead in the grass. She had indeed been raped, then left behind to die. Her body was still warm, the blood not yet dried on her thin, childish thighs.

Grief and anger so overwhelmed her that Maria erupted into a sorrowful wailing derived from some ancient instinct which, until now, she had never realized she possessed. As she wept and wailed over the child, Diego had to wrestle with Santelmo to stop him from slashing himself repeatedly with one of the sharpened flints he carried in a waist pouch.

"Remember Blue Water!" he sharply admonished her brother. "If your wife still lives, she needs you now more than ever."

"They have tortured and slain my daughter!" Santelmo shouted. "She was hardly more than a babe, and see what they have done to her!"

"I see," Diego grimly responded. "And I will help you avenge this terrible atrocity. I am with you now, Santelmo, as I never thought I could be. Once, I myself failed to prevent the rape and abuse of several young women. I acted too late to stop their tormentors, and did not punish them as I should have. *No more.* I will not let this pass as I did the other. Let us hurry and cover her body with stones, then resume our search for Blue Water."

"Her body must go back to the Valley of Green Grass to

be hidden in a cleft among the rocks. I will not leave her lying out here on the plain to be dug up by wolves.''

"After we have rescued Blue Water, we will return for her remains. For now, we must press onward.''

Diego's arguments roused Maria from her fit of weeping and forced her to think about what must still be done. Soon, they were once again trailing the child-murderers. They rode all day, stopping frequently to dismount and examine the ground, but again, darkness fell before they found anything.

During the night, the buffalo came. They awoke to find themselves and their horses on the wrong side of a passing herd of buffalo numbering at least a thousand. Santelmo was almost irrational in his fury.

"We will lose the trail for certain now! The passage of so many wooly cows will wipe it out entirely.''

Rubbing the sleep from her eyes, Maria scrambled to her feet and then had to fight a wave of dizziness and cramping in her stomach. They had eaten nothing for two days now, and the effects of abstinence were catching up with her. A scant moment before she toppled to the ground, Diego caught her by the arm and held her upright.

"Santelmo, this is an opportunity to secure meat for our journey. Maria must eat soon. So must we, if we are to retain our strength for this endeavor.''

"My child is dead, and my wife is in the hands of my enemies! Who can think of hunting or eating at such a moment? Stay here and see to your own needs if you must. I am riding ahead to find Blue Water.''

Santelmo stalked over to La Reina, who grazed nearby, still bridled, her reins tied around her neck so she could eat grass. He leapt aboard her and, wheeling the mare about, galloped off toward the buffalo, heading straight toward the center of the herd.

"He has lost his reason!'' Diego exploded. "And he is about to kill himself and the finest mare I have ever known.''

"What can we do to stop him?'' Maria clutched at Diego's arm. "Should we not go after him?''

"And get ourselves killed along with him? What good will

that do? 'Tis sheer folly to gallop into the middle of a herd of
a thousand buffalo. Stay here while I try to bring down some
fresh meat. Once we have eaten, we will continue the chase. I
hope we will catch up to Santelmo before he attacks those
vaqueros. The way he is going, if he does not get trampled to
death, he will wind up a prisoner heading back to slavery and
the wrath of your father.''

"Oh, Diego! I hate to think of what my father will do to
him if he ever gets his hands on him. Especially if the *vaqueros*
see him riding La Reina.''

"Then you had better pray hard that he comes to his senses,"
Diego snapped, hurrying toward El Cid.

Diego succeeded in bringing down a small buffalo whose
meat fed them for the next five days. For five days, they searched
without success for Santelmo, neither of them willing to admit
that when her brother had disappeared among the buffalo, he
had disappeared from the face of the earth, and La Reina along
with him. Neither did they discover any sign of Blue Water or
the *vaqueros.*

"We will keep riding south," Diego told Maria. " 'Tis all
we can do. And we will continue watching for signs that horses
have passed this way."

She nodded and kept her worries to herself. The last thing
she wanted to do was return to *Dehesa de Oro,* but they could
hardly go back to the Indians without knowing what had happened to Santelmo and Blue Water. Maria wondered if they
could even find the Indians again, but if they kept riding south
she knew they would eventually encounter Spaniards.

Her father's land claims were enormous. He liked to boast
that only the King of Spain possessed more land than he did.
He owned land he had never seen, defining his boundaries by
such vague generalities as: ". . . all the land between here and
the sunset. I have claimed it on behalf of the monarchy and
my heirs—if I ever have any."

They might already be riding on her father's land. The
thought gave Maria a chill that mocked the day's heat. As they

rode south, the heat had once again become unbearable. Only the nights were cool and pleasant. Maria tried her best to enjoy them. She knew her time alone with Diego was coming to an end. They could hardly wander the plains forever; the hot season was passing. Before the nights grew frosty, they must have shelter and a plan for surviving the winter.

On the sixth day, quite unexpectedly, they discovered what they were looking for. They crested a slight rise on the plain and spotted a distant group of men on horseback. A single man on foot stumbled along behind the riders, his hands bound behind his back, his neck attached to the front of one of the rider's saddles by a long rope. No sooner had they seen the party than the prisoner stumbled and fell to his knees. The rider dragged him a short distance before stopping, and Maria unthinkingly urged her horse forward to rescue him.

"Get back out of sight!" Diego hissed, blocking her view of the scene with El Cid.

Maria did not argue. Heart pounding, she turned her horse and did as she was told. Diego rode back with her on El Cid, swung off the stallion's back, and handed her his reins.

"Hold him while I crawl up that rise again and study the situation. At this distance, 'tis difficult to recognize the men, but I think I can identify the horses. One of them looked like La Reina."

"If the mare is among them, the bound man can only be Santelmo. Diego, they were *dragging* him by the neck!"

"Hush! Keep your voice down. 'Tis what I want to check—the identity of their prisoner. Stay here unless I motion for you to do otherwise."

She nodded and glanced worriedly at El Cid. "Will he remain silent? If the other horses interest him—"

"He has a mare right here to hold his interest. Besides, he is well-trained. El Cid will make no fuss about other horses unless I set him free to indulge his own whims."

Diego left her, but returned a short time later.

"The prisoner is indeed Santelmo. Miguel and the other *vaqueros* have captured him. They have now slung him across La Reina's back and tied his hands and feet beneath her belly."

"My poor brother! But where is Blue Water?"

Diego shook his head. "I have no idea. Tonight, after dark, I will spy on them some more. Perhaps that will answer our questions. We must think about how we can rescue him—and decide if we even *can* rescue him."

"But we *must* rescue him!"

"Only if we can do so without getting ourselves killed. I have only enough powder to fire a single shot with my *pistola.* 'Tis all that is left, Maria. Even if I had more, a single *pistola* is no match for their more powerful weapons. Our lack of weapons is why I did not pursue them when they first deserted us, remember?"

That night proved to be the longest of Maria's entire life. She and Diego kept their distance from the party until well after dark. Even then, they feared approaching too closely. The *vaqueros,* on the other hand, lit a fire, as if they had no fear of attack by Indians.

Leaving the horses with Maria, Diego set off on foot to learn what he could about Santelmo's capture and Blue Water's disappearance. Tired as she was, Maria could not even think about sleeping. She lay looking up at the stars and counting the moments until Diego's return. After a while, she ceased counting and sat up, too restless and impatient to lie still any longer.

Fear nibbled at her insides; she worried about Diego, Santelmo, Blue Water, and even herself. She now believed her friend was dead. It was the only explanation. If Diego tried to free Santelmo, especially out here in the open, he risked being killed by Pedro, Ignacio, Fernandez, or Miguel. They were all good shots . . . and unlike Diego, probably had powder and balls to spare.

Unless a natural site for an ambush presented itself, Diego stood little or no chance of emerging victorious from a confrontation with the *vaqueros,* especially with Santelmo weak and injured. There was also the problem of what would happen later if he attacked Spaniards in order to free a renegade Indian. Once Diego betrayed his own heritage, he could never return to the Spanish. Maria understood his dilemma better than he did. They had not had time to discuss the matter, but it was clear he would be doomed to live forever among the Indians, and she knew he was not yet ready to take such a drastic step.

The night passed slowly, and sometime before dawn, Diego finally returned.

"Come," he whispered to Maria. "We must leave before it grows light enough for them to see us riding away."

"Where are we going?" she whispered back. "What did you learn?"

"I will tell you later. All you need to know for now is that we are going to try to reach *Dehesa de Oro* before they do."

Forgetting to whisper, Maria exclaimed: *"What?"*

Diego clapped his hand over her mouth to silence her. "Be still! Will you risk your life or Santelmo's, when I cannot promise I will be able to save you? Just come with me quickly and quietly, and I will explain when we are out of earshot."

By the time the sun rose, they could no longer see anyone on the plain, and Maria could contain herself no longer.

"Why must we return to *Dehesa de Oro?*"

" 'Tis the only way to save your brother. Fighting the *vaqueros* out here is much too risky. They will do all in their power to kill me, and if they succeed, you and Santelmo will be at their mercy. They will rape and kill *you,* as they did Blue Water and Grasshopper. Santelmo they will haul back to your father, which they are doing now, in expectation of a rich reward. But if I get there first and explain what happened . . . how they abandoned the search for your father's horses in order to look for gold, and how they ran out on us—"

"You cannot tell my father you have become friends with the *Indios!* You especially cannot tell him you taught them how to ride horses."

"I have no intention of telling him all that." Diego made a gesture of impatience. "Let me explain, will you? I intend to behave as if I am outraged by all that has happened. I will try to act pleased that they have captured your brother, but furious that they abandoned us. Neither your father nor Miguel and the others must suspect that I plan to free Santelmo at the first opportunity. We need only bide our time, Maria, and we can put Santelmo on a fast horse—not La Reina, but another good animal—and he will be able to escape and return to Scar-Face and the others."

And us. What about us?

Maria was too afraid to ask the question, for she dreaded hearing the answer. So she asked another question instead. "Why not La Reina? She is the fastest horse my father owns, and Santelmo is accustomed to riding her."

"Because then your father would never give up. He would continue to send out more men to retrieve his best horse. This way, if Santelmo takes a lesser horse, there is a chance I can persuade Gonzalo to let the matter rest. I will explain to him the difficulties of ever finding Santelmo again, especially when winter comes."

"I doubt your plan will work, Diego."

His decision to return to her father, regardless of her feelings in the matter, left Maria feeling fearful and contentious. "When my father lays eyes on Santelmo—and hears that he was indeed the one who stole La Reina in the first place—he may slay him on the spot."

"Which is precisely why we have to hurry and get to him first. He needs time to digest the news before Santelmo suddenly appears. Do not worry, Maria. I can handle your father."

"You do not know him as well as I do."

"Perhaps not, but I know he will be furious that his *vaqueros* disobeyed his orders and were more interested in gold than his precious horses."

"Oh, he will be angry about that! But his anger will die when they suddenly appear with Santelmo and La Reina."

"We shall see." Diego's tone held a trace of smugness. "In any case, I will make those men pay for what they did to Blue Water and Grasshopper."

"How do you know for certain that Blue Water is dead? Did you hear them mention her?"

"The *vaqueros* taunted your brother with descriptions of all they had done to her before she died. They never even covered her body with stones or buried her. Like Grasshopper, they left her lying where she fell when they were done with her. Two days later, Santelmo finally caught up with them and rushed in like a fool to try and kill them with his puny weapons. He is badly hurt, Maria. He may have broken bones. But they will keep him alive to deliver to your father. They laughed and joked and made bets with one another on the size of the reward they expect to receive. Your brother's injuries are another reason why I hesitate to try to rescue him out here. He could never make good an escape just now."

"And us," Maria at last found the courage to venture. "Do they know about us? Do they realize we are still alive?"

"I think not. Unless Santelmo mentioned us—which I doubt—they have no idea where we are or where we have been. They probably think we are dead by now. They will be greatly surprised to find us awaiting them at *Dehesa de Oro*."

She almost confided her fears then—almost refused to return to her father's house. But she knew she could never leave Diego and her brother. Whether for good or ill, her future was bound to Diego's, and she must help him to free Santelmo, but oh, how she dreaded seeing her father and stepmother again! Knowing that Diego would once again be under their influence was almost more than she could bear. He would be the grand *hidalgo*, the Master of Horses, the heir-in-waiting, and she would be . . . nothing. She would be right where she had always been: dependent on the whims of a powerful Spaniard—just like her mother.

Diego claimed to love her, but how long would his infatuation last? . . . And how long before she became pregnant? Once she had children, she would truly be dependent upon Diego's good will, or lack of it. Good intentions aside, he might come to regard her as an embarrassment—a mistake—the way her father had come to view her mother. All her old fears resurfaced, and she rode back to *Dehesa de Oro* with a sad and heavy heart.

"Those traitorous scoundrels!" Don Gonzalo waved a goblet and sloshed brandy all over his bedclothes. "You say they rode off during the night to search for gold, and left you and Maria alone to face the Indians and the elements by yourselves?''

Diego nodded. He was not surprised to find Gonzalo still recovering from his injuries, but his host's deterioration *did* surprise him. Confined to bed now, Gonzalo had aged ten years, and his temper had definitely worsened. Before granting Diego admittance to her husband's bedchamber, Doña Inez had told him that her husband lived only for revenge now. He had ordered the rations for the Indians at the silver mine cut in half. And if any of them broke the rules, they were to be starved or beaten to death. She had shared her hope that Diego's reappearance would raise Gonzalo's spirits and give him a new reason for living—perhaps even get him out of bed.

"We are fortunate to be alive," Diego told the old man, "and even more fortunate to have found our way back to *Dehesa de Oro.*''

"But you say you never found those thieving *Indios* who stole my horses?" Gonzalo gazed petulantly at him from his nest of pillows and bolsters. "All this time, and you never found them?''

"The Ocean of Grass is bigger than you imagine, Gonzalo. We suffered much wandering on it. The fight for survival took all our efforts. Bartolomeo died before he could show us the way. Then we were on our own. Finding food and water was our first necessity. Without the old *Indio* to guide or help us, locating the thieves and retrieving the horses was out of the question. I am only one man," he reminded his host. "And your *vaqueros* took all our supplies. They left me a single *pistola,* but very little gunpowder. I was hard put to hunt game and protect us from wolves.''

" 'Tis indeed a wonder you were able to find your way back here," Doña Inez remarked from the foot of the bed where she stood guard over her husband. "I am surprised Maria survived the journey. But then, being half-*Indio,* she is more accustomed to hardship than a Spaniard.''

"Maria was wonderful," Diego defended. "Without her, I myself might be dead. When we could find no meat, she searched for tubers which kept up our strength. And she often caught small game with a snare. Bartolomeo taught her the skill.''

"Well, you are safely home now and can forget all your trials and tribulations." Doña Inez sniffed. "Gonzalo, we can wait no longer. Now that Diego has returned to us, we must proceed with our plans. We cannot risk losing him again. I urge to you get out of bed, my husband, and help me secure your empire before 'tis too late. Then we can remove ourselves to Santa Barbola, where—"

"Too late?" Diego questioned. "What do you mean—too late?''

"She means before I die," Gonzalo grumbled. "I have come close to dying now on several occasions, with no definite plans made for the disposition of my worldly goods. Doña Inez has been angry with me that I risked your life in this whole endeavor. We had begun to despair we would ever see you again. She made me promise that if you returned, we would move quickly to secure your future as my heir."

"Gonzalo, forgive me if I seem ungrateful, but I have no wish to be your heir. I prefer making my own fortune, and—"

"Nonsense! Why should you struggle to build all that I have already built in this land? When I die, *before* I die, it will all be yours. The only thing I ask in return is that after I am gone, you take care of Doña Inez and provide her with the style of living to which she is accustomed."

"Of course, I will take care of her, but—"

"You have no choice! I am determined to leave everything to you, whether you desire it or not. In time, you will be delighted. Any sane man would be. I am just sorry we have lost La Reina, for we can never replace her . . . or perhaps we can. I will write to your father and implore him to send me the very best mares he can find, so you may breed them to your stallion. You will live here at *Dehesa de Oro* and manage my holdings, including the breeding of fine horses, while Doña Inez and I retire to our house in the south, among more civilized people. 'Tis what my wife has always wanted, and what I want, too—now that I can barely get out of bed."

"Gonzalo, we must discuss this further," Diego insisted, for he knew how Maria would feel about all this. His own feelings were in turmoil. He was being handed the keys to a kingdom, given a new start in a world he already knew. The trouble was he wanted a *new* world now, one where . . .

"There is nothing to discuss, Diego. I intend you should be my heir and assume the management of *Dehesa de Oro*. My silver mine will one day be yours, as well. But for now, I need your help with the ranch and the horses. How can you refuse?"

Indeed, how could he? Gonzalo had offered him a haven when he most needed it. Much as he disliked the man, he could not abandon him in his hour of need. Maria would have to understand this and grant him some freedom in determining their future. As soon as Don Gonzalo and Doña Inez departed *Dehesa de Oro,* he could begin at once to make changes. In time, he would be able to change things at the silver mine, too. The cruelties and injustices must end; *this* was his chance— and Maria's—to abolish them forever.

"Well, my son, what do you say?" Gonzalo pressed him.

"I am deeply indebted to you, Gonzalo. You *know* that. Whatever you need, I am bound to provide."

"Good! Excellent. We must celebrate this great moment."

Doña Inez's eyes lit up. "We will have a *festividad* to announce you as my husband's heir! The cream of society will attend, and we will have dancing, music, and contests of skill among the *vaqueros—*"

"No, please don't." Diego could well imagine Maria's reaction. He must assure her that none of this in any way altered his feelings for her. Their relationship would remain the same.

"Don Diego, we must now find you a *wife!*" Doña Inez exclaimed with a sly sparkle in her eyes. "The *festividad* will be an opportunity for you to meet every eligible girl in the region and take your pick of the prettiest to be your wife and give you heirs of your own."

"I do not want a wife! I have Maria. You gave her to me, and she is all I will ever want or need."

"You cannot marry the daughter of an *Indio!*" Doña Inez exclaimed.

"She can be your mistress. No one is taking her away from

you," Don Gonzalo drawled with another wave of his hand and a sloshing of his brandy. "Give your wife her own quarters, and keep Maria separate from her. Who will know or care? No one will expect you to rid yourself of Maria, for she is my daughter. They will understand you must provide for her, too. You need only be discreet, and you can do whatever you wish. Just be sure you choose someone young and malleable to marry, a girl who will not argue or insist you give up your mistress. 'Tis all that is necessary, Diego. *You* will be master, after all. Not only the Master of Horses, but master of everyone who sets foot on *Dehesa de Oro.*"

"I oppose taking a wife," Diego insisted. "You can parade anyone you wish before me, but I will not consent to marry."

"You will change your mind!" Gonzalo chortled. "A man needs children—*legitimate* children—heirs to inherit his kingdom. Maria is hardly in a position to protest. I myself will tell her she must accept the inevitable."

"You will not say a word to her! If I marry anyone, it will be Maria."

"No, Diego. Think on what you are saying." Gonzalo wearily shook his head. "If Maria gives you children, they cannot inherit, for her children will not be pure-blooded Spaniards. Must I remind you? *Indios* or part-*Indios* cannot own land, or even ride horses. I never intended you should marry my daughter. I only intended you should *enjoy* her and look after her when I am gone. Continue bedding her, but think not of wedding her. Your duty is to pick a wife with the proper bloodlines. If she has a huge dowry or brings you more land or horses, so much the better. You will hardly need it, for you have wealth enough of your own now."

"I cannot allow you to manage my whole life," Diego bit out. "When I marry—*if* I marry—I will make my own choices."

"Diego, of *course,* you will choose your own wife!" Doña Inez gushed. "Let us not argue. 'Tis so silly to argue. Let me plan my *festividad,* to be held in one month's time. You will then have the opportunity to look over the marriageable daughters of our finest families. If you do not see one you like, we will forget about marriage for the time being. But do not deny us the pleasure of celebrating the fact that you have become our heir. My husband must settle his affairs at long last. This will give him peace of mind, and the freedom to go south where life will be easier, and he need not spend all his time worrying about *Indios* stealing his horses."

Diego reluctantly agreed. For now, he must go along with their plans, though he already knew there would be no one among the daughters of the *hidalgos* to compete with Maria. He could not imagine taking anyone else for a wife. As for society's rules about Indians, society would have to change. He would help bring about those changes—beginning with freeing Santelmo at the first opportunity. If *Dehesa de Oro* were going to be his, he would run it the way he saw fit, and get rid of any men who disagreed with him. As soon as Don Gonzalo and Doña Inez went south to Santa Barbola, he could begin. Now that he thought about it, he could scarcely wait to initiate reforms both here and at the silver mine.

It was only later, after he had taken his leave of Gonzalo and Doña Inez, that he realized how much his own life was about to change: Had he truly abandoned the idea of returning home again and regaining his own inheritance from his father? Had he given up the thought of vengeance against his cousin, Evaristo? By agreeing to become Gonzalo's heir, he was consenting to remain forever in the New World. He was trading one *Dehesa de Oro* for another.

He knew how Maria would feel about all this. Should he even tell her? Or should he wait until after he had freed her brother? Coward that he was, he dreaded telling her that he must remain here at *Dehesa de Oro* and never return to the Indians. She would hate the idea, but if he did not immediately tell her, she would find out soon enough for herself. The news of the *festividad* to celebrate his announcement as her father's heir would be all over the ranch within hours.

He decided he must tell her everything—or nearly everything, leaving out only the part about Doña Inez wanting to find him a proper wife. Yes, he would tell her, but *Dios!* he was not looking forward to it.

Chapter Twenty-one

Late in the evening of their first night back at *Dehesa de Oro*, in the privacy of Diego's quarters, Maria quietly listened to all Diego had to say. What he said was distressing enough, but what he did *not* say truly worried her.

He told her he had agreed to become her father's heir and take over the management of *Dehesa de Oro,* and that a *festividad* would be held to announce the event. He revealed that her father and stepmother intended to retire to the south, and that he himself had all but abandoned the idea of ever again returning to Spain. He described how angry Gonzalo had been with Miguel and the others, and how cleverly he had arranged things so the *vaqueros* would find themselves unwelcome when they returned. He reminded her that as soon as her brother recovered from the abuse he had suffered, he would help Santelmo escape. And he assured her that before too long, *Dehesa de Oro* would be a new place altogether.

But he did *not* tell her what the nature of their relationship would be from now on. He never mentioned marriage, and avoided the topic of returning to the Indians altogether. He knew how she felt about living among the Spanish—how she had always intended to make a new life for herself among her mother's people—but he never said one word about *her* dreams and desires. It was as if she had none, or he expected her to embrace his.

"Come to bed now, Maria," he urged. "The hour is late. You must be exhausted. Besides, I have a great need to hold you in the comfort of a soft bed, instead of on the hard ground."

She wanted to protest that she much preferred the hard ground over a soft bed, for the former meant freedom while the latter meant bondage. No matter what he thought or intended, her life would turn out to be just like her mother's. She did not think she could bear it, even for the sake of sharing Diego's bed every night.

"Diego," she murmured as he pulled her toward the bed and began undressing her.

"Naked," he whispered. "I would have you lie down with me naked, the way you were that first night I saw you."

"Diego, we must talk," she protested.

"I already know what you are going to say, Maria. It all comes down to trust. I have told you this before. You *must* trust me. You must believe me when I tell you I love you, and I will never do anything to hurt you. If I am to free your brother I must play a part that contradicts both my own feelings and what you expect from me. In order to help your people, I must behave as your father and stepmother desire, but as soon as I have the chance—as soon as they leave *Dehesa de Oro*—trust me, Maria. Believe in me. Do not force me to explain every single thing I do and withhold your love from me because you are always expecting the worst."

"But Diego, I am so afraid! I have so many questions, so many fears." She clung to him as he removed her clothing then drew her down to lie on the bed with him.

"Forget them, Maria." He kissed her brow and then her eyelids. He nuzzled her neck and trailed a line of kisses down to her breasts. "Trust only what you feel when I make love to you—when I hold you in my arms and *show* you what you mean to me. The world cannot hurt us, my beautiful little madonna. Only *we* can hurt us by our lack of trust. Help me shut out all the things that threaten to tear us apart."

"Diego, I do want to trust you and believe what you say, but changing things will not be as easy as you think!"

"Hush, now. I will make you forget all your fears. Lie still and relax. Surrender your mind and body. I will not disappoint you, Maria. This, I promise . . ."

His voice trailed off as his mouth moved across her body. He took his time and stoked her passion to a raging inferno that consumed all her fears, doubts, and hesitations. Later, when she lay limp and sated in his arms, she could scarcely remember why she had been so fearful. Diego loved her. That was all that mattered. He would protect and shield her. He would love their children, the beautiful daughters and stalwart sons she hoped to give him. He would claim them proudly, and her life would *never* be like her mother's. Her children would never suffer as she had. She must dwell on their love, not on her fears. Love was all they needed.

Two days later, the *vaqueros* arrived and dumped a half-dead Santelmo in the courtyard. Doña Inez rushed outside and started shrieking. Everyone in the house hurried to see what was happening, and Don Gonzalo demanded that he be carried outside to witness the cause of the commotion.

Maria ran to her brother's side. At this hour, Diego was down at the stable, but he must have seen the *vaqueros* ride up and would surely come to the house in time to stop her father from killing his long-lost son.

"Don Gonzalo!" Miguel shouted as two servants helped her father to a bench in the courtyard. "We have returned with the thief who stole your horses, and we have brought back La Reina. Unfortunately, we could not find the others."

"Who is it?" her father asked in a wavering voice. "Maria, get away from the scoundrel! Do you know the thief who lies unmoving in my courtyard?"

"Give her a moment, and she will soon recognize him." Miguel looked momentarily surprised and chagrinned to see her, but quickly recovered his confidence. Swinging down from his horse, he kept a steady hand on La Reina's reins, for the mare was skittish amidst all the furor. " 'Tis your own son, Don Gonzalo—Santelmo. He has been living all these years among the *Indios*. We captured his wife and child, but they did not survive the journey home. Santelmo himself is near death. We have done our best to keep him alive to suffer whatever punishment you deem fit for a horse thief."

"You have beaten him unmercifully!" Maria accused. " 'Tis a wonder he still lives. Look at these frightful injuries! Did you force him to fight all four of you?"

Kneeling on the cobblestones beside her bruised, bleeding unconscious brother, Maria glared at the four men in turn. Except for Miguel, they would not meet her gaze. "Yes, I am still alive," she spat. "Were you expecting otherwise? If so you will be greatly disappointed to hear that Don Diego lives also."

"I can speak for myself, Maria," Diego interrupted, emerging from the crowd and coming toward her. "So you found the horse thief, did you?"

He bent down, seized Santelmo by his long black hair, and lifted his head. "He looks more dead than alive, Gonzalo. Would you have me put him out of his misery now—or do you intend he should first recover, so he can suffer more later?"

His callousness sent a shiver down Maria's spine. She knew he was only acting, but his contempt for her brother seemed so real. His behavior was exactly what she might expect from an *hidalgo*.

"Miguel!" Diego let go of Santelmo's head, waiting a moment for Maria to catch it before it fell to the stones. "Did you find any of *my* horses? Or were you too busy looking for gold to worry about the rest of the animals?"

Miguel's sun-browned features paled as he returned Diego's murderous gaze. "We searched everywhere, *señor,* but we found neither horses nor gold. Only La Reina, and the man responsible for stealing the horses in the first place. I tried to persuade him to cooperate and tell us where to look for the others, but he refused. 'Tis why we had to beat him."

"Santelmo," Gonzalo muttered. "Once again, I see my traitorous son. As a man, he *continues* to betray me."

With great effort, Gonzalo rose from the bench and made his way over to Santelmo's battered figure. Maria immediately put herself between her father and her brother.

"Father, he is near death. Be merciful! He cannot hurt you now. Surely, he has paid for his crimes with the suffering he has endured at the hands of your men."

"Bah!" Gonzalo scoffed. "His suffering has only begun. Since you care so much for his welfare, you yourself will nurse him back to health, Maria. When he is strong enough, I will send him to the silver mine to spend the remainder of his days laboring in the darkness. He will never again see the sunlight or feel the breeze on his face. . . . What do you think, Diego? Is that not a worthy punishment for a son who betrays his father, not once but twice?"

"No!" Maria screamed, playing her own part, which was easy. All she had to do was express the horror she felt.

"To me, it sounds good," Diego said. "The mine is the perfect place for him. Give him back his life, and then make him regret it. 'Tis a punishment that fits the crime of horse stealing."

"Put him in the potting shed," Doña Inez directed the two servants who had assisted her husband. "I myself will keep the door locked. Maria, you will tend him twice daily. If he dies, it was meant to be. If he lives, the mine will be his just reward."

"And what about *our* reward, Don Gonzalo?" Miguel demanded. "We brought him back, along with La Reina, your finest mare. What reward will you give to us?"

Gonzalo staggered back to his bench before answering. "Diego, *you* decide. *Dehesa de Oro* is yours, now. Will you reward these men, and keep them to work for you? Or will you send them away with nothing, which is only what they deserve for abandoning you and my daughter in the wilderness? You have my blessing to kill them, if you prefer. I wonder what story they would have told if you had not arrived before they did."

"We would have told the truth, *patrón*. We are not murderers. We only wanted the gold for *your* sake. We thought you would want us to search for gold, since it can buy many more horses than you lost.''

"Enough lies," Diego growled. "You wanted the gold for yourselves. Leave at once, and never again show your faces, or I will shoot you on sight. Shooting you now would be preferable, but also stooping to *your* level. Be glad I am not sending you away on foot. The idea tempts me, but without horses you would not get very far, and I hope never to see you again.''

"You ought not to send us away at all!" Miguel's indignant cry drowned out the wails of several women. "We did nothing wrong. We could have stolen *your* horse, and left *you* afoot.''

"You could not have laid a hand on El Cid, and well you know it. You left us little enough to ensure our survival." A muscle ticked in Diego's jaw as he strode over to the *arrendador* and seized La Reina's reins. "Be gone now, before I change my mind. Nothing would give me greater pleasure than to treat you as you treat *Indios.*''

"*Indios,*" Miguel sneered. "The world would be better off without *any* of them.''

Maria clenched her hands together. From Diego's expression she knew he felt the same disgust and need for revenge that she did. But they must think of Santelmo now; it was too late to help Blue Water or little Grasshopper—and her father watched with great interest. Diego dare not show compassion for her brother.

"You have until the sun rises tomorrow morning to leave *Dehesa de Oro,*" Diego responded. "If you are still on this land by then, I will shoot you down like wild dogs.''

" 'Tis not fair! Don Gonzalo's holdings are too vast. One can ride for days and still be on his land.''

"Then I suggest you set out at once. Watch for me behind you. If I appear, you will know you are dead men.''

"We are dead men, anyway. We have no food, and are short of water. We also need more gunpowder. Ours will soon be gone.''

"Strange, is it not? 'Tis exactly how you left me. If anyone lifts a finger to help you, they will join you in your banishment

I will send them with you. Get out of here, now. I despise the sight of you."

From the corner of her eye, Maria saw Pedro lift his *pistola*. Diego saw the movement, too.

"Shoot me, and you will need to shoot all of us, Pedro. Every *hidalgo* in the New World will come after you. We *hidalgos* stick together. We do not tolerate being gunned down on our own lands. Did you learn any survival skills from this wretched *Indio*? I sincerely hope you did, for you will need them now. Put that *pistola* away, and ride off while you still can. My patience wears thin."

Without saying a word, Pedro shoved his *pistola* back in its holster. Red-faced, he turned away, and the others followed. Not sparing them another glance, Maria turned her attention to her brother. Santelmo's survival appeared strongly in doubt.

Santelmo did not die, but his injuries were so extensive that Maria feared he would never again be the same man. He would always walk with a limp and have limited use of one arm. He was forced to stop and think before he spoke, for his speech was slurred and slow in returning, and he had frequent headaches.

Still, by the time of the *festividad,* little more than a fortnight later, he was much improved, able to hobble across the potting shed, turn around, and hobble back again to his pallet. He did not say much, however. Whenever Maria gazed into his eyes she glimpsed his despair, and had to assure him Diego would arrange his escape as soon as he was well enough to sit a horse and look after himself.

In the meantime, he must strive to get better—while she herself strove to quell her own fears that Diego was fast being gobbled up by his new responsibilities and falling prey to the plans her father and Doña Inez were making for him.

On the afternoon of the first day of the *festividad,* she overheard her stepmother and her father talking. All day long, men on horseback and carriages bearing beautifully dressed women had been arriving. Among them were many lovely young girls of marriageable age. Maria had already guessed that her stepmother was plotting to marry Diego off to the daughter of some *hidalgo*. Now she learned which particular young woman Doña Inez had in mind.

"What do you think of *Señorita* Eugenia as a wife for Diego?" Doña Inez asked Maria's father as they sat together in the courtyard greeting newly arrived guests and directing them to their quarters.

Maria ducked behind a latticework of greenery. Her arms filled with bedding, she waited breathlessly to hear his answer. The entire house as well as the stable had been converted to provide sleeping quarters for the guests during this three-day event, and she had been working unceasingly since well before dawn.

"Eugenia's a pretty enough girl," her father answered after a pause, "but is she quiet and biddable? Will she ignore Diego's association with Maria, or will she give way to a fit of weeping and screaming when she finds out?"

"If she does have a fit, Maria will simply have to move out of the house and take up residence in a hut somewhere on the grounds. Diego can visit her there, if he must. Her removal from the house might be a good idea, anyway. He will be quite busy for a time when he takes a lovely young wife to his bed. He may even forget about Maria. At least, his infatuation for her will dim."

"You are probably right, Inez," her father sighed. "Somehow, you are always right."

"I accept that as a compliment, my husband. 'Tis all working out according to plan. Eugenia will make Diego a wonderful wife. She brings a portion of her father's land as part of her dowry. We should insist that he add some of his best breeding stock to the bargain. He has some good horseflesh you have always coveted, does he not?"

"Yes, and Diego would like that. We need more mares to replace the ones those damn *Indios* still have."

"The wedding should take place immediately," Doña Inez continued. "What is the sense of sending everyone back home again—over such long distances—when they would only have to return again before winter? If Diego and Eugenia are marry, it must take place before winter. Spring is too long to wait. There is always too much to be done in the spring, anyway. Let us do it at once. I want grandchildren as soon as possible— *legitimate* grandchildren.''

"Are you not rushing things a bit, Inez? He has yet to meet the girl. And there are a half dozen other young women with the same goal as young Eugenia, to catch themselves a rich husband like Diego, preferably Diego himself.''

"Nothing good comes from sitting on one's hands, my husband. Leave everything to me. I can arrange it.''

"But what about Santelmo? I wanted him gone from here by now, and still, he lingers. Has he not recovered enough to be sent to the mine? That bit of unpleasantness should be taken care of before a new bride comes to stay in the house.''

"I will check on the situation, at once. If he is fit to travel, he can be taken under guard to the mine immediately following the *festividad*. I agree with you. The sooner he is gone from the house, the better. Eugenia's family would not be pleased to have their daughter living near a rogue, scoundrel, and horse thief. He is a reminder of your tainted past, my husband—an embarrassment, at the very least.''

"So is Maria,'' her father pointed out. "Indeed, the more I think on it, the more I worry about her influence on Diego. You wanted him to fall in love with her, Inez. Now that he has, it could prove to be a great inconvenience. He fancies himself loyal and faithful to her. He does *not* see himself wedding another.''

"Leave everything to me, my husband. Men lack inventiveness when it comes to affairs of the heart and the bedchamber. All of Eugenia's family are here, including her three strong brothers. If her reputation were to be in the least ... ah ... compromised, I doubt not they would see her wed at swordpoint, if need be.''

Gonzalo's chuckle set Maria's teeth on edge. "Ah, but you are a wicked conspirator, wife! I could almost feel sorry for Diego—except 'tis clear we know better than he does what is best for him. Ah, here come Eugenia's brothers and the rest of her family now.''

"And the lovely Eugenia herself," Doña Inez added in a whisper. "Tell me what you think, my husband. Is she not a beauty to make a man forget an ill-bred, half-*Indio?*

"*Dios!* She is incredible, Inez."

Maria walked a little farther down the length of the screen, to a point where she could peer through the latticework to study her rival. What she saw made her heart skip a beat: delicate ivory skin, flashing black eyes, and a manner that was at once innocent and mischievous. *Señorita* Eugenia had hair that shone like a raven's wing, and lips and cheeks that held the tint of roses.

She was the loveliest thing Maria had ever seen—impossibly graceful, perfectly proportioned, and already turned out in a bridal-white gown dripping with lace. From the way she was dressed, one might think she anticipated marriage in her immediate future.

Madre de Dios! How could she ever compete with *this?* In truth, she could not. It would make no difference, anyway, because she would not be here to try to compete with her. She would be somewhere far away on the Ocean of Grass with Santelmo.

As Diego finished dressing in a black velvet doublet trimmed with gold braid, he could not help wondering where Maria was. He had not seen her since early that morning, and he was hungry for the sight of her. He hated the idea of spending most of the night being charming and gracious to people he did not even know. He would much rather spend his time making love to Maria and reassuring her that nothing had changed between them. He loved her now more than ever, and they could live happy, fulfilling lives at *Dehesa de Oro*.

Society was bound to change sooner or later, and if he had anything to say about it—and he would—it would be sooner. She must begin practicing the patience she had so often preached.

A slight sound outside his bedchamber made him turn, expecting to see Maria. But a stranger stood in the doorway—

a lovely young woman looking as surprised to see him as he was to see her.

"Oh!" she exclaimed. "Pardon me. I seem to be lost. I thought Doña Inez's bedchamber was in this wing of the house. She left her shawl lying on the bed. The servants were all busy, so I offered to fetch it for her."

"You have entered the wrong wing," Diego informed her. "This is the west wing, and my quarters are the only ones here. You want the east wing. You had better turn around and go right back. There is no one else here but me, and you ought not to be alone with—"

"Eugenia!" called an impatient male voice. "Where have you gone off to now? Mother is looking all over for you."

"Oh, dear! 'Tis one of my brothers. I had better hide! If he should find me alone with you—"

"Wait!" Diego exclaimed as the girl darted behind the wooden door and pressed her finger to her lips to warn him to silence.

A moment later, an elegantly dressed, distracted-looking young man with a mustache appeared in the same doorway the girl had just vacated.

"Oh!" he said, echoing his sister's reaction. "Excuse me. I am looking for my sister, Eugenia. She is forever going off alone in complete disregard for her safety and reputation. Not that she has anything to fear in *this* house, of course, but she keeps all of us—her brothers—busy keeping track of her whereabouts. She went off on her own over an hour ago, leaving our poor mother in a state of extreme agitation."

"Well, as you can see," Diego drawled, indicating the empty room with a sweep of his hand, "she is not here."

Just then, the girl coughed. Diego heard it clearly—and so did her brother. Suspicion flared in his eyes. Stepping into the room, he closed the door behind him, revealing his cowering sister.

"Eugenia! I *knew* you would one day go too far with your mischief. Now, look what you have done! Your reputation is ruined." The young man turned to Diego. "Whoever you are, señor . . . You will have to answer for this."

"For what?" Diego snapped. "I did nothing. Nor did your sister. She only came here to fetch a shawl for Doña Inez."

He felt as if he were playing a part in a dream—or had suddenly been transported back in time to another incident when being in the wrong place at the wrong time had convicted him of a crime he had never committed. That incident had changed his entire life, and so might this one.

"A shawl!" the young man scoffed. "I see no shawl. If your story is true, why is my sister hiding behind the door? And why did you lie to me—telling me no one was here?"

"Because I thought . . ." Diego paused to gather his wits. "I knew how it would look if she were found here alone in my bedchamber, and I did not wish to get her in trouble."

"She is already in trouble! No young woman of good family would *dare* be found alone with a man in his bedchamber. Who else will want her now? Her reputation is destroyed."

"But nothing happened!" Diego grated. "Ask your sister. See what she says. I never touched her."

"Eugenia?" The young man rounded on his sister, scowling and waiting for an answer.

The girl looked discomfitted . . . but also guilty. She gazed first at her brother and then at Diego. She neither confirmed nor denied her brother's accusation. In the end, she only shrugged her shoulders.

An alarm clanged in Diego's head. Then he heard the voice of Doña Inez. "Diego, where are you? I want everyone to meet you. We are all awaiting your presence."

"I am here, Doña Inez," he answered, "and I wish to ask you about your shawl."

"Shawl?" Sweeping into the room in a rustle of black velvet and lace, she looked questioningly from one to the other. She seemed surprised to see them all standing there. "What shawl? I have my shawl right here."

She patted the square of lace covering her shoulders and gave Diego a triumphant smile. " 'Tis chilly tonight, and I have been wearing it all evening."

Chapter Twenty–two

The noise and commotion of the *festividad* combined with the darkness gave Maria the perfect opportunity to put her plan into action. It was an easy matter to steal the key to the potting shed from Doña Inez's bedchamber. She had a more difficult time getting Santelmo from the potting shed down to the stable. Bridling two horses and putting her brother up on one proved next to impossible. She did not know how she managed to do all this without being seen, but she did. Desperation fueled her efforts. She had to act quickly; there was neither time nor opportunity to tell Diego what she was doing and why. He had a new life now, anyway. It was all planned for him, and she was the only obstacle.

As she hiked up her skirts and climbed aboard a horse, she told herself it was better this way. She preferred to part now, while he still loved her, than to wait until he began to look at her with regret in his eyes, wishing he was free to live the life to which he had been born.

She could not stay here and watch the tragedy unfold; it would be too painful. Santelmo needed to escape *now,* before they took him to the mine and sealed him in a tomb forever. No Indian ever left the mine alive; they stayed there until they died from too much work, too little food, and frequent beatings. She would not let this happen to her brother.

She urged her horse into a trot, but Santelmo cried out in pain, and she had to drop back to a walk.

"Santelmo, you must be quiet. No matter how much it hurts, you must restrain yourself, or someone will hear us."

"I will t-try," her brother groaned. "B-but you should stay here. Diego will . . . look after you, m-my sister."

She had not told Santelmo everything—not about the beautiful young woman her stepmother intended for Diego to marry, or the plan to remove her from the house. She did not tell him now. Until they skirted all the outbuildings and reached the Ocean of Grass, they should not be talking at all.

"Hush," she whispered. "Save your strength for riding. We have a long way to go tonight."

No sooner had she finished speaking than a figure on horseback, barely visible in the darkness, hailed them. "Who are you? Identify yourselves, or I will shoot."

It was a lone *vaquero* keeping watch for late arriving guests. Maria did not dare identify herself or her brother.

"Santelmo, hold on! We must get away from here at once."

His answer was lost as she urged her horse into a flat-out gallop. The man behind her began shouting. A shot rang out. Voices of other men joined the shouts of the first man.

Dios! How many men were there?

She could not stop to look—nor even to see if Santelmo followed close behind her. She could only hope that his horse would keep up with her horse for fear of being left behind.

"Follow me, Santelmo!" she screamed. "Follow me as we race for freedom!"

"I will not marry her," Diego emphatically stated. "You cannot force me into it."

"Can we not?" Eugenia's father asked. "Look around you, Don Diego. There are three swords and a *pistola* aimed at your midsection. There could be more. I have many relatives and loyal friends."

The weapons did not bother Diego; what hurt were the disapproving glances. Virtually every person there eyed him with a contempt bordering on insult. In their minds, he had dishonored the daughter of a family they knew and trusted, and was now refusing to do right by her. If he did *not* marry the girl, he would be alienating potential friends, neighbors, and people with whom he hoped to conduct business. For as long as he lived here in the New World, they would never forget this. If they did not kill him, they would shun him. He would be unwelcome wherever he went.

For the second time in his life, he faced becoming an outcast—a man everyone despised and no one would ever call friend. Having once again made enemies of all his peers, where could he run and hide this time?

"We did nothing wrong," he repeated for the third—or was it the fourth?—time. "This was all arranged for the sole purpose of forcing me into marriage." He gazed pointedly at Doña Inez. "Someone . . . has convinced this young woman that she can succeed in trapping me into wedding her."

"My sister has no need to trap any man," one of Eugenia's brothers—the man who had found them—sneered. "She is the most beautiful *señorita* in the region. She has many suitors. Why would she even *want* to marry a man who lives at the edge of the world, where attacks by *Indios* are always a danger, and her own family is so far away?"

"Perhaps you should ask *her*. She should have thought of all that before she came bursting into my bedchamber and hid behind my door when she heard you coming."

"She says you *invited* her into your quarters and assured her she would not be alone with you. She claims you tried to seduce her and would not listen when she begged you to stop. If I had failed to come along when I did—"

"She lies."

"She was found alone with you!" Eugenia's father bellowed, while her mother wept copiously in the arms of another female guest and Eugenia herself appeared close to swooning. "Her whole life is ruined. No other man of good family will have her now."

"B-but Father!" Eugenia sniffed. " 'Tis obvious Don Diego does not want me—at least, not now, though he seemed to want me enough when we were alone together."

An angry murmur rose among the onlookers.

"Whether he wants you or not hardly matters! Honor demands he marry you here and now, before the day is out."

Diego wondered why he alone was the only one who could see that the girl was lying. Doña Inez had put her up to this, but no one else seemed to realize it—or care.

"I agree he must marry your daughter, Don Constantino, but he cannot do so tonight," Doña Inez interrupted. "We must send for a priest. It will take a week or more for one to arrive."

"Then we will avail ourselves of your fine hospitality, until a priest can be found," Don Constantino said. "We will not leave here until our daughter is wed to this man. He does not deserve her, but he must accept her or face the consequences."

"He is my heir," Gonzalo stated, opening his mouth for the first time since the incident had happened. "That is why you were all invited—so I could announce my decision to retire to the south and leave everything in the hands of Don Diego. He is a Master of Horses, an *arrendador* of incomparable skill, a true gentleman and a man of honor. Forgive his reluctance in this matter, but I am sure that when he has had time to think about it he will agree he must marry your daughter."

"I will never agree," Diego insisted.

"But of course you will!" Gonzalo disputed. "Must I watch your blood be spilled here on my floor? I hardly think so. We will send for the priest, and *he* will convince you. If he does not—if all of us fail—I myself will take up a sword and prod you to the altar. 'Tis your duty to marry her."

"He does not want me!" Eugenia sobbed, covering her face with her hands. "How can he not want me? I am so ashamed."

As well you should be, Diego thought in disgust. The girl had made a great mistake entrusting her future to Doña Inez. In a way, he almost felt sorry for her; she was being manipulated as much as he was.

Doña Inez put her arms around the distraught girl and comforted her. "There, there, my dear. Of course, he wants you.

You are so beautiful! No man could help but want you. Don
Diego need only accustom himself to the idea of wedding you,
and the two of you will be divinely happy. Fear not for your
future, my dear. I shall be ecstatic to call you my daughter-in-
law, even as I call Diego my son.''

She smiled encouragingly at the gathering. ''Come along
everyone, and let us go to supper. Take my arm, sweet Eugenia.
Better yet, take Diego's. Dry your tears and *smile*, my dear.
There is nothing to worry about.''

When Diego did not offer his arm to the girl, her father and
brothers pressed closer. One of them pricked him in the back
with the tip of his sword.

''You have the manners of a swine!'' he hissed. ''Can you
not at least take my sister's arm and lead her into supper?''

''*That* I can do,'' Diego growled. ''As for the rest—''

''You will do it or die!'' the girl's father retorted. ''I curse
the hour I set foot in this household.''

''Now, now, *señors*,'' Don Gonzalo placated. ''You cannot
mean that. My house is *your* house. While you are my guests,
all I own I gladly put at your disposal.''

He motioned to his servants to come and pick up his wooden
chair and carry him after the others. This was how he got
around these days—and why he wanted Diego's future carved
in stone. They all meant to force him into marriage; his only
other choice was to free Santelmo, take Maria, and run with
both of them back to the Indians.

And that is what I will do, he decided. He would not be
manipulated or forced into anything—particularly marriage.
The only vows he would ever make would be to Maria.

Until his plans were in place, he had to pretend to yield to
this foolishness. Gonzalo and Doña Inez had no idea how he
truly felt about Maria, or they would never have tried to trap
him like this. Well, soon they would know the truth of the
matter. He had promised Maria he would never hurt her, and
he never would. He regretted losing *Dehesa de Oro* and the
opportunity to change things, but he would never regret spending the rest of his life with the woman he loved. He wanted to
be wherever *she* was. She, at least, would be delighted to return

to her beloved Indians. Tonight, he would tell her. They would
plan it together. They did not have much time—a week, Doña
Inez had said—before a priest could make the journey here.
By then, Santelmo should be strong enough to travel, and they
could flee. He would take El Cid, La Reina, and one other
horse, the fastest he could find.

Somehow, Diego managed to survive the rest of the evening.
By the time he was free to return to his bedchamber, the hour
was late. He expected Maria to be sleeping in his bed, but to
his great surprise and disappointment she was neither in his
bed, nor anywhere else in his quarters. After searching them
thoroughly, he headed for the rest of the house to look for her.
Eugenia's vigilant brother stopped him at the entrance to the
west wing.

"Looking for another young victim whose reputation you
can ruin?" Slurring his words, the man drunkenly waved his
sword about. "Wherever you are going, I am going with you.
Until you marry my sister, one of my family will accompany
you wherever you go . . . and we will allow no other young
women to enter your quarters."

"This is outrageous!" Diego exclaimed. "I am only looking
for a servant to . . . to bring me some water."

"I will have water sent to you. I will bring you some myself.
But I will not let you go anywhere alone, Don Diego. I would
sooner run you through with my sword."

"What if I fetch a sword of my own? Will you fight me
when the odds are equal?"

"My brothers and I will *all* fight you. So will my father and
uncles. 'Tis a matter of honor, Don Diego, a concept you seem
not to understand. Before you become my brother-in-law, I
will teach it to you."

Diego sighed. "Forget the water. I am going to bed now.
You should go, too. Honor can be very tiring."

The man snapped his heels together. "Not for me, *señor.*
The most important thing a man possesses is his honor. Once
lost, it can never be regained."

"So I have been told—repeatedly. Believe me. I know all
about honor."

"Then you will marry my sister without all this bother?" He looked suddenly hopeful.

"If I had truly done what you accuse me of doing, I would marry your sister without a single protest. As it is, I am bound to resist right up until the moment you force me to say my vows."

"Force you I shall, *señor.*"

"I am sure you will try. *Buenas noches, señor.*"

Maria awoke to darkness and the clank of a chain. She and Santelmo had been bound hand and foot in chains and tossed inside some sort of shed or hut. The smell of manure was overwhelming, and she suddenly realized where they were—in Bartolomeo's little house by the manure pile.

Light seeping through the brush-covered roof indicated morning—or at least, daytime. She had no idea how long they had been there, but her muscles were cramped and aching and her mouth filled with grit. She longed for a drink of water, and wondered whether her brother was sleeping, unconscious, or perhaps even dead.

"Santelmo!" she whispered. "Santelmo, wake up."

He groaned and moved a little.

"Are you all right?"

A long moment passed before he found strength to answer. "I am no worse off . . . than I was before. I still live . . . unfortunately."

" 'Tis not unfortunate! While we live, there is hope."

"Somehow . . . I doubt that."

The fragile door of sticks suddenly opened, and a familiar figure stepped through it. With one hand, Doña Inez held up her skirts. With the other, she pressed a kerchief to her nose. The *vaquero* who had called his companions to help capture them accompanied her.

"You have put them in a proper place here, Manuel. The air is so foul I can scarcely breathe," Doña Inez complained. "You say someone actually lives inside this pig sty?"

"*Sí, Señora,* the *Indio* who was brought from the silver mine to take the place of the old man who once tended the manure pile," the *vaquero* answered.

Maria did not know Manuel; he was one of several newly hired *vaqueros*. Nor had she met the Indian of whom he spoke.

"This place is fit only for hogs and *Indios*," Doña Inez grumbled. "I would have you take them somewhere else while I speak to them, but I want no one to see us. . . . Worthless One! Wake up."

Maria struggled to face her stepmother in an upright position. Her chains impeded her, and her wrists stung from the abrasion of the heavy iron metal. She managed to sit up and straighten her back, but standing required more effort than she could muster.

"What a mess you are!" her stepmother observed. "I have never seen you look so dirty or unkempt. If Diego saw you now, he would be only too happy to wed the young woman I have picked out for him."

Maria thought of the lovely Eugenia in her spotless white gown. She wrinkled her nose against her own ripe odor, but somehow found the courage to ask the question uppermost in her mind. "Where is Don Diego?"

She was so hoarse she could hardly speak. She knew Doña Inez understood, because her lips curved in a malicious smile. "Well, he is not pining for you, my dear, if that is what you wish to know. Indeed, before the day is out I expect him to announce his intention to wed a certain young woman—a clean young woman, the sweet-smelling daughter of a very rich *hidalgo*. She is the perfect match for him."

Maria refused to react to her stepmother's cruelty. "He will be wondering where I am. I imagine he is looking all over for me, and will not rest until he finds me."

"You flatter yourself. He is not looking for you. I have already informed him that you are missing—you and your brother both, along with a couple of horses. He is hurt and angry that you chose to leave him and run away with your brother. What he does *not* know is that you were captured."

"Why keep it a secret?" Maria squinted to see her stepmother better in the gloom.

Doña Inez had pushed the stick door partially shut. She was dressed in her usual black, and seemed more like a dark specter than a woman—a specter from a bone yard, perhaps.

"Because he must never discover what really happened to you. He will think you and Santelmo are living happily among the savages, but you will actually spend the remainder of your days in the silver mine."

"N-not Maria!" Santelmo rattled his chains in protest. "I . . . will go willingly, if only . . . you will spare her."

"Oh, I do not intend she will work in the bowels of the earth at your side, Santelmo. I have a much better punishment in mind for *her*. I will give her to the guards. They have so little female companionship. They can all take turns with her. Each night, she can amuse a different man."

"Does my father know about this?" Maria demanded. "Have you told *him* we were captured?"

"One of these days, I may tell him. Like Diego, he thinks you have fled for good. He wants to send *vaqueros* after you, but Diego has dissuaded him from that. Nor does Diego himself intend to pursue you. Your lover is nursing a wounded heart, my dear, and never wants to see you again. I was searching for a way to make him fall out of love with you, and you kindly provided it. He despises you now, and hopes never to lay eyes on you again."

Tears welled in Maria's eyes, but she would not give her stepmother the satisfaction of seeing them. She turned her face away from the meager light. "When will you send us to the mine? Santelmo is still too weak to make such an arduous journey."

"Oh, I intend he shall have a few days rest. I dare not do it while I still have so many guests who might witness your departure. You can lie here in your chains for a while, smelling this awful stench and contemplating your futures. However, I *will* remove you before Diego's wedding. Before he exchanges vows with the young woman I have chosen for him, I want you both gone from here. Picturing you suffering at the mine will enhance my enjoyment of the nuptial festivities."

"You finally have your heart's desire." Maria could not

contain her bitterness. "You have rid yourself of me and my brothers, and your son has been replaced by another. Now, you have a *new* son."

"And a daughter-in-law of whom I can be proud . . . yes, and grandchildren, too. Now, I will have beautiful grandchildren I can visit whenever I please. But I myself—and your father—will be living in the south among genteel society. I will never again have to see an *Indio*, much less smell one. I must remember to make my grandchildren come visit *me*, for when I leave *Dehesa de Oro*, it will be forever. Never again will I set foot in this godforsaken wilderness. My exile here is ending."

How odd that they should share a common desire to never again set foot on the lands of *Dehesa de Oro!* If only she and Santelmo had escaped . . . if only Diego would guess what had really happened . . . but he might refuse to help them even if he *knew* they were bound in chains and headed for the silver mine. He was probably glad to finally be rid of her. In her haste to rescue her brother, she had demonstrated an appalling lack of trust. Her actions spoke more loudly than words that she wanted nothing more to do with Diego.

He had not betrayed *her:* she had betrayed *him.* She had doubted their love and counted it insufficient to overcome their problems. She saw it all clearly now: She had no one but herself to blame for the way it had all turned out. This was the opportunity her stepmother had long been awaiting. Now, she and Santelmo would die slow, lingering deaths, and Diego would never even know they had gone to the silver mine.

"Get out of here, Doña Inez! You have said what you came here to say—why do you remain? What more is there to add?"

"Oh, there is always more, my dear. 'Tis so enjoyable to gloat. My only regret is the pain I have caused poor Diego. But he will soon forget you. When he lies beside his beautiful new wife, your memory will quickly fade. And when she gives him a child, he will be glad he can offer the babe everything your father did not dare offer you. What a pity you will no live long enough to see *that,* Worthless One. I believe it would hurt more than being raped by the prison guards."

"Nothing can hurt me any more. Do you not understand

what you have done this day? I am dead inside. My body is
only a shell. I no longer feel anything."

"It would seem I have gone too far, then," Doña Inez
sneered. "But if we stop at the silver mine on our way south,
I will be sure and ask the guards whether or not you scream
when they abuse you, or if you ever weep or cry out in your
sleep. Any such sign of life will please me immensely. *Adios,*
Worthless One. I doubt we will meet again."

"Unless we meet in your Christian hell," Maria retorted.

"Do not set your hopes too high, my dear. Even in hell,
Indios will have a lesser place than Spaniards. How could it
be otherwise?"

Doña Inez left then, shutting the door behind her, and Maria
succumbed to bitter, silent tears.

Never had Diego felt so bereft, not even when his father
refused to listen to his explanation about the murder he had
been accused of committing. He could not understand what
had driven Maria to flee with Santelmo—to leave *Dehesa de
Oro* without him! No one had yet mentioned taking her brother
to the silver mine. Even if they had, she had known he intended
to rescue him. It would not have happened during the *festividad,*
anyway; her father and stepmother would not have wanted their
guests to be aware of the awkward situation.

As for the scandal involving Eugenia, Diego could not see
how Maria could have known about it before she made her
plans. The incident had not happened until nightfall—around
the same time she and Santelmo must have been busy stealing
horses. If she *had* known about it, she ought to have realized
he was innocent. Why would he yearn for another, when he
already slept every night with the most beautiful woman in the
world?

Her behavior baffled him. Yet she was gone, and so was
Santelmo, along with two horses. Gonzalo still wanted him to
send *vaqueros* after them, but Doña Inez was more concerned
about keeping the matter a secret from their guests. She claimed
she wanted no more embarrassments.

Diego spent three days brooding and thinking. During that time, he refused to join the others for meals or sporting events on horseback. For the most part, he remained alone in his quarters, guarded by Eugenia's brothers. All he did was pace the floor—and refuse to accept the truth. Maria had not trusted him. She had not believed in his promise to rescue Santelmo. He had failed to convince her that he was sincere in his desire to make changes.

On the evening of the third day of the *festividad,* Eugenia herself, accompanied by her brothers, begged him to come out and sit with her at dinner. He refused. An hour later, it finally struck him why Maria had really left. What he had offered was not enough. She wanted *more.* She yearned for a wedding, just like Eugenia. Marriage was the one thing he had never offered—the one thing he could not yet promise.

She was unwilling to wait or take the risk of losing him. So she had made up her own mind and plotted her own course. She lacked not only trust, but love; she did not love him enough to give him a chance to prove himself.

Why was he torturing himself over her defection? She was gone. Their relationship was over. She demanded he give up everything for *her,* but was apparently unwilling to give up anything for *him.* She required freedom, not fidelity. He had offered her the wrong thing altogether.

Had she come to him and begged him to go away with her he might have considered it, but she had not given him the choice. Part of him was cold and dead, but the rest of him needed to go on living. With a heavy heart, he went to his door, opened it, and walked out past Eugenia's most zealous brother.

"Where are you going?" the man demanded, stepping in front of him.

"To see your sister. I think, if I am to wed her, I ought to at least get to know her first."

"Madre de Dios! Have you at last come to your senses?"

Diego nodded. "I think so. Or if I have not, I can at least give a beautiful young woman a chance to persuade me."

"You will not be sorry, Don Diego. Eugenia will make you a fine wife."

"So everyone seems to think." *Even Maria. If Maria had known about this match, her departure meant she approved of it.*

Pain twisted anew in his heart, but Diego steadfastly ignored it. She had made her choice. Now, he must make his. He would be a fool to turn his back on *Dehesa de Oro* for the sake of a woman who could not find it in her heart to trust him. He had lost the first *Dehesa de Oro* through circumstances beyond his control; he would not lose this one.

Chapter
Twenty–three

A full week passed, and Fray Leonido, the priest Doña Inez
had sent for, did not appear. Diego had begun taking part in
the meals and various amusements available to the guests, but
still the *hidalgos* were getting restless. Cooler weather reminded
them that preparations for winter had to be made at their own
haciendas. Eugenia's family, in particular, was impatient for
the wedding to take place. They rejoiced that Diego was no
longer resisting it—and indeed, was paying court to their sister.

Under the watchful eyes of her brothers, Diego made an
honest effort to get to know the girl, despite the fact that he
could not help comparing her to Maria and finding her lacking.
Though beautiful, Eugenia had no substance. All her life she
had been pampered, petted, sheltered, and adored. Other than
her own personal amusement, which she pursued with enthusiasm, she had no interests, plans, or goals, except to marry a
rich, handsome *hidalgo*.

The only fire or spirit she had thus far shown was to plot
with Doña Inez to entrap him. When he gazed into Eugenia's
eyes, he did not see mystery, excitement, or that indefinable
energy that drew him like a moth to a flame with Maria. There
was no fox fire—only a self-absorbed emptiness, and he knew

that his life with her would be empty, too. Marrying her would in no way betray his feelings for Maria; other than boredom, he could never have any feelings for this girl. In Spain, he had known a thousand women just like her . . . but there was only *one* Maria.

On the eighth day, a message arrived from Fray Leonido. An outbreak of fever in Santa Barbola had detained him. Several people had died, and he had to conduct funerals and administer last rites to the stricken. When he was sure the epidemic had passed, he would come at once for the wedding.

The news greatly upset all the guests, and they rushed to depart.

"We must return home to check on our own households and servants," one of them said, echoing the sentiments of all. "If the fever comes here, it could wipe out too many *hidalgos* at one time. 'Tis better if we separate, and each family returns to its own *hacienda*. Hopefully, the infection will spread no further than the town itself. We will avoid passing through there on our way home and pray for the best."

The family of Don Constantino could not decide whether to go or stay. Doña Inez finally solved the problem by suggesting that the family go, but Eugenia remain.

"Have no fear the marriage will not take place. I myself will see to it," Diego overheard Inez assuring them. "Don Diego has accepted his responsibility. Even if he had not, I am sure we could have persuaded him. Gonzalo still has to sign the papers giving him complete control over *Dehesa de Oro*."

She laughed, as if making a joke, but Diego took it the way he was sure she meant it—as a threat.

Don Constantino seemed to agree. "Then we will leave our daughter in your capable hands, Doña Inez. With such a strong inducement, I cannot imagine he will change his mind after we are gone."

"You would do better to accept *my* assurances of what I will do or not do," Diego informed them. "I presume I have your permission to wed your daughter, with or without your attendance at the actual ceremony."

"Do not make light of this matter, *señor!*" Don Constantino snapped. "When the priest comes, if you should refuse to marry her my sons and I will return here, and you will not be pleased to see us."

"You need say no more. I understand your position. Please excuse me now. I must see to the proper exercising of my horses. Recent events have caused me to neglect my duties."

It was the last he saw of Eugenia's family, or indeed, of any of the guests. By the end of the day, they had all departed. Diego was relieved to return to the work he best knew and loved: riding and training horses.

He concentrated on refreshing El Cid's memory of the advanced movements, which he had not had time to practice lately. One never knew when they might be needed. With that in mind, he started working again with La Reina. Several days passed in these pleasant endeavors, and then another message arrived from Fray Leonido.

No new deaths had occurred; the fever seemed contained. He was now ready to travel to *Dehesa de Oro* to conduct the wedding.

"Eugenia, we must begin at once to plan the ceremony!" Doña Inez gleefully announced at the noonday meal. "As there will be no guests, we will keep it simple, but I see no reason why it cannot be elegant. In the spring, we will hold another *festividad* to celebrate your nuptials. After that, Don Gonzalo and I should be ready to turn the house over to you newlyweds while we retire to our home in Santa Barbola."

Avid delight flooded the girl's pretty face, and Diego felt the sudden need to escape both women. Once again, he took refuge down at the stables, strolling among the corrals and looking over the horses. He soon found himself wondering which horses Maria and Santelmo had taken. A quick head count of the animals confirmed the proper number and led him to call over a nearby *vaquero,* one of a half dozen new men hired while he and Maria had been gone for so long.

"Are any horses missing that ought to be here?" he asked the man, who seemed surprised by the question.

The *vaquero* shook his head. *"No, señor.* All the horses a

here who should be here, including your fierce white stallion
and the beautiful mare called La Reina.''

"I see," Diego murmured. *"Gracias."*

Walking onward, he puzzled over the situation. If Maria and
Santelmo had stolen two horses, there ought to be two less in
the corrals, and any man assigned to care for them should know
which ones were missing. Intending to discuss the matter with
Gonzalo, he started toward the house . . . only to stop short
when he suddenly saw a strange man, an *Indio,* hauling a
handcart heaped high with manure over to the manure pile.

The presence of an unknown *Indio* at *Dehesa de Oro* piqued
his curiosity. Walking over to him, Diego greeted him in Spanish. The man lifted his head and stared at him a moment, then
hurried about his business. Another of the new *vaqueros* offered
an explanation.

"That *Indio* does not understand Spanish, *señor.* He speaks
only his own *lengua.* Fortunately, he comprehends the language
of a bullwhip. 'Tis the best way to communicate with him.''

"I am sorry to hear that. I would like to discuss something
with him."

Diego did not mention that he could understand a bit of the
Indian dialect. He could also speak it—not much, but enough
to make himself understood. He had learned while living among
Santelmo's people. It suddenly occurred to him that perhaps
he should direct his questions to the Indian instead of to Gonzalo, or even Doña Inez. He was far more likely to get truthful
answers.

He decided to watch for an opportunity to confront the man
privately and see what he had to say about the fact that no
horses were missing. Few things had ever escaped Bartolomeo's
notice, especially when it came to animals. Diego suspected
that this man was just as observant. In the meantime, he must
prepare for his unwanted wedding.

Maria and Santelmo spent most of their time in the darkened
hut trying to stretch their cramped muscles—no easy task, as
each wore a length of chain attached to a cuff around one ankle.

The chain was fastened to an immovable stake in the center of the hut, an arrangement which gave them a limited amount of freedom. They could reach the slop pail in the corner, but not the door.

They had been warned that if they made any noise they would once again be bound hand and foot—and gagged for good measure. Thus, they conversed only in whispers and tried not to rattle their chains. Any day now, they expected to be sent to the silver mine, for Diego's wedding should be fast approaching. Santelmo's improvement was also becoming apparent. In front of the *vaquero* assigned to guard them, he tried to conceal it, but his dogged efforts to regain his strength were yielding remarkable results.

Day and night, he worked at flexing his muscles, telling Maria that if an opportunity for escape ever again presented itself, he wanted to be better prepared than he had been the last time. They both knew how hopeless their situation was, but they continued to hope. The instinct to keep fighting was as powerful as the urge to breathe.

"Work on your legs in particular," Maria urged her brother one morning after they had eaten the food a *vaquero* had brought them. "Remember how much trouble you had mounting a horse when we tried to escape the last time?"

"I would not count on riding this time." Santelmo gave her a mocking glance. "They will not let us . . . near a horse."

Even his speech had improved, she thought. Soon, it would be normal.

"Probably not. But we must be ready, just in case."

"The last time, we should have taken La Reina. Then they never would have . . . caught us."

"And never stopped trying, either. Diego himself warned me not to take La Reina."

Diego! she thought, her heart wrenching. Had he married and no one told them? Or was he delaying the wedding because he could not bring himself to welcome another woman into his bed? Wishful thinking, she decided. He must not be married yet; her stepmother had said she wanted them gone by the time of the wedding. Besides, Doña Inez would never waste such an opportunity to gloat.

As Maria sat thinking, the door swung open and a *vaquero* stuck his head inside.

"Here," he said, tossing her a wad of clothing. "The *patrón's* wife sent these down to you. She said you were to make yourself presentable for your new duties at the silver mine. You will leave before dawn tomorrow morning."

"The wedding!" Maria blurted. "That means the wedding will soon be taking place."

"Day after tomorrow," the *vaquero* confirmed. "But why should the personal affairs of the Master of Horses be of interest to one such as *you?*"

He obviously knew nothing about their situation.

"We are not full-blooded *Indios*, as you no doubt believe. I am the daughter of Don Gonzalo, and this man is his son," she said. "Did you not know that? Have you not wondered why we are being held here, or sent to the silver mine?"

She was looking for an ally, but the man quickly dashed her budding hopes. "When I was hired in Santa Barbola, I was told to keep my mouth closed and do as I was told, or I would not last long with this *patrón*. So that is what I do, *señorita*. I speak little to anyone, and they do not speak to me. I only know that any man who helps you escape will never again work for an *hidalgo*. If no *patrón* will have me, I will starve, and my woman along with me."

"Then you are not that much better off than me," Maria sighed, reaching for the clothing.

Anyone who was not a member of the ruling class had similar problems. How could Diego ever believe he could change this society? His chances of changing it were about as good as Santelmo's chances for escape—and her own.

Before dawn the next morning, a *vaquero* rudely awakened them. Iron cuffs were applied to Santelmo's right wrist and her left one. The ends of both their ankle and wrist chains were then fastened together by a large iron lock. The lock ensured that neither could go anywhere without the other, rendering escape more difficult. Reminded to be quiet or they would be gagged, they were led out to a cart hitched to a jackass.

By the light of a single torch held by a *vaquero*, Maria took one last look at her former home. She could not see much because of the darkness. In the direction of the big house, everything was black. Nothing moved, except for the shadowy figures of the three men assigned the task of transporting them to the mine.

Then Maria noticed another figure—an *Indio!* She had never seen the man before, but his ragged dress, facial features, and yes, even his smell, proclaimed him an Indian. He stood silently watching as she and Santelmo stepped into the conveyance and sat down on the floor behind the low seat where the driver waited to haul them away. Producing another lock, one of the *vaqueros* secured their chains to an iron ring in the floor of the cart, and they were ready to go.

Maria wished she could speak to the *Indio*, ask him questions . . . even help him escape. She had already guessed his purpose; like Bartolomeo, he reeked of manure. He would spend the remainder of his life as his predecessor had done, hauling manure and tending the manure pile.

Despair settled over her like a shroud. Escape was impossible. She and Santelmo—as well as the Indian who watched them— were all doomed. The last flicker of hope she had so carefully nurtured died out like a flame snuffed by a breeze. As the cart rumbled away, accompanied by two riders, she closed her eyes and sought solace in her memories of freedom on the Ocean of Grass . . . but the memories would not come. They, too, had died.

A full day and a night later, after being jostled until Maria thought their bones would break, they arrived at the silver mine. The *vaqueros* must have been ordered not to stop for the night, for they had allowed only short periods of rest for the jackass and their own horses, including the spare tied to the back of the cart. Maria and Santelmo had little time to stretch their legs or get down from the cart. Even then, they were kept chained together and had to suffer the embarrassment of performing bodily functions in full view of each other and the *vaqueros*.

Once away from the house, the *vaqueros* had given them permission to speak, but Maria had nothing to say, and neither did Santelmo. They both knew that trying to convince their captors to release them would be a wasted effort.

Now, the ugly reality of the mine faced them. The *vaqueros* unhitched the jackass, but left them sitting in the tilted cart in an inner courtyard, while they went inside a stone building to converse with the guards and locate the mine overseer. The gate to the courtyard stood wide open, but their chains prevented any chance of escape. Nor could the *Indios* Maria saw all around them take advantage of the open gate.

They were all locked in cages lining either side of the enclosure. Most of the cages held men, but one contained a dozen or more women. Maria could only stare at them and wonder if she herself would soon be thrust among them, sharing their crowded quarters. The conditions in the cages horrified her: both the sleeping pallets and the minimal garments of the inhabitants consisted of filthy rags. Each cage held a large, clay water urn and one or two overflowing slop buckets, but no tables, chairs, or other furnishings. The cages had roofs, but no walls or fire pits.

In the early morning silence, the Indians lounged on their meager pallets. Looking hopeless and forlorn, they showed no interest in Maria or Santelmo. Most of them never raised their heads. Some had open sores or wounds. Lash marks crisscrossed their arms and legs. All were painfully thin, and none were old. Apparently, they died before they reached old age. Maria saw no children or babies.

It was worse than she remembered. When she had visited here as a girl she had only glimpsed the cages, for they had used a different entrance, graced by trees and flowers. She did recall the huge furnaces where the ore was processed and had never forgotten the experience of descending into the depths of the mine itself. The vacant expressions on the faces of the Indians had haunted her. She had never imagined that she herself would one day become one of these poor, hopeless creatures.

The *vaqueros* finally departed the stone building and silently untied the jackass from the hitching post, mounted their horses, and rode away, taking the jackass with them. Maria could not blame them for their eagerness to be gone. They had done their duty. The mine was a depressing place to visit, and they surely wanted to leave it as soon as possible. In the pale light of the rising sun, she bowed her head and fought to get a grip on her emotions. Whatever happened next, she resolved to conceal her fear.

Her stomach lurched at the sound of male voices. She looked up to see a half dozen men emerging from the stone building. Taking their time, they strolled over to the cart and made a great show of leaning over the low sides and peering into it.

"A couple of prime ones this time, eh, *señors?*" one burly fellow exclaimed. He lacked two front teeth and was ugly besides. His arms and shoulders reminded Maria of a powerful ox. "Look at the *señorita!* 'Tis been a long time since I have seen such a tasty morsel."

Maria cringed as he reached out and curled a finger around a lock of her tangled, dirty hair. She had not been able to groom herself properly since she and Santelmo had tried to escape. Her stepmother's gift of new clothing had been a subtle mockery; Doña Inez must have relished the idea of providing new garments without first giving her the chance to bathe or comb her hair.

"Leave her alone." Santelmo's chains rattled as he tried to put himself between Maria and the big burly fellow.

"Or you will do what?" the man demanded, and he burst out laughing. "Maybe you want to watch while we give the little *señorita* a proper welcome to San Martin!"

When he stopped laughing, he shoved a key into the lock securing the chain to the ring in the bottom of the cart. With the same key, he unlocked the chain fastening them together. Shoving Santelmo to one side, he grabbed Maria by the hand and dragged her over the side of the cart.

"Come here, *puta!* I will remove these chains, so they do not get in our way."

Santelmo made a noise of protest, and three of the guards leapt to restrain him. Maria said not a word. She closed her eyes and let them do whatever they wanted. It was useless to fight. If she were lucky, they would kill her this very day—and Santelmo along with her.

After a bit of pounding with a hammer and chisel, the cuffs fell away from her wrist and ankle. As hard hands began to grope her body, a commotion broke out in the cart behind her. Holding her breath, she prayed: *Dios! Let us die together, and let it be over quickly.*

Hoofbeats suddenly clattered on stone.

At first, Maria thought she was imagining them, but a startled shout roused her from the submissive lethargy into which she had sunk. Opening her eyes, she saw a lone horseman riding a familiar horse—El Cid!

The white stallion came galloping into the courtyard, followed by another familiar, but riderless horse—La Reina. The stallion's rider wore an armored breastplate and a metal helmet. Beneath the helmet, a gauzy piece of fabric stretched across his face, concealing his identity, but she did not need to see his features to know who he was. Diego had come to rescue them!

Caught by surprise, the guards failed to react immediately. Anticipating no trouble, they had come out unarmed, and had not even bothered to lock the gate behind the departing *vaqueros.* One of them made a belated grab for La Reina's reins, while another launched himself at Diego.

The stallion reared, came down on his front legs, and kicked out with his hind—catching the fellow squarely in the midsection with a resounding thud. Whirling about, El Cid reared a second time. His flailing hooves sent two more men flying across the courtyard.

Maria suddenly understood the reasoning behind the "airs above the ground." The techniques Diego had taught the horse each had a purpose. In a battle at close quarters, the stallion became a lethal weapon—easily dispersing slower and weaker human adversaries.

Frightened and demoralized, the remaining guards fell back. Their thoughts shown on their faces: Only the most accomplished equestrians—the highest members of the aristocracy—could control a horse like this and make him perform with such deadly accuracy. Several men now writhed in pain on the cobblestones, but those who could still run did so. Racing for the entrance to the mine, they shouted for help to fight off the masked intruder on the vicious horse.

"Maria! Come up here with me." Diego lifted her onto the saddle in front of him. "Santelmo, hurry and take La Reina!"

"My chains!" Santelmo struggled to remove the restraints.

"Bring the hammer and chisel! We will deal with them later." Diego held La Reina's reins out to Santelmo, but he brother did not take them.

"Go ahead—both of you. I will free . . . the *Indios* first."

"There is no time for that!" Diego argued, but then he swung down from El Cid, leaving Maria in charge of both horses. "All right, we will do it. Look there!"

He pointed to a bunch of keys lying beside a fallen guard. "Let us hope they are the ones we need."

Maria had to control both prancing, excited horses, while Diego ran from cage to cage, fitting keys into locks. Santelmo hobbled along behind him, opening gates as he went. By the time the guards returned with reinforcements, they had managed to free most of the *Indios*.

"Diego! Santelmo, come! We must flee."

Maria expected the slaves to join them in racing toward the open gate. But the men and women, who only moments before had looked so defeated and helpless, suddenly came to life. With a collective roar of rage, they turned on the guards and attacked them with flailing fists, lengths of chain, and anything else they could get their hands on to use for weapons.

Pistolas fired, and a couple of *Indios* fell, but the guards had no time to reload before the enraged horde overwhelmed them. Ignoring the ensuing slaughter, Diego mounted behind Mar and waited a moment to be sure Santelmo managed to mount La Reina. Then all of them galloped out of the courtyard.

They had gone a long way before Maria noticed that something was wrong with her brother. Looking back over her shoulder, she spotted blood on Santelmo's arm and a pallor on his determined features.

"Diego, stop! Santelmo is hurt."

Diego immediately checked the stallion. Clawing at the thin fabric still wrapped around his face, he tore the mask away and tossed it to the ground, then turned back toward her brother. Santelmo swayed dangerously in the saddle. Only sheer effort of will kept him mounted on La Reina.

"You were shot back there! Why did you not say something?" Diego shouted in exasperation, but Santelmo only shook his head and grimaced.

"He prefers death to capture," Maria explained. "So would you, Diego, if you faced spending the remainder of your life in the bowels of a silver mine."

Dismounting, they helped Santelmo get down from La Reina, and together laid her brother on the ground and examined his wound. He had a deep, raw crease in his upper arm. The injury would not kill him, unless it became infected or he lost too much blood. Diego used the remnants of his mask to bind it up tightly and stop the bleeding.

"Can you still ride?" he asked Santelmo. "We dare not linger here, this close to the mine or even to *Dehesa de Oro*. We must pass by your father's house on our way to the Ocean of Grass."

"I can ride." Santelmo's face and eyes were grim. "I refuse . . to be caught again. This time . . . I will fight until my last breath. They will have to kill me to take me back to San Martin."

"Then let us ride." Diego looked at Maria. "We have a long way to go to get you both home again."

Despite Santelmo's condition, Maria's spirits soared. Her heart felt light as air as they remounted their horses and set out for the Ocean of Grass. "How did you know we were at the mine?" she asked later as they slowed to a walk to rest the horses.

"I asked the Indian who took Bartolomeo's place what he could tell me about the fact that no horses were missing from *Dehesa de Oro.*"

"No horses—you noticed that none were gone?"

Diego nodded, then pushed back the brim of his metal hat. "I am the Master of Horses. 'Tis my job to notice."

"But, the *Indio,* does he speak Spanish? How were you able to converse with him?"

"I am not entirely ignorant of your *lengua,* Maria. While I lived among your people, I was learning—storing words and phrases in my head. I am not yet fluent, but I can manage well enough. Once the Indian understood I was not his enemy, he proved to be a great help."

"How did you convince him you meant no harm?"

"Simple. I offered to free him. If he told me all I wished to know, I promised to take him up on El Cid and ride far out into the wilderness and release him. 'Tis a promise I still must keep."

"Then . . . you intend to return to *Dehesa de Oro.*" Her elation faded as she grappled with this disturbing notion.

" 'Tis my intention," he confirmed. "I still have business at *Dehesa de Oro.*"

She turned in the saddle to look him in the eye. "What business, Diego? I thought . . . since you came for us, and freed us. . ."

She suddenly realized why he had worn a mask while he had done so. His identity had been a mystery to everyone but her and Santelmo. The *vaqueros* would have recognized El Cid and La Reina at once, just as she had, but Diego had been careful not to appear until *after* the *vaqueros* departed. *What would he have done,* she wondered, *if the gates had been locked?* Knowing Diego, he would have come up with something.

"I will not explain myself, Maria. You would not believe

me anyway. I begged you to trust me, but you took matters into your own hands and fled without even telling me.''

"You were going to marry that girl, Eugenia! Do you deny it? *Today* is supposed to be your wedding day.''

"Yes,'' he conceded. "But I only consented to the wedding *after* you and Santelmo tried to escape.''

"And . . . now? What will you do now?''

"Now, I have unfinished business back at *Dehesa de Oro*. I will accompany you and Santelmo only until I am certain you can go the rest of the way by yourselves. Then I must return.''

"I see.'' Maria almost choked on the huge lump in her throat. "And La Reina? Will you let us have her, or will you take her back with you?''

Diego sighed. "Do you think I will leave you horseless and alone on the plain, especially with winter coming? I brought the mare because she can outrun anything with four legs, except for El Cid. I thought about bringing a third horse, but that would have complicated an already difficult situation. Your journey back to the Indians will not be an easy one, particularly now that Santelmo is wounded, but you can do it, Maria. You will *have* to do it, because I must return to *Dehesa de Oro*.''

He fell silent then, and Maria knew he would say no more about his plans for the future. Obviously, they did not include *her*—and why should they? Her own plans had not included him. She could only hope he would eventually find it in his heart to forgive her.

"I am sorry, Diego,'' she murmured. "I am so very sorry.''

"So am I, Maria. So am I.''

Chapter Twenty-four

Diego remained with Maria and Santelmo for the next fou
days. Each night seemed a little chillier, and the days wer
growing shorter as well. On the morning of the fifth day c
their journey they awoke to find a light frost on the grounc
and Diego knew that if he were going to return to *Dehesa d
Oro,* he must go now. It was early for frost, but the furthe
north they went the sooner they could expect it, and not lon
thereafter, the onset of winter.

In the far distance, a cloak of mist hid the high sierra
toward which they were heading. At least now, with Santelmo
guidance, Diego had a better idea of the most direct route t
the Indians' stronghold. Before their first encounter with tl
Indians, he and Maria had been wandering aimlessly. Now, l
had little fear of getting lost. Indeed, if he left now, he stoc
a good chance of being able to return to *Dehesa de Oro,* tal
care of business, and still make it back to Maria before wint
shut down the plains entirely.

But he was not going to tell her all this and risk disappointir
her, especially when he could not be certain he could achie
that goal. Then, too, he was still smarting from the sting of h
rejection, when she had gone off without him. If she did n

know when—or if—he was coming, his sudden appearance would be all the sweeter, a lesson taught in the value of trusting.

Fortunately, Santelmo's wound was giving him little trouble. Diego knew he could depend on Maria's brother to look after her and keep her safe on the rest of their journey. So he said his farewells, mounted El Cid, and turned him southeast, while Maria and Santelmo prepared to double up on La Reina and ride in the opposite direction.

Both the stallion and the mare whinnied a protest over the parting, and the look in Maria's eyes almost made Diego relent. He could tell she doubted she would ever see him again—and he dare not make any promises he might not be able to keep. It all depended on what happened at *Dehesa de Oro*.

Eugenia had to agree to release him from his commitment to wed her. True, she had conspired with Doña Inez to trap him into marriage, but in the end he had given his consent. Honor now demanded that before he sought to wed another, she release him from the promise. He would tell her he could never love her, and that she would be better off admitting to her family what she had done and seeking another husband.

He especially felt the need to confront Don Gonzalo: A man who would condemn his own flesh and blood to the silver mine deserved no heirs to his empire. Nor did Diego intend to return La Reina to him. When he took his final leave of the man, he would tell him he was going to keep the mare and take several others, as well—compensation for the wrongs done to Maria and Santelmo. To ensure that Gonzalo would leave the Indians alone from now on, he would offer him the first foal produced by a cross between El Cid and La Reina, plus the chance to purchase other promising foals in the future. He himself would need a source of income to build his own empire further north in the Sea of Grass.

Diego still could not imagine living the rest of his life as an Indian. He wanted at least some of the comforts of civilization for himself and his family, should Maria give him children. He planned to settle somewhere *between* the Indians and the Spanish, far enough away from both sides so that he and Maria could lead their own lives, but close enough that they could

bridge the gap between the two cultures and conduct busines
with both. He would keep the peace, continue teaching th
Indians how to breed and train horses, and hire those willin
to work for him—show them how to survive in the new wor
that awaited all of them. Sooner or later, the various tribe
would obtain horses, anyway. They would either steal them
trade for them. Diego had finally seen the error of his ow
thinking—the horse was a wondrous animal who belonged
all people, not just to a single race.

The great Sea of Grass and whatever lay beyond was t
vast a land to be managed solely by the Spanish aristocrac
They would try their best to control it, but the boundaries
the known world would keep expanding, beyond their capaci
to enforce their laws and customs. Diego knew he would n
be the last man to break free of the old ways and embrace t
new. He believed he was the first of many who would sei
the opportunities the New World offered.

He wanted to be part of the exciting future, and needed
mate who shared his vision. That woman was *not* Eugenia. I
doubted she would attempt to hold him once she realized
was refusing Gonzalo's wealth. In order to settle matters befo
the onset of winter, he had to hurry. Still, it was hard to ri
away when the woman he loved and wanted to marry sto
gazing after him as if her heart were breaking.

Wheeling around, he cantered back to Maria, slid off El C
and gathered her into his arms.

"Once again, I ask you to believe in me, Maria. Trust n
If your father does not kill me first, I will return."

"Oh, Diego!" she sobbed, and hugged him tightly. "I w
wait for you! I promise you I will wait forever. Never ag:
will I doubt your love!"

"I hope to return before the snow flies. If I do not, look
me in the spring. If summer comes, and I have not appear
promise me you will wed another. You will need a hunter a
a protector."

"Until you return to us, she has me," Santelmo growl
"I no longer have a wife or family to feed, but if I did I wo

still bring my sister meat and defend her . . . as I will you, my brother. If anyone harms you, count on my revenge.''

"Thank you." Diego clapped him on the shoulder. "Look after Maria for me. But do not endanger yourself seeking revenge if I fail to return. Instead, find your sister a worthy husband. I want Maria to be happy, to have children and a man of her own. If not me, then someone else. She deserves love, not loneliness. And so do you, Santelmo. Do not be afraid to take another wife. Blue Water would want *you* to be happy, too."

"You are the only man I will ever love or want for a husband!" Maria cried, embracing him anew. "Come back to me, Diego. Without you, I cannot be fully alive."

"Nor am I alive without you, my love."

He bent and kissed her one last time. Then, before he could change his mind, he swiftly mounted El Cid and rode off without looking back.

"You have returned, Don Diego! *Dios* be praised. Gonzalo and I had so feared you were dead."

Doña Inez grabbed Diego by the arm and all but pulled him through the doorway of the ruined and partially burnt-out house. "Gonzalo will be so pleased. He is dying, Diego—those wretched *Indios!* They attacked us as we lay sleeping in our beds. *This* is how they repay us for all we try to do for them. . . . Can you believe it? Gonzalo and I are fortunate to still be alive. I wish I could say the same for your poor Eugenia! She panicked when the savages rampaged across *Dehesa de Oro*—slaying our cattle, stealing our horses, setting fire to the grasslands, and even trying to burn the house itself. Gonzalo and I fled to the potting shed and hid like terrified rats, but the foolish girl ran outside screaming for help and made a spectacle of herself. I know not what she expected. The Indios got her. They even tore her hair from her head, put it on a pole, and danced around waving it!"

When Diego had first discovered the devastation both in and around *Dehesa de Oro*, it had not been difficult to guess what

had happened. Even so, the extent of the damage shocked him
Of all Don Gonzalo's fine horses, only three could now b
found grazing outside the corrals; they seemed reluctant t
leave the only home they had ever known. He had searched i
vain for a *vaquero* or a servant and spotted not a single one
Had they not fought back?. . . . Or had they simply been unpre
pared for so many Indians to show up at one time, with murde
mayhem, and revenge on their minds?

"I am sorry to hear about Eugenia," he murmured, and h
truly was sorry. "However foolish she may have been, she di
not deserve to die such a violent death."

"May *Dios* have mercy on her." Doña Inez quickly crosse
herself. "I sorely grieve for her, but in truth she lacked th
sense to do what I told her, so she suffered the consequences.

"If she had refused to do what you told her in the first plac
she would not have been here," Diego drily pointed out. "Sl
would have been safe at home with her family."

"Perhaps—but you—where have *you* been? We thoug
you had changed your mind about the wedding and gone in
hiding. When you disappeared so suddenly, Eugenia was deva
tated. She wept for three days. I kept telling her you on
needed time to think, and you would hurry back to do yo
duty. Then, when the *Indios* attacked, I thought you must ha
fallen prey to them. We still do not know how they manag
to escape the silver mine. They must have slain the guards a
the overseer. We had no warning they were even coming he
They took us all by surprise, attacking in the wee hours of t
morning. There was no time to take refuge in the blockhous
or plan a proper defense. Our cowardly *vaqueros* were far mc
interested in saving their own hides than in sparing ours. Wh
they saw the Indians lighting grass fires to burn us out, th
mounted their horses—bareback—and fled into the darkne
You will have to find them and severely punish them for th
appalling lack of loyalty. Otherwise, we *hidalgos* will ne
again be able to get a good night's sleep. We will live in fe
for our lives, which is exactly what we have been doing sir
all of this happened."

Diego debated how much he should tell her. If she did

know—or had not guessed by now—that *he* had freed the Indians, he saw no sense in enlightening her. He was not supposed to know about Maria and Santelmo, so she had no reason to suspect him of going to the mine to rescue them. *She* was the one who had lied. Let her keep her secrets, and he would keep his.

"Did you not send for help to Santa Barbola?" he finally asked.

"How could we, when everyone was either dead or had disappeared?" Fury twisted Doña Inez's thin lips. "Except for me and Gonzalo, there is no one left. I have been desperately waiting for someone to come check on us. I have heard nothing from Eugenia's family. You would expect them to be anxious about her welfare and eager to know whether or not the wedding took place. We are almost out of food, and I grow weary of doing all the work myself."

"You look as if you have suffered." Diego suddenly noticed the shabbiness of her appearance. Normally, she had not a hair out of place. Now, her black gown was badly soiled and wrinkled, and her hair disheveled. Dark circles ringed her eyes, and she seemed thinner, older, and even less attractive than he remembered.

"Well, you look fit enough! I ask you again, Diego: Where have you been all this time?"

"I left with El Cid and La Reina," Diego began.

"Yes! Gonzalo was unhappy to hear you took his best mare. He worried you were gone for good. I assured him you had packed none of your things nor taken food for a long journey, so you could not have intended to go far. Also, you gave your word you would marry Eugenia!"

"'Tis why I have returned," Diego explained. "To ask Eugenia to release me from my promise of marriage. Since she is dead, there is no reason for me to stay—nor to tell you where I have been."

"No reason! What are you talking about? Of course, there's a reason. You are now officially our heir! Gonzalo has signed all the papers. As I said, he is dying, and there is no one to whom he wishes to leave our estate but you. You will need to rebuild the house, of course, and capture more slaves before you can reopen the silver mine, but—''

"I do not want the house or the silver mine," Diego grimly announced, "nor even the land. I had hoped to negotiate for more horses, but I see there are few remaining."

"What are you saying? You cannot think to abandon us! As soon as Gonzalo passes, I need someone to take me to Santa Barbola. Where will you go, Diego? What will you do? Without *me*, you have no life and no future."

"Ah, but I do, Doña Inez. I have found my own land, far to the north. 'Tis ideal for my purposes, to breed fine horses, raise them, and train them. I may even raise cattle. I saw some wandering out on the plain. In the spring, I will gather them and put my own brand on them."

"No doubt they are wearing my husband's brand!"

"Then I will wait until next year and gather the young ones who are yet unbranded. If you want them yourself, you will have to gather them first, Doña Inez."

"You fool! They will be yours anyway! As for me, I will not be here, but in Santa Barbola."

"For your sake, I hope so. I am sorry, but I cannot take you there. My own duties call me."

"You would leave without greeting my dying husband who claimed you as his cherished son?"

Diego could not quite bring himself to do so. He must at least *see* Don Gonzalo, though he no longer intended to reveal his plans or chide the man for his sins.

"I cannot linger, but I *will* bid him farewell. Lead the way if you will."

Doña Inez straightened her shoulders and marched past him toward the east wing. Regal as a queen, she swept into his chambers ahead of him. He had to give her credit for maintaining her poise and haughtiness. She was a worthy adversary for any man, and he would be relieved to see the last of her.

"Gonzalo!" she shouted. "Rouse yourself. Diego is here."

"What? . . . Diego?"

Diego hardly recognized the old man in the huge, rumpled

bed. Gonzalo had a withered, sunken look about him, and his eyes held a wild expression.

"Katerina!" he called out suddenly. "Katerina, where are you? My little dove . . . my sweet, precious love. Come to me, Katerina. Hold my hand. I beg of you—come to me now!"

Diego glanced questioningly at Doña Inez. Her eyes glittered, and her lips thinned. She had grown pale. "When we stumbled into the potting shed, fleeing for our lives, he fell and hit his head. He has not been himself since. Sometimes, he knows me. Other times, like now, he does not."

"But . . . to whom is he speaking?"

"Katerina! Maria's mother, the bitch who bore her and his two horrid sons. He weeps for her all the time. Tears roll down his cheeks, and he begs her forgiveness. He—*the great Don Gonzalo—begs the forgiveness of a lowly Indio!* When I try to comfort him, he does not recall my face or name and only hollers all the louder for Katerina."

Then you have both gotten what you deserve, Diego thought. Having no appetite for rubbing Doña Inez's nose in her own misery, he held his tongue. These two had caused so much misery for others, but in the end they had been amply repaid. Revenge was unnecessary—as it would be for his own cousin, he suddenly realized. He would not be there to witness Evaristo's downfall, might never even hear about it, but Evaristo, too, would eventually pay for his crimes. People drew to themselves the same heartache—or happiness—they gave to others.

Diego bent over the bed, where Gonzalo wept for the woman whose love and loyalty he had betrayed. Taking the dying man's hand, he said softly: "Farewell, Gonzalo. We will not see each other again in this lifetime."

Gonzalo appeared not to hear him. He stared at the ceiling, his eyes filled with anguish. "Katerina . . ." he moaned. "What have I done to you and our children? You are the only person I ever loved—but *Madre de Dios!* I did not realize it until too late!"

"Both of you are fools!" Doña Inez spat. "You even more so than he. You think you have discovered a new life somewhere. You think you are better than *we* are—more noble, less

selfish and greedy. You think you can live happily now." Her
eyes narrowed as if a new thought had just occurred to her.
"Have you somehow found your little *Indio?* Is that it? You
have found Maria and think you will live in everlasting bliss
with her, as Gonzalo tried to do with *his* little savage. It will
not happen, Diego."

She burst out laughing. "Trust me. It will *never* happen, not
when I give you *this.*"

She stalked over to a heavy wooden cupboard, yanked open
the door, and rummaged among some folded garments. With
a look of triumph, she pulled out a packet. Diego immediately
recognized the broken wax seal on it. It was his family seal:
the mark of generations of Iberras. Only his father—or someone
appointed by him—could use it.

"Shall I tell you what it says?" Doña Inez crowed. "It came
while you were off searching for the horses with Maria and
that smelly old *Indio* who used to haul away manure. After
reading it, I knew better than to tell my husband . . . and of
course, I did not tell *you.*"

"I care not what it says," Diego told her. "My plans are
made. I will not change them for any reason."

"Yes, you will! I know you, Don Diego. You are one of
us—an *hidalgo* to the bone." Grinning wickedly, she held the
packet out to him. "Take it and be damned, oh great Master
of Horses!"

Snatching the packet from her hand, Diego stalked from the
room and went to retrieve his horse for the journey back to
Maria.

He did not open the packet until he was within a day or two
of the Valley of Green Grass. Driving the three horses ahead
of him that he had taken from *Dehesa de Oro,* he headed El
Cid into a cold bitter wind beneath a leaden sky that hinted of
snow. He was still a long way from shelter. If it did start to
snow, he knew he might die out here on the open plain. Indeed
he might have to kill one of the horses just to survive before
he reached the sierras. He was unprepared for such a cold, har

ourney. Not much had been left at *Dehesa de Oro* to take with
aim.

His hands were almost too cold to open the packet, but he
lecided he might as well see what it said. Reaching beneath
ais cloak and leather doublet, he withdrew the packet with
umbling fingers, unwrapped it, and peered at the writing on
he first sheet. He did not recognize the script; it had not been
vritten in his father's hand, as he had been hoping.

*To the most honorable and distinguished Don Diego de
berra . . .* it started out. *Most esteemed Sir:*

The greeting puzzled him. No one in Spain considered him
aonorable, distinguished, or esteemed. Frowning, he read fur-
aer, holding the pages tightly lest they be torn from his hands
y the wind.

*I regret to inform you of your father's untimely passing. It
ame only six days after your mother succumbed to a mysterious
aalady. I will tell you first about her. Not long after your
'eparture for the New World, she became ill and died. When
our father displayed the same symptoms, his devoted servant,
)ario, secretly summoned a physician. . . . I say secretly,
ecause he had been expressly forbidden to do so by our mutual
ousin, Don Evaristo de Iberra.*

Diego paused to regain his composure. The news hit him
ard. His parents must have died before he had even arrived
ere! All this time, he had been picturing them as he had last
en them. All this time, they had been lying in their tombs,
ad he had not even known it.

Wiping the moisture from his eyes, he continued: *After much
eliberation, the physician concluded that your father was
eing poisoned with a diabolical and slow-acting substance
ttle known to anyone outside his own profession. He sum-
oned the authorities at once. To spare you a long recitation
` the details, I will only say that your cousin has since been
und guilty of poisoning both your mother and your father.
ae king has ordered his execution, and by the time you receive
is it will have been carried out.*

*Before your father died, he attempted to rearrange his affairs.
ae king appointed me to help him. I am another one of your*

cousins, Roberto, son of your deceased uncle, Vitorio. You will perhaps remember me as an eager young lad hanging over the balcony overlooking the arena where you often trained horses. I always watched you with unbridled awe (forgive the word play) and a sense of worshipfulness. To my great dismay, my family visited yours but rarely. I never got to know you well, but trust me when I say I never forgot you.

Diego again paused, searching his memory for an image of a boy he only vaguely remembered. Roberto had to be the wide-eyed child with the unruly mop of curls that made him look like a wayward cherub. Yes, he did recall him.

Before continuing my tale, I must tell you that your father deeply regretted all that had passed between the two of you. Most especially, he regretted not having listened to you when you tried to inform him of Evaristo's devious nature. He died with your name on his lips. Just prior to his expiration, he begged me to make things right again—to handle his affairs until this news reached you and you could return to claim your inheritance.

I myself am a second son with little of importance to occupy my time, so I am happy to be of use to someone. I have spent my entire life attempting to perfect my equestrian skills, so you will not laugh at me if you ever see me on a horse. For that reason alone, because of my great admiration for your horsemanship, I will do all in my power to safeguard your magnificent Iberran horses and your beloved Dehesa de Oro until you return. . . .

The letter continued for two more pages. Diego only scanned them before he quit reading altogether. There were a few details regarding the day-to-day management of the estate, but everything seemed to be in order, with Roberto in control and not in the least inclined to take after Evaristo. It would all be there for him whenever he wanted it.

But he was not going back!

Once, it had been all he could think about: to return to the land of his birth and regain all he had lost. Now, all he could think about was reaching Maria before he froze to death. His hands were numb from the cold. He attempted to refold the pages of the letter, but the wind whipped a couple sheets from his fingers, and they scattered behind him like huge white flakes of snow.

Thrusting the remaining sheet back into his doublet, he debated whether he ought to stop and gather them up again—and decided against it. He already knew what they said; he did not need to reread them. If he survived until spring, he would think about returning south and posting a letter to his half-forgotten cousin.

As a second son, Roberto had little, if any, inheritance of his own. Perhaps he would like to continue managing Diego's. He would give him complete freedom—including the right to live at *Dehesa de Oro* and oversee the breeding and training of the Iberran horses.

All Diego would demand in return was a periodic accounting of the young man's efforts—and a regular advancement of a set amount of ducats to be used for the expansion of Iberran interests in the New World. Diego himself would handle those interests. He would also insist upon the importation of several prime horses each year, so new blood lines would be added to those he hoped to establish here.

Diego meant to become the major breeder of the finest horses to be found in either the New World or Spain. If he survived the winter . . . if he ever made it back to Maria . . . if the snows did not come and bury him on the open plain first . . .

Rousing himself, he urged El Cid into a canter.

Chapter Twenty-five

For a full day and a night it had been snowing. Snow now blanketed the Valley of Green Grass, along with the surroundin sierra. Maria had never seen so much snow. She was unaccu tomed to such frigid weather. At *Dehesa de Oro*, it had nev snowed like this, nor been this cold during the daylight hour The nights were often bitter, but during the day, when the su shone, she had rarely noticed the cold.

Diego must not be coming. She did not even want to thin about him alone on the plain, at the mercy of the wind's fu and the sky's determination to smother the earth. Even th Indians stayed close to their hide dwellings. The shelters we surprisingly warm and comfortable in any kind of weathe During winter, the Indians relied upon the caches of dried me and other foodstuffs collected and processed during the h season. Most of the structures had special storage places ho lowed out of the earth beneath them; Maria's was no exceptio and thanks to the Indians, hers was full.

Several highly successful hunts had resulted in a surplus meat and hides, which the tribe members had stored in bo her own quarters and her brother's—in hopes that they wou eventually return and make use of the supplies. As usual, Ma despaired of adequately repaying her friends and neighbors for their foresight and generosity. If Diego returned, she would need everything they had given her . . . but she was beginning to doubt he would ever come.

He could be dead by now—both he and his faithful stallion. Next summer, she might find the bones of a man and his horse somewhere out on the open plain. The thought brought tears to her eyes, and she dashed them away before entering her brother's dwelling to see how he had fared the storm.

As she leaned down to open the flap of the dwelling, she suddenly heard voices. One belonged to her brother; the other she could not immediately identify. She paused, listening, not wanting to interrupt.

"You should consider taking my sister for a wife," a voice was saying. "Since her husband was killed on that buffalo hunt at the end of summer, she has had no one but me to keep her in meat. I do not mind, nor does my wife, though we have two mouths to feed already—and another one soon to arrive. 'Tis you yourself I am thinking of, Santelmo. You need a woman to warm your buffalo robes at night, and to cook for you, bear you sons and daughters, and—"

"I am not yet ready to take another wife," her brother protested. "When I am ready, I will let you know, Black Loon. Your sister is a good woman."

She is more than good, Maria thought. White Antelope was handsome, sweet, and gentle. She had not been married long before her husband's death, and her eyes still held a sadness that spoke more eloquently than words of her love for him.

Maria mentally scolded herself for not having suggested this match before now. She herself should have seen how perfect it was; if she had not been spending all her time brooding over Diego and watching the horizon for any sign of his return, she would have realized how badly her brother needed a wife this winter, and White Antelope needed a husband.

As she stood in the swirling snow berating herself for her selfishness, the flap was drawn back, and Black Loon emerged from the dwelling. He nodded to Maria, then held the flap open so she could get down on her hands and knees to enter. This

was one thing she disliked about the small, snug shelters: They
had very low entrances and once inside, there was little room
for people to move around.

Now, only her brother remained—hunkered over a tiny,
banked fire. At his side was her old friend, Caobo. The dog
shot her a mournful look, when she quickly knelt down and
extended her reddened hands to the smoldering coals. The
staghound had been greatly disappointed when they returned
to the Indians without Diego. Tail madly wagging, he had run
back and forth between her and Santelmo, then stopped and
gazed in the direction they had come, apparently looking for
his old master. He had even whined plaintively, a reaction with
which Maria could identify.

"How long do you think this storm will last, Santelmo?"
she asked her brother by way of greeting.

Santelmo glanced up as if only just noticing her. "Who
knows? It may end today or continue for several more days.
If Diego is not here by now, he is not coming, Maria. He may
never come. He may be dead, or he may have decided he cannot
bear to give up his life as an *hidalgo*. You must prepare yourself
to accept the fact that you will never see him again."

"'Tis far too soon to accept it! If you and your dog wish
to be gloomy, I will return to my own shelter. I have no need
for dismal company. The weather is dismal enough."

He smiled at that and scratched between Caobo's ears. "For-
give me for allowing my loneliness to affect my view of life.
Even Black Loon thinks I brood too much. He has suggested
I marry his sister."

"I think you should," Maria said. "White Antelope would
make any man a wonderful wife—even one who likes to sit
around feeling sorry for himself."

"True. But she is not Blue Water. I do not feel the same
way about her. I doubt I ever will."

"Santelmo, that does not mean the two of you cannot be
happy or comfortable together. She may never feel the same
way about you that she did for her first husband, but in your
loneliness you can console each other."

His face brightened. "I never thought of that. She, too, has lost someone, so she will understand my lack of enthusiasm for a match with another woman. I never want to care that much for anyone again. It hurts too much when you lose them.''

Considering how she felt about the prospect of losing Diego—never again seeing him or being held in his arms—Maria found it difficult to reassure her brother that he *could* learn to care for another. But she made the effort.

"Santelmo, does it not demean what we feel for our loved ones, when we hesitate to love again for fear of getting hurt? If that which a man feels for a woman and a woman feels for a man is truly wonderful, then we should be *eager* to experience it again. We should not hold ourselves aloof from others.''

He gave her a sly mocking glance. "Oh, I agree. But let us see how eager you are to marry a man other than Diego when the hot season comes again.''

"My case is different,'' she argued. "You *know* that Blue Water is dead.''

"If Diego does not appear by spring, you will know that *he* is dead—or married to someone else.''

"If he should die or marry another, I will know it in my heart,'' she whispered. "I will feel it deep inside me.''

She remained silent for a moment, thinking of what she had just said. . . . What was her heart telling her now? What was this . . . this strange feeling of anticipation?

Lifting her head, she listened intently for a moment. Her senses strained to capture some outward—or inner—message. Amazingly, Caobo seemed to share her sudden feeling that something was wrong. Raising his head, ears and eyes alert, he watched the entrance, as if he expected to see someone.

"What is it?'' Santelmo studied her intently. "You look so different. Your eyes . . . your face—''

"He needs me,'' she blurted. *"He needs me.''*

She leapt to her feet, her heart racing, her entire being vibrating with an awful certainty. "Santelmo, he needs us both! We must go to him—find him. He is dying somewhere out in the snow!''

"Maria, wait! Where are you going?''

But she was already running, Caobo at her heels. Scrambling

out of the shelter, she obeyed the call of her innermost instincts
She did not know how she knew it, but Diego was nearby, i‚
mortal danger, and only *she*—and Caobo—could save him.

Diego lay in the snow where he had fallen when he topple‚
from his horse. Snow fell wet and heavy on his face, but h‚
was too stiff and cold to lift his hand to brush it away fron
his mouth and eyes. His limbs refused to obey his wishes. Fo
what seemed like an eternity, he had been riding . . . riding . .
swaying to El Cid's motion.

The stallion must be as tired as he was! Diego felt a sof‚
velvety nose nuzzle his cheek, and a warm breath caress hi‚
numb cheekbones. El Cid snorted in his ear, his message clea‚
"Get up! Do you not know you will die if you do not get u‚
and climb back into my saddle?"

No man could have a better friend than this stallion, Dieg‚
thought. He had long since lost track of the other horses. The‚
had disappeared in the swirling wall of white that had engulfe‚
him two—or was it three—days ago? He had lost track ‚
time, and had not dared to stop or dismount. He knew he coul
not have remounted.

He had hoped he would somehow find Maria before he froz‚
to death, but now, it appeared, he was finished. He would nev‚
make it. He had no idea where he was, or how much farth‚
he had to go. The snow had obliterated everything. Since t‚
onset of the storm, he had been depending on the stallion‚
instincts to take him where he wanted to go . . . if El C‚
remembered. Diego knew it was asking a lot of an animal—
even a horse as wonderful as El Cid—to carry him to warm‚
and safety among other human beings. It was far more like‚
that the stallion would head for the Canyon of Horses and oth‚
horses.

El Cid would not have forgotten where he had left a bun‚
of mares; his instincts would guide him. He would want ‚
drive these other mares toward his herd. Was that not wha‚
stallion would do?

Diego's thoughts jumbled together. Besides being cold a‚

numb, he was sleepy. All he wanted to do was sleep. No longer was he even hungry. In sleep, he could forget about impending death and the pain of losing Maria. Memories of Maria were all that comforted him now. Her smile, her scent, her fox fire eyes, the feel of her silky skin beneath his hands—he remembered all of it!

He never wanted to forget. She had taught him what really mattered in life—not wealth, gold, reputation, or even beautiful, blooded horses. All that mattered was the depth of feeling and commitment between one human being and another. If a man had love in his life, he needed nothing else. If he lacked it, possessing neither family, wife, or child, he could own the biggest gold mine in the world, and it would not be enough. Witness Don Gonzalo! Don Gonzalo had had it all, but as he lay dying, he had wept for the one thing he had wasted and could never regain—his chance at love.

Losing Maria would be worse than dying. Scalding-hot tears formed in Diego's eyes. As the tears dribbled down his cheeks, he could feel them freezing on his face. Ah, well . . . it was over now. He must bid farewell to his woman and his horse. Then he would die. He just hoped Maria would not think he had changed his mind and chosen to stay and marry Eugenia, after all!

When he failed to return, she might imagine he craved her father's wealth too much to ever give it up. He regretted his inability to assure her that he loved her above all else. Now, he would always wonder, always doubt. He knew her too well. She had doubted him once; she would doubt him again. And that doubt would keep her from ever again risking her heart and loving another.

Yet he had meant what he had told her: He wanted her to know the happiness of being loved and of loving another. If he could not have her for himself, he did not want her to be lonely. Love left no room for selfishness; it meant putting the good of another ahead of one's *own* good.

The thought riveted him: *I have discovered the most precious secret in the universe!*

Intense joy flowed over and through him. Peace flooded his

soul. No longer was he cold or hungry; no longer did he fee
alone. He sensed the presence of someone who loved him. I
his mind, he heard her call his name. He even saw her face—
Maria! She was racing toward him—coming to rescue him.

She had come for him . . . and would take him home.

Warmth. Light. Heat. Comfort. Diego wondered if he ha
died and gone to heaven. He wanted to open his eyes and chec
his surroundings, but for the moment, he was too content t
move. He just wanted to lie there and float—bask in the softnes
and warmth. He could hear voices murmuring above hin
Angels? No—impossible. One was a woman's. Anothe
belonged to a man. Then a second woman spoke.

He knew her voice. He had heard it a thousand times in h
dreams. He wanted to speak, but kept slipping in and out e
consciousness. One moment, he was almost there—awake ar
fully aware. The next, he was drifting away on a deep, so
cloud. Warm hands moved across his body.

"He has something inside his doublet," he heard a wom;
say. *His* woman. He knew that much. She belonged to hi
alone.

"What is it?" a man asked.

"It has words on it. Let me see if I can read them. Mar
years have passed since I attended Antonio at his lessons.
learned then how to read Spanish, but . . . snow has faded t
ink on this, and I may not be able to decipher the words."

There was a short silence and then an exclamation. "O
This is from someone who knows Diego's family. His fath
and mother are dead, and their murderer has been execute
No longer is he an outcast. His land and titles have been return
to him. Someone named Roberto is taking care of things un
. . . until he can return to Spain."

"To Spain!"

"Yes, to Spain. I . . . I wonder if he came all this way
tell me he is going back to Spain."

*No! 'Tis not why I came. What is the matter with you, Mari
What more must I do to prove my love for you? . . . Maria*

He tried to form her name with his lips. Tried to open his eyes. Weakness almost defeated him. He was so damn weak!

"Santelmo, look! He is moving. Diego is awakening at last!"

The other woman spoke, her words unintelligible. Then the man spoke, the one called Santelmo. . . . *Yes, Santelmo, Maria's brother.*

Someone nudged his shoulder. "My brother, wake up! If you wish to make love to Maria again, you must wake up."

"Santelmo!" Maria sounded shocked.

"He needs a reminder of all he is missing," Santelmo defended. "The man lies near death. He must fight to wake up or he *will* never make love to you again."

"Diego," Maria whispered, her mouth close to his ear. "My dearest love, wake up. Are you still cold? If so, I will warm you. We have already built the fire high, my love, and rubbed your body all over."

All over? No, they could not have done that. He would have remembered.

"Please, my love. Come back to us. Give me some sign that you hear us."

Maria, he said, but his lips would not move. They felt fat and awkward. He wiggled his bottom lip and then his upper. He tried to open his mouth. *Maria!*

Was that any better?

He tried one more time. "M—ma . . ."

"Santelmo, he is saying my name!"

A Dios gracias.

It would be all right now. She was kissing and hugging him. Stroking his hair and face. He tried a smile—a very small one—and struggled to open his eyes. It was still too difficult. *Later. He would do it all later. Smile. Talk. Laugh. And make love to his woman.*

He could hardly wait.

"Diego, you almost died! You must not get up yet. You are still too weak." Maria pushed Diego down onto his buffalo robe, but he tried to pull her down on top of him.

"No, I am not. I will soon show you how strong I hav
become. 'Tis long past time I renewed our acquaintance. Afte
all, I came a long way to see you again—and hold you."

She nimbly eluded him. "Not yet, my love. *I* will decid
when you can risk leaving your buffalo robes—or doing any
thing else that might delay your recovery."

"Listen to me, woman!" Diego caught her hand. Try thoug
she might, she could not wrench it away from him. "I am
man—not a child. If nothing else, I must get up and see to th
needs of my horse."

"Santelmo has already seen to your horses. El Cid and th
others are all safe in the Canyon of Horses. The snow there
not so deep. The horses can easily paw through it to find gras
They can even break the ice on the stream to drink. Did yo
think we would ignore the needs of such precious animals?"

Diego's grin showed through his thick beard. Indians almo
never grew beards; if a few stray hairs did appear, they quick
plucked them out. The beard reminded Maria that Diego w
no Indian—he was a rich *hidalgo,* with land, horses, and a li
of ease awaiting him in Spain.

"No, I knew they would be well taken care of—but a hors
man can never truly abandon his duties to others. He mu
always see for himself that his horse is thriving."

"Only yesterday, when the sun finally showed its face, Sa
telmo went out to the Canyon of Horses. All the horses we
thriving. Winter or summer, the canyon is the perfect shel
for them."

"Then I need not go there today yet. Come and sit with i
then, Maria. I am growing restless in this confinement."

"Perhaps tomorrow, if it is warmer, you may go outside
she agreed, sitting down beside him on the thick buffalo rob

"Whether 'tis warmer or not, I will go outside," Die
corrected her. "I am strong enough now. I must work to rega
all the strength I have lost."

"You are too impatient," she chided.

"Yes, I suppose so." He lifted his hand to run a finger alo
the curve of her cheek. "I am impatient to wed my beauti

Maria and spend all my nights—and half my days—showing her how much I cherish her.''

Maria gently removed his hand. The moment had come. It was time to tell Diego what she knew about his family. She had been using her concerns about his strength to keep him at arm's length, but it was really her other concerns that prevented her from joining him in his bed.

These last few days, while he had been recovering, she had thought long and hard about his future—and hers. It was wrong to expect him to give up everything for her sake. He was not an *Indio.* He deserved better. He had been born to a different life. When he thought he had lost that life forever, he had been so bitter! She well remembered his bitterness.

Now, his old life had been restored to him—a life in which she had no place. She belonged here, on the Sea of Grass. He belonged in Spain.

''Diego . . .'' She looked down at his hand, and the sight of increased her certainty.

He had the hand of an *hidalgo,* not an Indian. He possessed long, elegant fingers and well-shaped nails. His skin was roughened and chapped, but not hardened and callused from years of exposure to the elements. He normally wore leather gloves, even in the hot season, while every other man in the encampment, including her own brother, had hands that had never seen the inside of gloves.

''What is wrong, Maria? You look so pensive and unhappy. Why? I am here now, and our whole lives lie ahead of us. I have many plans I wish to share with you—''

''I already know your plans, Diego. Rather, I know what your plans *should* be.''

''No,'' he disputed. ''You do not. I cannot live as an *Indio,* Maria, but neither will I live as your father did.''

''You are returning to Spain.''

''Spain!'' He shook his head and laughed. ''Never. *This* is my home now: this land of the future. I have no wish to return to the past.''

''But you need not remain here! Your inheritance has been restored.''

He stared at her incredulously, struggling to recall a dream he had when he was ill. "How do you know this? What strange powers do you possess? First, you found me in the snow—led Santelmo straight to me—and now, you tell me what no one but myself and your stepmother knows. Are those fox fire eyes of yours a sign of supernatural powers?"

It was her turn to laugh. "No, my love, no! I have no special powers, supernatural or otherwise. It was Caobo who found you in the snow, not me."

That was not precisely true; she *had* sensed his need of her, but she could not explain it. At the mention of his name, Caobo lifted his head and thumped his tail, then returned to dozing by the fire. Apparently Caobo could not explain it either.

"I *can,* however, read," she continued. "And I found—"

"That letter from my cousin, Roberto! I lost half of it on the plain."

"I found the half you did not lose, and I read it. You should return to Spain, Diego, and reclaim your birthright."

"You could not force me if you aimed a *pistola* at my head," he said solemnly. Then he told her what he intended to do with his fortune.

As he spoke Diego's face lit with a radiance that betrayed his great excitement. His own brand of fox fire shone in his eyes, and Maria realized that he really did want to remain here and build a new life on the Sea of Grass. She herself had nothing to do with it; he wanted it *apart* from her, though indeed he expected her to share it.

"Then you are not staying here for *my* sake," she said, seeking to confirm her conclusions.

"No, but if you intend to go somewhere else, I will follow you, Maria. You will never be rid of me. Having found you, I will not let you go."

Maria could not restrain herself. She promptly burst into tears. "Oh, Diego, my love!"

"I am right here." He drew her into his arms. "And here I will stay, Maria. If *Dios* be willing, we will grow old together, you and I. We will live to see our children and grandchildren galloping horses across the Sea of Grass."

"Along with Santelmo's children and grandchildren!"

"Santelmo's? Do you know something I do not, Maria?"

She told him then—how Santelmo had decided to take White ntelope for a wife, and White Antelope had agreed. Diego emembered White Antelope, and recalled that she was a hand-me woman. He thought they would make good mates for ch other.

" 'Tis the beginning of a new era, Maria." He took her hand d again gently tugged her downward. "For us, for Santelmo, d for the world. Now that the Indian has the horse, the world ll never again be the same."

"I know," she whispered.

As he slid his arms around her, she realized that the prospect making love with Diego thrilled her far more than the arrival a new epoch in history. Her own Master of Horses had turned, and their future was a bright shining star streaking ross the night sky into the unknown. Suddenly, she no longer ared it—and no longer doubted that Diego was where he longed.

" 'Tis the beginning of a new era," she agreed. "Yours and ne. *Our* time together."

Smiling into Diego's eyes, she sank down with him into the ftness of the buffalo robe. "So let us not waste a single ment of it."

And they did not.

Afterword

When the American Indian obtained the horse, the cours
of history was indeed forever changed. The Horse Barbarian
as they became known, ruled the western half of America f
centuries thereafter, evolving into the Comanche, Shoshon
Apache, Cheyenne, and other well-known tribes. The begin
nings of these tribes and exactly how they obtained the hor
are a matter of conjecture: No one really knows for certain.

We do know that the Indian adopted the culture of the hor
from the Spanish. The forerunners of the American mustan
the stock horse, and various color breeds such as Paints ar
Pintos were originally brought to the New World by the Spa
ish. The Iberian mustang (or *mesteno*) had a dash of Arabi
blood, combined with hardy North African barb.

My own interest in the history of different breeds of hors
fueled this story and others, including *Windsong, Ride the Win
Race the Dawn,* and *Painted Horse.* Watch for the next Kath
rine Kincaid historical romance involving horses, coming so
from Kensington Publishing.